NATURE AND ART

broadview editions
series editor: L.W. Conolly

NATURE AND ART

Elizabeth Inchbald

edited by Shawn Lisa Maurer

broadview editions

NATIONAL LIBRARY OF CANADA CATALOGUING IN PUBLICATION DATA

Inchbald, Mrs., 1753-1821.
Nature and art / by Elizabeth Inchbald ; edited by Shawn Lisa Maurer.

(Broadview editions)
Includes bibliographical references.
ISBN 1-55111-278-7

I. Maurer, Shawn L., 1960-   II. Title. III. Series.

PR3518.A725 2004   823'.6   C2004-905338-8

Broadview Press, Ltd. is an independent, international publishing house, incorporated in 1985. Broadview believes in shared ownership, both with its employees and with the general public; since the year 2000 Broadview shares have traded publicly on the Toronto Venture Exchange under the symbol BDP.

The Broadview Editions Series represents the ever-changing canon of literature by bringing together texts long regarded as classics with valuable lesser-known works.

We welcome comments and suggestions regarding any aspect of our publications—please feel free to contact us at the addresses below or at broadview@broadviewpress.com / www.broadviewpress.com

North America
Post Office Box 1243,
Peterborough, Ontario, Canada K9J 7H5
TEL (705) 743-8990; FAX (705) 743-8353

3576 California Road,
Orchard Park, New York, USA 14127

E-MAIL customerservice@broadviewpress.com

United Kingdom and Europe
NBN Plymbridge.
Estover Road, Plymouth PL6 7PY, UK
TEL   44(0) 1752 202301
FAX   44 (0) 1752 202331
FAX ORDER LINE   44 (0) 1752 202333
CUST. SERVICE cservs@nbnplymbridge.com
ORDERS orders@nbnplymbridge.com

Australia & New Zealand
UNIREPS University of New South Wales
Sydney, NSW 2052
TEL 61 2 9664099; FAX 61 2 9664520
E-MAIL infopress@unsw.edu.au

Advisory Editor for this volume: Michel W. Pharand

Cover design by Lisa Brawn
Typeset by Liz Broes Black Eye Design

Printed in Canada

for Anya and Aidan

Contents

Acknowledgments

My acquaintance with *Nature and Art* dates back to my days as a graduate student at the University of Michigan, where I was introduced to the novel by Carol Barash. Since that time, many people have supported the project of making Inchbald's second novel available to a modern audience. I first edited *Nature and Art* for Pickering Women's Classics; work on that edition was generously supported by colleagues, research assistants, and the English Department at Texas A&M University. I am also grateful to the staff at the British Library, the Bodleian Library's Abinger Collection, and the Victoria and Albert Museum's Foster Collection as well as to my valued eighteenth-century colleagues Jill Campbell and George Haggerty. The College of the Holy Cross provided research support for the current edition; for their help I would also like to thank my Holy Cross colleagues Paige Reynolds and Lisa Kasmer, as well as Sister Irene Mizula from the college's Interlibrary Loan office. I am thankful to Broadview Press's Julia Gaunce for her patience and understanding, and to Barbara Conolly for timely word processing assistance. As always, I owe my greatest debt to my husband, Brittain Smith.

Shawn Lisa Maurer
College of the Holy Cross

Introduction

As struggling actress, theatre critic, commercially successful playwright, acclaimed novelist, and much-fêted woman of letters, Elizabeth Inchbald stood at the center of late eighteenth-century London's literary and intellectual life. And yet, despite continued interest through the nineteenth century, her work—consigned to expensive facsimile editions or out of print altogether—has been largely ignored through most of the twentieth century, and her life has been reduced to a series of anecdotes describing her Catholicism, her captivating beauty, her early marriage and untimely widowhood, and finally, her relationships with the actor John Philip Kemble and the philosopher William Godwin. Recently, however, owing to the revival of "forgotten" women writers by feminist scholarship and the subsequent availability, in an affordable edition, of her powerful first novel *A Simple Story* (1791),[1] Inchbald has experienced a well-deserved renaissance, both in criticism and in the classroom. Yet critics' almost exclusive focus on this one work has seriously distorted our understanding of both Inchbald's biography and her literary output. By reading the novel's heroine, the society flirt Miss Milner, as a portrait of Inchbald herself, critics have inadvertently marginalized those works that manifest other, equally significant aspects of the author's character and artistic concerns. Inchbald's second novel, *Nature and Art* (1796), represents the writer's most concerted attempt to analyze the effects of education, wealth, power, and privilege upon human behavior. Extraordinarily broad in scope, Inchbald's narrative examines such important issues as the sexual double standard, infanticide, along with gender and class conditioning; the work also explicitly condemns British imperialism, the country's legal system, and aristocratic educational practices and codes of honor. Moreover, by focusing upon the story of two brothers, William and Henry Norwynne, along with the sons who bear their names, the novel provides an opportunity for scrutinizing masculinity, in addition to femininity, as a crucial site of gender construction.[2] Demonstrating the links between personal experience and institutional oppression, *Nature and Art*,

---

1 Issued by Oxford University Press in 1965, *A Simple Story* appeared in paperback, with a new introduction by Jane Spencer, in 1991.
2 See Maurer, "Masculinity and Morality in Elizabeth Inchbald's *Nature and Art*" in *Women, Revolution, and the Novels of the 1790s*, ed. Linda Lang-Peralta (East Lansing: Michigan State University Press, 1999) 155–76.

no less than *A Simple Story*, commands a central place both in Inchbald's oeuvre and in the history of the English Jacobin novel.

The novel relies upon the opposition between the upbringing and actions of the younger Henry, a "child of nature" who has been reared without books on an African island, and the artificial manners and corrupted conduct of his cousin William. A child of "art" in the sense of artifice, William, raised under the pernicious influence of parents and tutors who teach him to imitate rather than understand, is incapable of thinking for himself; thus his adult life merely perpetuates the callous irresponsibility of the supposedly civilized upper classes. Henry, by contrast, sees through the norms of aristocratic society because he is not yet inured to them; moreover, the values these forms represent contradict the principles taught to him by his benevolent father. A manifest demonstration of "The Prejudice of Education"—an earlier title for *Nature and Art*[1]—both Henry's goodness and William's immorality testify that Inchbald, like her Jacobin contemporaries, affirmed the power of education to effect important social change.

Attending to the significant ideological components of *Nature and Art* should not, however, blind us to Inchbald's aesthetic accomplishments. The theme of judgment, subtly woven throughout the text, demonstrates how the novel's structure supports its polemical content. By employing the concept in its legal sense—William and his father are magistrates—as well as in the more general sense of passing judgment, Inchbald's narrative demonstrates, again and again, that those who have been accorded the role of evaluating others are often the least fit for such assessment. *Nature and Art* skillfully renders all arbiters of justice, whether empowered by rank, sex, or profession, unjust by virtue of their patent inability to judge themselves and their motives. Inchbald's irony deftly deploys the novel's most disfranchised characters, the cultural outsider Henry and the uneducated young village woman, Hannah Primrose, to launch her most scathing critique of social injustice. Expanding upon the established literary conventions of the noble savage[2] and the seduced maiden,[3] these characters evince, in very different ways, the biased and inhuman standards by which

---

1   James Boaden, *The Memoirs of Mrs. Inchbald* (London: Bentley, 1833) I: 346. For related works addressing the topic of education, see Appendix B.

2   For a different version of this trope in Robert Bage's novel *Hermsprong*, see Appendix C.1.

3   For an analysis of Hannah Primrose's place within this tradition, see Susan Staves, "British Seduced Maidens," *Eighteenth-Century Studies* 14 (1980–81): 109–34. See Appendix C.3 for two additional representations of the seduced maiden paradigm in novels by Mary Wollstonecraft and Mary Hays.

they are judged. Whereas the ostensibly naive Henry can expose the false assumptions that sustain British society, the equally innocent Hannah, impregnated and abandoned by an unscrupulous William, is eventually destroyed by them. In the novel's most famous passage, William, now a London magistrate, unknowingly sentences to death the woman whose ruin he had himself precipitated.

Yet this scene is only one of many to illustrate the hypocritical standards of a society that confuses justice with affluence. The impoverished Hannah has, in fact, already been condemned by William's own father, who castigates Hannah and her infant instead of the son who has deserted them, as well as by the prospective employers who refuse to shelter a woman with an illegitimate child; in the most ironic turn of all, she has even been condemned by her own conscience, as she internalizes the values of her corrupted judges. Hannah, however, is not the novel's only victim. Chapter by chapter, Inchbald builds a case for the pervasive cruelty perpetrated, almost instinctively, by all of the book's privileged characters. Inchbald's narrative thus transforms the novel's readers into the ultimate arbiters who, through the act of reading, are impelled not only to judge for themselves those in the novel who judge others, but also to examine their own attitudes and actions in light of those characters' questionable behavior.

Although critics traditionally view the figure of Hannah Primrose as deriving from the destitute life of the author's younger sister Debby,[1] Inchbald too was no stranger to misfortune and hardship. Having lost her father at the age of eight, Elizabeth Simpson, the future Mrs. Inchbald, while still in her teens and despite a pronounced stutter established herself in the arduous and socially problematic world of provincial theatre. Her husband Joseph, whom she married at nineteen in part as protection against harassment, died suddenly seven years later, leaving her devastated and, as an attractive woman of the theatre, especially vulnerable to unwanted sexual advances. Seeking financial independence as well as a

---

1   Inchbald's sister followed her to London, where she became a persistent source of worry, as she turned from a barmaid to outright prostitution. Despite her misgivings, Inchbald gave her sister constant and generous financial assistance; she attended Debby during her final illness and paid her sister's funeral expenses. Yet Inchbald's biographer Boaden speculates that in spite of these final attentions, the writer was haunted by her harsh treatment of the difficult Debby (see especially I: 332–33). It seems highly plausible that Inchbald's experience with Debby, who died in 1794, the year *Nature and Art* was first drafted, influenced not only the creation of the figure of Hannah Primrose, but also lent power to her portrayal of bad conscience in the characters of William and his son.

means of aiding the needy friends and family who increasingly flocked to her, Inchbald turned to writing. Her first efforts, dramatic as well as novelistic, met with repeated rejection, but, by the early 1790s, her farces, comedies, and adaptations, on the one hand, and her first novel, on the other, achieved both popular and critical success, affording her entrée into the foremost social and intellectual circles.

An obvious disappointment to those readers eager for another production in the manner of *A Simple Story*, *Nature and Art* has heretofore occupied a tenuous place in Inchbald's oeuvre. Although both works revolve around familial disjunction—*A Simple Story* contrasts a mother and daughter, *Nature and Art* two very different brothers and their equally disparate sons—the latter novel moves quickly from the domestic to the polemical. Inchbald's critics have tended to dismiss *Nature and Art* as aberrational, arguing that the writer, inflamed by Jacobin fervor, produced a treatise warped by the philosophies of Rousseau and Godwin. Yet we do well to take seriously Inchbald's choice of both subject matter and literary form. Stimulated by the artistic and political possibilities furnished by the novel genre, Inchbald returned to the form that, as she complained bitterly to Godwin in November of 1792, she found both financially unrewarding and emotionally debilitating:

> I was ten months, unceasingly, finishing my novel, notwithstanding the plan (such as you saw it) was formed, and many pages written. My health suffered much during this confinement, my spirits suffered more on publication; for though many gentlemen of the first abilities have said to me things high in its favour, it never was liked by those people who are the readers and consumers of novels; and I have frequently obtained more pecuniary advantage by ten days' labour in the dramatic way than by the labour of this ten months.[1]

As Godwin himself observed,[2] the novel enabled Inchbald to "expand her genius" by elaborating themes and structures already present in her dramas. We find *Nature and Art*'s overtly political critique clearly foreshadowed in such early plays as *Such Things Are* (1787), an original comedy

---

1 C. Kegan Paul, *William Godwin: His Friends and Contemporaries* (Boston: Roberts Brothers, 1876) 74–75. The complete letter is reprinted in Appendix A.2.a.
2 After reading a fragment of *Nature and Art*, Godwin wrote to Inchbald: "It seems to me that the drama puts shackles upon you, and that the compression it requires prevents your genius from expanding itself" (cited in Boaden, II: 354).

juxtaposing the pretentious would-be courtier, Twineall, with the benevolent Haswell, a character based upon the prison reformer John Howard; *Next Door Neighbours* (1791), an adaptation of two French plays contrasting the fortunes of a dissipated aristocrat with the misfortunes of a virtuous yet indigent middle-class family;[1] and *The Massacre* (1792), a tragedy set in seventeenth-century France censuring the recent slaughter of Royalist prisoners.[2] Didactic in intent, political in commitment, dualistic in structure, *Nature and Art* exhibits ideological and formal concerns prominent throughout Inchbald's work.

Moreover, the novel genre's extended chronological and dramatic scope allowed Inchbald to develop, rather than simply present, *Nature and Art*'s wide range of characters. While certain figures, like the aptly named Lord Bendham, a sycophantic courtier, behave more as type than character, others afford valuable insight into the enmeshed relationship between private needs and public persona. In what is arguably the novel's most complex portrayal, that of the elder William, Inchbald reveals how insecurity and resentment can determine the course of a man's life. The son of an impoverished shopkeeper, William obtains an elevated position in the church—culminating in a bishop's seat—only through the private negotiations of his less educated brother, a popular musician. However, rather than being grateful for Henry's assistance, William feels humiliated by his own impotence. He assuages his wounded self-importance by increasing, at every turn, the distance between himself and the brother through whom he had benefited: he marries a vain and shallow but aristocratic wife, allows himself to be blatantly exploited by the aristocratic bishop who is his church superior, and, perhaps most consequentially, fosters disastrous pride in the son who bears his name. Inchbald's complex depiction of "things as they are," no less than Godwin's,[3] probes the construction of the oppressor as well as of his victim.

Inchbald's pointed examination of her society's debased principles emerged from a particularly volatile historical moment. First copied out for press in January of 1794, *Nature and Art* sits on the cusp of England's

---

1   See Boaden, who notes correspondences between *Next Door Neighbours* and Inchbald's novel in terms of character development and plot, as well as dialogue (I: 294).

2   Although the play had already been typeset, Godwin, Holcroft, and the lawyer George Hardinge—the men to whom Inchbald would later submit the manuscript of *Nature and Art*—all advised that the tragedy be suppressed owing to its incendiary political content. *The Masssacre* had its first publication in Boaden's *Memoirs*. Inchbald refers to the play in the letter printed in Appendix A.2.b.

3   *Things As They Are; or, The Adventures of Caleb Williams* was the original title of Godwin's influential 1794 novel; it became simply *Caleb Williams* for the 1831 edition.

changing reception of the French Revolution. Initially, the developments in France seemed to sanction radical hopes for the overthrow of the old order and its replacement by a society comprised of rational individuals who might live, like Inchbald's two Henrys, "exempt both from patronage and from controul" (ch. 47). Subsequently, however, the bloody turn of events in France not only proved a sobering draught to the radical thinkers themselves, but also inspired increasing reactionary terror on the part of the British government. At the end of 1794, the year in which Inchbald was circulating her manuscript among various literary advisors, her close friend and erstwhile suitor, Thomas Holcroft, was imprisoned along with eleven others on a charge of High Treason;[1] Habeas Corpus was suspended, and libel suits proliferated.[2] Although Inchbald's biographers can provide little information about this phase of Inchbald's writing life,[3] we know from an undated letter discussing the composition of "A Satire on the Times," probably an earlier version of *Nature and Art*, that the author was fully aware that her subject matter was inflammatory, and that she herself might be subject to imprisonment, for she acknowledges revising some passages "having Newgate before my eyes."[4] It seems likely, therefore, that the politically astute Inchbald deliberately postponed the publication of her own novel to a less dangerous moment.[5]

Despite its delayed release, *Nature and Art* shares with the works of Inchbald's radical contemporaries an abiding faith in human reason and a

---

1 Inchbald visited Holcroft in prison, despite the fact that she had earlier broken off relations with him after his publication of his novel *Hugh Trevor* (Boaden, I: 330). Holcroft published the first three volumes of that novel in 1794 and the novel in its entirety in 1797. See Appendix C.2.a for examples of Holcroft's exposure of hypocrisy within both church and state.

2 For a recent account of Inchbald's relation to the Treason Trials, see the biography by Annibel Jenkins, *I'll Tell You What: The Life of Elizabeth Inchbald* (Lexington: University of Kentucky Press, 2003) 358–64.

3 Boaden evinced minimal interest in this facet of Inchbald's work; indeed, he classes "A Satire on the Times" with "some of those political writings which were of a temporary nature, and have happily perished in the furious season that gave birth to them" (I: 330). As subsequent critics have noted, Boaden wished to downplay such purportedly unladylike aspects of Inchbald's character and career as an interest in politics; clearly Inchbald herself was forced to negotiate the delicate balance between what was and what was not acceptable to her readers as well as to her government. Although Inchbald's latest biographer, Annibel Jenkins, finds Boaden "serious and rather dull," lacking "real understanding of Inchbald and her friends" (326), she nevertheless can offer little new knowledge about this period of Inchbald's writing.

4 This undated letter to William Godwin is printed in full in Appendix A.2.c. Newgate was the central London prison during this period.

5 *Nature and Art* was eventually purchased by Inchbald's "steady friend Robinson," her usual publisher, on 11 January 1796 (Boaden, II: 3).

vehement repudiation of those bastions of privilege that perpetuate oppression. Through pivotal relationships with William Godwin and Thomas Holcroft, two of the most instrumental proponents of the Jacobin cause, Inchbald imbibed revolutionary sentiments not as abstract ideas, but as part of intense—and mutual—intellectual debate. Godwin first encountered Inchbald in 1790 when he read the manuscript of *A Simple Story* for her publishers; by 1792 the relationship had blossomed into a friendship and, some have surmised, a romance.[1] During the period around which *Nature and Art* was composed, Godwin was clearly one of Inchbald's most valued readers: in addition to advising her to suppress from publication her play *The Massacre*, he consulted with her upon her memoirs, and proffered criticism as well as encouragement of the work that became *Nature and Art*.

Inchbald met Holcroft in the early days of her acting career; like her, he came from a modest background (his father was a shoemaker, hers a farmer), was largely self-taught, and soon turned from acting to playwriting, where his dramas enjoyed popular success. His most well-known novel, *Anna St. Ives* (1792), utilizes an epistolary structure to trace the scandalous, for the time, relationship of its exemplary upper-class heroine with a steward's son; in *Hugh Trevor* (1794–97), the eponymous hero's search for a profession sparks a relentless attack upon the institutions of law, church, and politics as well as condemning the university system and the aristocracy. Dogged by a reputation damaged by the Treason Trials, Holcroft died destitute, but the reformatory thrust of his works, their concern with the effects of conscience upon character, undeniably supported Inchbald's own didactic efforts.

As her friends, admirers, and, perhaps most importantly, her literary reviewers, Holcroft, and particularly Godwin, unquestionably influenced the course of Inchbald's work.[2] Too often, however, critics have branded Inchbald the callow pupil of these two opinionated men, the beautiful woman who accepted their radical beliefs along with their admiration.

---

1   Godwin's intimacy with Inchbald has been noted by biographers and critics alike. For the most recent depiction of Godwin's relation to Inchbald, see Jenkins, *I'll Tell You What*. Jenkins writes that "Holcroft had already proposed to [Inchbald] in the summer of 1793 and Godwin in the fall soon after" (364). For an additional, usefully consolidated account of the Inchbald-Godwin relationship, see Roger Manvell, *Elizabeth Inchbald: England's Principal Woman Dramatist and Independent Woman of Letters in 18th-Century London* (Lanham, MD and London: University Press of America, 1987) 94–108.

2   See, for example, Jenkins: "All during these months [late 1794 through 1795] when Godwin called on Mrs. Inchbald, she was working on her novel, and no doubt they discussed it while they had tea and conversation" (368).

But in fact Inchbald's first novel, *A Simple Story*, published in 1791 prior to the advent of English Jacobinism, exerted a pioneering influence upon the development of the movement.[1] Moreover, biographical evidence shows that during this period, Inchbald scrutinized the work of Holcroft and Godwin as painstakingly, and as authoritatively, as they did hers. In 1794, for example, Inchbald read Godwin's *Caleb Williams* in manuscript. While she praised the novel's macabre power, she also, out of fear for her friend's safety, advised him to expunge the work's overt polemicism.[2] Although he failed to take her advice in this case, Godwin clearly valued her critical acumen: more than twenty years later, and despite the estrangement precipitated by his marriage with Mary Wollstonecraft,[3] Godwin entreated Inchbald to peruse his latest work, the novel *Mandeville*, with the same care she had earlier given to *Caleb Williams*.[4] Just as in her personal and professional relations with Godwin and Holcroft, Inchbald maintains her integrity, so too does her writing stand on its own merits. *Nature and Art* no doubt shares themes and values with the works of Inchbald's Jacobin contemporaries. Yet, the novel is the product primarily of the author's own artistic vision, and not, as critics would have it, the result of derivative borrowings from her male counterparts. Moreover, viewing *Nature and Art* exclusively through the prism of English Jacobinism has led readers to emphasize the novel's reformist agenda at the cost of neglecting its psychological insight and emotional impact.

---

1   In *The English Jacobin Novel*, Gary Kelly argues that Inchbald, along with Robert Bage, "founded the English Jacobin novel. At a time when the English popular novel was going through a period of vulgar commercial formula and low critical esteem, Holcroft and Godwin, two of the most important novelists of the 1790s, had the benefit of direct acquaintance with both Mrs. Inchbald and her novel *A Simple Story*. They saw in *A Simple Story* and its author a prime example of the central English Jacobin doctrine, that circumstances form character.... Within a short time both Holcroft and Godwin had begun novels of their own. Not only did they imitate particular aspects of *A Simple Story*, they took up and made the most of the potential which Mrs. Inchbald's novel had made plain" (Oxford: Clarendon Press, 1976, 113).

2   "I shudder lest for the sake of a few sentences, (and these particularly marked for the reader's attention by the purport of your preface) a certain set of people should hastily condemn the whole work as of immoral tendency, and rob it of a popularity which no other failing it has could I think endanger" (quoted in Kegan Paul, I: 139). This letter and one that followed are reprinted in Appendix A.2.b.

3   Inchbald effectively broke off relations with Godwin upon his marriage, and refused to renew the friendship upon its former close terms even after Wollstonecraft's sudden death in the same year. Although Godwin continued to solicit Inchbald's company and criticism, their relationship never returned to its previous intimacy.

4   For the text of that letter, see Appendix A.2.d.

In the two hundred years since its publication, a number of other questionable assumptions have also contributed to a critical underestimation of *Nature and Art*. First, by considering the work as little more than a fleshing out of Rousseau's theory of the noble savage, readers disregard two far more interesting and subtle components of the novel. What precedes and follows the tale of two cousins, namely, the story of the personal and professional advancement of the brothers themselves, and the description of the increasing misfortunes of the seduced woman, Hannah Primrose, are integral to Inchbald's social and artistic project. Indeed these sections of the novel, more than the clever scenes involving the innocent Henry, contain the work's most profound, as well as dramatically moving, passages. Once the formerly destitute William begins to prosper, in possession of a deanery and a noble wife, he callously spurns the unassuming brother who made his advancement possible. The ingratitude that stems from his insecurity translates, in the public sphere, into a necessary blindness towards his own entitlement and an assumption that those who lack such privilege are therefore undeserving of it. Inchbald's portrait of the senior William thus adroitly combines psychological insight with social critique, as she leads us to understand the ways in which the character's actions result from the specific circumstances of his experience; she also demonstrates the inevitable impact of that behavior in the broader cultural realm.

In the narrative of Hannah Primrose, Inchbald anticipates recent feminist criticism by demonstrating the crucial intersection of gender and class. For Hannah the two are inseparable: she is victimized not solely because she is a woman, for as Mona Scheuermann has pointed out, women are also the victimizers in this book,[1] but because she is poor *and* a woman. The guileless Hannah, unlearned in social forms, operates as Henry's double, but with a twist: while his position as cultural outsider is positional—a function of his upbringing—hers is rather personal—ascribed to her at and by birth. As an outsider, lacking any stake in the status quo, Henry can speak, boldly and often wittily, for the poor and dispossessed; Hannah, deprived of education by her poverty and of authority by her sex, has no voice with which to speak. While some have criticized the plot's reliance upon coincidence—Hannah is sentenced to death by the younger William, who has become, at thirty-eight, "raised to preferment, such as rarely falls to the share of a man of his short experience—he found

---

1   "Inchbald sees class rather than gender as the determinant of victimization: rich women are as obnoxious as rich men." *Her Bread to Earn: Women, Money, and Society from Defoe to Austen* (Lexington: University of Kentucky Press, 1994) 169.

himself invested with a judge's robe" (ch. 39)—the concurrence emphasizes the fact that Hannah's misfortunes are inseparable from the professional fortunes of her seducer. Thus while society might condone William's maltreatment of the working-class Hannah, his conduct destroys him along with her. Doomed to live out the remainder of his life in misery, envying Hannah "the death to which he first exposed, then condemned her" (ch. 42), William provides the novel's most potent demonstration of the brutal cost of exploitation.

Secondly, the novel's protean form resists any clear or simple generic categorization. In contrast with *A Simple Story*, whose family structure and psychological complexities place the novel within the tradition of "domestic" or "realistic" fiction, *Nature and Art* veers from satire to melodrama, employing here the terse vocabulary of the allegory, there a grammar of acute psychological penetration. Roger Manvell's apt, oxymoronic characterization of the novel as a "sociopolitical fable"[1] contains a key to the novel's generic intractability: both treatise and tragedy, *Nature and Art* speaks in the timeless voice of the fairy tale, yet its incidents depend upon a historically specific engagement with contemporary concerns. The novel's opening chapter, which contains a précis of the narrative as a whole, illustrates the tension between these two elements. As in a fairy tale, two brothers set off in the world to make their fortune after their father's death. Such action could take place any time, anywhere. Yet their journey is also situated historically: moving from an unnamed country town to London, they are part of a wave of urban migration that transpired during the long eighteenth century, a result, at least in part, of such economic changes as the increased enclosure of common land. Moreover, the brothers are neither any nor everyman; the narrator's description of their father as "a country shopkeeper who had lately died insolvent" places them into the low end of the middle ranks. Their apprehensive passage into London finds a parallel in the comparable journey made by Hannah Primrose and her illegitimate son in the novel's second volume. Indeed the last sentence of the first chapter foretells William's success as well as Hannah's downfall: London is "that metropolis, which has received for centuries past, from the provincial towns, the bold adventurer of every denomination; has stampt his character with experience and example; and, while it has bestowed on some coronets and mitres—on some the lasting fame of genius—to others has dealt beggary, infamy, and untimely death."

---

1 Manvell, 109.

Most readers of *Nature and Art* have been troubled by the apparent split between the two halves of the novel. They find a problematic dissonance between the largely satirical first volume, with its account of the two brothers, their divergent careers and marriages, and the upbringing of their respective sons, culminating in those sons' very different sexual relationships, and the tragic, sentimental, indeed even at times melodramatic second volume, which centers primarily upon the declining fortunes of Hannah Primrose and which reaches its tragic apotheosis in the scene where William, elevated to a magistrate, condemns Hannah to death. One of the novel's early reviewers thought the "abrupt" transitions from one part of the history to the other "the principal defect of the work on the whole;"[1] in 1935 William McKee complained even more adamantly that Hannah's story "violates [Inchbald's] original intention." I cite his criticism at some length because it typifies the way most readers have conceived these seemingly incompatible parts of the novel: "She begins with Rousseau's idea of the man of *nature* and the man of *art*. When she is half way through the novel the fate of the heroine so absorbs her interest that she largely forgets her sociological intent, and, instead of making the novel a treatise upon the disasters resulting from a false system of education, she makes it a tragedy of an outcast in the London streets.... Unity of design has been destroyed."[2] By contrast, I contend that what have been commonly viewed as the disparate, indeed disjunctive parts of the novel—the satirical attack on English mores provided by the contrasting upbringings, attitudes, and behaviors of the two cousins and the pitiful tale of the seduced and abandoned cottager's daughter—are instead inextricably bound by Inchbald's penetrating critique of language. Operating through the method Victor Shklovsky has termed "ostraneniye"—defamiliarization[3]—Inchbald wields language as a means of cutting down pretense, of questioning what common usage has made unquestionable.

Thus while the novel's privileged characters seem, on the surface, to be able to get away with everything, Inchbald uses the character of Henry, as well as the ironic voice of her narrator, to uncover the sanctioned deceit that is the prerogative of the élite, both male and female. Henry's lack of knowledge about traditional behavior means that he does not share the same susceptibility to received opinion as his brainwashed cousin.

---

1   *The Analytical Review*, Vol. 23 (1796): 511; the review can be found in Appendix E.1.
2   *Elizabeth Inchbald, Novelist* (Washington: Catholic University of America, 1935) 67.
3   See "Art as Technique" (1917) in *Russian Formalist Criticism: Four Essays* (Lincoln: University of Nebraska Press, 1965) 3–24.

Unmasking, rather than capitulating to, the key terms in the social system, Henry, in his wise innocence, can call a spade a spade, or a wig a wig:

> Having been told, that every morning on first seeing his uncle he was to make a respectful bow, and coming into the dean's dressing room just as he was out of bed, his wig lying on the table, Henry appeared at a loss which of the two he should bow to—at last he gave the preference to his uncle; but afterwards, bowed reverently to the wig. In this, he did what he conceived was proper, from the introduction which the dean, on his first arrival, had given him to this venerable stranger; for in reality Henry had a contempt for all finery; ... But being corrected in this disrespect, ... he now believed there was great worth in glittering appearances, and respected the ear-rings of Lady Clementina almost as much as he respected herself. (ch. 12)

By respecting objects "almost as much" as the people who wear them, Henry exposes these status symbols as so much inflated currency, devoid of any moral underpinnings. Focusing particularly upon the seductive properties of language as a tool both to manipulate reality and to uncover such manipulation, the novel's plot and structure execute the unmasking process that Henry performs linguistically.[1] While Inchbald's use of the noble savage trope is certainly not original, her employment of Henry as an instrument for critique is both entertaining and efficacious. Henry, who can both see and reveal the emperor's nakedness, becomes the vehicle of the narrator's irony:

> In addition to his ignorant conversation upon many topics, Henry had an incorrigible misconception and misapplication of many *words*—...
>
> He would call *compliments, lies—Reserve*, he would call *pride—stateliness, affectation*—and for the words *war* and *battle*, he constantly substituted the word *massacre*. (ch. 14)

Nature and Art's plot lays bare a society in which such concepts as love, honor, and virtue have become hollow, "void of all the sentiment"—the

---

1 Inchbald here foreshadows George Orwell's famous essay "Politics and the English Language" in disclosing the cover-up entailed by semantic complicity. (In *Shooting an Elephant and Other Essays* [New York: Harcourt, Brace and Company, 1950] 77–92.)

phrase the narrator uses to describe the ape-like mannerisms of the younger William (ch. 9). Indeed the novel's fallen woman, the poor cottager's daughter Hannah Primrose, is the victim of her seducer's words as much as of his deportment; Inchbald renders Hannah complicit less in a sexual than in a class sense, insofar as she buys the rhetoric that William's status allows him to assume. Hannah sacrifices her own honor—in this case, her physical chastity—by falling for William's words of love, as she is seduced by the expectation that, as a gentleman, those words are honorable, i.e., backed up by virtuous action.

Inchbald's didactic stance is not unique: she follows a long line of middle-class moralists who attempted, in the early- and mid-eighteenth century, to refigure the concept of honor by configuring it in terms that appealed to both Christian virtue and burgeoning commercial values. Such writers as Richard Steele and Samuel Richardson argued that honor was to be found not in a man's status but in his deportment: the *Tatler*'s Isaac Bickerstaff maintained that "It is to me a very great Meanness, ... to rank a Man among the Vulgar for the Condition of Life he is in, and not according to his Behavior, his Thoughts and Sentiments, in that Condition."[1] Attacking notions of honor derived from a feudal ethos, one that endorsed bragging, aggression, and competition and was exemplified most powerfully in the code of honor that not only condoned but demanded the barbarous practice of duelling, these writers proffered an alternative form of heroism, one manifested in humility, charity, and benevolence as well as in the particularly commercial values of honesty and credibility. Their works challenged the belief that aristocratic birth entails noble behavior, as well as the view that the well-born are the only people capable of virtuous thought and action.

Inchbald's two brothers illustrate this revision process. Through education, career, marriage, and association, William elevates himself to the ranks of the élite, but despite his ecclesiastic position, he is far less ethical than his brother Henry, a musician who possesses "the virtues of humility and charity, far above William, who was the profest teacher of them" (ch. 5). Although William apparently uses his intimate relationship with

---

1   No. 69 (17 September 1709). (*The Tatler*, ed. Donald F. Bond, 3 vols. [London: Clarendon Press, 1987] I: 477.) Among numerous other works, essays by both Steele and Joseph Addison in the *Tatler*, *Spectator*, and *Guardian* papers; Steele's play *The Conscious Lovers* (1722) and Richardson's final novel, *The History of Sir Charles Grandison* (1753–54), deal explicitly with the attempt to reconstruct honor. For an analysis of these earlier literary efforts, see Chapter 4 of Maurer, *Proposing Men: Dialectics of Gender and Class in the Eighteenth-Century English Periodical* (Stanford: Stanford University Press, 1998).

the noble bishop to advance his career, the alliance that should ideally confer distinction upon the dean functions instead to infantilize and demean him. Likened by the narrator to "an apt boy at school" with regard to "the rich dunces" (ch. 15), William performs his homage oblivious to the moral implications of his actions.

In his dealings with Hannah Primrose, William inherits his father's ability to manipulate language for his own purposes. In spite of his avowal to Henry that Hannah acts out of "free choice," William artfully maneuvers that choice by waiting to disclose his own situation (he loves her but cannot marry her) until it was "evident that he had obtained her heart, her whole soul entire—so that loss of innocence would be less terrifying than separation from him" (ch. 21). Left at the summer's end to mourn her lost virginity and approaching motherhood once William has returned to London, Hannah waits in agony for a letter; after two months one indeed arrives, making her feel "rich as an empress with a new-acquired dominion" (ch. 22). Inchbald's simile emphasizes the way in which William's letter—which is to say his words—possess an almost monetary value for Hannah; once deciphered, however, those words turn out to be nothing more than "cold civility." In a distressing example of women's internalized oppression, Hannah blames not William but herself: "'He has only the fault of inconstancy, ... and that has been caused by *my* change of conduct—had I been virtuous still, he had still been affectionate'" (Ibid.). Yet Hannah's rationalization has a harrowing element of truth. In a society that reifies female chastity as property, Hannah's honor is her only dowry; once that has been spent, she becomes unfit for private ownership and must live out her days as a "public" woman, which is to say, a prostitute. While Hannah's betrayal must then necessarily follow her sexual seduction, only her impassioned love for William, and thus her unconditional acceptance of the bankrupt code of honor he both represents and perpetuates, makes that seduction possible.

Through the multiple failures of her privileged characters to operate from any motives other than self-love, Inchbald shows that, given the shift from an agrarian to a commercial economy in late eighteenth-century England, élite status has become both severed from, and inimical to, virtuous action. Revealing the void within traditional usages of such terms as honor, Inchbald then attempts to rewrite—and re-right—those concepts through her humble characters, the two Henrys. In the middle-class redefinition of honor, genuine honor manifests itself as the ability to judge for oneself, to act upon personal conviction rather than established code. As opposed to the aristocrat whose worth must be validated by the opinion of others, the truly honorable man or woman is emotionally and psychologically self-sufficient. Thus while the senior William's vain wife, Lady Clementina, lives her life "much less for the pleasure of *seeing* than for that of being *seen*" (ch. 15), Henry, upon his first entrance into his uncle's house, "walked into the room, not with a dictated obeisance, but with a hurrying step, a half pleased, yet a half frightened look, an instantaneous survey of every person present; not as demanding 'what they thought of him,' but expressing, almost as plainly as in direct words, 'what he thought of them'" (ch. 11).[1] Throughout the novel, Henry's supposed ignorance functions to realign appearance with reality, for he would "venture to give his opinion, contradict, and even act in opposition to persons, whom long experience and the approbation of the world had placed in situations which claimed his implicit reverence and submission" (ch. 18). His cousin William, by contrast, only mimics conventions already emptied of any content. Thus William, the narrator informs us, "inherited all the pride and ambition of the dean—Henry, all his father's humility" (Ibid.).

Like his father before him, the younger Henry is one whose "affectionate heart ... loved *persons* rather than *things*" (ch. 39). In a narrative comprised of emotional fracture—family members die, leave, or are believed dead; lovers are separated or estranged—the book's concluding reunion between father and son manifests, more powerfully than any other event in the novel, a vision of community. When Henry, who has left behind his beloved Rebecca in order to sail to Africa in search of his father, rushes from the boat to fall at his father's feet, exclaiming, "'My father! oh! my father!,'" the narrator comments: "William! dean! bishop! what are your honors, what your riches, what all your possessions, compared to the happiness, the transport bestowed by this one sentence, on your poor brother Henry?" (ch. 37). In their ability to function independently while simultaneously maintaining the deepest possible connections, Henry and his father exemplify what Inchbald holds to be authentic pride. The humble and contented Henrys thus stand in direct opposition to their successful counterparts, whose desire for rank and privilege has led to prosperous careers yet miserable lives.

The exemplary peace of mind experienced by the two Henrys and the faithful Rebecca is both cause and function of their economic situation, for upon returning to England, they "planned the means of their future support, independent of their kinsman William—not only of him, but of every person and thing, but their own industry" (ch. 46). In her descrip-

---

1 See the comparable passage in Rousseau's *Émile*, Appendix B.1.

tion of their secluded life, Inchbald stresses the link between material and psychological self-reliance:

> By forming an humble scheme for their remaining life, a scheme depending upon their *own* exertions alone, on no light promises of pretended friends, and on no sanguine hopes of certain success; but with prudent apprehension, with fortitude against disappointment, Henry, his son, and Rebecca, (now his daughter) found themselves, at the end of one year, in the enjoyment of every comfort which such distinguished minds knew how to taste.
>
> Exempt both from patronage and from controul—healthy—alive to every fruition with which nature blesses the world; dead to all out of their power to attain, the works of art—susceptible of those passions which endear human creatures to one another, insensible to those which separate man from man—they found themselves the thankful inhabitants of a small house or hut, placed on the borders of the sea. (ch. 47)

"Distinguished" not by rank, profession, or notoriety but by their capacity to eschew "public opinion" in the name of "private happiness" (ch. 23), Henry and his father withdraw from a society fueled by relentless maneuvering for wealth and status to one in which daily labor satisfies everyday needs. Critics have frequently dismissed this ending, labelling it overly simplistic. However, once readers regard Inchbald within the concrete historical situation with which she so actively engaged, the progressive, far-reaching implications of her conclusion begin to emerge more clearly. By positing an ideal community in which her characters can live independently, Inchbald responds to the unprecedented rise in consumerism that had taken a firm hold in Britain by the late eighteenth century.

Mercantile expansion, the growth of London as a center for international commerce, and the burgeoning of domestic enterprise meant that goods and services previously available only to the most affluent were becoming increasingly accessible. In other words, the expenditure and display that had previously distinguished the upper classes from those in the middle station were, ironically, turning into the means by which those in the middle ranks could catapult themselves into the élite. Inchbald's character, the senior William, exemplifies this progress in his calculated rise from obscure poverty to a position of religious, economic, and political power. Not only does William advance himself through career, marriage, and contacts, but he also reinforces his acquired status by the purchase of a country estate. In this second residence, where he lives like a rural squire, William further boosts his own and his family's position by cultivating first an acquaintance, then an alliance, with the village's first family, Lord and Lady Bendham, when their niece marries the younger William. Born the son of an indigent shopkeeper, William dies in possession of a bishop's palace.

Through the course of the eighteenth century, numerous authors responded to this kind of social transformation by employing the literary convention of rural retreat as a means of upholding the agrarian ethos of an earlier epoch.[1] Their works operate conservatively, advocating withdrawal from the corruption of modern urban life to the supposed harmony of rural existence. Inchbald, however, offers a different vision. Looking forward rather than harkening back, Inchbald attempts to transcend the city/country dualism by envisioning a new society altogether—a society of equals, unstructured by rank or fortune. Henry and son's seclusion is characterized not by a longing for rusticity, but by its provision of material and emotional self-sufficiency.

Inchbald's biography affirms her adherence to the moderate existence celebrated at the end of *Nature and Art*. A committed Londoner, Inchbald spent her adulthood at the hub of international as well as domestic commerce; her wide-ranging contacts among the élite—including theatrical colleagues, respected professionals, and the nobility—constantly positioned her in the midst of fashionable London life. Yet despite the splendor that often surrounded her, Inchbald was renowned for her frugality: in one letter she describes herself "scouring my bed-chamber while a coach with a coronet and two footmen waited at the door to take me an airing."[2] Inchbald, like her characters, successfully resisted the innumerable material temptations of her society; her life privileged familial connection and self-sufficiency over lavish display. Although vain about her beauty, her dress, according to one account, was "very seldom worth so much as eight-pence."[3] Writing at the age of fifty-two to her close friend

---

1 Consider, for example, *Spectator* No. 15 (1711); Alexander Pope's "Epistle to Burlington" (1731); the character of Lord Munodi in Part III of Jonathan Swift's *Gulliver's Travels* (1726); Samuel Johnson's poem "London" (1738); the rural retirement of Joseph, Fanny, and the Wilsons at the end of Henry Fielding's *Joseph Andrews* (1742); and the conclusions of Johnson's *Rasselas* (1759), Voltaire's *Candide* (1759), and Tobias Smollett's *Humphry Clinker* (1771).

2 26th May, 1796 (cited in Boaden, II: 55).

3 From a catalogue of Inchbald's person written by "a decided admirer" and "endorsed" by the author, who titled it "DESCRIPTION OF ME" (cited in Boaden, I: 175–76).

John Taylor, Inchbald noted that her temperate style of living subjected her to constant reproach:

> Because I choose that retirement suitable to my years, and think it my duty to support two sisters, instead of one servant, I am accused of madness. I might plunge into debt, be confined in prison, a pensioner on "The Literary Fund," or be gay as a girl of eighteen, and yet be considered as perfectly in my senses; but because I choose to live in independence, affluence to me, with a mind serene and prospects unclouded, I am supposed to be mad.[1]

Rendered wealthy by literary success and sound investments—she died with an estate worth over £5000—Inchbald consistently adopted restraint over expenditure, valuing the charity it made possible as much as the tranquility it produced. Her characters' retreat at the conclusion of *Nature and Art* reflects a comparable endeavor to attain happiness by choosing the lasting comfort of human relations over the temporary solace of commodities. Whereas at first glance Inchbald's conclusion seems to advocate the very kind of withdrawal proposed by her conservative predecessors, her characters' humble status—they are farmers and fishermen, not rural landowners—directly challenges those authors' representation of an idealized past by eliminating, rather than attempting to reinstate, class divisions.

In her fervent commitment to change, Inchbald imagined that such a community presented a viable solution to social ills. In retrospect, her proposal might appear forbiddingly utopian; yet, her idealistic scheme was in fact shared by some of the most forward-looking thinkers of her day. The Pantisocratic movement promoted most prominently in the last decade of the eighteenth century by Samuel Taylor Coleridge and Robert Southey, who met for the first time in June of 1794, represented a serious attempt to found a society upon the principles of "equal government of all" as well as upon the "generalization of individual property."[2] Through the autumn and winter of 1794, Coleridge and Southey were deeply engaged in planning and proselytizing the American community to be located on the banks of the Susquehannah River in rural Pennsylvania. Their design, modeled upon principles espoused in Godwin's *Political*

---

1 John Taylor, *Records of My Life* (London, 1832) 405 (quoted in Manvell, 157).
2 Letter from Robert Southey to Thomas Southey, 7 September 1794, *New Letters of Robert Southey*, ed. Kenneth Curry (New York: Columbia University Press, 1965) 75.

Justice, was encouraged by Godwin as well as by Holcroft. "From the writings of William Godwin and yourself," Robert Lovell, another member of the Pantisocratic movement, wrote to Holcroft, "our minds have been illuminated."[1] While there is as yet no evidence that Inchbald encountered personally any of the participants in the drive toward Pantisocracy, it seems highly plausible that as Godwin's close friend she would be well-acquainted with the project as well as with its underlying aim: "to realize a state of society free from the evils and turmoils that then agitated the world, and present an example of the eminence to which men might arrive under the unrestrained influence of right principles."[2] Moreover, although their plans never materialized, Southey's description of his "visionary" society as a place "where men's abilities would insure respect; where society was upon a proper footing, and man was considered as more valuable than money; and where I could till the earth, and provide by honest industry the meat which my wife would dress with pleasing care—"[3] is remarkably similar to Inchbald's own depiction of the life of her model characters:

> Each morning wakes the father and the son to cheerful labour
> in fishing, or the tending of a garden, the produce of which
> they carry to the next market town. The evening sends them
> back to their home in joy; where Rebecca meets them at the
> door, affectionately boasts of the warm meal that is ready, and
> heightens the charm of conversation with her taste and judg-
> ment. (ch. 47)

If the Pantisocrats looked originally to America as the earthly paradise in which to found their ideal society, Inchbald imagined that a classless Eden might be enjoyed within England itself. Yet the practical calculations of the Pantisocrats find no parallel in *Nature and Art*. In fact, the surprising lack of detail regarding the characters' final retreat echoes an earlier moment in the novel—the elder Henry's abrupt removal to an island off

---

1   *Memoirs of Thomas Holcroft*, ed. William Hazlitt (London, 1930) III: 278–79; cited in M. Ray Adams, *Studies in the Literary Backgrounds of English Radicalism* (New York: Greenwood, 1968 [1947]) 134.

2   The Bristol publisher Joseph Cottle, a prospective joiner in the scheme, describing a conversation with Robert Lovell at the end of 1794. (*Early Recollections, chiefly relating to the late Samuel Taylor Coleridge* [London, 1837] I: 2–4; cited in Adams, 135.)

3   Letter to Horace Walpole Bedford, 13 November 1793; cited in *The Life and Correspondence of Robert Southey*, ed. Charles Cuthbert Southey (New York: Harper and Brothers, 1851) 68.

the coast of Africa. Initially, Henry's flight seems to partake in the nostalgic yearning that characterizes the noble savage tradition: after having lost his young wife, the affection of his brother, and his livelihood, he hopes to recapture his lost innocence on an island of peace and plenty, far removed from society. Yet the events that transpire quickly thwart his expectations, along with those of the reader: his fellow travelers are brutally murdered by the native inhabitants who, while sparing Henry and his child, retain them as captives. Narrated only retrospectively in the form of a letter Henry sends with his son to England, Henry's island existence remains geographically remote and textually oblique, jettisoned, by its very obscurity, to the realm of myth.[1]

This chimerical quality permeates Inchbald's characterization of the younger Henry as well. Sharing Godwin's conviction that "our virtues and vices may be traced to the incidents that make the history of our lives,"[2] Inchbald nevertheless provides only the smallest glimpse of the events that contribute to the shaping of Henry. In and of itself, the fact that Inchbald devotes so little attention to the upbringing of her natural man is not a problem; indeed as one critic has remarked, "*Nature and Art* is no *Émile* in English clothing."[3] What is questionable, however, is the situation set up by the absence of such information. Because Henry's education remains abstract, little more than a general indoctrination in the golden rule, his goodness emerges as an inherent quality rather than a learned behavior. Like other noble savages, Henry appears good because he is uncorrupted by the evils of civilization. Thus Henry embodies a kind of pure "nature"—an uncorrupted innocence contrasted, through much of the novel, with the artifice inculcated in his cousin William. The presentation of Henry's virtue as innate rather than learned contradicts what is arguably the novel's most important point, that "the characters of men originate in their external circumstances."[4] Inchbald's portraits of William and his son are forceful precisely because they demonstrate that there can be no such thing as nature unmediated by culture. Inchbald clearly believes that the younger William possesses the potential for goodness,

---

1 There is, however, one moment in Henry's letter that responds directly to contemporary events. Henry's reaction to the slaying of his comrades offers, undoubtedly, a critique of the assumptions underlying British imperialism when he remarks that "'I do not know that the savages were much to blame—we had no business to invade their territories; and if they had invaded England, we should have done the same by them'" (ch. 10).

2 *Political Justice* (1793), Book I, Ch. III, 18.

3 Manvell, 114.

4 Godwin employs this phrase as the heading of Book I, Chapter IV in the third (1798) edition of *Political Justice*.

for she posits his adult depravity as a direct result of the education that "taught him to walk, to talk, to ride, to think like a man—a foolish man, instead of a wise child, as nature intended him to be" (ch. 9). William even commands our sympathy because the novel has demonstrated exactly how external circumstances made him what he is. Indeed the novel's ultimate power emanates more from Inchbald's complex and ambivalent rendering of William and his father than from her more monochromatic portrait of the benevolent Henry and his son.

Like her representations of Henry's island existence and his son's early education, Inchbald's depiction of her characters' final retreat collapses under the weight of its own contradictions. Henry and his father, disgusted by the disorder and corruption they discover upon their much-delayed return to England, found a new society "on the borders of the sea"—at the farthest reaches of civilization. Inchbald clearly presents their simple existence as a potential solution to societal ills; yet that existence, as represented in the novel, cannot function as any kind of social blueprint. Because it relies too heavily upon an abstract—and impossible—notion of goodness, Inchbald's proposed resolution to the dilemma of how to live virtuously in a corrupt world remains unsatisfactory. Yet it is important that she raises the question, for the issues she addresses have only intensified in the more than two hundred years since *Nature and Art* was published. Technological developments mean a relentless barrage by the ubiquitous advertising that supports consumer capitalism; moreover, the growth of multinationalism has created even more economic disparity among classes and between sexes. In her own life, Inchbald managed to combine vigorous independence, both economic and intellectual, with an extraordinarily wide range of human attachments; her fiction, ironically, envisions that such harmony could transpire only in a community utterly removed from social structures. *Nature and Art*'s provocative critique of a society driven by competition and consumption remains, however, exceedingly relevant, as we continue to struggle with the challenges posed by Inchbald's final novel.

Elizabeth Inchbald: A Brief Chronology

1753   Born 15 October in Standingfield, near Bury St. Edmunds (40 miles from London), second youngest of John and Mary Simpson's eight children. Catholic farmers.

1761   Death of father. Mother perseveres with farm; elder sisters marry.

1762   Publication of Rousseau's *Émile*.

1770   Brother George becomes actor in Norwich company. Elizabeth, beautiful but with stammer, applies unsuccessfully to Norwich manager Richard Griffith.

1771   First trip to London. Stays with sister; there meets Joseph Inchbald, 36, actor, painter, and Catholic.

1772   9 June, marries Inchbald. September: Theatrical debut in Bristol—plays Cordelia to Inchbald's Lear. October: Inchbalds tour Scotland with West Digges's company (until 1776).

1776   July: Inchbalds go to Paris, he to study painting and she French. October: Join Younger's company at Liverpool. Inchbald meets actress Sarah Siddons, who was to become life-long friend.

1777   Meets Siddons's brother, John Philip Kemble, model for Dorriforth in *A Simple Story*. July: Inchbalds at Canterbury. Thomas Holcroft (1745–1809), who was to become a literary advisor to Inchbald, acts with them at this time. October: Join Tate Wilkinson's company at Hull.

1778   At work on early drafts of novel that was to become *A Simple Story*.

1779   Sudden death of Joseph Inchbald, aged 44. Novel rejected by London publisher Stockdale; Inchbald at work on farces.

1780   October: First appearance on London stage: Bellario (breeches part) in Fletcher's *Philaster* at Covent Garden.

1783   Summer: creates minor sensation by appearing on stage without wig and with natural hair exposed.

1784   Brilliant success of her farce, *A Mogul Tale* (publ. as *The Mogul Tale*, Dublin 1788, London 1796), for George Colman the Elder at Little Theatre in the Haymarket; Inchbald in part of Selina.

1785   *I'll Tell You What* (publ. 1786) favorably received; *Appearance is Against Them* adopted by Harris for Covent Garden—first of plays to appear in print (1785).

1786   *The Widow's Vow*, adapted from Patrat's *L'Heureuse erreur* (publ. 1786).

1787   *Such Things Are*—based in part on life of prison reformer John Howard (publ. 1788); *The Midnight Hour*, adapted from Dumaniant's *Guerre ouverte* (publ. 1787); *All on a Summer's Day* (not published). Until 1811 engaged in continuous literary and editorial production.

1788   *Animal Magnetism*, adapted from Dumaniant's *Le Médecin malgré tout le monde* (publ. Dublin 1788); *The Child of Nature*, adapted from Mme. de Genlis's *Zélie, ou l'Ingénue* (publ. 1788).

1789   *The Married Man*, adapted from Destouches' *Le Philosophe marié* (publ. 1789). Retires from stage. Fall of Bastille.

1791   Robinson publishes *A Simple Story*, pays £200 for rights. *Hue and Cry*, adapted from Dumaniant's *La Nuit aux aventures* (not published); *Next-Door Neighbours*, adapted from Mercier's *L'Indigent* and Destouches' *Le Dissipateur* (publ. 1791) acted with great applause: character of Henry Wilford foreshadows Henry of *Nature and Art*. Performance of Holcroft's most successful play, *The Road to Ruin*.

1792   *Young Men and Old Women* (also called *Lovers No Conjurors*), altered and adapted from Gresset's *Le Méchant* (not published). Begins intimate friendship and correspondence with Jacobin philosopher and author, William Godwin (1756–1836); withdraws *The Massacre*, three-act tragedy set in seventeenth-century France and never acted, from publication on advice of Godwin and others (Boaden to publish in *Memoirs*). Holcroft's epistolary novel *Anna St. Ives*; Mary Wollstonecraft, *A Vindication of the Rights of Woman*.

1793   *Every One Has His Fault* (publ. 1793) attacked in conservative journal, *The True Briton*. Execution of Louis XVI and Marie-Antoinette. Godwin publishes his influential *Enquiry Concerning Political Justice*; he proposes to Inchbald on 16 September. August: Holcroft presses suit, also unsuccessfully.

1794   January: completes draft of early version of *Nature and Art* (previous titles: "A Satire upon the Times" and "The Prejudice of Education") and submits ms. to Holcroft, Godwin, George Hardinge for readings. *The Wedding Day* (publ. 1794). Death of sister Debby, whom Inchbald supported for much of life. Godwin publishes most famous novel *Caleb Williams*—Inchbald read and commented on proofs [included in

Appendix A.2.b]. Holcroft publishes first three volumes of *The Adventures of Hugh Trevor*; he is indicted for High Treason and spends eight weeks in Newgate, then acquitted without trial.

1796   January: *Nature and Art* purchased by Robinson for £150. Robert Bage's novel, *Hermsprong, or Man As He Is Not*. First meeting with Prince Hoare, publisher of *The Artist*.

1797   Second and revised edition of *Nature and Art. Wives as They Were, and Maids As They Are* (publ. 1797). Holcroft publishes last three volumes of *Hugh Trevor*, reissues first three as "second edition." Godwin marries Mary Wollstonecraft, causes rift with Inchbald.

1798   *Lovers' Vows*, adapted from Kotzebue's *Das Kind der Liebe* (publ. 1798) (play rehearsed in Jane Austen's *Mansfield Park*, 1814). Godwin's posthumous publication of Wollstonecraft's *The Wrongs of Woman: or, Maria*.

1799   *The Wise Man of the East*, adapted from Kotzebue's *Das Schreiberpult, oder Die Gefahren der Jugend* (publ. 1799). Godwin's *St. Leon*; Mary Hays's *The Victim of Prejudice*.

1802   Publisher bids £1000 for her *Memoirs*, sight unseen, but Inchbald refuses to sell; continues work on memoir, but destroys ms. in 1819 on advice of her confessor.

1805   *To Marry or Not To Marry* (publ. 1805).

1806–8   *The British Theatre; or, A Collection of Plays, … with Biographical and Critical Remarks by Mrs. Inchbald*, 25 vols.

1807   Untitled essay on novel writing for Prince Hoare's *The Artist* 14 (13 June) [included in Appendix A].

1809   Inchbald's *Collection of Farces and Afterpieces*, 7 vols. (selected by her). Declines editorship of John Bell's magazine *La Belle Assemblée*; Richard Lovell Edgeworth sends copy of Maria's *Tales of Fashionable Life* for Inchbald's comments (corrects *Patronage* for publishers in 1814).

1810   Sells copyright of two novels to Longman and Co.; revised third edition of *Nature and Art* published with introductory preface by Mrs. Barbauld in Vol. 27 of her *British Novelists* series [included in Appendix E].

1811   Inchbald's *Modern Theatre*, 10 vols. (plays selected by her).

1819   Retires to Kensington House.

1820   Fourth edition of *Nature and Art* published in *British Novelists*.

1821   Dies 1 August of inflammation of intestines, aged 69. Her estate was valued at over £5000.

1833 Boaden's *Memoirs of Mrs Inchbald* in two volumes, taken from large store of manuscript materials. Includes first publications of *The Massacre* (written 1792) and *A Case of Conscience* (written 1800).

A Note on the Text

This edition of *Nature and Art* is based on the novel's second edition, published in two volumes by G.G. and J. Robinson of Paternoster Row, London, in 1797. With the exception of the long "s," I have retained the spelling and punctuation of the original, but have silently restored missing quotation marks. This "corrected and improved" second edition of the novel introduced hundreds of grammatical, stylistic, and contextual revisions of the first edition published in 1796 by the same firm of G.G. and J. Robinson. In 1810 Inchbald once again emended her novel, this time for inclusion in Anna Laetitia Barbauld's *British Novelist* series. Although touted on the title page as "A New Edition," the third rendering, except for substituting the name "Agnes" for "Hannah" Primrose, offers little that is actually new. Despite its claim of presenting "the Last Corrections by the Author," the variant lacks, in my judgment, much of the vitality that infuses the two earlier versions of the text. For a description of changes from the first to the second edition of the novel, see Appendix A.

NATURE AND ART

IN TWO VOLUMES

by

MRS. INCHBALD

VOL. I

———————————

SECOND EDITION,

CORRECTED AND IMPROVED

———————————

LONDON:

Printed for G.G. and J. ROBINSON,
PATERNOSTER ROW.

1797.

CHAPTER I.

AT a time when the nobility of Britain were said, by the Poet Laureate, to admire and protect the arts, and were known by the whole nation to be the patrons of music—William and Henry, youths under twenty years of age, brothers, and the sons of a country shopkeeper who had lately died insolvent, set out on foot for London, in the hope of procuring by their industry a scanty subsistence.

As they walked out of their native town, each with a small bundle at his back, each observed the other drop several tears: but, upon the sudden meeting of their eyes, they both smiled with a degree of disdain at the weakness in which they had been caught.

"I am sure," said William (the elder) "I don't know what makes me cry."

"Nor I neither," said Henry: "for though we may never see this town again, yet we leave nothing behind us to give us cause to lament."

"No," replied William; "nor any body who cares what becomes of us."

"But I was thinking," said Henry, now weeping bitterly, "that, if my poor father were alive, *he* would care what was to become of us: he would not have suffered us to begin this long journey without a few more shillings in our pockets."

At the end of this sentence, William, who had with some effort suppressed his tears while his brother spoke, now uttered, with a voice almost inarticulate,—"Don't say any more; don't talk any more about it. My father used to tell us, that when he was gone we must take care of ourselves: and so we must. I only wish," continued he, giving way to his grief, "that I had never done any thing to offend him while he was living."

"That is what I wish too," cried Henry. "If I had always been dutiful to him while he was alive, I would not shed one tear for him now that he is gone: but I would thank heaven that he had escaped from his creditors."

In conversation such as this, wherein their sorrow for their deceased parent seemed less for his death, than because he had not been so happy when living, as they ought to have made him; and wherein their own outcast fortune was less the subject of their grief, than the reflection "what their father would have endured, could he have beheld them in their present situation;" in conversation such as this, they pursued their journey till they arrived at that metropolis, which has received for centuries past, from the provincial towns, the bold adventurer of every denomination; has stampt his character with experience and example; and, while it has bestowed on some coronets and mitres[1]—on some the lasting fame of genius—to others has dealt beggary, infamy, and untimely death.

CHAPTER II.

AFTER three weeks passed in London, a year followed, during which, William and Henry never sat down to a dinner, or went into a bed, without hearts glowing with thankfulness to that providence who had bestowed on them such unexpected blessings; for they no longer presumed to expect (what still they hoped they deserved) a secure pittance in this world of plenty. Their experience, since they came to town, had informed them, that to obtain a permanent livelihood, is the good fortune but of a part of those who are in want of it: and the precarious earning of half a crown, or a shilling, in the neighbourhood where they lodged, by an errand, or some such accidental means, was the sole support which they at present enjoyed.

They had sought for constant employment of various kinds, and even for servants' places; but obstacles had always occurred to prevent their success. If they applied for the situation of a clerk to a man of extensive concerns, their qualifications were admitted; but there must be security given for their fidelity:—they had friends, who would give them a character, but who would give them nothing else.

If they applied for the place even of a menial servant, they were too clownish and awkward for the presence of the lady of the house;—and once, when William (who had been educated at the free grammar-school[2] of the town in which he was born, and was an excellent scholar) hoping to obtain the good opinion of a young clergyman whom he solicited for the favour of waiting upon him, acquainted him "That he understood Greek and Latin," he was rejected by the divine, "because he could not dress hair."

Weary of repeating their mean accomplishments of "honesty, sobriety, humility," and on the precipice of reprobating such qualities,—which, however beneficial to the soul, gave no hope of preservation to the body,—they were prevented from this profanation by the fortunate remembrance of one qualification, which Henry, the possessor, in all his distress, had never till then called to his recollection; but which, as soon as

---

1   A tall headdress worn by a bishop as a symbol of episcopal office (*OED*).
2   Schools founded in the sixteenth century for the teaching of Latin; the term "grammar" was often understood to mean Latin grammar or language.

remembered and made known, changed the whole prospect of wretchedness placed before the two brothers; and they never knew want more.

Reader—Henry could play upon the fiddle.

CHAPTER III.

NO sooner was it publicly known that Henry could play most enchantingly upon the violin, than he was invited into many companies where no other accomplishment could have introduced him. His performance was so much admired, that he had the honour of being admitted to several tavern feasts, of which he had also the honour to partake without partaking of the expense. He was soon addressed by persons of the very first rank and fashion, and was once seen walking side by side with a peer.[1]

But yet, in the midst of this powerful occasion for rejoicing, Henry, whose heart was particularly affectionate, had one grief which eclipsed all the happiness of his new life:—his brother William could *not* play on the fiddle!—consequently, his brother William, with whom he had shared so much ill, could not share in his good fortune.

One evening, Henry, coming home from a dinner and concert at the Crown and Anchor,[2] found William, in a very gloomy and peevish humour, poring over the orations of Cicero.[3] Henry asked him several times "How he did;" and similar questions, marks of his kind disposition towards his beloved brother: but all his endeavours, he perceived, could not soothe or soften the sullen mind of William. At length, taking from his pocket a handful of almonds, and some delicious fruit (which he had purloined from the plenteous table, where his brother's wants had never been absent from his thoughts) and laying them down before him, he exclaimed, with a benevolent smile, "Do, William, let me teach you to play upon the violin."

William—full of the great orator whom he was then studying, and still more alive to the impossibility that *his* ear, attuned only to sense, could ever descend from that elevation, to learn mere sounds—William caught up the tempting presents which Henry had ventured his reputation to obtain for him, and threw them all indignantly at the donor's head.

---

1   A member of one of the degrees of nobility in Great Britain; a duke, marquis, earl, viscount, or baron (*OED*).

2   Tavern on the Strand at Arundel Street; from 1710–90 the location of a highly successful school for singing conducted by the Academy of Antient Music; in the 1790s the tavern also served as a popular meeting place for reforming groups.

3   Roman writer, statesman, and orator (106–43 BCE), renowned for his prose style.

Henry felt too powerfully his own superiority of fortune, to resent this ingratitude; he patiently picked up the repast, and laying it again upon the table, placed by its side a bottle of claret,[1] which he held fast by the neck, while he assured his brother, that, "although he had taken it while the waiter's back was turned, yet it might be drank with a safe conscience by them; for he had not himself tasted one drop at the feast, on purpose that he might enjoy a glass with his brother at home, and without wronging the company who had invited him."

The affection Henry expressed as he said this,—or the force of a bumper of wine, which William had not seen since he left his father's house,—had such an effect in calming the displeasure he was cherishing, that, on his brother's offering him the glass, he took it; and he deigned even to eat of his present.

Henry, to convince him that he had stinted himself to obtain for him this collation, sat down and partook of it.

After a few glasses, he again ventured to say, "Do, brother William, let me teach you to play on the violin."

Again his offer was refused, though with less vehemence; at length they both agreed that the attempt could not prosper.

"Then," said Henry, "William, go down to Oxford, or to Cambridge. There, no doubt, they are as fond of learning, as in this gay town they are of music. You know you have as much talent for the one as I for the other: do go to one of our universities, and see what dinners, what suppers, and what friends *you* will find there."

CHAPTER IV.

WILLIAM *did* go to one of those seats of learning, and would have starved there, but for the affectionate remittances of Henry, who shortly became so great a proficient in the art of music, as to have it in his power not only to live in a very reputable manner himself, but to send such supplies to his brother, as enabled him to pursue his studies.[2]

---

1 General term for red wine, especially from Bordeaux.

2 As Annibel Jenkins, Inchbald's recent biographer, has noted, "Professional musicians could, in the late eighteenth century, become quite celebrated, for this was the period when the opera flourished and concerts were a part of both public and private entertainment." However, while Henry could certainly earn a living as a musician, "he could never attain a proper social standing" (*I'll Tell You What: The Life of Elizabeth Inchbald* [Lexington: University Press of Kentucky, 2003] 374).

With some, the progress of fortune is rapid. Such is the case when, either on merit or demerit, great patronage is bestowed. Henry's violin had often charmed, to a welcome forgetfulness of his insignificance, an effeminate lord; or warmed with ideas of honour, the head of a duke, whose heart could never be taught to feel its manly glow. Princes had flown to the arms of their favourite fair-ones, with more rapturous delight, softened by the masterly touches of his art: and these elevated personages, ever grateful to those from whom they receive benefits, were competitors in the desire of heaping favours[1] upon him. But he, in all his advantages, never once lost for a moment the hope of some advantage for his brother William: and when at any time he was pressed by a patron to demand a "token of his regard," he would constantly reply:

"I have a brother, a very learned man, if your lordship (your grace, or your royal highness) would confer some small favour on him——"

His lordship would reply, "He was so teased and harassed in his youth by learned men, that he had ever since detested the whole fraternity."

His grace would inquire "If the learned man could play upon any instrument."

And his highness would ask "If he could sing."

Rebuffs such as these poor Henry met with in all his applications for William, till one fortunate evening, at the conclusion of a concert, a great man shook him by the hand, and promised a living of five hundred a year[2] (the incumbent of which was upon his death-bed) to his brother, in return for the entertainment that Henry had just afforded him.

Henry wrote in haste to William, and began his letter thus: "My dear brother, I am not sorry you did not learn to play upon the fiddle."

---

1   In her Preface to *A Bold Stroke for a Husband* (*British Theatre*, XIX, 4), Inchbald observes that "The part of Don Vicenzo was certainly meant as a moral satire upon the extravagant love, or the foolish affectation, of pretending to love, to extravagance—music. This satire was aimed at so many, that the shaft struck none. The charm of music still prevails in England, and the folly of affected admirers."

2   After completing his university studies, a priest in the Anglican Church would become ordained and take holy orders. The living offered to William is a relatively generous one: Dr. Blick, in Robert Bage's *Hermsprong*, makes £1000 by combining three livings (see Appendix C.2.b), while the Delaford living that Colonel Brandon offers to Edward Ferrars in Jane Austen's *Sense and Sensibility* (1811) brings only £200 a year.

CHAPTER V.

THE incumbent of this living died—William underwent the customary examinations, obtained successively the orders of deacon and priest;[1] then as early as possible came to town, to take possession of the gift, which his brother's skill had acquired for him.

William had a steady countenance, a stern brow, and a majestic walk; all of which this new accession, this holy calling to religious vows, rather increased than diminished. In the early part of his life, the violin of his brother had rather irritated than soothed the morose disposition of his nature: and though, since their departure from their native habitation, it had frequently calmed the violent ragings of his hunger, it had never been successful in appeasing the disturbed passions of a proud and a disdainful mind.

As the painter views with delight and wonder the finished picture, expressive testimony of his taste and genius: as the physician beholds with pride and gladness the recovering invalid, whom his art has snatched from the jaws of death: as the father gazes with rapture on his first child, the creature to whom he has given life—so did Henry survey, with transporting glory, his brother, drest for the first time in canonicals,[2] to preach at his parish church. He viewed him from head to foot—smiled—viewed again—pulled one side of his gown a little this way, one end of his band a little that way—then stole behind him, pretending to place the curls of his hair, but in reality, to indulge, and to conceal, tears of fraternal pride and joy.

William was not without joy: neither was he wanting in love or gratitude to his brother—but his pride was not completely satisfied.

"I am the elder," thought he to himself, "and a man of literature; and yet am I obliged to my younger brother, an illiterate man."—Here he suppressed every thought which could be a reproach to that brother. But there remained an object of his former contempt, now become even detestable to him—ungrateful man! the very agent of his elevation was now so odious to him, that he could not cast his eyes upon the friendly violin, without instant emotions of disgust.

In vain would Henry at times endeavour to subdue his haughtiness, by a tune on this wonderful machine.—"You know I have no ear," William would sternly say, in recompense for one of Henry's best solos. Yet was William enraged at Henry's answer, when, after taking him to hear him

---

1   The first two orders in the church hierarchy.
2   The articles of clothing worn by clergy according to the dictates of canon (ecclesiastical) law.

preach, he asked him "how he liked his sermon," and Henry modestly replied (in the technical phrase of his profession) "You know, brother, I have no ear."

Henry's renown in his profession daily increased; and with his fame, his friends. Possessing the virtues of humility and charity, far above William, who was the profest teacher of those virtues, his reverend brother's disrespect for his vocation never once made him relax for a moment in his anxiety to gain him advancement in the church. In the course of a few years, and in consequence of many fortuitous circumstances, he had the gratification of procuring for him the appointment to a deanery;[1] and thus at once placed between them an insurmountable barrier to all friendship, that was not the effect of condescension on the part of the dean.

William would now begin seriously to remonstrate with his brother "upon his useless occupation," and would intimate "the degradation it was to him, to hear his frivolous talent spoken of in all companies." Henry believed his brother to be much wiser than himself, and suffered shame that he was not more worthy of such a relation. To console himself for the familiar friend, whom he now perceived he had entirely lost, he searched for one of a softer nature—he married.

CHAPTER VI.

AS Henry despaired of receiving his brother's approbation of his choice, he never mentioned the event to him: but William, being told of it by a third person, inquired of Henry, who confirmed the truth of the intelligence, and acknowledged, that, in taking a wife, his sole view had been, to obtain a kind companion and friend, who would bear with his failings, and know how to esteem his few qualifications; therefore, he had chosen one of his own rank in life, and who, having a taste for music, and, as well as himself, an obligation to the art——

"And is it possible," cried the dean, "that what has been hinted to me is true? Is it possible that you have married a public singer?"

"She is as good as myself," returned Henry: "I did not wish her to be better, for fear she should despise me."

---

1 "The group of parishes, forming a division of a diocese, over which a rural dean presides" (*OED*). As assistant to the bishop (the third order in the church ranking), a dean held a position of power.

"As to despise," (answered the dean) "heaven forbid that we should despise any one—That would be acting unlike a christian—But do you imagine I can ever introduce her to my intended wife, who is a woman of family?"

Henry had received in his life many insults from his brother: but, as he was not a vain man, he generally thought his brother in the right, and consequently submitted with patience—but, though he had little self-love, he had for his wife an unbounded affection: on the present occasion, therefore, he began to raise his voice, and even (in the coarse expression of clownish anger) to lift his hand—but the sudden and affecting recollection of what he had done for the dean—of the pains, the toils, the hopes, and the fears he had experienced when soliciting his preferment—this recollection overpowered his speech—weakened his arm—and deprived him of every active force, but that of flying out of his brother's house (in which they then were) as swift as lightning, while the dean sat proudly contemplating—"that he had done his duty."

For several days Henry did not call, as was his custom, to see his brother: William's marriage drew near, and he sent a formal card to invite him on that day; but not having had the condescension to name his sister-in-law in the invitation, Henry thought proper not to accept it; and the joyful event was celebrated without his presence. But the ardour of the bridegroom was not so vehement as to overcome every other sensation—he missed his brother—that heart-felt cheerfulness with which Henry had ever given him joy upon every happy occasion—even amidst all the politer congratulations of his other friends—seemed to the dean mournfully wanting. This derogation from his felicity he was resolved to resent—and for a whole year these brothers, whom adversity had entwined closely together, prosperity separated.

Though Henry, on his marriage, paid so much attention to his brother's prejudices, as to take his wife from her public employment, this had not so entirely removed the scruples of William, as to permit him to think her a worthy companion for Lady Clementina, the daughter of a poor Scotch earl, whom he had chosen, merely that he might be proud of her family; and, in return, suffer that family to be ashamed of *his*.

If Henry's wife were not fit company for Lady Clementina, it is to be hoped she was company for angels—she died within the first year of her marriage, a faithful, an affectionate wife, and a mother.

When William heard of her death, he felt a sudden shock—and a kind of fleeting thought glanced across his mind, that

"Had he known she had been so near her dissolution, she might have been introduced to Lady Clementina; and he himself would have called her sister."

That is (if he had defined his fleeting idea) "They would have had no objection to have met this poor woman for the *last time*; and would have descended to the familiarity of kindred, in order to have wished her a good journey to the other world."

Or, is there in death something which so raises the abjectness of the poor, that, on their approach to its sheltering abode, the arrogant believer feels the equality he had before denied, and trembles?

CHAPTER VII.

THE wife of Henry had been dead near six weeks before the dean heard the news: a month then elapsed in thoughts by himself, and consultations with Lady Clementina, how he should conduct himself, on this occurrence. Her advice was,

"That, as Henry was the younger, and by their stations, in every sense, the dean's inferior, he ought first to make overtures of reconciliation."

The dean answered, "He had no doubt of his brother's good will to him; but that he had reason to think, from the knowledge of his temper, he would be more likely to come to him upon an occasion to bestow comfort, than to receive it: for instance, if I had suffered the misfortune of losing you, my brother, I have no doubt, would have forgotten his resentment, and ———"

She was offended that the loss of the vulgar wife of Henry should be compared to the loss of her—she lamented her indiscretion in forming an alliance with a family of no rank, and implored the dean to wait till his brother should make some concession to him, before he renewed the acquaintance.

Though Lady Clementina had mentioned on this occasion her *indiscretion*, she was of a prudent age—she was near forty—yet, possessing rather a handsome face and person, she would not have impressed the spectator with an idea that she was near so old, had she not constantly attempted to appear much younger. Her dress was fantastically fashionable, her manners affected all the various passions of youth, and her conversation was perpetually embellished with accusations against her own "heedlessness, thoughtlessness, carelessness, and childishness."

There is perhaps, in each individual, one parent motive to every action, good or bad: be that as it may, it was evident, that with Lady Clementina, all she said or did, all she thought or looked, had but one foundation—vanity.—If she were nice,[1] or if she were negligent, vanity was the cause of both; for she would contemplate with the highest degree of self-complacency "what such a one would say of her elegant preciseness, or what such a one would think of her interesting neglect."

If she complained she was ill, it was with the certainty that her languor would be admired; if she boasted she was well, it was that the spectator might admire her glowing health; if she laughed, it was because she thought it made her look pretty; if she cried, it was because she thought it made her look prettier still.—If she scolded her servants, it was from vanity, to show her knowledge superior to theirs; and she was kind to them from the same motive, that her benevolence might excite their admiration.—Forward, and impertinent in the company of her equals from the vanity of supposing herself above them, she was bashful even to shamefacedness in the presence of her superiors, because her vanity told her she engrossed all their observation. Through vanity she had no memory; for she constantly forgot every thing she heard others say, from the minute attention which she paid to every thing she said herself.

She had become an old maid from vanity, believing no offer she received worthy of her deserts; and when her power of farther conquest began to be doubted, she married from vanity, to repair the character of her fading charms. In a word, her vanity was of that magnitude, that she had no idea but that she was humble in her own opinion; and it would have been impossible to have convinced her that she thought well of herself, because she thought *so well*, as to be assured, that her own thoughts undervalued her.

CHAPTER VIII.

THAT, which in a weak woman is called vanity, in a man of sense is termed pride—make one a degree stronger, or the other a degree weaker, and the dean and his wife were infected with the self-same folly. Yet, let not the reader suppose that this failing (however despicable) had erased from either bosom all traces of humanity. They are human creatures who are meant to be pourtrayed in this little book: and where is the human creature who has not some good qualities to soften, if not counterbalance his bad ones?

1 Particular, but also in the sense of fastidious, difficult to please, refined.

The dean, with all his pride, could not wholly forget his brother, nor eradicate from his remembrance the friend he had been to him—he resolved therefore, in spite of his wife's advice, to make him some overture, which he had no doubt but Henry's good nature would instantly accept. The more he became acquainted with all the vain and selfish propensities of Lady Clementina, the more he felt a returning affection for his brother: but little did he suspect how much he loved him, till (after sending to various places to enquire for him) he learned—that on his wife's decease, unable to support her loss in the surrounding scene, Henry had taken the child she brought him in his arms, shaken hands with all his former friends—passing over his brother in the number—and set sail in a vessel bound for Africa, with a party of Portuguese and some few English adventurers,[1] to people there the uninhabited part of an extensive island.

This was a resolution, in Henry's circumstances, worthy a mind of singular sensibility: but William had not discerned, till then, that every act of Henry's was of the same description; and more than all, his every act towards him.—He staggered when he heard the tidings; at first thought them untrue; but quickly recollected that Henry was capable of surprising deeds! He recollected, with a force which gave him torture, the benevolence his brother had ever shown towards him—the favours he had heaped upon him—the insults he had patiently endured in requital!

In the first emotion, which this intelligence gave the dean, he forgot the dignity of his walk and gesture—He ran with frantic enthusiasm to every corner of his house where the least vestige of what belonged to Henry, remained—He pressed close to his breast, with tender agony, a coat of his, which by accident had been left there—He kissed and wept over a walking-stick which Henry once had given him—He even took up with delight, a music-book of his brother's—nor would his poor violin have then excited anger.

When his grief became more calm, he sat in deep and melancholy meditation, calling to mind, when, and where he saw his brother last. The recollection gave him fresh cause of regret. He remembered they had parted on his refusing to suffer Lady Clementina to admit the acquaintance of Henry's wife.—Both Henry and his wife he now contemplated

---

1 The term "adventurer," with its implications both of danger—"One who seeks adventures, or who engages in hazardous enterprises" and commerce—"One who undertakes, or shares in, commercial adventures or enterprises; a speculator" (OED)—suggests that the people with whom Henry travels may have been involved in the slave trade. During the sixteen century the Portuguese held a near monopoloy on the African slave trade; by the eighteenth century, that position was held by the British. For texts related to the West African settlement of Sierra Leone, see Appendix D.

beyond the reach of his pride; and he felt the meanness of his former haughtiness towards them.

To add to his self-reproaches, his tormented memory presented to him the exact countenance of his brother at their last interview, as it changed, while he censured his marriage, and treated with disrespect the object of his conjugal affection. He remembered the anger repressed, the tear bursting forth, and the last glimpse he had of him, as he left his presence, most likely for ever.

In vain he now wished, that he had followed him to the door—that he had once shaken hands and owned his obligations to him before they had parted. In vain he wished too, that, in this extreme agony of his mind, he had such a friend to comfort him, as Henry had ever proved.

CHAPTER IX.

THE avocations of an elevated life erase the deepest impressions—the dean, in a few months, recovered from those which his brother's departure first made upon him; and would now at times even condemn, in anger, Henry's having so hastily abandoned him and his native country, in resentment, as he conceived, of a few misfortunes which his usual fortitude should have taught him to have borne. Yet, was he still desirous of his return, and wrote two or three letters expressive of his wish, which he anxiously endeavoured should reach him. But many years having elapsed without any intelligence from him, and a report having arrived that he, and all the party with whom he went, were slain by the savage inhabitants of the island, William's despair of seeing his brother again, caused the desire to diminish; while attention and affection to a still nearer and dearer relation than Henry had ever been to him, now chiefly engaged his mind.

Lady Clementina had brought him a son, on whom, from his infancy, he doated—and the boy, in riper years, possessing a handsome person and evincing a quickness of parts, gratified the father's darling passion, pride; as well as the mother's vanity.

The dean had, besides this child, a domestic comfort highly gratifying to his ambition: the bishop of **** became intimately acquainted with him soon after his marriage, and from his daily visits had become, as it were, a part of the family. This was much honour to the dean, not only as the bishop was his superior in the church, but was of that part of the bench[1] whose blood is ennobled by a race of ancestors, and to which, all wisdom on the plebeian side crouches in humble respect.

Year after year rolled on in pride and grandeur; the bishop and the dean passing their time in attending levees[2] and in talking politics; Lady Clementina passing hers in attending routs[3] and in talking of *herself*, till the son arrived at the age of thirteen.

Young William passed *his* time, from morning to night, with persons who taught him to walk, to ride, to talk, to think like a man—a foolish man, instead of a wise child, as nature designed him to be.

This unfortunate youth was never permitted to have one conception of his own—all were taught him—he was never once asked "what he thought?" but men were paid to tell him "how to think." He was taught to revere such and such persons, however unworthy of his reverence; to believe such and such things, however unworthy of his credit; and to act so and so, on such and such occasions, however unworthy of his feelings.

Such were the lessons of the tutors assigned him by his father—Those masters whom his mother gave him, did him less mischief; for though they distorted his limbs and made his manners effeminate, they did not interfere beyond the body.

Mr. Norwynne (the family name of his father, and though but a schoolboy, he was called *Mister*) could talk on history, on politics, and on religion; surprisingly to all who never listened to a parrot or magpie—for he merely repeated what had been told to him, without one reflection upon the sense or probability of his report. He had been praised for his memory; and to continue that praise, he was so anxious to retain every sentence he had heard or he had read, that the poor creature had no time for one native idea, but could only re-deliver his tutors' lessons to his father, and his father's to his tutors. But, whatever he said or did, was the admiration of all who came to the house of the dean, and who knew he was an only child—Indeed, considering the labour that was taken to spoil him, he was rather a commendable youth; for, with the pedantic folly of his tutors, the blind affection of his father and mother, the obsequiousness of the servants, and flattery of the visitors, it was some credit to him that

---

1 I.e., order of bishops, from those who occupy the bishop's bench in the House of Lords.
2 Derived from the French *lever*, to rise: a reception of visitors on rising from bed; more specifically, as here, "The concourse of those who croud round a man of power in a morning (Johnson's *Dictionary* [1755]) or "an assembly held (in the early afternoon) by the sovereign or his representatives, at which men only are received" (*OED*). Inchbald's point is that the dean and his superior spend their time attending to political rather than spiritual matters.
3 Fashionable assemblies or gatherings, large evening parties or receptions.

he was not an ideot, or a brute—though when he imitated the manners of a man, he had something of the latter in his appearance—for he would grin and bow to a lady, catch her fan in haste when it fell, and hand her to her coach, as thoroughly void of all the sentiment, which gives grace to such tricks, as a monkey.

CHAPTER X.

ONE morning in winter, just as the dean, his wife, and darling child, had finished their breakfast at their house in London, a servant brought in a letter to his master, and said "The man waited for an answer."

"Who is the man?" cried the dean, with all that terrifying dignity, with which he never failed to address his inferiors, especially such as waited on his person.

The servant replied with a servility of tone equal to the haughty one of his master "he did not know; but that the man looked like a sailor, and had a boy with him."

"A begging letter, no doubt," cried Lady Clementina.

"Take it back," said the dean, "and bid him send up word who he is, and what is his errand."

The servant went; and returning said "He comes from on board a ship; his captain sent him, and his errand is, he believes, to leave a boy he has brought with him."

"A boy!" (cried the dean) "what have I to do with a boy? I expect no boy. What boy? What age?"

"He looks about twelve or thirteen," replied the servant.

"He is mistaken in the house," (said the dean). "Let me look at the letter again."

He did look at it, and saw plainly it was directed to himself—Upon a second glance, he had so perfect a recollection of the hand as to open it instantaneously; and after ordering the servant to withdraw, he read the following.

"Zocotora Island,[1] April 6th.

"MY DEAR BROTHER WILLIAM,

"It is a long time since we have seen one another, but I hope not so long, that you have quite forgotten the many happy days we once passed together.

---

1   A fictitious island off the west coast of Africa.

"I did not take my leave of you when I left England, because it would have been too much for me—I had met with a great many sorrows just at that time, one of which was, the misfortune of losing the use of my right hand by a fall from my horse, which accident robbed me of most of my friends, for I could no longer entertain them with my performance as I used to do; and so I was ashamed to see them or you; and that was the reason I came hither to try my fortune with some other adventurers.

"You have, I suppose, heard that the savages of the island put our whole party to death. But it was my chance to escape their cruelty. I was heart-broken for my comrades, yet upon the whole I do not know that the savages were much to blame—we had no business to invade their territories; and if they had invaded England, we should have done the same by them.—My life was spared, because, having gained some little strength in my hand, during the voyage, I pleased their king when I arrived there, with playing on my violin.

"They spared my child too, in pity to my lamentations, when they were going to put him to death.—Now, dear brother, before I say any more to you concerning my child, I will first ask your pardon for any offence I may have ever given you in all the time we lived so long together—I know you have often found fault with me, and I dare say I have been very often to blame; but I here solemnly declare that I never did any thing purposely to offend you, but mostly all I could, to oblige you—and I can safely declare, that I never bore you above a quarter of an hour's resentment, for any thing you might say to me which I thought harsh.

"Now, dear William, after being in this island eleven years, the weakness in my hand has unfortunately returned; and yet there being no appearance of complaint, the un-informed islanders think it is all my obstinacy, and that I *will not* entertain them with my music, which makes me say that I *cannot*; and they have imprisoned me, and threaten to put my son to death if I persist in my stubbornness any longer.

"The anguish I feel in my mind takes away all hope of the recovery of strength in my hand; and I have no doubt but that they intend in a few days to put their horrid threat into execution.

"Therefore, dear brother William, hearing in my prison of a most uncommon circumstance, which is, that an English vessel is lying at a small distance from the island, I have entrusted a faithful negro to take my child to the ship, and deliver him to the captain, with a request that he may be sent (with this letter) to you, on the ship's arrival in England.

"Now, my dear dear brother William, in case the poor boy should live to come to you, I have no doubt but you will receive him; yet, excuse a poor fond father, if I say a word or two which I hope may prove in his favour.

"Pray, my dear brother, do not think it the child's fault, but mine, that you will find him so ignorant—he has always shown a quickness and a willingness to learn, and would, I dare say, if he had been brought up under your care, have been by this time a good scholar—but you know I am no scholar myself. Besides, not having any books here, I have only been able to teach my child by talking to him; and in all my conversations with him, I have never taken much pains to instruct him in the manners of my own country; thinking, that if ever he went over, he would learn them soon enough; and if he never *did* go over, that it would be as well he knew nothing about them.

"I have kept him also from the knowledge of every thing which I have thought pernicious in the conduct of the savages, except that I have now and then pointed out a few of their faults, in order to give him a true conception and a proper horror of them. At the same time I have taught him to love, and to do good to his neighbour, whoever that neighbour may be, and whatever may be his failings. Falsehood of every kind I included in this precept as forbidden, for no one can love his neighbour and deceive him.

"I have instructed him too, to hold in contempt all frivolous vanity, and all those indulgences which he was never likely to obtain. He has learned all that I have undertaken to teach him; but I am afraid you will yet think he has learned too little.

"Your wife, I fear, will be offended at his want of politeness, and perhaps proper respect for a person of her rank; but indeed he is very tractable, and can, without severity, be amended of all his faults; and though you will find he has many, yet, pray my dear brother, pray my dear brother William, call to mind he has been a dutiful and an affectionate child to me; and that, had it pleased heaven we had lived together for many years to come, I verily believe that I should never have experienced one mark of his disobedience.

"Farewel for ever, my dear dear brother William—and if my poor, kind, affectionate child should live to bring you this letter, sometimes speak to him of me; and let him know, that for twelve years he was my sole comfort; and that, when I sent him from me, in order to save his life, I laid down my head upon the floor of the cell in which I was confined, and prayed that heaven might end my days before the morning."

* * *

This was the conclusion of the letter, except four or five lines which (with his name) were so much blotted, apparently with tears, that they were illegible.

CHAPTER XI.

WHILE the dean was reading to himself this letter, his countenance frequently changed, and once or twice the tears streamed from his eyes. When he was finished, he exclaimed

"My brother has sent his child to me, and I will be a parent to him." He was rushing towards the door when Lady Clementina stopped him.

"Is it proper, do you think, Mr. dean, that all the servants in the house should be witnesses to your meeting with your brother and your nephew in the state in which they must be at present?—send for them into a private apartment."

"My brother!" (cried the dean) "Oh! that it *were* my brother! The man is merely a person from the ship, who has conducted his child hither."

The bell was rung, money was sent to the man, and orders given that the boy should be shown up immediately.

While young Henry was walking up the stairs, the dean's wife was weighing in her mind, in what manner it would most redound to her honour to receive him; for her vanity taught her to believe that the whole inquisitive world pried into her conduct, even upon every family occurrence.

Young William was wondering to himself what kind of an unpolished monster his beggarly cousin would appear; and was contemplating how much the poor youth would be surprised, and awed by his superiority.

The dean felt no other sensation than an impatient desire of beholding the child.

The door opened—and the son of his brother Henry, of his benefactor, entered.

The habit he had on when he left his father being worn out by the length of the voyage, he was in the dress of a sailor-boy. Though about the same age with his cousin, he was something taller: and though a strong family resemblance appeared between the two youths, he was handsomer than William; and from a simplicity spread over his countenance, a quick impatience in his eye, which denoted anxious curiosity, and childish surprise at every new object which presented itself, he appeared younger than his informed, and well-bred cousin.

He walked into the room, not with a dictated obeisance, but with a hurrying step, a half pleased, yet a half frightened look, an instantaneous survey of every person present; not as demanding "what they thought of him," but expressing, almost as plainly as in direct words, "what he thought of them." For all alarm in respect to his safety and reception seemed now wholly forgotten, in the curiosity which the sudden sight of strangers, such as he had never seen in his life before, excited: and as to *himself,* he did not appear to know there was such a person existing: his whole faculties were absorbed in *others.*[1]

The dean's reception of him did honour to his sensibility, and his gratitude to his brother.—After the first affectionate gaze, he ran to him, took him in his arms, sat down, drew him to him, held him between his knees, and repeatedly exclaimed, "I will repay to you, all I owe to your father."

The boy, in return, hugged the dean round the neck, kissed him, and cried,

"Oh! you *are* my father—you have just such eyes, and such a forehead—indeed you would be almost the same as he, if it were not for that great white thing[2] which grows upon your head!"

Let the reader understand, that the dean, fondly attached to every ornament of his dignified function, was never seen (unless caught in bed) without an enormous wig—with this, young Henry was enormously struck; having never seen so unbecoming a decoration, either in the savage island from whence he came, or on board the vessel in which he sailed.

"Do you imagine" (cried his uncle, laying his hand gently on the revered habiliment) "that this grows?"

"What is on *my* head grows," said young Henry, "and so does what is upon my father's."

"But now you are come to Europe, Henry, you will see many persons with such things as these, which they put on and take off."

"Why do you wear such things?"

"As a distinction between us and inferior people: they are worn to give an importance to the wearer."

---

1   Note Rousseau's comparable depiction of the behavior of his fictional pupil Émile in Appendix B.1.

2   Most probably a massive full-bottomed periwig, which consisted of elaborate powdered curls falling from a center part to the shoulders and framing the face. In 1795, Pitt's tax on hair powder made wigs such as William's unfashionable. The use of powder was also diminishing for women: in 1783 Inchbald was "among the first to try the effect of her natural hair upon the stage" (Boaden, I: 173).

"That is just as the savages do; they hang brass nails, wire, buttons, and entrails of beasts all over them, to give them importance."

The dean now led his nephew to Lady Clementina, and told him "She was his aunt, to whom he must behave with the utmost respect."

"I will, I will," he replied; "for she, I see, is a person of importance too—she has, very nearly, such a white thing upon her head as you have!"

His aunt had not yet fixed, in what manner it would be advisable to behave; whether with intimidating grandeur, or with amiable tenderness. While she was hesitating between both, she felt a kind of jealous apprehension, that her son was not so engaging either in his person or address as his cousin; and therefore she said

"I hope, dean, the arrival of this child will give you a still higher sense of the happiness we enjoy in our own—what an instructive contrast between the manners of the one, and of the other!"

"It is not the child's fault," returned the dean, "that he is not so elegant in his manners as his cousin;—had William been bred in the same place, he would have been as unpolished as this boy."

"I beg your pardon, sir," (said young William with a formal bow and a sarcastic smile). "I assure you, several of my tutors have told me, that I appear to know many things as it were by instinct."

Young Henry fixed his eyes upon his cousin while with steady self-complacency he delivered this speech; and no sooner was it concluded than Henry cried out in a kind of wonder

"A little man! as I am alive, a little man! I did not know there were such little men in this country! I never saw one in my life before!"

"This is a boy" (said the dean) "a boy not older than yourself."

He put their hands together, and William gravely shook hands with his cousin.

"It *is* a man," continued young Henry—then stroked his cousin's chin. "No no, I do not know whether it is or not."

"I tell you again," said the dean, "he is a boy of your own age—you and he are cousins, for I am his father."

"How can that be?" (said young Henry) "he called you *Sir*."

"In this country," said the dean, "polite children do not call their parents *father* and *mother*."

"Then don't they sometimes forget to love them as such?" asked Henry.

His uncle became now impatient to interrogate him in every particular concerning his father's state—Lady Clementina felt equal impatience to know where the father was: whether he were coming to live with them, wanted any thing of them, and every circumstance in which her vanity was interested. Explanations followed all these questions; but which, exactly agreeing with what the elder Henry's letter has related, require no recital here.

CHAPTER XII.

THAT vanity which presided over every thought and deed of Lady Clementina's was the protector of young Henry within her house: it represented to her how amiable her conduct would appear in the eye of the world, should she condescend to treat this destitute nephew as her own son,—what envy such heroic virtue would excite in the hearts of her particular friends, and what grief in the bosoms of all those who did not like her.

The dean was a man of acute penetration; he understood the thoughts which, upon this occasion, passed in the mind of his wife; and in order to insure her kind treatment of the boy, instead of reproaching her for the cold manner in which she had at first received him, he praised her tender and sympathetic heart, for having shown him so much kindness: and thus stimulated her vanity to be praised still more.

William, the mother's own son, far from apprehending a rival in this savage boy, was convinced of his own preeminence, and felt an affection for him; though rather as a foil, than as a cousin. He sported with his ignorance upon all occasions, and even lay in wait for circumstances that might expose it: while young Henry, strongly impressed with every thing which appeared new to him, expressed, without reserve, the sensations which those novelties excited; and felt little care what construction was put upon his observations.

He never appeared offended, or abashed when laughed at, but still pursued his questions, and still discovered his wonder at many replies made to him, though "simpleton," "poor silly boy," and "ideot," were vociferated around him from his cousin, his aunt, and their constant visitor the bishop.

His uncle would frequently undertake to instruct him; so indeed would the bishop; but Lady Clementina, her son, and the greatest part of her companions, found something so irresistibly ridiculous in his remarks, that nothing but immoderate laughter followed: they thought such folly had even merit in the way of entertainment, and they wished him no wiser.

Having been told, that every morning on the first seeing his uncle he was to make a respectful bow, and coming into the dean's dressing-room just as he was out of bed, his wig lying on the table, Henry appeared at a loss which of the two he should bow to—at last he gave the preference to his uncle; but, afterwards, bowed reverently to the wig. In this, he did what he conceived was proper, from the introduction which the dean, on his first arrival, had given him to this venerable stranger; for in reality, Henry had a contempt for all finery; and had called even his aunt's jewels, when they were first shown to him, "trumpery," asking "what they were good for?" But being corrected in this disrespect, and informed of their high value, he, like a good convert, gave up his reason to his faith: and becoming, like all converts, over zealous, he now believed there was great worth in glittering appearances, and respected the ear-rings of Lady Clementina almost as much as he respected herself.

CHAPTER XIII.

IT was to be lamented, that when young Henry had been several months in England, had been taught to read, and had of course, in the society in which he lived, seen much of the enlightened world, yet the natural expectation of his improvement was by no means answered.

Notwithstanding the sensibility, which upon various occasions he manifested in the most captivating degree, notwithstanding the seeming gentleness of his nature upon all occasions, there now appeared, in most of his enquiries and remarks, a something which demonstrated either a stupid, or troublesome disposition; either dulness of conception, or an obstinacy of perseverance in comments, and in arguments, which were glaringly false.

Observing his uncle one day offended with his coachman, and hearing him say to him in a very angry tone, "You shall never drive me again"—The moment the man quitted the room, Henry (with his eyes fixed in the deepest contemplation) repeated five or six times in a half whisper to himself

"*You shall never drive me again.*"

"*You shall never drive me again.*"

The dean at last called to him "what do you mean by thus repeating my words?"

"I am trying to find out what *you* meant," said Henry.

"What! don't you know," cried his enlightened cousin, "Richard is turned away?—he is never to get upon our coach-box again, never to drive any of us any more."

"And was it pleasure to drive us, cousin?—I am sure I have often pitied him—it rained sometimes very hard when he was on the box—and sometimes Lady Clementina has kept him a whole hour at the door all in the cold and snow—was that a pleasure?"

"No," replied young William.

"Was it honour, cousin?"

"No," exclaimed his cousin with a contemptuous smile.

"Then why did my uncle say to him as punishment "he should never"——

"Come hither, child," said the dean, "and let me instruct you—your father's negligence has been inexcusable.—There are in society" (continued the dean) "rich and poor; the poor are born to serve the rich."

"And what are the rich born for?"

"To be served by the poor."

"But suppose the poor would not serve them?"

"Then they must starve."

"And so poor people are permitted to live, only upon condition that they wait upon the rich?"

"Is that a hard condition? or if it were, they will be rewarded in a better world than this."

"Is there a better world than this?"

"Is it possible you do not know there is?"

"I heard my father once say something about a world to come; but he stopt short, and said I was too young to understand what he meant."

"The world to come" (returned the dean) "is where we shall go after death; and there no distinction will be made between rich and poor—all persons there will be equal."

"Aye, now I see what makes it a better world than this. But cannot this world try to be as good as that?"

"In respect to placing all persons on a level, it is utterly impossible— God has ordained it otherwise."

"How! has God ordained a distinction to be made, and will not make any himself?"

The dean did not proceed in his instructions; he now began to think his brother in the right, and that the boy was too young, or too weak, to comprehend the subject.

CHAPTER XIV.

IN addition to his ignorant conversation upon many topics, young Henry had an incorrigible misconception and misapplication of many *words*—his father having had but few opportunities of discoursing with him upon account of his attendance at the court of the savages; and not having books in the island, he had consequently many words to learn of this country's language when he arrived in England: this task his retentive memory made easy to him; but his childish inattention to their proper signification still made his want of education conspicuous.

He would call *compliments, lies*—*Reserve*, he would call *pride*—*stateliness, affection*—and for the words *war* and *battle*, he constantly substituted the word *massacre*.

"Sir," said William to his father, one morning as he entered the room, "do you hear how the cannons are firing, and the bells ringing?"

"Then I dare say," cried Henry, "there has been another massacre."

The dean called to him in anger "Will you never learn the right use of words? You mean to say a battle."

"Then what is a massacre?" cried the frightened, but still curious Henry.

"A massacre," replied his uncle, "is when a number of people are slain—"

"I thought," returned Henry, "soldiers had been people!"

"You interrupted me," said the dean, "before I finished my sentence—certainly, both soldiers and sailors are people, but they engage to die by their own free will and consent."

"What! all of them?"

"Most of them."

"But the rest are massacred?"

The dean answered, "The number who go to battle unwillingly, and by force, are few; and for the others, they have previously sold their lives to the state."

"For what?"

"For soldiers' and sailors' pay."

"My father used to tell me, we must not take away our own lives; but he forgot to tell me, we might sell them for others to take away."

"William," (said the dean to his son, his patience tired with his nephew's persevering nonsense) "explain to your cousin the difference between a battle and a massacre."

"A massacre," said William, rising from his seat, and fixing his eyes alternately upon his father, his mother, and the bishop (all of whom were present) for their approbation, rather than the person's to whom his instructions were to be addressed—"a massacre," said William, "is when human beings are slain, who have it not in their power to defend themselves."

"Dear cousin William," (said Henry) "that must ever be the case, with every one who is killed."

After a short hesitation, William replied, "In massacres, people are put to death for no crime, but merely because they are objects of suspicion."

"But in battle," said Henry, "the persons put to death are not even suspected."

The bishop now condescended to end this disputation by saying emphatically

"Consider, young savage, that in battle neither the infant, the aged, the sick, nor infirm are involved, but only those in the full prime of health and vigour."

As this argument came from so great and reverend a man as the bishop, Henry was obliged, by a frown from his uncle, to submit, as one refuted; although he had an answer at the veriest tip of his tongue, which it was torture to him not to utter. What he wished to say must ever remain a secret.—The church has its terrors as well as the law; and Henry was awed by the dean's tremendous wig, as much as Pater-noster Row is awed by the attorney-general.[1]

CHAPTER XV.

IF the dean had loved his wife but moderately, seeing all her faults clearly as he did, he must frequently have quarrelled with her: if he had loved her with tenderness, he must have treated her with a degree of violence in the hope of amending her failings: but having neither personal nor mental affection towards her sufficiently interesting to give himself the trouble to contradict her will in any thing, he passed for one of the best husbands in the world. Lady Clementina went out when she liked, staid at home when she liked, dressed as she liked, and talked as she liked, without a word of disapprobation from her husband, and all—because he cared nothing about her.

---

1 Paternoster Row was the center of London's book trade; the attorney general, Sir John Scott, was notorious for his prosecutions for libel.

Her vanity attributed this indulgence to inordinate affection: and observers in general thought her happier in her marriage, than the beloved wife who bathes her pillow with tears by the side of an angry husband, whose affection is so excessive, that he unkindly upbraids her because she is—less than perfection.

The dean's wife was not so dispassionately considered by some of his acquaintance as by himself; for they would now and then hint at her foibles; but this great liberty she also conceived to be the effect of most violent love, or most violent admiration; and such would have been her construction, had they commended her follies—had they totally slighted, or had they beaten her.

Amongst those acquaintances, the bishop of****, by far the most frequent visitor, did not come merely to lounge an idle hour, but he had a more powerful motive; the desire of fame, and dread of being thought a man receiving large emolument for unimportant service.

The dean, if he did not procure him the renown he wished, still preserved him from the apprehended censure.

The elder William was to his negligent or ignorant superiors in the church, such as an apt boy at school is to the rich dunces—William performed the prelates' tasks for them, and they rewarded him—not indeed with toys or money, but with their countenance, their company, their praise.—And scarcely was there a sermon preached from the patrician part of the bench, in which the dean did not fashion some periods,[1] blot out some uncouth phrases, render some obscure sentiments intelligible, and was the certain person, when the work was printed, to correct the press.

The Honourable and Right Reverend Bishop of**** delighted in printing and publishing his works; or rather the entire works of the dean, which passed for his:[2]—and so degradingly did William, the shopkeeper's son, think of his own honest extraction, that he was blinded, even to the loss of honour, by the lustre of this noble acquaintance: for, though in other respects a man of integrity, yet, when the gratification of his friend was in question, he was a liar; he not only disowned his giving him aid in any of his publications, but he never published any thing in his own name, without declaring to the world "That he had

---

1   In other words, write concluding sentences.
2   Holcroft's novel, *Hugh Trevor* (1794–97), contains a comparable portrait of ecclesiastical plagiarism. According to Gary Kelly, both Inchbald's and Holcroft's bishops, as well as the odious Dr. Blick in Bage's *Hermsprong* (1796), were modelled after the Reverend Samuel Horsley, bishop of Rochester (157–58). Passages from both novels are printed in Appendix C.2.

been obliged for several hints on the subject, for many of the most judicious corrections, and for those passages in page so and so (naming the most eloquent parts of the work) to his noble and learned friend the bishop."

The dean's wife being a fine lady—while her husband and his friend pored over books or their own manuscripts at home, she ran from house to house, from public amusement to public amusement; but much less for the pleasure of *seeing* than for that of being *seen*. Nor was it material to her enjoyment whether she were observed, or welcome, where she went, as she never entertained the smallest doubt of either; but rested assured that her presence roused curiosity and dispensed gladness all around.

One morning she went forth to pay her visits, all smiles, such as she thought captivating: she returned, all tears, such as she thought no less endearing.

Three ladies accompanied her home, entreating her to be patient under a misfortune to which even kings are liable,—namely, defamation.

Young Henry, struck with compassion at grief, of which he knew not the cause, begged to know "What was the matter?"

"Inhuman monsters, to treat a woman thus!" cried his aunt in a fury—casting the corner of her eye into a looking-glass to see how rage became her.

"But, comfort yourself:" (said one of her companions) "few people will believe you merit the charge."

"But few! if only one believe it, I shall call my reputation lost, and I will shut myself up in some lonely hut, and for ever renounce all that is dear to me!"

"What! all your fine cloaths?" said Henry in amazement.

"Of what importance will my best dresses be, when nobody would see them?"

"You would see them yourself, dear aunt: and I am sure nobody admires them more."

"Now you speak of that," said she, "I do not think this gown I have on becoming—I am sure I look——"

The dean, with the bishop (to whom he had been reading a treatise just going to the press, which was to be published in the name of the latter, though written by the former) now entered, to enquire why they had been sent for in such haste.

"Oh dean! Oh my lord!" she cried, resuming that grief which the thoughts of her dress had for a time dispelled—"My reputation is destroyed—a public print has accused me of playing deep[1] at my own house, and winning all the money."

"The world will never reform," said the bishop: "all our labour, my friend, is thrown away."

"But is it possible," cried the dean, "that any one has dared to say this of you?"

"Here it is in print." Said she, holding out a newspaper.

The dean read the paragraph, and then exclaimed "I can forgive a falsehood *spoken*—the warmth of conversation may excuse it—but to *write* and *print* an untruth is unpardonable—and I will prosecute this publisher."

"Still the falsehood will go down to posterity," (said Lady Clementina) "and after ages will think I was a gambler."

"Comfort yourself, dear madam," said young Henry, wishing to console her: "perhaps after ages may not hear of you; nor even the present age think much about you."

The bishop now exclaimed, after having taken the paper from the dean, and read the paragraph, "It is a libel, a rank libel, and the author must be punished."

"Not only the author, but the publisher." Said the dean.

"Not only the publisher, but the printer." Continued the bishop.

"And must my name be bandied about by lawyers in a common court of justice?" cried Lady Clementina. "How shocking to my delicacy!"

"My lord, it is a pity we cannot try them by the ecclesiastical court,"[2] said the dean, with a sigh.

"Or by the India delinquent bill,"[3] said the bishop with vexation.

"So totally innocent as I am!" she vociferated with sobs. "Every one knows I never touch a card at home, and this libel charges me with playing at my own house—and though, whenever I do play,—I own I am apt to win, yet it is merely for my amusement."

"Win or not win, play or not play," exclaimed both the church-men, "this is a libel: no doubt, no doubt, a libel."

Poor Henry's confined knowledge of his native language tormented him so much with curiosity upon this occasion, that he went softly up

---

1 Gambling for high stakes. In Inchbald's play *Next Door Neighbours* (1791), Lady Caroline Seymour's waiting woman declares that her mistress "loves gaming to distraction, and plays deep, yet she never loses."

2 Courts for administering clerical ecclesiastical law and maintaining the discipline of the Established Church, as contrasted to judicial courts.

3 Possibly a reference to one of the restrictions imposed upon the Indian press.

to his uncle, and asked him in a whisper, "What is the meaning of the word libel?"

"A libel," replied the dean, in a raised voice, "is that which one person publishes to the injury of another."

"And what can the injured person do" (asked Henry) "if the accusation should chance to be true?"

"Prosecute." Replied the dean.

"But then, what does he do if the accusation be false?"

"Prosecute likewise." Answered the dean.

"How, uncle! is it possible that the innocent behave just like the guilty?"

"There is no other way to act."

"Why then, if I were the innocent, I would do nothing at all, sooner than I would act like the guilty. I would not persecute——"

"I said *prosecute*." (Cried the dean in anger) "Leave the room, you have no comprehension."

"Oh yes, now I understand the difference of the two words—but they sound so much alike, I did not at first observe the distinction. You said "the innocent *prosecute*, but the guilty *persecute*." He bowed (convinced as he thought) and left the room.

After this modern star-chamber,[1] which was left sitting, had agreed on its mode of vengeance, and the writer of the libel was made acquainted with his danger, he waited, in all humility, upon Lady Clementina, and assured her, with every appearance of sincerity——-

"That she was not the person alluded to by the paragraph in question, but that the initials which she had conceived to mark out her name, were, in fact, meant to point out Lady Catharine Newland."

"But, Sir," cried Lady Clementina, "what could induce you to write such a paragraph upon Lady Catharine? She *never* plays."

"We know that, madam, or we dared not to have attacked her. Though we must circulate libels, madam, to gratify our numerous read-ers, yet no people are more in fear of prosecutions than authors and edi-tors; therefore, unless we are deceived in our information, we always take care to libel the innocent—we apprehend nothing from them—their own characters support them—but the guilty are very tenacious; and what they cannot secure by fair means, they will employ force to accomplish. Dear

---

1   A criminal court developed in the fifteenth century from the judicial sittings of the King's Council in the Star Chamber at Westminster. The abuse of this court's power in the seven-teenth century made it a proverbial type of arbitrary and oppressive tribunal. It was abolished by an Act of the Long Parliament in 1641.

madam, be assured I have too much regard for a wife and seven small children, who are maintained by my industry alone, to have written any thing in the nature of a libel upon your ladyship."

CHAPTER XVI.

ABOUT this period the dean had just published a pamphlet in his own name, and in which that of his friend the bishop was only mentioned with thanks for hints, observations, and condescending encouragement to the author.

This pamphlet glowed with the dean's love for his country; and such a country as he described, it was impossible *not* to love. "Salubrious air, fertile fields, wood, water, corn, grass, sheep, oxen, fish, fowl, fruit, and vegetables," were dispersed with the most prodigal hand—"valiant men, virtuous women; statesmen wise and just; tradesmen abounding in merchandise and money; husbandmen possessing peace, ease, plenty: and all ranks, liberty."—This brilliant description, while the dean read the work to his family, so charmed poor Henry that he repeatedly cried out

"I am glad I came to this country."

But it so happened that a few days after, Lady Clementina, in order to render the delicacy of her taste admired, could eat of no one dish upon the table, but found fault with them all. The dean at length said to her,

"Indeed you are too nice—reflect upon the hundreds of poor creatures who have not a morsel or a drop of any thing to subsist upon, except bread and water; and even of the first a scanty allowance, but for which they are obliged to toil six days in the week, from sun to sun."

"Pray, uncle," cried Henry, "in what country do these poor people live?"

"In this country." Replied the dean.

Henry rose from his chair, ran to the chimney-piece, took up his uncle's pamphlet, and said, "I don't remember your mentioning them here."

"Perhaps I have not." Answered the dean coolly.

Still Henry turned over each leaf of the book; but he could meet only with luxurious details of the "fruits of the earth, the beasts of the field, the birds of the air, and the fishes of the sea."

"Why here is provision enough for all the people," said Henry: "why should they want? why do not they go and take some of these things?"

"They must not," said the dean, "unless they were their own."

"What! uncle, does no part of the earth, nor any thing which the earth produces, belong to the poor?"

"Certainly not."

"Why did not you say so then in your pamphlet?"

"Because it is what every body knows."

"Oh, then, what you have said in your pamphlet, is only what—nobody knows."

There appeared to the dean, in the delivery of this sentence, a satirical acrimony, which his irritability as an author could but ill forgive.

An author, it is said, has more acute feelings in respect to his works, than any artist in the world besides.

Henry had some cause, on the present occasion, to think this observation just; for no sooner had he spoken the foregoing words, than his uncle took him by the hand out of the room; and leading him to his study, there he enumerated his various faults, and having told him "it was for all those, too long permitted with impunity, and not merely for the *present* impertinence, that he meant to punish him," ordered him to close confinement in his chamber for a week.

In the mean time the dean's pamphlet (less hurt by Henry's critique than *he* had been) was proceeding to the tenth edition, and the author acquiring literary reputation beyond what he had ever conferred on his friend the bishop.

The style, the energy, the eloquence of the work, was echoed by every reader who could afford to buy it—some few enlightened ones excepted, who chiefly admired the author's *invention*.

CHAPTER XVII.

THE dean, in the good humour which the rapid sale of his book produced, once more took his nephew to his bosom; and although the ignorance of young Henry upon the late occasions, had offended him very highly, yet that self-same ignorance, evinced a short time after upon a different subject, struck his uncle, as productive of a most rare and exalted virtue.

Henry had frequently in his conversation betrayed the total want of all knowledge in respect to religion or futurity; and the dean for this reason delayed taking him to church, till he had previously given him instructions *wherefore* he went.

A leisure morning arrived, on which he took his nephew to his study, and implanted in his youthful mind the first unconfused idea of the Creator of the universe!

The dean was eloquent, Henry was all attention: his understanding, expanded by time, to the conception of a God—and not warped by custom, from the sensations which a just notion of that God inspires, dwelt with delight and wonder on the information given him!—lessons, which, instilled into the head of a senseless infant, too often produce, throughout his remaining life, an impious indifference to the truths revealed.

Yet, with all that astonished, that respectful sensibility which Henry showed on this great occasion; he still expressed his opinion, and put questions to the dean, with his usual simplicity, till he felt himself convinced.

"What!" cried he—after being informed of the attributes inseparable from the Supreme Being, and having received the injunction to offer prayers to him night and morning, "What! am I permitted to speak to power divine?"

"At all times." Replied the dean.

"How! whenever I like?"

"Whenever you like." Returned the dean.

"I durst not" (cried Henry) "make so free with the bishop: nor dare any of his attendants."

"The bishop" (said the dean) "is the servant of God, and therefore must be treated with respect."

"With more respect than his master?" asked Henry.

The dean not replying immediately to this question, Henry in the rapidity of enquiry ran on to another: "But what am I to say, when I speak to the Almighty?"

"First, thank him for the favours he has bestowed on you."

"What favours?"

"You amaze me" (cried the dean) "by your question! Do not you live in ease, in plenty, and happiness?"

"And do the poor, and the unhappy, thank him too, uncle?"

"No doubt—every human being glorifies him, for having been made a rational creature."

"And does my aunt and all her card parties glorify him for that?"

The dean again made no reply—and Henry went on to other questions, till his uncle had fully instructed him as to the nature and the form of *prayer*—and now putting into his hands a book, he pointed out to him a few short prayers which he wished him to address to heaven in his presence.

Whilst Henry bent his knees, as his uncle had directed, he trembled—turned pale—and held, for a slight support, on the chair placed before him.

His uncle went to him, and asked him "What was the matter?"

"Oh!" cried Henry, "when I first came to your door with my poor father's letter, I shook for fear you would not look upon me—and I cannot help feeling, even more now, than I did then."

The dean embraced him with warmth—gave him confidence—and retired to the other side of the study, to observe his whole demeanour on this new occasion.

As he beheld his features varying between the passions of humble fear, and fervent hope,—his face sometimes glowing with the rapture of thanksgiving, and sometimes with the blushes of contrition, he thus exclaimed apart:

"This is the true education on which to found the principles of religion—The favour conferred by heaven in granting the freedom of petitions to its throne, can never be conceived with proper force, but by those, whose most tedious moments during their infancy, were *not* passed in prayer. Unthinking governors of childhood! to insult the Deity with a form of worship, in which the mind has no share; nay worse, has repugnance; and by the thoughtless habits of youth, prevent, even in age, devotion."

Henry's attention was so firmly fixed, that he forgot there was a spectator of his fervour; nor did he hear young William enter the chamber and even speak to his father.

At length closing his book, and rising from his knees, he approached his uncle and cousin with a sedateness in his air, which gave the latter a very false opinion of the state of his youthful companion's mind.

"So, Mr. Henry," cried William, "you have been obliged to say your prayers at last."

The dean informed his son, "That to Henry, it was no punishment to pray."

"He is the strangest boy I ever knew!" Said William inadvertently.

"To be sure," said Henry, "I was frightened when I first knelt; but when I came to the words *Father which art in heaven*, they gave me courage; for I know how merciful and kind a *father* is, beyond any one else."

The dean again embraced his nephew; let fall a tear to his poor brother Henry's misfortunes; and admonished the youth to show himself equally submissive to other instructions, as he had done to those, which inculcate piety.

CHAPTER XVIII.

THE interim between youth and manhood was passed by young William and young Henry in studious application to literature; some casual mistakes in our customs and manners on the part of Henry, some too close adherences to them on the side of William.

Their different characters when boys, were preserved when they became men: Henry still retained that natural simplicity which his early destiny had given him; he wondered still at many things he saw and heard, and at times would venture to give his opinion, contradict, and even act in opposition to persons, whom long experience and the approbation of the world had placed in situations which claimed his implicit reverence and submission.

Unchanged in all his boyish graces, young William, now a man, was never known to infringe upon the statutes of good-breeding, even though sincerity, his own free will, duty to his neighbour, with many plebeian virtues and privileges, were the sacrifice.

William inherited all the pride and ambition of the dean—Henry, all his father's humility. And yet, so various and extensive is the acceptation of the word pride, that, on some occasions, Henry was proud even beyond his cousin. He thought it far beneath his dignity, ever to honour or contemplate with awe, any human being in whom he saw numerous failings. Nor would he, to ingratiate himself into the favour of a man above him, stoop to one servility, such as the haughty William daily practised.

"I know I am called proud." One day said William to Henry.

"Dear cousin," replied Henry, "it must be only, then, by those who do not know you: for to me you appear the humblest creature in the world."

"Do you really think so?"

"I am certain of it; or would you always give up your opinion to that of persons in a superior state, however inferior in their understanding? Would, else, their weak judgment immediately change yours, though, before, you had been decided on the opposite side? Now indeed, cousin, I have more pride than you; for I never will stoop to act or to speak contrary to my feelings."

"Then you will never be a great man."

"Nor ever desire it, if I must first be a mean one."

There was in the reputation of these two young men another mistake, which the common retailers of character committed. Henry was said to be wholly negligent, while William was reputed to be extremely fond, of the other sex. William indeed was gallant, was amorous, and indulged his inclination to the libertine society of women; but Henry it was who *loved* them. He admired them at a reverential distance, and felt so tender an affection for the virtuous female, that it shocked him to behold, much more to associate with, the depraved and vicious.

In the advantages of person, Henry was still superior to William; and yet the latter had no common share of those attractions which captivate weak, thoughtless, or unskillful minds.

CHAPTER XIX.

ABOUT the time that Henry and William quitted college and had arrived at their twentieth year, the dean purchased a small estate in a village near to the country residence of Lord and Lady Bendham; and in the total want of society, the dean's family were frequently honoured with invitations from the great house.

Lord Bendham, besides a good estate, possessed the office of a lord of the bed-chamber to his majesty. Historians do not ascribe much importance to the situation, or to the talents of nobles in this department, nor shall this little history.[1] A lord of the bed-chamber is a personage well known in courts, and in all capitals where courts reside; with this advantage to the inquirer, that in becoming acquainted with one of those noble characters, he becomes acquainted with all the remainder; not only with those of the same kingdom, but those of foreign nations; for, in whatever land, in whatever climate, a lord of the bed-chamber must necessarily be the self-same creature: one, wholly made up of observance, of obedience, of dependance, and of imitation—a borrowed character—a character formed by reflection.

The wife of this illustrious peer, as well as himself, took her hue, like the chameleon, from surrounding objects; her manners were not governed by her mind, but were solely directed by external circumstances. At court, humble, resigned, patient, attentive—At balls, masquerades, gambling-tables, and routs, gay, sprightly, and flippant—At her country seat, reserved, austere, arrogant, and gloomy.

Though in town her timid eye, in presence of certain persons, would scarcely uplift its trembling lid, so much she felt her own insignificance; yet, in the country, till Lady Clementina arrived, there was not one being

---

1 In an undated letter to William Godwin discussing the manuscript of "A Satire on the Times," most probably an early version of *Nature and Art*, Inchbald describes a "Lord Rinforth," possibly a precursor to Lord Bendham. See Appendix A.2.c.

of consequence enough to share in her acquaintance; and she paid back to her inferiors there, all the humiliating slights, all the mortifications, which in London she received from those to whom *she* was inferior.

Whether in town or country, it is but justice to acknowledge, that in her own person she was strictly chaste; but in the country she extended that chastity even to the persons of others; and the young woman who lost her virtue in the village of Anfield, had better have lost her life. Some few were now and then found hanging or drowned, while no other cause could be assigned for their despair, than an imputation on their character, and dread of the harsh purity of Lady Bendham. She would remind the parish priest of the punishment allotted for female dishonour,[1] and by her influence had caused many an unhappy girl to do public penance in their own or the neighbouring churches.

But this country rigour, in town, she could dispense withal; and like other ladies of virtue, she there visited and received into her house the acknowledged mistresses of a man in elevated life: it was not therefore the crime, but the rank which the criminal held in society, that drew down Lady Bendham's vengeance: she even carried her distinction of classes in female error to such a very nice point, that the adulterous concubine of an elder brother was her most intimate acquaintance, whilst the less guilty unmarried mistress of the younger, she would not sully her lips to exchange a word with.

Lord and Lady Bendham's birth, education, talents, and propensities, being much on the same scale of eminence, they would have been a very happy pair, had not one great misfortune intervened—The lady never bore her lord a child.—While every cottage of the village was crammed with half-starved children, whose father from week to week, from year to year, exerted his manly youth and wasted his strength in vain to protect them from hunger; whose mother mourned over her new-born infant as a little wretch, sent into the world to deprive the rest of what already was too scanty for them; in the castle which owned every cottage and all the surrounding land, and where one single day of feasting would have nourished for a month all the poor inhabitants of the parish, not one child was given to partake of the plenty. The curse of barrenness was on the family of the lord of the manor—the curse of fruitfulness upon the famished poor.

---

1 Women convicted of fornication—sexual intercourse outside of marriage—were condemned to stand in public wrapped in a white sheet as atonement for their misconduct.

This lord and lady, with an ample fortune both by inheritance and their sovereign's favour, had never yet the oeconomy to be exempt from debts; still, over their splendid, their profuse table, they could contrive and plan excellent schemes "how the poor might live most comfortably with a little better management."

The wages of a labouring man with a wife and half a dozen small children Lady Bendham thought quite sufficient, if they would only learn a little oeconomy.

"You know, my lord, those people never want to dress—shoes and stockings, a coat and a waistcoat, a gown and a cap, a petticoat and a handkerchief, are all they want—fire, to be sure, in winter—then all the rest is merely for provision."

"I'll get a pen and ink," said young Henry, (one day when he had the honour of being at their table) "and see what the *rest* amounts to."

"No, no accounts," cried my lord, "no summing up: but if you were to calculate, you must add to the receipts of the poor my gift at Christmas—Last year, during the frost, no less than a hundred pounds."

"How benevolent!" Exclaimed the dean.

"How prudent!" Exclaimed Henry.

"How do you mean by prudent?" asked Lord Bendham. "Explain your meaning."

"No, my lord," replied the dean, "do not ask for an explanation: this youth is wholly unacquainted with our customs; and though a man in stature, is but a child in intellects. Henry, have not I often cautioned you——"

"Whatever his thoughts are upon this subject," cried Lord Bendham, "I desire to know them."

"Why then, my lord," answered Henry, "I thought it was prudent in you to give a little; lest the poor, driven to despair, should take all."[1]

"And if they had, they would have been hanged."

"Hanging, my lord, our history, or some tradition, says, was formerly adopted as a mild punishment, in place of starving."

"I am sure," cried Lady Bendham, (who seldom spoke directly to the argument before her) "I am sure they ought to think themselves much obliged to us."

---

1 In *Social Protest in the Eighteenth-Century English Novel*, Mona Scheuermann points to the "inflammatory, even revolutionary" nature of this statement: "*Nature and Art* was published only seven years after the French Revolution, and one can guess which poor Inchbald might have had in mind" (185).

"That is the greatest hardship of all." Cried Henry.

"What, sir?" Exclaimed the earl.

"I beg your pardon—my uncle looks displeased—I am very ignorant—I did not receive my first education in this country—and I find I think so differently from every one else; that I am ashamed to utter my sentiments."

"Never mind, young man," answered Lord Bendham: "we shall excuse your ignorance for once. Only inform us what it was you just now called, *the greatest hardship of all.*"

"It was, my lord, that what the poor receive to keep them from perishing, should pass under the name of *gifts* and *bounty*. Health, strength, and the will to earn a moderate subsistence, ought to be every man's security from obligation."[1]

"I think a hundred pounds a great deal of money," cried Lady Bendham; "and I hope my lord will never give it again."

"I hope so too," cried Henry; "for if my lord would only be so good as to speak a few words for the poor as a senator,[2] he might possibly for the future keep his hundred pounds, and yet they never want it."

Lord Bendham had the good-nature only to smile at Henry's simplicity, whispering to himself, "I had rather keep my——" His last word was lost in the whisper.

CHAPTER XX.

IN the country—where the sensible heart is still more susceptible of impressions; and where the unfeeling mind, in the want of other wits to invent, forms schemes for its own amusement—our youths both fell in love; if passions that were pursued on the most opposite principles can receive the same appellation. William, well versed in all the licentious theory, thought himself in love, because he perceived a tumultuous

---

1   Note the comparable argument in Godwin's *Political Justice* (1793): "But, while religion inculcated on mankind the impartial nature of justice, its teachers have been too apt to treat the practice of justice, not as a debt, which it ought to be considered, but as an affair of spontaneous generosity and bounty. They have called on the rich to be clement and merciful to the poor. The consequence of this has been that the rich, when they bestowed the most slender pittance of their enormous wealth in acts of charity, as they were called, took merit to themselves for what they gave, instead of considering to themselves as delinquents for what they withheld" (Bk. 8, Ch. 1).

2   A term often applied to a member of either House of the British Parliament; thus, Lord Bendham's position in the House of Lords.

impulse cause his heart to beat, while his fancy fixed on a certain object, whose presence agitated yet more his breast.

Henry thought himself not in love, because, while he listened to William on the subject, he found their sensations did not in the least agree.

William owned to Henry, that he loved Hannah, the daughter of a cottager in the village, and hoped to make her his mistress.

Henry felt that his tender regard for Rebecca, the daughter of the curate of the parish, did not inspire him even with the boldness to acquaint her with his sentiments, much less to meditate one design that might tend to her dishonour.

While William was cautiously planning, how to meet in private, and accomplish the seduction of the object of his passion, Henry was endeavouring to fortify the object of *his* choice with every virtue. He never read a book from which he received improvement, that he did not carry it to Rebecca—never knew a circumstance which might assist towards her moral instruction, that he did not haste to tell it her—and once when William boasted

"He knew he was beloved by Hannah;"

Henry said, with equal triumph, "he had not dared to take the means to learn, nor had Rebecca dared to give one instance of her partiality."

Rebecca was the youngest, and by far the least handsome daughter of four, to whom the Reverend Mr. Rymer, a widower, was father. The other sisters were accounted beauties; and she, from her comparative want of personal charms, having been less beloved by her parents, and less caressed by those who visited them, than the rest, had for some time past sought other resources of happiness than the affection, praise, and indulgence of her fellow-creatures.[1] The parsonage house in which this family lived, was the forlorn remains of an ancient abbey: it had in later times been the habitation of a rich and learned rector, by whom, at his decease, a library was bequeathed for the use of every succeeding resident. Rebecca, left alone in this huge ruinous abode, while her sisters were paying stated visits in search of admiration, passed her tedious hours in

---

1   Compare Richard Steele's tale of two sisters in *Spectator* No. 33 (7 April 1711): Laetitia, who is extremely beautiful, hears nothing but praise all her life; Daphne, who is plain, must cultivate other charms. As in Inchbald's novel, in the end it is Daphne who gets her man: a young gentleman, first smitten by the beautiful sister, soon tires of her "haughty Impertinence" and can then appreciate the "good Humour" and "agreeable Conversation" of Daphne.

reading.[1] She not merely read—she thought—the choicest English books from this excellent library taught her to *think*, and reflection fashioned her mind to bear the slights, the mortifications of neglect, with a patient dejection, rather than with an indignant or a peevish spirit.

This resignation to injury and contumely gave to her perfect symmetry of person, a timid eye, a retiring manner, and spread upon her face a placid sweetness, a pale serenity mixed with sense and taste, which no wise connoisseur in female charms would have exchanged for all the sparkling eyes and florid tints of her vain and vulgar sisters.—Henry's soul was so much enamoured of her gentle deportment, that in his sight she appeared beautiful; while she, with an understanding competent to judge of his worth, was so greatly surprised, so prodigiously astonished at the distinction, the attention, the many offices of civility paid her by him in preference to her idolized sisters, that her gratitude for such unexpected favours had sometimes (even in his presence, and in that of her family) nearly drowned her eyes with tears. Yet, they were only trifles, in which Henry had the opportunity or the power to give her testimony of his regard—trifles, often more grateful to the sensible mind than efforts of high importance; and by which, the artist in the human heart will accurately trace a passion, wholly concealed from the dull eye of the unskilled observer.

The first cause of amazement to Rebecca in the manners of Henry was, that he talked with *her* as well as with her sisters; no visitor else had done so. In appointing a morning's or an evening's walk, he proposed *her* going with the rest; no one had ever required her company before. When he called and she was absent, he asked where she was; no one had ever missed her before.—She thanked him from her very heart, and soon perceived, that, at those times when he was present, company was more pleasing even than books.

Her astonishment, her gratitude, did not stop here—Henry proceeded in attention—he soon selected her from her sisters to tell her the news of the day when he chanced to call; answered her observations the first; once gave her a sprig of myrtle from his bosom in preference to another who

1 These two sentences were added to the second edition. By locating the parsonage house in "the forlorn remains of an ancient abbey" replete with a fine library, Inchbald develops her portrayal of the self-educated Rebecca and also creates a more plausible environment in which Rebecca will later conceal Hannah's infant. In these changes, Inchbald was perhaps addressing the *Monthly Review*'s mention of "some improbabilities" and "some impossibilities" in the novel (April 1796: 453; see Appendix E.4).

had praised its beauty; and once—never to be forgotten kindness—sheltered her from a hasty shower with his *parapluie*,[1] while he lamented to her drenched companions

"That he had but *one* to offer."

From a man whose sense and person they admire, how dear, how impressive on the female heart is every trait of tenderness! Till now, Rebecca had experienced none; not even of the parental kind; and merely from the overflowings of a kind nature (not in return for affection) had she ever loved her father and her sisters. Sometimes, repulsed by their severity, she transferred the fulness of an affectionate heart upon animals: but now, her alienated mind was recalled and softened by a sensation that made her long to complain of the burthen it imposed—those obligations which exact silence, are a heavy weight to the grateful—Rebecca longed to tell Henry "that her life would be too little to express the full sense she had of the respect he paid to her." But as modesty forbade not only every kind of declaration, but every insinuation purporting what she felt,[2] she wept through sleepless nights from a load of suppressed explanation; yet still she would not have exchanged this trouble, for all the beauty of her sisters.

CHAPTER XXI.

OLD John and Hannah Primrose, a prudent hardy couple, who, by many years of peculiar labour and peculiar abstinence, were the least poor of all the neighbouring cottagers, had an only child called after the mother, Hannah: and this cottage girl was reckoned, in spite of the beauty of the elder Miss Rymers, by far the prettiest female in the village.

Reader of superior rank, if the passions which rage in the bosom of the inferior class of human kind are beneath your sympathy, throw aside this little history, for Rebecca Rymer and Hannah Primrose are its heroines.

But you, unprejudiced reader, whose liberal observations are not confined to stations, but who consider all mankind alike deserving your investigation; who believe that there exist in some, knowledge without the advantage of instruction; refinement of sentiment independent of elegant

---

1 Umbrella.

2 In her groundbreaking essay, "Ev'ry Woman is at Heart a Rake," Patricia Meyer Spacks emphasizes the rigidity of attitudes toward female sexuality throughout the eighteenth century: "Men were the wooers, women the wooed; a woman who allowed her interest in a man to become apparent before he declared his in her risked disgrace" (*Eighteenth-Century Studies*, Vol. 8 [1974–75] 27).

society; honourable pride of heart without dignity of blood; and genius destitute of art to render it conspicuous—*You* will, perhaps, venture to read on; in hopes that the remainder of this story may deserve your attention, just as the wild herb of the forest, equally with the cultivated plant in the garden, claims the attention of the botanist.

When young William saw Hannah, he thought her even more beautiful than she was thought by others; and on those days that he felt no inclination to ride, to shoot, or to hunt, he would contrive, by some secret device, the means to meet with her alone,[1] and give her tokens (if not of his love) at least of his admiration of her beauty, and of the pleasure he enjoyed in her company.

Hannah listened with a kind of delirious enchantment to all her elevated and eloquent admirer uttered; and in return for his praises of her charms, and his equivocal replies in respect to his designs towards her, gave to him her most undisguised thoughts, and her whole enraptured heart.

This, to her apparently harmless, intercourse had not lasted many weeks before she loved him—she even confessed she did, every time that any unwonted mark of attention from him, struck with unexpected force her infatuated senses.

It has been said by a celebrated writer, upon the affection subsisting between the two sexes, "that there are many persons who, if they had never heard of the passion of love, would never have felt it."[2] Might it not with equal truth be added, that—there are many more, who having heard of it, and believing most firmly that they feel it, are nevertheless mistaken? Neither of these cases was the lot of Hannah. She experienced the sentiment before she ever heard it named in that sense in which it possessed her—and it possessed her as genuine love alone exists—joined with numerous other sentiments: for love, however rated by many, as the chief passion of the human heart, is but a poor dependant, a retainer upon other passions; admiration, gratitude, respect, esteem, pride in the object:—divest the boasted sensation of these, and it is no more than the impression of a twelve-month, by courtesy, or vulgar error, termed love.

Hannah was formed by the rarest structure of the human frame, and fated by the tenderest thrillings of the human soul, to inspire and to experience real

---

1 According to eighteenth-century mores, a young woman's solitary meetings with a young man, like any written correspondence between them, signified dangerous, because morally lax, behavior. In Eliza Haywood's didactic novel, *Betsy Thoughtless* (1751), the heroine's near-rape in an Oxford garden results, in large part, from her unchaperoned engagements with her brother's friends.

2 François de la Rochefoucauld (1613–80), *Maximes*, No. 136.

love—but her nice taste, her delicate thoughts, were so refined beyond the sphere of her own station in society, that nature would have produced this prodigy of attraction in vain, had not one of superior education and manners assailed her heart: and had she been accustomed to the conversation of men in William's rank of life, she had, perhaps, treated William's addresses with indifference; but in comparing him with her familiar acquaintance, he was a miracle! His unremitting attention seemed the condescension of a superior being, to whom she looked up with reverence, with admiration, with awe, with pride, with sense of obligation—and all those various passions which constitute true, and *never* to be eradicated, love.

But in vain she felt and even avowed with her lips what every look, every gesture, had long denoted; William, with discontent, sometimes with anger, upbraided her for her false professions, and vowed "That while one tender proof, which he fervently besought, was wanting, she did but aggravate his misery by less endearments."

Hannah had been taught the full estimation of female virtue; and if her nature could have detested any one being in a state of wretchedness, it would have been the woman who had lost her honour: yet, for William, what would not Hannah forfeit? The dignity, the peace, the serenity, the innocence of her own mind, love soon encouraged her to fancy she could easily forego—and this same overpowering influence at times so forcibly possessed her, that she even felt a momentary transport in the idea "of so precious a sacrifice to him."—But then she loved her parents; and their happiness she could not prevail with herself to barter even for *his*. She wished he would demand some other pledge of her affection; for there was none but this, her ruin in no other shape, that she would deny at his request. While thus she deliberated, she prepared for her fall.

Bred up with strict observance both of his moral and religious character, William did not dare to tell an unequivocal lie even to his inferiors—he never promised Hannah he would marry her; nay even, he paid so much respect to the forms of truth, that no sooner was it evident that he had obtained her heart, her whole soul entire—so that loss of innocence would be less terrifying than separation from him—no sooner did he perceive this, than he candidly told her he "could never make her his wife."—At the same time he lamented "the difference of their births, and the duty he owed his parents' hopes," in terms so pathetic to her partial ear, that she thought him a greater object of compassion in his attachment, even than herself; and was now urged by pity to remove the cause of his complainings.

One evening Henry accidentally passed the lonely spot where William and she constantly met—he observed his cousin's impassioned eye, and her affectionate, yet fearful glance. William, he saw, took delight in the agitation of mind, in the strong apprehension mixed with the love of Hannah; this convinced Henry that either he, or himself, was not in love: for his heart told him he would not have beheld such emotions of tenderness mingled with such marks of sorrow, upon the countenance of Rebecca, for the wealth of the universe.

The first time he was alone with William after this, he mentioned his observation on Hannah's apparent affliction, and asked "Why her grief was the result of their stolen meetings?"

"Because," replied William, "her professions are unlimited, while her manners are reserved; and I accuse her of loving me with unkind moderation, while I love her to distraction."

"You design to marry her then?"

"How can you degrade me by the supposition?"

"Would it degrade you more to marry her than to make her your companion? To talk with her for hours in preference to all other company? To wish to be endeared to her by still closer ties?"

"But all this is not raising her to the rank of my wife."

"It is still raising her to that rank for which wives alone were allotted."

"You talk wildly!—I tell you I love her; but not enough, I hope, to marry her."

"But too much, I hope, to undo her?"

"That must be her own free choice—I make use of no unwarrantable methods."

"What are the warrantable ones?"

"I mean, I have made her no false promises—offered no pretended settlement—vowed no eternal constancy."

"But you have told her you love her; and, from that confession, has she not reason to expect every protection which even promises could secure?"

"I cannot answer for her expectations—but I know if she should make me happy as I ask, and I should then forsake her, I shall not break my word."

"Still she will be deceived; for you will falsify your looks."

"Do you think she depends on my looks?"

"I have read in some book, *Looks are the lover's sole dependence.*"[1]

"I have no objection to her interpreting mine in her favour: but then for the consequences, she will have herself, and only herself, to blame."

"Oh! heaven!"

---

1 Quotation not identified.

"What makes you exclaim so vehemently?"

"An idea of the bitterness of that calamity which inflicts self-reproach! Oh rather deceive her—leave her the consolation to reproach *you*, rather than *herself*."

"My honour will not suffer me."

"Exert your honour, and never see her more."

"I cannot live without her."

"Then live with her by the laws of your country; and make her and yourself both happy."

"Am I to make my father and my mother miserable? They would disown me for such a step."

"Your mother, perhaps, might be offended, but your father could not. Remember the sermon he preached but last Sunday, upon—*the shortness of this life: contempt of all riches and worldly honours in balance with a quiet conscience*—and the assurance he gave us—*that the greatest happiness enjoyed upon earth, was to be found under an humble roof with heaven in prospect.*"

"My father is a very good man," said William; "and yet, instead of being satisfied with an humble roof, he looks impatiently forward to a bishop's palace."

"He is so very good then," said Henry, "that perhaps, seeing the dangers to which men in exalted stations are exposed, he has such extreme philanthropy, and so little self-love, he would rather that *himself* should brave those perils incidental to wealth and grandeur, than any other person."

"You are not yet civilised," said William; "and to argue with you, is but to instruct, without gaining instruction."

"I know, Sir," replied Henry, "that you are studying the law most assiduously, and have vast prospects of rising to eminence in your profession: but let me hint to you—that though you may be perfect in the knowledge how to administer the commandments of men, unless you keep in view the precepts of God, your judgment, like mine, will be fallible."

CHAPTER XXII.

THE dean's family passed this first summer at the new-purchased estate so pleasantly, that they left it with regret when winter called them to their house in town.

But if some felt concern on quitting the village of Anfield, others who were left behind felt the deepest anguish. Those were not the poor—for rigid attention to the morals of people in poverty, and total neglect of their bodily wants, was the dean's practice. He forced them to attend church every sabbath; but whether they had a dinner on their return, was too gross and temporal an enquiry for his spiritual fervour. Good of the *soul* was all he aimed at; and this pious undertaking, besides his diligence as a pastor, required all his exertion as a magistrate—for to be very poor and very honest, very oppressed yet very thankful, is a degree of sainted excellence not to be attained without the aid of zealous men to frighten into virtue.

Those then, who alone felt sorrow at the dean's departure, were two young women, whose parents, exempt from indigence, preserved them from suffering under his unpitying piety; but whose discretion had not protected them from the bewitching smiles of his nephew, and the seducing wiles of his son.

The first morning that Rebecca rose and knew Henry was gone till the following summer, she wished she could have lain down again and slept away the whole long interval. Her sisters' peevishness, her father's austerity, she foresaw, would be insupportable now that she had experienced Henry's kindness, and he was no longer near to fortify her patience. She sighed—she wept—she was unhappy.

But if Rebecca awoke with a dejected mind and an aching heart, what were the sorrows of Hannah? The only child of two doating parents, she never had been taught the necessity of resignation—untutored, unread, unused to reflect, but knowing how to *feel*; what were her sufferings when, on waking, she called to mind that "William was gone," and with him gone all that excess of happiness which his presence had bestowed, and for which she had exchanged her future tranquility?

Loss of tranquility even Rebecca had to bemoan—Hannah had still more—the loss of innocence!

Had William remained in the village, shame, even conscience, perhaps had slept; but separated from her betrayer, parted from the joys of guilt, and left only to its sorrows, every sting which quick sensibility could sharpen, to torture her, was transfixed in her heart. First came the recollection of a cold farewell from the man whose love she had hoped her yielding passion had for ever won—next, flashed on her thoughts her violated person—next, the crime incurred—then her cruelty to her parents—and last of all the horrors of detection.

She knew that as yet, by wariness, care, and contrivance, her meetings with William had been unsuspected; but in this agony of mind her fears foreboded an informer who would defy all caution; who would stigmatise her with a name—dear and desired by every virtuous female—abhorrent to the blushing harlot—the name of mother.

That Hannah, thus impressed, could rise from her bed, meet her parents and her neighbours with her usual smile of vivacity, and voice of mirth, was impossible—to leave her bed at all, to creep down stairs, and reply in a faint broken voice to questions asked, were, in her state of mind, mighty efforts; and they were all to which her struggles could attain for many weeks.

William had promised to write to her while he was away: he kept his word; but not till the end of two months did she receive a letter.—Fear for his health, apprehension of his death during this cruel interval, caused an agony of suspense, which, by representing him to her distracted fancy in a state of suffering, made him, if possible, still dearer to her. In the excruciating anguish of uncertainty, she walked with trembling steps through all weathers (when she could steal half a day while her parents were employed in labour abroad) to the post town[1] at six miles distance, to enquire for his long expected, long wished for letter. When at last it was given to her, that moment of consolation seemed to repay her for the whole time of agonising terror she had endured. "He is alive!" she said, "and I have suffered nothing."

She hastily put this token of his health and his remembrance of her into her bosom, rich as an empress with a new-acquired dominion. The way from home, which she had trod with heavy pace, in the fear of renewed disappointment, she skimmed along on her return swift as a doe—the cold did not pierce, neither did the rain wet her.—Many a time she put her hand upon the prize she possessed, to find if it were safe—once, on the road, she took it from her bosom, curiously viewed the seal and the direction, then replacing it, did not move her fingers from their fast gripe, till she arrived at home.

Her father and her mother were still absent. She drew a chair, and placing it near to the only window in the room, seated herself with ceremonious order; then, gently drew forth her treasure; laid it on her knee; and with a smile that almost amounted to a laugh of gladness, once more inspected the outward part, before she would trust herself with the excessive joy of looking within.

At length the seal was broken—but the contents still a secret. Poor Hannah had learned to write as some youths learn Latin: so short a time had

---

1   A town with a head post office, to which letters could be directed. As a small village, Anfield would have had no post office of its own.

been allowed for the acquirement, and so little expert had been her master, that it took her generally a week to write a letter of ten lines, and a month to read one of twenty. But this being a letter on which her mind was deeply engaged, her whole imagination aided her slender literature, and at the end of a fortnight she had made out every word.—They were these,

"D^r. HANNAH,
  "I HOPE you have been well since we parted—I have been very well myself, but I have been teazed with a great deal of business, which has not given me time to write to you before—I have been called to the bar, which engages every spare moment—but I hope it will not prevent my coming down to Anfield with my father in the summer.
  "I am, D^r. Hannah,
  "With gratitude for all the favours you have conferred on me,
  "Yours, &c.
  "W.N."

To have beheld the illiterate Hannah trying for two weeks, day and night, to find out the exact words of this letter, would have struck the spectator with amazement, had he also understood the right, the delicate, the nicely proper sensations with which she was affected by every sentence it contained.

She wished it had been kinder, even for his sake who wrote it—because she thought so well of him, and desired still to think so well, that she was sorry at any faults which rendered him less worthy of her good opinion. The cold civility of his letter had this effect—her clear, her acute judgement felt it a kind of prevarication *to promise to write—and then write nothing that was hoped for.* But, enthralled by the magic of her passion, she shortly found excuses for the man she loved, at the expence of her own condemnation:

"He has only the fault of inconstancy," she cried; "and that has been caused by *my* change of conduct—had I been virtuous still, he had still been affectionate." Bitter thought!

Yet there was a sentence in the letter, that, worse than all the tenderness left out, wounded her sensibility—and she could not read the line, *gratitude for all the favours conferred on me,* without turning pale with horror, then kindling with indignation at the common-place thanks which insultingly reminded her of her innocence, her peace of mind, given in exchange for unmeaning acknowledgement.

CHAPTER XXIII.

ABSENCE is said to encrease strong and virtuous love, but to destroy that which is weak and sensual. In the parallel between young William and young Henry, this was the case; for Henry's real love encreased, while William's turbulent passion declined in separation: yet had the latter not so much abated that he did not perceive a sensation, like a sudden shock of sorrow, on a proposal made him by his father, of entering the marriage state with a young woman, the dependent niece of Lady Bendham;[1] who, as the dean informed him, had signified her lord's and her own approbation of his becoming their nephew.

At the first moment William received this intimation from his father, his heart revolted with disgust from the object, and he instantly thought upon Hannah, with more affection than he had done for many weeks before. This was from the comparison between her and his proposed wife; for he had frequently seen Miss Sedgeley at Lord Bendham's, but had never seen in her whole person, or manners, the least attraction to excite his love. He pictured to himself an unpleasant home with a companion so little suited to his taste, and felt a pang of conscience, as well as of attachment, in the thought of giving up poor Hannah.

But these reflections, these feelings lasted only for the moment: no sooner had the dean explained why the marriage was desirable, recited what great connections, and what great patronage it would confer upon their family, than William listened with eagerness, and both his love and his conscience were, if not wholly quieted, at least for the present hushed.

Immediately after the dean had expressed to Lord and Lady Bendham his son's "sense of the honour and the happiness conferred on him by their condescension in admitting him a member of their noble family"— Miss Sedgeley received from her aunt, nearly the same shock as William had done from his father. *For she had frequently seen the dean's son at Lord Bendham's, but had never seen in his whole person or manners the least attraction to excite her love—she pictured to herself an unpleasant home with a companion so little suited to her taste:* and at this moment she felt a more than usual partiality to the dean's nephew, finding the secret hope she had long indulged, of winning his affections, so near being thwarted.

But Miss Sedgeley was too much subjected to the power of her uncle and aunt to have a will of her own, at least, to dare to utter it. She

---

1 As a woman who possesses no independent income, Miss Sedgeley is both financially and psychologically "dependent" upon Lady Bendham.

received the commands of Lady Bendham with her accustomed submission, while all the consolation for the grief they gave her was, "that she resolved to make a very bad wife."

"I shall not care a pin for my husband," said she to herself; "and so I will dress and visit, and do just as I like—he dares not be unkind because of my aunt.—Besides, now I think again, it is not so disagreeable to marry *him* as if I were obliged to marry into any other family, because I shall see his cousin Henry as often, if not oftener than ever."

For Miss Sedgeley—whose person he did not like, and with her mind thus disposed—William began to force himself to shake off every little remaining affection, even all pity, for the unfortunate, the beautiful, the sensible, the doating Hannah; and determined to place in a situation to look down with scorn upon her sorrows, this weak, this unprincipled woman.

Connections, interest, honours, were powerful advocates—his private happiness William deemed trivial, compared to public opinion—and to be under obligations to a peer his wife's relation, gave greater renown in his servile mind, than all the advantages which might accrue from his own intrinsic independent worth.

In the usual routine of pretended regard, and real indifference, sometimes disgust, between parties allied by what is falsely termed *prudence*, the intended union of Mr. Norwynne with Miss Sedgeley proceeded in all due form; and at their country seats at Anfield, during the summer, their nuptials were appointed to be celebrated.

William was now introduced into all Lord Bendham's courtly circles—his worldly soul was entranced in glare and show—he thought of nothing but places, pensions, titles, retinues:—and stedfast, alert, unshaken in the pursuit of honours, neglected not the lesser means of rising to preferment—his own endowments. But in this round of attention to pleasures and to study, he no more complained to Hannah of "excess of business." Cruel as she had once thought that letter in which he thus apologised for neglecting her, she at last began to think it was wondrous kind; for he never found time to send her another. Yet she had studied with all her most anxious care to write him an answer; such a one as might not lessen her understanding, which he had often praised, in his esteem.

Ah William! even with less anxiety your beating ambitious heart panted for the admiration of an attentive auditory, when you first ventured to harangue in public!—With far less hope and fear (great as yours were) did you first address a crowded court, and thirst for its approbation on your efforts, than Hannah sighed for your approbation, when she took a pen and awkwardly scrawled over a sheet of paper. Near twenty times she began—but to a gentleman—and one she loved like William—what could she dare to say? Yet she had enough to tell, if shame had not interposed—or, if remaining confidence in his affection had but encouraged her.

Overwhelmed by the first, and deprived of the last, her hand shook, her head drooped, and she dared not communicate what she knew must inevitably render her letter unpleasing: and still more depreciate her in his regard, as the occasion of encumbrance, and of injury to his moral reputation.

Her free, her liberal, her venturous spirit subdued, intimidated by the force of affection, she only wrote—

"SIR,

"I am sorry you have so much to do, and should be ashamed if you put it off to write to me. I have not been at all well this winter—I never before passed such a one in all my life, and I hope you will never know such a one yourself in regard to not being happy—I should be sorry if you did— think I would rather go through it again myself than you should. I long for the summer, the fields are so green, and every thing so pleasant at that time of the year—I always do long for the summer, but I think never so much in my life as for this that is coming—though sometimes I wish that last summer had never come. Perhaps you wish so too—and that this summer would not come either.

"Hope you will excuse all faults, as I never learnt but one month.
                    "Your obedient humble servant,
                              "H.P."

CHAPTER XXIV.

SUMMER arrived—and lords and ladies who had partaken of all the dissipation of the town, whom opera-houses, gaming-houses, and various other houses had detained whole nights from their peaceful home, were now poured forth from the metropolis, to imbibe the wholesome air of the farmer and peasant, and disseminate in return moral and religious principles.

Among the rest, Lord and Lady Bendham, strenuous opposers of vice in the poor, and gentle supporters of it in the rich, never played at cards, or had concerts on a Sunday, in the village, where the poor were spies—*he*, there, never gamed, nor drank, except in private—and *she*, banished from her doors every woman of sullied character. Yet poverty and idiotism are not the same—the poor can hear, can talk, sometimes can reflect—servants will tell their equals how they live in town—listeners will smile and shake their heads—and thus, hypocrisy, instead of cultivating, destroys every seed of moral virtue.

The arrival of Lord Bendham's family at Anfield, announced to the village that the dean's would quickly follow. Rebecca's heart bounded with joy at the prospect—Poor Hannah felt a sinking, a foreboding tremor, that wholly interrupted the joy of *her* expectations—She had not heard from William for five tedious months—she did not know whether he loved or despised—whether he thought of, or had forgotten her. Her reason argued against the hope that he loved her—yet hope still subsisted—she would not abandon herself to despair while there was doubt—she "had frequently been deceived by the appearance of circumstances, and perhaps he might come all kindness—perhaps—even not like her the less, for that indisposition which had changed her bloom to paleness, and the sparkling of her eyes to a pensive languor."

Henry's sensations on his return to Anfield were the self-same as Rebecca's were: sympathy in thought, sympathy in affection, sympathy in virtue, made them so. As he approached near the little village, he felt more light than usual. He had committed no trespass there, dreaded no person's reproach or enquiries; but his arrival might prove, at least to one object, the cause of rejoicing.

William's sensations were the reverse of these. In spite of his ambition, and the flattering view of one day accomplishing all to which it aspired, he often, as they proceeded on their journey, envied the gaiety of Henry, and felt an inward monitor that told him, "he must first act like Henry, to be as happy."

His intended marriage was still, to the families of both parties, (except to the heads of the houses) a profound secret. Neither the servants, nor even Henry, had received the slightest intimation of the designed alliance; and this to William was matter of some comfort.

When men submit to act in contradiction to their principles, nothing is so precious as a secret. In their estimation, to have their conduct *known* is the essential mischief—while it is hid, they fancy the sin but half committed; and to the moiety of a crime they reconcile their feelings, till, in progression, the whole, when disclosed, appears trivial. He designed that Hannah should receive the news from himself by degrees, and in such a manner as to console her, or at least to silence her complaints: and with the wish to soften, the something like, regret, which he still felt on the prudent necessity of yielding her up when his marriage should take place, he promised to himself some intervening hours of private meetings, which he hoped would produce satiety.

While Henry flew to Mr. Rymer's house with a conscience clear, and a face enlightened with gladness; while he met Rebecca with open-hearted friendship and frankness which charmed her soul to peaceful happiness; William skulked around the cottage of Hannah, dreading detection; and when towards midnight he found the means to obtain the company of the sad inhabitant, he grew so impatient at her tears and sobs, at the delicacy with which she with-held her caresses, that he burst into bitter upbraidings at her coyness; and at length (without discovering the cause of her peculiar agitation and reserve) abruptly left her, vowing "never to see her more."

As he turned away, his heart even congratulated him, "that he had made so discreet a use of his momentary disappointment, as thus to shake her off at once without farther explanation or excuse."

She, ignorant and illiterate as she was, knew enough of her own heart to judge of his, and to know, that such violent affections and expressions, above all, such a sudden, heart-breaking, manner of departure, were not the effects of love: not even of humanity. She felt herself debased by a ruffian—yet still, having loved him when she thought him otherwise, the blackest proof of the deception could not erase a sentiment, formed whilst she was deceived.

She passed the remainder of the night in anguish—but with the cheerful morning some cheerly thoughts arose. She thought "perhaps William by this time had found himself to blame—had conceived the cause of her grief and her distant behaviour, and had pitied her."

The next evening she waited with anxious heart for the signal that had called her out the foregoing night—in vain she watched, counted the hours, and the stars, and listened to the nightly stillness of the fields around: they were not disturbed by the tread of her lover.—Day-light came; the sun rose in its splendour; William had not been near her, and it shone upon none so miserable as Hannah.

She now considered his word, "never to see her more," as solemnly passed—she heard anew the impressive, the implacable tone in which the sentence was pronounced; and could look back on no late token of affection, on which to found the slightest hope that he would recall it.

Still, reluctant to despair—in the extremity of grief, in the extremity of fear for an approaching crisis which must speedily arrive, she (after a few days had elapsed) trusted a neighbouring peasant with a letter to deliver to Mr. Norwynne in private.

This letter, unlike the last, was dictated without the hope to please—no pains were taken with the style, no care in the formation of the letters—the words flowed from necessity; strong necessity guided her hand.

"SIR,

"I beg your pardon—pray don't forsake me all at once—see me one time more—I have something to tell you—it is what I dare tell nobody else—and what I am ashamed to tell you—yet pray give me a word of advice—what to do I don't know—I then will part if you please, never to trouble you, never any more—but hope to part friends—pray do if you please—and see me one time more.

"Your obedient,
"H.P."

These incorrect inelegant lines produced this immediate reply:—

"TO HANNAH PRIMROSE.

"I have often told you that my honour is as dear to me as my life—my word is a part of that honour—you heard me say *I would never see you again*—I shall keep my word."

CHAPTER XXV.

WHEN the dean's family had been at Anfield about a month—One misty morning, such as portends a sultry day, as Henry was walking swiftly through a thick wood on the skirts of the parish, he suddenly started on hearing a distant groan, expressive, as he thought, both of bodily and mental pain.—He stopped to hear it repeated, that he might pursue the sound. He heard it again; and though now but in murmurs, yet as the tone implied excessive grief, he directed his course to that part of the wood from which it came.

As he advanced, in spite of the thick fog, he discerned the appearance of a female stealing away on his approach. His eye was fixed on this object; and regardless where he placed his feet, soon he shrunk back with horror, on perceiving they had nearly trod upon a new-born infant, lying on the ground!—a lovely male child, entered on a world where not one preparation had been made to receive him.

"Ah!" cried Henry, forgetting the person who had fled, and with a smile of compassion on the helpless infant, "I am glad I have found you—

you give more joy to me, than you have done to your hapless parents. Poor dear," (continued he, while he took off his coat to wrap it in,) "I will take care of you while I live—I will beg for you, rather than you shall want—but first, I will carry you to those who can at present do more for you than myself."

Thus Henry said and thought, while he inclosed the child carefully in his coat, and took it in his arms. But about to walk his way with it, an unlucky query struck him, *where he should go.*

"I must not take it to the dean's," he cried, "because Lady Clementina will suspect it is not nobly, and my uncle will suspect it is not lawfully, born.[1] Nor must I take it to Lord Bendham's for the self-same reason—though, could it call Lady Bendham mother, this whole village, nay the whole country round, would ring with rejoicings for its birth. How strange!" continued he, "that we should make so little of human creatures, that one sent among us, wholly independent of his own high value, becomes a curse instead of a blessing by the mere accident of worthless circumstances."

He now, after walking out of the wood, peeped through the folds of his coat to look again at his charge—He started, turned pale, and trembled to behold what, in the surprise of first seeing the child, had escaped his observation. Around its little throat was a cord entwined by a slipping noose, and drawn half way—as if the trembling hand of the murderer had revolted from its dreadful office, and he or she had left the infant to pine away in nakedness and hunger, rather than *see* it die.

Again Henry wished himself joy of the treasure he had found; and more fervently than before; for he had not only preserved one fellow creature from death, but another from murder.

Once more he looked at his charge, and was transported to observe, upon its serene brow and sleepy eye, no traces of the dangers it had passed—no trait of shame either for itself or its parents—no discomposure at the unwelcome reception it was likely to encounter from a proud world!—He now slipped the fatal string from its neck; and by this affectionate disturbance causing the child to cry, he ran (but he scarce knew whither) to convey it to a better nurse.

---

1   For a useful analysis of some of the often conflicting attitudes towards illegitimate children during this period, see the essay by Alan Macfarlane, "Illegitimacy and Illegitimates in English History" in the collection entitled *Bastardy and its Comparative History*, ed. Peter Laslett, et al. (Cambridge: Harvard UP, 1980).

He at length found himself at the door of his dear Rebecca—for so very happy Henry felt at the good luck which had befallen him, that he longed to bestow a part of the blessing upon her he loved.

He sent for her privately out of the house to speak to him.—When she came,

"Rebecca," said he (looking around that no one observed him) "Rebecca, I have brought you something you will like."

"What is it?" She asked.

"You know, Rebecca, that you love deserted birds, strayed kittens, and motherless lambs—I have brought something more pitiable than any of these. Go, get a cap and a little gown, and then I will give it you."

"A gown!" exclaimed Rebecca. "If you have brought me a monkey,[1] much as I should esteem any present from *you*, indeed I cannot touch it."

"A monkey!" repeated Henry, almost in anger—then changing the tone of his voice, exclaimed in triumph

"It is a child!"

On this he gave it a gentle pinch, that its cry might confirm the pleasing truth he spoke.

"A child!" Repeated Rebecca in amaze.

"Yes, and indeed I found it."

"Found it?"

"Indeed I did. The mother, I fear, had just forsaken it."

"Inhuman creature!"

"Nay, hold Rebecca! I am sure you will pity her when you see her child—you then will know she must have loved it—and you will consider how much she certainly had suffered, before she left it to perish in a wood."

"Cruel!" Once more exclaimed Rebecca.

"Oh! Rebecca, perhaps, had she possessed a home of her own, she would have given it the best place in it—had she possessed money, she would have dressed it with the nicest care—or had she been accustomed to disgrace, she would have gloried in calling it hers! But now, as it is, it is sent to us, to you and me, Rebecca, to take care of."

---

1   Rebecca's refusal of what she supposes to be Henry's gift provides further indication of her good sense: pet monkeys, like lap-dogs in earlier decades, epitomized frivolous affectation. Compare the scene in Frances Burney's *Evelina* (1778), in which Captain Mirvan taunts the ridiculous fop, Mr. Lovel, by presenting him with a monkey "fully dressed, and extravagantly *à-la-mode*" as a mirror image of Lovel himself (Vol. III, Letter XXI). Recall as well the narrator's description of the young William in Chapter 9: "he would grin and bow to a lady, and catch her fan in haste when it fell, and hand her to her coach, as thoroughly void of all the sentiment, which gives grace to such tricks, as a monkey."

Rebecca, soothed by Henry's compassionate eloquence, held out her arms and received the important parcel—and, as she kindly looked in upon the little stranger,

"Now are not you much obliged to me," said Henry, "for having brought it to you? I know no one but yourself to whom I would have trusted it with pleasure."

"Much obliged to you," repeated Rebecca with a very serious face, "if I did but know what to do with it—where to put it—where to hide it from my father and sisters."

"Oh! any where"—returned Henry. "It is very good—It will not cry—Besides, in one of the distant unfrequented rooms of your old abbey, through the thick walls and long gallery, an infant's cry cannot pass.[1] Yet, pray be cautious how you conceal it: for if it should be discovered by your father or sisters, they will take it from you, prosecute the wretched mother, and send the child to the workhouse."

"I will do all I can to prevent them," said Rebecca; "and I think I call to mind a part of the house where it *must* be safe. I know, too, I can take milk from the dairy, and bread from the pantry, without its being missed, or my father much the poorer.—But if—"

That instant they were interrupted by the appearance of the stern curate at a little distance—Henry was obliged to run swiftly away, while Rebecca returned by stealth into the house with her innocent burthen.

END OF THE FIRST VOLUME.

---

1 In keeping with the earlier transformation of the parsonage house (see the note to ch. 20, above), this sentence was added to the novel's second edition. See also the changes to ch. 27.

NATURE AND ART

IN TWO VOLUMES

by

MRS. INCHBALD

VOL. II

SECOND EDITION,

CORRECTED AND IMPROVED

LONDON:

Printed for G.G. and J. ROBINSON,
PATERNOSTER ROW.

1797.

CHAPTER XXVI.

THERE is a word in the vocabulary more bitter, more direful in its import, than all the rest.—Reader, if poverty, if disgrace, if bodily pain, even if slighted love be your unhappy fate, kneel and bless heaven for its beneficent influence, so that you are not tortured with the anguish of—*remorse.*

Deep contrition for past offences had long been the punishment of unhappy Hannah; but, till the day she brought her child into the world, *remorse* had been averted. From that day, life became an insupportable load, for all reflection was torture! To think—merely to think, was to suffer excruciating agony—yet, never before was *thought* so intrusive—it haunted her in every spot, in all societies—sleep was no shelter—she never slept but her racking dreams told her——"she had slain her infant."

They presented to her view the naked innocent whom she had longed to press to her bosom, while she lifted up her hand against its life—They laid before her the smiling babe whom her eye-balls strained to behold once more, while her feet hurried her away for ever.

Often had Hannah, by the winter's fire, listened to tales of ghosts—of the unceasing sting of a guilty conscience—often had she shuddered at the recital of murders—often had she wept over the story of the innocent put to death; and stood aghast that the human mind could perpetrate the heinous crime of assassination!

From the tenderest passion the most savage impulse may arise—In the deep recesses of fondness, sometimes is implanted the root of cruelty—and from loving William with unbounded lawless affection, she found herself depraved so as to become the very object, which could most of all excite her own horror!

Still, at delirious intervals, that passion, which like a fatal talisman had enchanted her whole soul, held out the delusive prospect that—"William might yet relent"—for though she had for ever discarded the idea of peace, she could not force herself to think, but that, again blest with his society, she should, at least for the time that he was present, taste the sweet cup of "forgetfulness of the past," for which she so ardently thirsted.

"Should he return to me," she thought in those paroxysms of delusion, "I would to *him* unbosom all my guilt; and as a remote, a kind of innocent accomplice in my crime, his sense, his arguments, ever ready in making light of my sins, might afford a respite to my troubled conscience."

While thus she unwittingly thought, and sometimes watched through the night, starting with convulsed rapture at every sound, because it might possibly be the harbinger of him; *he* was busied in carefully looking over marriage articles, fixing the place of residence with his destined bride, or making love to her in formal process.—Yet, Hannah, vaunt!—he sometimes thought on thee—he could not witness the folly, the weakness, the vanity, the selfishness of his future wife, without frequently comparing her with thee. When equivocal words, and prevaricating sentences fell from her lips, he remembered with a sigh thy candor—that open sincerity which dwelt upon thy tongue, and seemed to vie with thy undisguised features, to charm the listener even beyond the spectator. While Miss Sedgeley eagerly grasped at all the presents he offered, he could not but call to mind "that Hannah's declining hand was always closed, and her looks forbidding, every time he proffered such disrespectful tokens of his love." He recollected the softness which beamed from Hannah's eyes, the blush on her face at his approach, while he could never discern one glance of tenderness from the niece of Lord Bendham: and the artificial bloom on her cheeks was nearly as disgusting as the ill-conducted artifice with which she attempted gentleness and love.

But all these impediments were only observed as trials of his fortitude—his prudence could overcome his aversion, and thus he valued himself upon his manly firmness.

'Twas now, that having rid himself, by Hannah's peevishness, most honourably of all future ties to her; and the day of his marriage with Miss Sedgeley being fixed, Henry, with the rest of the house, learnt, what, to them, was news.—The first dart of Henry's eye upon William, when, in his presence, he was told of it, caused a reddening on the face of the latter: he always fancied Henry saw his thoughts; and he knew that Henry in return would give him *his*. On the present occasion, no sooner were they alone, and Henry began to utter them, than William charged him

"Not to dare to proceed; for that, too long accustomed to trifle, the time was come when serious matters could alone employ his time; and when men of approved sense must take place of friends and confidents like him."

Henry replied, "The love, the sincerity of friends, I thought, were their best accomplishments; these I possess."

"But you do not possess knowledge."

"If that be knowledge which has of late estranged you from all who bear you a sincere affection; which imprints every day more and more upon your features the marks of gloomy inquietude, am I not happier in my ignorance?"

"Do not torment me with your ineffectual reasoning."

"I called at the cottage of poor Hannah the other day," returned Henry: "Her father and mother were taking their homely meal alone; and when I asked for their daughter, they wept and said—Hannah was not the girl she had been."

William cast his eyes on the floor.

Henry proceeded—"They said a sickness, which they feared would bring her to the grave, had preyed upon her for some time past. They had procured a doctor; but no remedy was found, and they feared the worst."

"What worst?" cried William, (now recovered from the effect of the sudden intelligence, and attempting a smile) "Do they think she will die? And do you think it will be for love? We do not hear of these deaths often, Henry."

"And if *she* die, who will hear of *that*? No one but those interested to conceal the cause: and thus it is, that dying for love becomes a phenomenon."

Henry would have pursued the discourse farther; but William, impatient on all subjects, except where his argument was the better, retired from the controversy, crying out "I know my duty, and want no instructor."

It would be unjust to William, to say he did not feel for Hannah's reported illness—he felt, during that whole evening, and part of the next morning—but business, pleasures, new occupations, and new schemes of future success, crowded to dissipate all unwelcome reflections; and he trusted to her youth, her health, her animal spirits, and above all, to the folly of the gossips' story of *dying for love*, as a surety for her life, and a safeguard for his conscience.

CHAPTER XXVII.

THE child of William and Hannah[1] was secreted by Rebecca in a distant chamber belonging to the dreary parsonage, near to which scarcely any part of the family ever went. There she administered to all its wants, visited every hour of the day, and at intervals during the night,—viewed almost with the joy of a mother its health, its promised life,—and in a short time found she loved her little gift, better than any thing on earth, except the giver.

---

1   In the first edition, this paragraph reads as follows: "The child of William and Hannah was
·   secreted by Rebecca in her own chamber, a garret, and at some distance from where her sisters slept. There she administered to all its wants, viewed almost with the joy of a mother ..."

Henry called the next morning, and the next, and many succeeding times, in hopes of an opportunity to speak alone with Rebecca, to enquire concerning her charge, and consult when, and how, he could privately relieve her from her trust; as he now meant to procure a nurse for wages. In vain he called or lurked around the house—for near five weeks all the conversation he could obtain with her was in the company of her sisters, who beginning to observe his preference, his marked attention to her, and the languid half-smothered transport with which she received it, indulged their envy and resentment at the contempt shown to their charms, by watching her steps when he was away, and her every look and whisper while he was present.

For five weeks, then, he was continually thwarted in his expectation of meeting her alone; and at the end of that period, the whole design he had to accomplish by such a meeting, was rendered abortive.

Though Rebecca had with strictest caution locked the door of the room in which the child was hid, and covered each crevice, and every aperture through which sound might more easily proceed; though she had surrounded the infant's head with pillows to obstruct all noise from his crying, yet one unlucky night, the strength of his voice encreasing with his age, he was heard by the maid, who slept the nearest to that part of the house.

Not meaning to injure her young mistress, the servant next morning simply related to the family what sounds had struck her ear during the night, and whence they proceeded.—At first she was ridiculed "for supposing herself awake when in reality she must be dreaming." But steadfastly persisting in what she had said, and Rebecca's blushes, confusion, and eagerness to prove the maid mistaken, giving suspicion to her charitable sisters, they watched her the very next time she went by stealth to supply the office of a mother; and breaking abruptly on her while feeding and caressing the infant, they instantly concluded it was her *own*; seized it, and, in spite of her tears, carried it down to their father.[1]

That account which Henry had given Rebecca "of his having found the child," and which her own sincerity, joined to the faith she had in his word, made her receive as truth, she now felt would be heard by the present auditors with contempt, even with indignation, as a falsehood.—Her affright is better to be conceived than described.

Accused, and dragged by her sisters along with the child before the curate, his attention to their representation, his crimsoned face, knit brow,

---

1 The first edition reads: "But stedfastly persisting in what she had said, and Rebecca's confusion giving much colour to the improbable tale, her chamber was searched by her sisters, the infant discovered, and brought down to their father."

and thundering voice, struck with terror her very soul—Innocence is not always a protection against fear—sometimes less bold than guilt.

In her father and sisters, she saw, she knew the suspicious, partial, cruel, boisterous natures by whom she was to be judged; and timid, gentle, oppressed, she fell trembling on her knees, and could only articulate "Forgive me."

The curate would not listen to this supplication till she had replied to his question—"Whose child is this?"

She replied, "I do not know."

Questioned louder, and with more violence still, "How the child came there, wherefore her affection for it, and whose it was?" She felt the improbability of the truth still more forcibly than before, and dreaded some immediate peril from her father's rage, should she dare to relate an apparent lie—she paused to think upon a more probable tale than the real one—and as she hesitated, shook in every limb—while her father exclaimed—

"I understand the cause of this terror! It confirms your sisters' fears, and your own shame[1]—From your infancy I have predicted that some fatal catastrophe would befall you—I never loved you like my other children—I never had the cause—you were always unlike the rest—and I knew your fate would be calamitous—but the very worst of my forebodings did not come to this—so young, so guilty, and so artful!—tell me this instant, are you married?"

Rebecca answered, "No."

The sisters lifted up their hands!

The father continued—"Vile prostitute, I thought as much.—Still I will know the father of this child."

She cast up her eyes to heaven, and firmly vowed she "did not know herself—nor who the mother was."

"This is not to be borne!" exclaimed the curate in fury. "Persist in this, and you shall never see my face again. Both your child and you I'll turn out of my house instantly, unless you confess your crime, and own the father."

Curious to know this secret, the sisters went up to Rebecca with seeming kindness, and—"Conjured her to spare her father still greater grief, and her own and her child's public infamy, by acknowledging herself its mother, and naming the man who had seduced her."

Emboldened by this insult from her own sex, Rebecca now began to declare the simple truth.—But no sooner had she said that—"The child

---

1   This sentence was added to the second edition.

was the gift of a young man who had found it——" than her sisters burst into laughter, and her father into redoubled rage.

Once more the women offered their advice—"To confess and be forgiven."

Once more the father raved.

Beguiled by solicitations, and terrified by threats, like women formerly accused of witchcraft, and other wretches put to the torture, she thought her present sufferings worse than any that could possibly succeed, and felt inclined to confess a falsehood, at which her virtue shrunk, to obtain a momentary respite from reproach;[1] she felt inclined to take the mother's share of the infant, but was at a loss to whom to give the father's. She thought that Henry had entailed on himself the best right to the charge; but she loved him, and could not bear the idea of accusing him falsely.

While, with agitation in the extreme, she thus deliberated, the proposition again was put

"Whether she would trust to the mercy of her father by confessing, or draw down his immediate vengeance by denying her guilt?"

She made choice of the former—and with tears and sobs "owned herself the mother of the boy."

But still—"Who is the father?"

Again she shrunk from the question, and fervently implored—"To be spared on that point."

Her petition was rejected with vehemence; and the curate's rage encreased till she acknowledged

"Henry was the father."

"I thought so." Exclaimed all her sisters at the same time.

"Villain!" cried the curate. "The dean shall know, before this hour is expired, the baseness of the nephew whom he supports upon charity: he shall know the misery, the grief, the shame he has brought on me, and know how unworthy he is of his protection."

"Oh! have mercy on him!" cried Rebecca as she still knelt to her father: "Do not ruin him with his uncle, for he is the best of creatures."

"Ay, ay, we always saw how much she loved him." Cried her sisters.

---

1 The section "like women … respite from reproach" was added to the second edition. As with her other revisions of this chapter, which accentuate both Rebecca's excessive caution in secreting the infant and her cruel treatment at the hands of her father and sisters, Inchbald may have been responding to the *Analytical Review*'s criticism of the scene (printed in full in Appendix E.1): "The making a young modest woman, with some powers of mind, acknowledge herself the mother of a child that she humanely fostered, in the presence of the man she loved, is also highly improbable, not to say unnatural" (January–June, 1796: 511).

"Wicked, undone girl!" said the clergyman (his rage now subsiding, and tears supplying its place) "you have drawn a curse upon us all—your sisters' reputation[1] will be stampt with the colour of yours—my good name will suffer—but that is trivial—your soul is lost to virtue, to religion, to shame—"

"No *indeed*!" cried Rebecca, "if you will but believe me."

"Do not I believe you? Have not you confessed?"

"You will not pretend to unsay what you have said:" cried her eldest sister: "that would be making things worse."

"Go, go out of my sight!" said her father. "Take your child with you to your chamber, and never let me see either of you again.—I do not turn you out of my doors to-day, because I gave you my word I would not if you revealed your shame—but by to-morrow I will provide some place for your reception, where neither I, nor any of your relations, shall ever see or hear of you again."

Rebecca made an effort to cling around her father, and once more to declare her innocence: but her sisters interposed, and she was taken, with her reputed son, to the chamber where the curate had sentenced her to remain, till she quitted his house for ever.

CHAPTER XXVIII.

THE curate, in the disorder of his mind, scarcely felt the ground he trod as he hastened to the dean's to complain of his wrongs. His name procured him immediate admittance into the library—and the moment the dean appeared, the curate burst into tears.—The cause being required of such "very singular marks of grief," Mr. Rymer described himself, "as having been a few months ago the happiest of parents, but that his peace and that of his whole family had been destroyed by Mr. Henry Norwynne, the dean's nephew."

He now entered into a minute recital of Henry's frequent visits there, and of all which had occurred in his house that morning, from the suspicion

---

1 Compare the situation of the Bennet sisters in Jane Austen's *Pride and Prejudice* (1813). Elizabeth, painfully aware of the way in which her younger sister's unruly behavior negatively affects her own reputation, attempts, albeit unsuccessfully, to convince her father not to allow Lydia to visit Brighton: "'If you were aware ... of the very great disadvantage to us all, which must arise from the public notice of Lydia's unguarded and imprudent manner; nay, which has already arisen from it, I am sure you would judge differently in the affair'" (ch. 41).

that a child was concealed under his roof, to the confession made by his youngest daughter of her fall from virtue, and of her betrayer's name.

The dean was astonished, shocked, and rouzed to anger: he vented reproaches and menaces on his nephew; and, "blessing himself in a virtuous son, whose wisdom and counsel were his only solace in every care," sent for William to communicate with him on the unhappy subject.

William came, all obedience, and heard with marks of amazement and indignation the account of such black villainy! In perfect sympathy with Mr. Rymer and his father, he allowed "no punishment could be too great for the seducer of innocence, the selfish invader of a whole family's repose."

Nor did William here speak what he did not think—he merely forgot his own conduct; or if he did recall it to his mind, it was with some fair interpretation in his own behalf; such as self-love ever supplies to those who wish to cheat their conscience.

Young Henry being sent for to appear before this triumvirate, he came with a light step and a cheerful face. But, on the charge against him being exhibited, his countenance changed—yet, only to the expression of surprise! He boldly asserted his innocence, plainly told the real fact; and with a deportment so perfectly unembarrassed, that nothing but the asseverations of the curate, "that his daughter had confessed the whole," could have rendered the story Henry told suspected; although some of the incidents he related were of no common kind. But Mr. Rymer's charge was an objection to his veracity, too potent to be overcome; and the dean exclaimed, in rage—

"We want not your avowal of your guilt—the mother's evidence is testimony sufficient."

"The virtuous Rebecca is not a mother." Said Henry, with firmness.

William here, like Rebecca's sisters, took Henry aside, and warned him not to "Add to his offence by denying what was proved against him."

But Henry's spirit was too manly, his affection too sincere, not to vindicate the chastity of her he loved, even at his own peril. He again and again protested "she was virtuous."

"Let her instantly be sent for," said the dean, "and this madman confronted with her." Then adding, that as he wished every thing might be conducted with secrecy, he would not employ his clerk on the unhappy occasion,—he desired William to draw up the form of an oath, which he would administer as soon as she arrived.

A man and horse were immediately dispatched to bring Rebecca; William drew up an affidavit as his father had directed him—*in Rebecca's name solemnly protesting she was a mother, and Henry, the father of her child—* and now, the dean, suppressing till she came the warmth of his anger, spoke thus calmly to Henry:

"Even supposing that your improbable tale of having found this child, and all your declarations in respect to it, were true, still you would be greatly criminal: what plea can you make for not having immediately revealed the circumstance to me or some other proper person, that the real mother might be detected and punished for her design of murder?"

"In that perhaps I was to blame:" returned Henry: "but whoever the mother was, I pitied her."

"Compassion on such an occasion was ill placed." Said the dean.

"Was I wrong, Sir, to pity the child?"

"No."

"Then how could I feel for *that*, and yet divest myself of all feeling for its mother?"

"Its mother!" (exclaimed William, in anger) "She ought to have been immediately pursued, apprehended, and committed to prison."

"It struck me, cousin William," replied Henry, "that the father was more deserving a prison: the poor woman had abandoned only *one*—the man, in all likelihood, had forsaken *two*."

William was pouring execrations "on the villain, if such there could be," when Rebecca was announced.

Her eyes were half-closed with weeping; deep confusion overspread her face; and her tottering limbs could hardly support her to the awful chamber where the dean, her father, and William sat in judgment, whilst her beloved Henry stood arraigned as a culprit, by her false evidence.

Upon her entrance, her father first addressed her, and said in a stern, threatening, yet feeling tone, "Unhappy girl, answer me before all present—Have you, or have you not, owned yourself a mother?"

She replied, stealing a fearful look at Henry,—"I have."

"And have you not," asked the dean, "owned that Henry Norwynne is the father of your child?"

She seemed as if she wished to expostulate——

The curate raised his voice—"Have you, or have you not?"

"I have." She faintly replied.

"Then here," cried the dean to William, "read that paper to her, and take the Bible."

William read the paper, which in her name declared a momentous falsehood: he then held the book in form, while she looked like one distracted—wrung her hands, and was near sinking to the earth.

At the moment the book was lifted up to her lips to kiss, Henry rushed to her—"Stop," he cried, "Rebecca! do not hurt your future peace. I plainly see under what prejudices you have been accused, under what fears you have fallen. But do not be terrified into the commission of a crime which hereafter will distract your delicate conscience. My requesting you of your father for my wife, will satisfy his scruples, prevent your oath—and here I make the demand."

"He at length confesses! Surprising audacity!—Complicated villainy!" exclaimed the dean—then added, "Henry Norwynne; your first guilt is so enormous; your second, in steadfastly denying it, so base; this last conduct so unaccountable! that from the present hour you must never dare to call me relation, or to consider my house as your home."

William, in unison with his father, exclaimed, "Indeed, Henry, your actions merit this punishment."

Henry answered with firmness, "Inflict what punishment you please."

"With the dean's permission then," (said the curate) "you must marry my daughter."

Henry started—"Do you pronounce that as a punishment? It would be the greatest blessing providence can bestow.—But how are we to live? My uncle is too much offended ever to be my friend again; and in this country, people of a certain class are so educated, they cannot exist without the assistance, or what is called the patronage, of others; when that is withheld, they steal or starve. Heaven protect Rebecca from such misfortune!—Sir, (to the curate) do you but consent to support her a year or two longer, and in that time I will learn some occupation that shall raise me to the eminence of maintaining both her and myself without one obligation, or one inconvenience to a single being."

Rebecca exclaimed, "Oh! you have saved me from such a weight of sin, that my future life would be too happy, passed as your slave."

"No, my dear Rebecca, return to your father's house, return to slavery but for a few years more, and the rest of your life I will make free."

"And can you forgive me?"

"I can love you; and in that is comprised every thing that is kind."

The curate, who, bating[1] a few passions and a few prejudices, was a man of some worth and feeling, had felt, in the midst of her distress, though the result of supposed crimes, that he loved this neglected daughter better than he had before conceived; and he now agreed "to take her home for a time, provided she were relieved from the child, and the

---

1   Excepting.

matter so hushed up, that it might draw no imputation upon the characters of his other daughters."

The dean did not degrade his consequence by consultations of this nature; but, having penetrated (as he imagined) into the very bottom of this intricate story, and issued his mandate against Henry—as a mark that he took no farther concern in the matter, he proudly walked out of the room without uttering another word.

William as proudly and as silently followed.

The curate was inclined to adopt the manners of such great examples—but, self-interest, some affection to Rebecca, and concern for the character of his family, made him wish to talk a little more with Henry; who now repeated what he had said respecting his marriage with Rebecca, and promised "to come the very next day in secret, and deliver her from the care of the infant, and the suspicion that would attend her nursing it."

"But above all," said the curate, "procure your uncle's pardon: for without that, without his protection, or the protection of some other rich man; to marry, to obey God's ordinance, *increase and multiply*, is to want food for yourself and your offspring."

CHAPTER XXIX.

THOUGH this unfortunate occurrence in the curate's family was, according to his own phrase, "to be hushed up," yet certain persons of his, of the dean's, and of Lord Bendham's house, immediately heard and talked of it. Among these, Lady Bendham was most of all shocked and offended; she "never could bear to hear Mr. Rymer either pray or preach again— he had not conducted himself with proper dignity either as a clergyman or a father—he should have imitated the dean's example in respect to Henry, and have turned his daughter out of doors."

Lord Bendham was less severe on the seduced, but had no mercy on the seducer— "a vicious youth, without one accomplishment to endear vice"— For vice, Lord Bendham thought (with certain philosophers), might be most exquisitely pleasing, in a pleasing garb. "But this youth sinned without elegance, without one particle of wit, or an atom of good breeding."

Lady Clementina would not permit the subject to be mentioned a second time in her hearing—extreme delicacy in woman she knew was bewitching; and the delicacy she displayed on this occasion went so far that she "could not even intercede with the dean to forgive his nephew, because the topic was too gross for her lips to name even in the ear of her husband."

Miss Sedgeley, though on the very eve of her bridal day with William, felt so tender a regard for Henry, that often she thought "Rebecca happier in disgrace and poverty, blest with the love of him, than she was likely to be in the possession of friends and fortune with his cousin."

Had Henry been of a nature to suspect others of evil, or had he felt a confidence in his own worth, such a passion as this young woman's would soon have disclosed its existence: but he, regardless of any attractions of Miss Sedgeley, equally supposed he had none in her eyes; and thus, fortunately for the peace of all parties, this prepossession ever remained a secret except to herself.

So little did William conceive that his clownish cousin could rival him in the affections of a woman of fashion, that he even slightly solicited his father "that Henry might not be banished from the house, at least till after the following day, when the great festival of his marriage was to be celebrated."

But the dean refused; and reminded his son, "That he was bound both by his moral and religious character, in the eyes of God, and still more, in the eyes of men, to shew lasting resentment of iniquity like his."

William acquiesced, and immediately delivered to his cousin the dean's "wishes for his amendment," and a letter of recommendation procured from Lord Bendham, to introduce him on board a man of war;[1] where, he was told, "he might hope to meet with preferment according to his merit as a sailor and a gentleman."

Henry pressed William's hand on parting—wished him happy in his marriage—and supplicated, as the only favour he would implore, an interview with his uncle—to thank him for all his former kindness, and to see him for the last time.

William repeated this petition to his father, but with so little energy, that the dean did not grant it. He felt himself compelled to resent that reprobate character in which Henry had appeared; and he feared—"lest the remembrance of his last parting from his brother might, on taking a formal leave of that brother's son, reduce him to some tokens of weakness, that would ill-become his dignity and just displeasure."

He sent him his blessing, with money to convey him to the ship—and Henry quitted his uncle's house in a flood of tears, to seek first a new protectress for his little foundling, and then to seek his fortune.

---

1   "A vessel equipped for warfare; a commissioned warship belonging to the recognized navy of a country" (*OED*).

CHAPTER XXX.

THE wedding day of Mr. William Norwynne with Miss Caroline Sedgeley arrived—and on that day, the bells of every parish surrounding that in which they lived, joined with their own, in celebration of the blissful union. Flowers were strewed before the new-married pair, and favours and ale made many a heart more gladsome, than that of either bridegroom or bride.

Upon this day of ringing and rejoicing, the bells were not muffled, nor was conversation on the subject withheld from the ear of Hannah! She heard like her neighbours; and sitting on the side of her bed in her little chamber, suffered, under the cottage roof, as much affliction as ever visited a palace.

Tyrants, who have embrued[1] their hands in the blood of myriads of their fellow creatures, can call their murders "religion, justice, attention to the good of mankind"—poor Hannah knew no sophistry to calm *her* conscience—she felt herself a harlot and a murderer—a slighted, a deserted wretch, bereft of all she loved in this world, all she could hope for in the next.

She complained bitterly of illness, nor could the entreaties of her father and mother prevail on her to share in the sports of this general holiday.— As none of her humble visitors suspected the cause of her more than ordinary indisposition, they endeavoured to divert it with an account of every thing they had seen at church—"What the bride wore, how joyful the bridegroom looked"—and all the seeming signs of that complete happiness, which they conceived was for certain tasted.

Hannah, who, before this event, had at moments suppressed the agonising sting of guilt, in the faint prospect of her lover one day restored; on this memorable occasion lost every glimpse of hope, and was weighed to the earth with an accumulation of despair.

Where is the degree in which the sinner stops? Unhappy Hannah! the first time you permitted indecorous familiarity from a man who made you no promise, who gave you no hope of becoming his wife, who professed nothing beyond those fervent though slender affections which attach the rake to the wanton—the first time you interpreted his kind looks and ardent prayers, into tenderness and constancy—the first time you descended from the character of purity, you rushed imperceptibly on the blackest crimes.—The more sincerely you loved, the more you

---

1   A variant of "imbrue": to stain or dye one's hands with blood.

plunged in danger—from one ungoverned passion proceeded a second and a third. In the fervency of affection, you yielded up your virtue!—In the excess of fear, you stained your conscience, by the intended murder of your child!—and now, in the violence of grief, you meditate—what?—to put an end to your existence by your own hand!

After casting her thoughts around, anxious to find some little bud of comfort on which to fix her longing eye; she beheld, in the total loss of William, nothing but a wide waste, an extensive plain of anguish.—"How am I to be sustained through this dreary journey of life?" she exclaimed.— Upon this question she felt, more poignantly than ever, her loss of innocence—innocence would have been her support—but, in place of this best prop to the afflicted, guilt flashed on her memory every time she flew for aid to reflection.

At length, from horrible rumination, a momentary alleviation came— "But one more step in wickedness," she triumphantly said, "and all my shame, all my sufferings are over." She congratulated herself upon the lucky thought—when, but an instant after, the tears trickled down her face for the sorrow her death, her sinful death, would bring to her poor and beloved parents.—She then thought upon the probability of a sigh it might draw from William; and the pride, the pleasure of that little tribute, counterpoised every struggle on the side of life.

As she saw the sun decline, "When you rise again," she thought, "when you peep bright to-morrow morning into this little room to call me up, I shall not be here to open my eyes upon a hateful day—I shall no more regret that you have waked me!—I shall be sound asleep, never to wake again in this wretched world—not even the voice of William would then awake me."

While she found herself resolved, and evening just come on, she hurried out of the house, and hastened to the fatal wood; the scene of her dishonour—the scene of intended murder—and now, the meditated scene of suicide.

As she walked along between the close-set trees, she saw, at a little distance, the spot where William first made love to her; and where, at every appointment, he used to wait her coming. She darted her eye away from this place with horror—but, after a few moments of emotion, she walked slowly up to it—shed tears, and pressed with her trembling lips that tree, against which he was accustomed to lean while he talked with her.—She felt an inclination to make this the spot to die in—but her preconcerted, and the less frightful death, of leaping into a pool on the other side of the wood, induced her to go onwards.

Presently, she came near the place where *her* child, and *William's*, was exposed to perish.—Here, she started with a sense of the most atrocious guilt; and her whole frame shook with the dread of an approaching, an omnipotent judge to sentence her for murder.

She halted, appalled! aghast! undetermined whether to exist longer beneath the pressure of a criminal conscience, or die that very hour, and meet her final condemnation.

She proceeded a few steps farther, and beheld the very ivy-bush close to which her infant lay, when she left him exposed—and now, from this minute recollection, all the mother rising in her soul, she saw, as it were, her babe again in its deserted state; and bursting into tears of bitterest contrition and compassion, she cried

"As I was merciless to *thee*, my child, thy father has been pitiless to *me*! As I abandoned *thee* to die with cold and hunger, he has forsaken, and has driven *me* to die by self-slaughter."

She now fixed her eager eyes on the distant pond, and walked more nimbly than before, to rid herself of her agonising sense![1]

Just as she had nearly reached the wished-for brink, she heard a footstep, and saw, by the glimmering of a clouded moon, a man approaching.—She turned out of her path for fear her intentions should be guessed at, and thwarted; but still, as she walked another way, her eye was wishfully bent towards the water that was to obliterate her love and her remorse—obliterate, for ever, William and his child.

It was now, that Henry—who, to prevent scandal, had stolen at that still hour of night to rid the curate of the incumbrance so irksome to him, and take the foundling to a woman whom he had hired for the charge—it was now that Henry came up, with the child of Hannah in his arms, carefully covered all over from the night's dew.

"Hannah, is it you?" (cried Henry, at a little distance) "Where are going thus late?"

"Home, Sir." Said she, and rushed among the trees.

"Stop, Hannah," he cried: "I want to bid you farewell—to-morrow I am going to leave this part of the country for a long time—So God bless you, Hannah!" Saying this, he stretched out his arm to shake her by the hand.

Her poor heart trusting that his blessing, for want of more potent offerings, might perhaps, at this tremendous crisis, ascend to heaven in her behalf,—she stopt, returned, and put out her hand to take his.

---

1   Here with the implication of (painful) self-awareness: "Emotional consciousness of something; a glad or sorrowful, grateful or resentful recognition" (*OED*).

"Softly!" said he: "don't wake my child—this spot has been a place of danger for him—for underneath this very ivy-bush it was that I found him."

"Found what?" Cried Hannah, with a voice elevated to a tremulous scream.

"I will not tell you the story," replied Henry, "for no one I have ever yet told of it, would believe me."

"I will believe you. I will believe you." She repeated with tones yet more impressive.[1]

"Why then," said Henry, "only five weeks ago———"

"Ah!" shrieked Hannah.

"What do you mean?" Said Henry.

"Go on." She articulated, in the same voice.

"Why then, as I was passing this very place, I wish I may never speak truth again, if I did not find"—(Here he pulled aside the warm rug in which the infant was wrapt)—"this beautiful child."

"With a cord?———"

"A cord was round its neck."

"'Tis mine—the child is mine—'tis mine—my child—I am the mother and the murderer—I fixed the cord, while the ground shook under me—while flashes of fire darted before my eyes!—while my heart was bursting with despair and horror.—But I stopt short—I did not draw the noose—I had a moment of strength, and I ran away. I left him living—he is living now—escaped from my hands—and I am no longer ashamed, but overcome with joy that he is mine! I bless you, my dear, my dear, for saving his life—for giving him to me again—for preserving *my* life, as well as my child's."

Here she took her infant, pressed it to her lips and to her bosom; then bent to the ground, clasped Henry's knees, and wept upon his feet.

He could not for a moment doubt the truth of what she said—her powerful, yet broken accents, her convulsive starts, even more than her declaration, convinced him.[2]

"Good heaven!" cried Henry, "and this is my cousin William's child!"

"But your cousin does not know it." Said she. "I never told him—he was not kind enough to embolden me—therefore do not blame *him* for *my* sin—he did not know of my wicked designs—he did not encourage me———"

---

1   Affecting, exciting deep feeling (i.e., in Henry).
2   See Appendix A.1.a for a passage deleted from the second edition.

"But he forsook you, Hannah."

"He never said he would not. He always told me he could not marry me."

"Did he tell you so at his first private meeting?"

"No."

"Nor at the second?"

"No, nor yet at the third."

"When was it he told you so?"

"I forget the exact time—but I remember it was on that very evening when I confest to him—"

"What?"

"That he had won my heart."

"Why did you confess it?"

"Because he asked me, and said it would make him happy if I would say so."

"Cruel! dishonourable!"

"Nay, do not blame him—he cannot help *not* loving me, no more than I can help *loving* him."

Henry rubbed his eyes.

"Bless me, you weep!—I always heard that you were brought up in a savage country; but I suppose it is a mistake; it was your cousin William."

"Will not you apply to him for the support of your child?" Asked Henry.

"If I thought he would not be angry."

"Angry!—I will write to him on the subject, if you will give me leave."

"But do not say it is by my desire. Do not say I wish to trouble him—I would sooner beg, than be a trouble to him."

"Why are you so delicate?"

"It is for my own sake—I wish him not to hate me."

"Then, thus you may secure his respect—I will write him, and let him know all the circumstances of your case; I will plead for his compassion on his child, but assure him that no conduct of his will ever induce you to declare (except only to me, who knew of your previous acquaintance) who is the father."

To this Hannah consented: but when Henry offered to take from her the infant and carry him to the nurse he had engaged; to this she would not consent.

"Do you mean then to acknowledge him yours?" Henry asked.

"Nothing shall force me to part from him. I will keep him, and let my neighbours judge of me as they please."

Here Henry caught at a hope he feared to name before. "You will then have no objection," said he, "to clear an unhappy girl to a few friends with whom her character has suffered by becoming, at my request, his nurse?"

"I will clear any one, so that I do not accuse the father."

"You give me leave, then, in your name, to tell the whole story to some particular friends, my cousin William's part in it alone excepted?"

"I do."

Henry now exclaimed "God bless you!" with greater fervour than when he spoke it before—and he hoped the night was nearly gone, that the time might be so much the shorter before Rebecca should be re-instated in the esteem of her father, and of all those who had misjudged her.

"God bless *you!*" said Hannah still more fervently, as she walked with unguided steps towards her home; for her eyes never wandered from the precious object which caused her unexpected return.

CHAPTER XXXI.

HENRY rose early in the morning, and flew to the curate's house, with more than even his usual thirst of justice, to clear injured innocence, to redeem from shame, her whom he loved. With eager haste he told—that he had found the mother, whose fall from virtue Rebecca, overcome by confusion and threats, had taken on herself.

Rebecca rejoiced—but her sisters shook their heads—and even the father seemed to doubt.

Confident in the truth of his story, Henry persisted so boldly in his affirmations, that if Mr. Rymer did not entirely believe what he said, he secretly hoped the dean and other people might; therefore he began to imagine, he could possibly shake from *his* family the present stigma, whether or no it belonged to any other.

No sooner was Henry gone, than Mr. Rymer waited on the dean to report what he had heard; and he frankly attributed his daughter's false confession to the compulsive methods he had adopted in charging her with the offence; upon this statement, Henry's love to her was also a solution of his seemingly inconsistent conduct on that singular occasion.

The dean immediately said—"I will put the matter beyond all doubt: for I will this moment send for the present reputed mother; and if she acknowledges the child, I will instantly commit her to prison for the attempt of putting it to death."

The curate applauded the dean's sagacity; a warrant was issued; and Hannah brought prisoner before the grandfather of her child.

She appeared astonished at the peril in which she found herself! Confused, also, with a thousand inexpressible sensations which the dean's presence inspired, she seemed to prevaricate in all she uttered.—Accused of this, she was still more disconcerted—said, and unsaid—confessed herself the mother of the infant, but declared she did not know—then owned she *did* know the name of the man who had undone her, but would never utter it.—At length, she cast herself on her knees before the father of her betrayer, and supplicated "he would not punish her with severity, as she most penitently confessed her fault, so far as it related to herself."

While Mr. and Mrs. Norwynne, just entered on the honey-moon, were sitting side by side enjoying with peace and with honour conjugal society; poor Hannah, threatened, reviled, and sinking to the dust, was hearing from the mouth of William's father, the enormity of those crimes to which his son had been accessary.—She saw the mittimus[1] written that was to convey her into a prison—saw herself delivered once more into the hands of constables, before her resolution left her, of concealing the name of William in her story.—She now, overcome with affright, and thinking she should expose him still more in a public court, if hereafter on her trial she should be obliged to name him—she now humbly asked the dean to hear a few words she had to say in private—where she promised she "would speak nothing but the truth."

This was impossible, he said—"No private confessions before a magistrate! All must be done openly."

She urged again and again the same request—it was denied more peremptorily than at first. On which she said,

"Then, Sir, forgive me, since you force me to it, if I speak before Mr. Rymer and these men, what I would for ever have kept a secret if I could.—One of your family is my child's father."

"Any of my servants?" Cried the dean.

"No."

"My nephew?"

"No; one who is nearer still."

"Come this way," said the dean, "I *will* speak to you in private."

---

1   From the Latin for "We send," a warrant from a justice of the peace to the keeper of a prison directing him to take an offender into custody. For a famous scene involving a mittimus (and criticizing the corruption of the legal system) see Book II, Chapter 11 of Henry Fielding's *Joseph Andrews* (1742).

It was not that the dean, as a magistrate, distributed partial decrees of pretended justice—he was rigidly faithful to his trust—he would not inflict punishment on the innocent, nor let the guilty escape—but in all particulars of refined or coarse treatment, he would alleviate or aggravate according to the rank of the offender. He could not feel that a secret was of equal importance to a poor, as to a rich person—and while Hannah gave no intimation but that her delicacy rose from fears for herself, she did not so forcibly impress him with an opinion that it was a case which had weighty cause for a private conference, as when she boldly said, "a part of *his* family, very near to him, was concerned in her tale."

The final result of their conversation in an adjoining room was—a charge from the dean, in the words of Mr. Rymer, "to hush the affair up;" and his promise that the infant should be immediately taken from her, and "she should have no more trouble with it."

"I have no trouble with it." Replied Hannah. "My child is now all my comfort: and I cannot part from it."

"Why, you inconsistent woman, did you not attempt to murder it?"

"That was before I had nursed it."

"It is necessary you should give it up—it must be sent some miles off—and then the whole circumstance will be soon forgotten."

"*I* shall never forget it."

"No matter—you must give up the child—Do not most of our first women of quality part with their children?"

"Women of quality have other things to love—I have nothing else."

"And would you occasion my son, and his new-made bride, the shame and the uneasiness——"

Here Hannah burst into a flood of tears; and being angrily asked by the dean "why she blubbered so?"——

"*I*—have had shame and uneasiness." She replied, wringing her hands.

"And you deserve them—they are the sure attendants of crimes such as yours.—If you allured, and entrapped a young man like my son——"

"I am the youngest by five years." Said Hannah.

"Well, well, repent;" returned the dean, "repent, and resign your child. Repent, and you may yet marry an honest man who knows nothing of the matter."

"And repent too?" Asked Hannah.

Not the insufferable ignorance of young Henry, when he first came to England, was more vexatious or provoking to the dean than the rustic folly of poor Hannah's uncultured replies. He at last, in an offended and determined manner, told her,

"That if she would resign the child, and keep the father's name a secret, not only the child should be taken care of, but she herself might, perhaps, receive some favours: but if she persisted in her imprudent folly, she must expect no consideration on her own account; nor should she be allowed, for the maintenance of the boy, a sixpence beyond the stated sum for a poor man's unlawful offspring."[1]—Hannah, resolving not to be separated from her infant, bowed resignation to this last decree; and, terrified at the loud words and angry looks of the dean, after being regularly discharged, stole to her home; where the smiles of her infant, and the caresses she lavished on it, repaid her for the sorrows she had just suffered for its sake.

Let it here be observed, that the dean, on suffering Hannah to depart without putting in force the law against her as he had threatened, did nothing, as it were, *behind the curtain*. He openly and candidly owned to Mr. Rymer, his clerk, and the two constables who were attending—"That an affair of some little gallantry, in which, he was extremely sorry to say, his son was rather too nearly involved, required, in consideration of his recent marriage, and an excellent young woman's (his bride's) happiness, that it should not be publicly talked of—Therefore he had thought proper only to reprimand the hussey, and send her about her business."

The curate assured the dean—"That upon this, and upon all other occasions, which should, would, or *could* occur, he owed to his judgment, as his superior, implicit obedience."

The clerk and the two constables most properly said—"His honour was a gentleman, and of course must know better how to act than they."

CHAPTER XXXII.

IT was not the pleasure of a mother that Hannah experienced, which could make her insensible to the sorrow of a daughter.

Her parents had received the stranger child along with a fabricated tale she told "of its appertaining to another," without the smallest suspicion; but, by the secret diligence of the curate; and the nimble tongues of his elder daughters, the report of all that had passed on the subject of this unfortunate infant, soon circulated through the village; and Hannah in a few weeks had seen her parents pine away in grief and shame at her loss of virtue.

---

1 According to the "poor law" of 1576 (18 Eliz. I, c. 3), the mother of an illegitimate child was obligated to name the father, who was then required to give a bond or weekly payment to the parish. Noncompliance could result in corporal punishment or prison terms for either parent.

She perceived the neighbours avoid, or openly sneer at *her*—but that was little—she saw them slight her aged father and mother upon her account: and she now took the resolution, rather to perish for want in another part of the country, than live where she was known, and so entail a curse upon the few who loved her. She slightly hoped, too, that by disappearing from the town and neigbourhood, some little reward might be allowed her for her banishment by the dean's family. In that she was deceived—No sooner was she gone, indeed, than her guilt was forgotten: but with her guilt her wants. The dean and his family rejoiced at her and her child's departure; but as this mode she had chosen, chanced to be no specified condition in the terms offered to her, they did not think they were bound to pay her for it; and while she was too fearful and bashful to solicit the dean, and too proud (forlorn as she was) to supplicate his son, they both concluded she "wanted for nothing;" for to be poor, and too delicate to complain, they deemed incompatible.

To heighten the sense of her degraded, friendless situation, she knew that Henry had not been unmindful of his promise to her, but that he had applied to his cousin in her and his child's behalf; for he had acquainted her that William's answer was—"all obligations on *his* part were now undertaken by his father; for Hannah having chosen (in a fit of malignity upon his marriage) to apprise the dean of their former intercourse, such conduct had for ever cancelled all attention due from him to her, or to her child, beyond what its bare maintenance exacted."

In vain had Henry explained to him the predicament in which poor Hannah was involved, before she consented to reveal her secret to his father; William was happy in an excuse to rid himself of a burthen, and he seemed to believe, what he wished to be true—that she had forfeited all claim to his farther notice.

Henry informed Hannah of this unkind reception of his efforts in her favour, in as gentle terms as possible, for she excited his deepest compassion.—Perhaps our *own* misfortunes are the cause of our pity for others, even more than *their* ills; and Henry's present sorrows had softened his heart to peculiar sympathy in woe. He had unhappily found, that the ardour which had hurried him to vindicate the reputation of Rebecca, was likely to deprive him of the blessing of her ever becoming his wife. For the dean, chagrined that his son was at length proved an offender instead of his nephew, submitted to the temptation of punishing the latter, while he forgave the former. He sent for Henry, and having coldly congratulated him on his and Rebecca's innocence, represented to him the impropriety of marrying the daughter of a poor curate, and laid his commands on him, "never to harbour such an intention more." Henry found this restriction so severe that he would not promise obedience; but on his next attempt to visit Rebecca, he met a positive repulse from her father, who signified to him, "that the dean had forbidden him to permit their farther acquaintance;" and the curate declared—"that, for his own part, he had no will, judgment, or faculties; but that he submitted in all things to the superior clergy."

At the very time young Henry had received the proposal from Mr. Rymer of his immediate union with his daughter, and the dean had made no objection, Henry waved the happiness for the time present, and had given a reason why he wished it postponed. The reason he then gave had its weight, but he had another concealed, of yet more import.—Much as he loved, and looked forward with rapture to that time when every morning, every evening, and all the day, he should have the delight of Rebecca's society; still there was one other wish nearer his heart than this—one desire which for years had been foremost in his thoughts, and which not even love could eradicate. He longed, he pined to know what fate had befallen his father. Provided he were living, he could conceive no joy so extreme as that of seeing him! If he were dead, he was anxious to pay the tribute of filial piety he owed, by satisfying his affectionate curiosity in every circumstance of the sad event.

While a boy, he had frequently expressed these sentiments to both his uncle and his cousin: sometimes they apprised him of the total improbability of accomplishing his wishes: at other times, when they saw the disappointment weigh heavy on his mind, they bade him—"wait till he was a man, before he could hope to put his designs in execution." He did wait. But on the very day he arrived at the age of twenty-one, he made a vow— "that to gain intelligence of his father should be the first act of his free will."

Previously to this time he had made all the enquiries possible, whether any new adventure to that part of Africa in which he was bred, was likely to be undertaken. Of this there appeared to be no prospect, till the intended expedition to Sierra Leone[1] was announced, which favoured his hope of being able to procure a passage, among those adventurers, so near to the island on which his father was (or had been) prisoner, as to obtain an opportunity of visiting it by stealth.

---

1   Gary Kelly observes that Inchbald "may have been alluding to the Sierra Leone expedition of 1791, a private venture by anti-slavery humanitarians" (*The English Jacobin Novel*, p. 102, n. 2). For a description of that venture, and a depiction of the settlers' life in the colony, see Appendix D.

Fearing contention, or the being dissuaded from his plans if he communicated them, he not only formed them in private, but he kept them secretly; and, his imagination filled with the kindness, the tenderness, the excess of fondness he had experienced from his father, beyond any other person in the world, he had thought with delight on the separation from all his other kindred, to pay his duty to him, or to his revered memory. Of late indeed, there had been an object introduced to his acquaintance, from whom it was bitter to part; but his designs had been planned and firmly fixed before he knew Rebecca; nor could he have tasted contentment even with her, at the expence of his piety to his father.

In the last interview he had with the dean, Henry—perceiving that his disposition towards him was not less severe than when a few days before he had ordered him on board a vessel—found this the proper time to declare his intentions of accompanying the fleet to Sierra Leone. His uncle expressed surprise! but immediately gave him a sum of money, such as he thought might defray his expences; and as he gave it, by his willingness, his look, and his accent, seemed to say, "I foresee this is the last you will ever require."

Young William, though a very dutiful son, was amazed when he heard of Henry's project, "as the serious and settled resolution of a man."

Lady Clementina, Lord and Lady Bendham, and twenty others, "wished him a successful voyage," and thought no more about him.

It was for Rebecca alone, to feel the loss of Henry—it was for a mind like hers alone, to know his worth—nor did this last proof of it, the quitting her, for one who claimed by every tie a preference, lessen him in her esteem.—When, by a message from him, she became acquainted with his design, much as it interfered with her happiness, she valued him the more for this observance of his duty,—the more she regretted his loss, and the more anxiously prayed for his return; which, in the following letter, written just before his departure, he taught her to hope for.

"MY DEAR REBECCA,

"I DO not tell you I am sorry to part from you—you know I am—and you know all I have suffered, since your father denied me permission to see you.

"But perhaps you do not know the hopes I enjoy, and which bestow on me a degree of peace—and those I am eager to tell you.

"I hope, Rebecca, to see you again—I hope to return to England, and overcome every obstacle to our marriage—and then, in whatever station we are placed, I shall consider myself as happy as it is possible to be in this world—I feel a conviction that you would be happy also.

"Some persons, I know, estimate happiness by fine houses, gardens, and parks—others, by pictures, horses, money, and various things wholly remote from their own species—but when I wish to ascertain the real felicity of any rational man, I always enquire *whom he has to love*. If I find he has nobody—or does not love those he has—even in the midst of all his profusion of finery and grandeur, I pronounce him a being in deep adversity. In loving you, I am happier than my cousin William; even though I am obliged to leave you for a time.

"Do not be afraid you should grow old before I return—age can never alter you in my regard. It is your gentle nature, your unaffected manners, your easy cheerfulness, your clear understanding, the sincerity of all your words and actions, which have gained my heart; and while you preserve charms like these, you will be dearer to me with white hairs and a wrinkled face, than any of your sex, who, not possessing all these qualities, possess the youth and bloom of perfect beauty.

"You will esteem me too, I trust, though I should return on crutches with my poor father, whom I may be obliged to maintain by daily labour.

"I will employ all my time, during my absence, in the study of some art which may enable me to support you both, provided heaven will bestow two such blessings on me. In the cheering thought that it will be so, and in that only, I have the courage, my dear, dear Rebecca, to say to you

"Farewell!
"H. NORWYNNE."

CHAPTER XXXIII.

BEFORE Henry could receive a reply to his letter, the fleet in which he sailed put to sea.

By his absence, not only Rebecca was deprived of the friend she loved, but poor Hannah lost a kind and compassionate adviser. Her parents, too, both sickened, and both died, in a short time after—and now, wholly friendless, and in her little exile where she could only hope for toleration, not being known, she was contending with suspicion, rebuffs, disappointments, and various other ills, which might have made the most harsh of her Anfield persecutors feel compassion for her, could they have witnessed the throbs of her heart, and have viewed the state of her agonising mind.

Still, there are few persons whom providence afflicts beyond the limits of *all* consolation—few cast so low, as not to feel pride on *certain* occasions—and Hannah felt a comfort and a dignity in the thought—that she had both a mind and a body capable of sustaining every hardship which her destiny might inflict, rather than submit to the disgrace of soliciting William's charity a second time.

This determination was put to a variety of trials—In vain she offered herself to the strangers of the village in which she was accidently cast, as a servant—her child, her dejected looks, her broken sentences, a wildness in her eye, a kind of bold despair which at times overspread her features, her imperfect story, who and what she was, prejudiced all those to whom she applied; and, after thus travelling to several small towns and hamlets, the only employer she could obtain was a farmer, and the only employment, to tend and feed his cattle, while his men were in the harvest, tilling the ground, or at some other labour which required, at that time, peculiar expedition.

Though Hannah was born of peasants, yet, having been the only child of industrious parents, she had been nursed with a tenderness and delicacy ill suited to her present occupation—but she endured it with patience; and the most laborious part would have seemed light, could she have dismissed the reflection—what it was that had reduced her to it.

Soon her tender hands became hard and rough, her fair skin burnt and yellow; so that when, on a Sunday, she has looked in the glass, she has started back as if it were some other face she saw instead of her own. But this loss of beauty gave her no regret—while William did not see her, it was matter of indifference to her, whether she were beautiful or hideous. On the features of her child only, she now looked with joy—there, she fancied she saw William at every glance—and in the fond imagination, felt, at times, every happiness short of seeing *him*.

By herding solely with the brute creation, she and her child were allowed to live together; and this was a state she preferred to the society of human creatures, who would have separated her from what she loved so tenderly.—Anxious to retain a place in which she possessed such a blessing, care and attention to her humble office caused her master to prolong her stay through all the winter—then, during the spring, she attended his yeaning[1] sheep—in the summer, watched them as they grazed—and thus season after season passed, till her young son could afford her assistance in her daily work.

---

1   Pregnant.

He now could charm her with his conversation as well as with his looks—a thousand times, in the transports of parental love, she has pressed him to her bosom, and thought, with an agony of horror—on her foul intent to destroy what was now so dear, so necessary to her existence.

Still the boy grew more like his father.—In one resemblance alone he failed—he loved Hannah with an affection totally distinct from the pitiful and childish gratification of his own self-love—he never would quit her side for all the tempting offers of toys or money—never would eat of rarities given to him, till Hannah took a part—never crossed her will, however contradictory to his own—never saw her smile that he did not laugh—nor did she ever weep, but he wept too.

CHAPTER XXXIV.

FROM the mean subject of oxen, sheep, and peasants, we return to personages—*i.e.* persons of rank and fortune. The bishop, who was introduced in the last volume, but who occupied a very small space there, is now mentioned in this, merely than the reader may know, he is at present in the same state as his writing—dying; and that his friend, the dean, is talked of as the most likely successor to his dignified office.

The dean, most assuredly, had a strong friendship for the bishop, and now, most assuredly, wished him to recover—and yet—when he reflected on the success of his pamphlet a few years past, and of many which he had written since on the very same subject, he could not but think "That he had more righteous pretensions to fill the vacant seat of his much beloved and reverend friend (should fate ordain it to be vacated) than any other man:" and he knew that it would not take one moment from that friend's remaining life, should he exert himself, with all due management, to obtain the elevated station when *he* should be no more.

In presupposing the death of a friend, the dean—like many other virtuous men—"always supposed him going to a better place." With perfect resignation, therefore, he waited whatever change might happen to the bishop; ready to receive him with open arms if he recovered, or equally ready, in case of his dissolution, to receive his dignities.

Lady Clementina displayed her sensibility and feeling for the sick prelate, by the disgusting extravagance of hysteric fits; except at those times when she talked seriously with her husband upon the injustice which she thought would be done to him, and to his many pamphlets and sermons, if he did not immediately rise to the episcopal honour.

"Surely, dean," said she, "should you be disappointed upon this occasion, you will write no more books for the good of your country?"

"Yes I will," he replied: "but the next book I write for the good of my country, shall be very different, nay the very reverse of those I have already written."

"How dean! would you show yourself changed?"

"No, but I will show that my country is changed."

"What! since you produced your last work? only six weeks ago!"

"Great changes may occur in six days;" replied the dean, with a threatening accent: "and if I find things *have* taken a new and improper turn, I will be the first to expose it."

"But before you act in this manner, my dear, surely you will wait——"

"I will wait till the See is disposed of to another." Said he.

He did wait—The bishop died—The dean was promoted to the See of * * *, and wrote a folio[1] on the prosperity of our happy country.

CHAPTER XXXV.

WHILE the bishop and his son were sailing before prosperous gales on the ocean of life, young Henry was contending with adverse winds, and many other perils, on the watery ocean—yet still, his distresses and dangers were less than those which Hannah had to encounter on land. The sea threatens an untimely death; the shore menaces calamities from which death is a refuge.

The afflictions Hannah had already experienced, could just admit of aggravation—the addition occurred.

Had the good farmer, who made her the companion of his flocks and herds, lived till now, till now she might have been secure from the annoyance of human kind: but, thrown once more upon society, she was unfit to sustain the conflict of decorum against depravity.—Her master, her patron, her preserver, was dead; and hardly as she had earned the pittance she received from him, she found, it surpassed all her power to obtain the like again. Her doubtful character, her capacious mind, her unmethodical manners, were still badly suited to the nice precision of a country housewife; and as the prudent mistress of a family sneered at her pretensions, she, in her turn, scorned the narrow-minded mistress of a family.

---

1 "A volume made up of sheets of paper folded once; a volume of the largest size" (*OED*).

In her enquiries how to gain her bread free from the cutting reproaches of discretion, she was informed, "that London was the only private corner where guilt could be secreted undisturbed—and the only public place where, in open day, it might triumphantly stalk, attended by a train of audacious admirers."

There was a charm to the ear of Hannah, in the name of London, which thrilled through her soul—William lived in London—and she thought, that, while she retired to some dark cellar with her offences, he probably would ride in state with his, and she at humble distance might sometimes catch a glance of him.

As difficult as to eradicate insanity from a mind once possessed, so difficult it is to erase from the lover's breast the deep impression of a *real* affection. Coercion may prevail for a short interval, still love will rage again. Not all the ignominy Hannah experienced in the place where she now was without a home—not the hunger which she at times suffered, and even at times saw her child endure—not every inducement for going to London, or motive for quitting her present desolate station, had the weight to affect her choice so much as—In London, she should live nearer William; in the present spot she could never hope to see him again; but there she might chance to pass him in the streets; she might pass his house every day unobserved; might enquire about him of his inferior neighbours, who would be unsuspicious of the cause of her curiosity.—For these gratifications, she should breathe another air; for these, she could bear all hardships which London threatened; and for these, she took a three weeks' journey to that perilous town on foot, cheering, as she walked along, her innocent and wearied companion.

William! in your luxurious dwelling! possessed of coffers filled with gold! relations, friends, clients, joyful around you! delicious viands and rich wines upon your sumptuous board! voluptuousness displayed in every apartment of your habitation!—contemplate, for a moment, Hannah, your first love, with her son, your first and only child, walking through frost and snow to London, with a foreboding fear on the mother—that, when arrived, they both may perish for the want of a friend.

But no sooner did Hannah find herself within the smoke of the metropolis, than the old charm was renewed; and scarcely had she refreshed her child at the poor inn at which she stopped, than she enquired—how far it was to that part of town where William, she knew, resided.

She received for answer, "about two miles."

Upon this information, she thought that she would keep in reserve, till some new sorrow befell her, the consolation of passing his door (perchance of seeing him), which must ever be an alleviation of her grief. It was not long before she had occasion for more substantial comfort. She soon found she was not likely to obtain a service here, more than in the country. Some objected that she could not make caps and gowns; some, that she could not preserve and pickle; some, that she was too young; some, that she was too pretty; and all declined accepting her, till at last a citizen's wife, on condition of her receiving but half the wages usually given, took her as a servant of all work.

In romances, and in some plays, there are scenes of dark and unwholesome mines, wherein the labourer works during the brightest day by the aid of artificial light. There are in London kitchens equally dismal, though not quite so much exposed to damp and noxious vapours. In one of these, under ground, hid from the cheerful light of the sun, poor Hannah was doomed to toil from morning till night, subjected to the command of a dissatisfied mistress; who, not estimating as she ought, the misery incurred by serving her, constantly threatened her servants "with a dismission;" at which the unthinking wretches would tremble merely from the sound of the words—for, to have reflected—to have considered what their purport was—"to be released from a dungeon, relieved from continual upbraidings, and vile drudgery," must have been a subject of rejoicing—and yet, because these good tidings were delivered as a menace, custom had made the poor creatures fearful of the consequence. So, death being described to children as a disaster, even poverty and shame will start from it with affright; when, had it been pictured with its benign aspect, it would have been feared but by few, and many, many would welcome it with gladness.

All the care of Hannah to please, her fear of offending, her toilsome days, her patience, her submission, could not prevail on her mistress to retain her one hour after by chance she had heard "that she was the mother of a child; that she wished it should be kept a secret; and that she stole out now and then to visit him."

Hannah, with swimming eyes and an almost breaking heart, left a place—where, to have lived one hour, would have plunged any fine lady in the deepest grief.

CHAPTER XXXVI.

HANNAH was driven from service to service—her deficiency in the knowledge of a mere drudge, or her lost character, pursued her wherever she went; and at length, becoming wholly destitute, she gladly accepted a place where the latter misfortune was not the least objection.

In one of those habitations where continual misery is dressed in continual smiles; where extreme of poverty is concealed by extreme of show; where wine dispenses mirth only by dispensing forgetfulness; and where female beauty is so cheap, so complying, that, while it inveigles, it disgusts the man of pleasure;—in one of those houses, to attend upon its wretched inhabitants, Hannah was hired.—Her feelings of rectitude submitted to those of hunger—Her principles of virtue (which the loss of virtue had not destroyed) received a shock when she engaged to be the abettor of vice, from which her delicacy, morality, and religion shrunk: but—persons of honour and of reputation would not employ her: was she then to perish? That perhaps was easy to resolve—but she had a child to leave behind! a child, from whom to part for a day was a torment.—Yet, before she submitted to a situation which filled her mind with a kind of loathing horror, often she paced up and down the street in which William lived, looked wistfully at his house, and sometimes, lost to all her finer feelings of independent pride, thought of sending a short petition to him—but, at the idea of a repulse, and of that frowning brow, which she knew William *could* dart on her, she preferred death, or the most degrading life, to the trial.

It was long since, that misfortune and dishonour had made her callous to the good or ill opinion of all the world, except *his*; and the fear of drawing upon her his encreased contempt was still, at the crisis of applying, so powerful, that she found she dared not even hazard a reproof from him in the person of his father; whose rigour she had already more than once experienced, in the frequent harsh messages conveyed to her with the poor stipend for her boy.

Awed by the rigid and pious character of the new bishop, the growing reputation and rising honours of his son, she mistook the appearance of moral excellence, for moral excellence itself; and felt her own unworthiness even to become the supplicant of those great men.

Day after day she watched those parts of the town through which William's chariot was accustomed to drive—but, to see the *carriage*, was all to which she aspired—a feeling, not to be described, forced her to cast her eyes upon the earth as it drew near to her—and when it had passed, she beat her breast and wept, that she had not seen *him*.

Impressed with the superiority of others, and her own abject and disgustful state, she cried—"Let me herd with those who won't despise me—let me only see faces whereon I can look without confusion and terror—let me associate with wretches like myself, rather than force my shame before those who are so good, they can but scorn and mock me."

With a mind thus languishing for sympathy in disgrace, she entered a servant in the house just now described. There accomplishing the fatal proverb against "*evil communications*,"[1] she had not the fortitude to be an exception to the general rule.—That pliant disposition which had yielded to the licentious love of William, stooped to still baser prostitution in company still more depraved.

At first she shuddered at those practices she saw, at those conversations she heard; and blest herself that poverty, not inclination, had caused her to be witness of such things, and had condemned her in this vile abode to be a servant, rather than in the lower rank of mistress.—Use softened those horrors every day—at length self-defence, the fear of ridicule, and the hope of favour, induced her to adopt that very conduct from which her heart revolted.

In her sorrowful countenance, and fading charms, there yet remained attraction for many visitors—and she now submitted to the mercenary profanations of love; more odious, as her mind had been subdued by its most sacred, most endearing joys.

While incessant regret whispered to her "that she ought to have endured every calamity rather than this," she thus questioned her nice sense of wrong—"Why, why respect myself, since no other respects me? Why set a value on my own feelings, when no one else does?"

Degraded in her own judgment, she doubted her own understanding when it sometimes told her she had deserved better treatment—for she felt herself a fool in comparison with her learned seducer, and the rest who despised her. "And why," she continued, "should I ungratefully persist to contemn women who alone are so kind as to accept for me a companion? Why refuse conformity to their customs, since none of my sex besides will admit me to their society a partaker of theirs?"

In speculation, these arguments appeared reasonable, and she pursued their dictates—but in the practice of the life in which she plunged, she

---

1   "Evil communication corrupts good manners"—I Corinthians 15: 33. The saying also appears in several contemporary works. In *Hermsprong*, Bage employs the maxim ironically by putting it into the mouth of the odious Sir Philip Chestrum (Ch. 47); in *Hugh Trevor*, Holcroft's protagonist uses the statement as a serious comment upon himself (Vol. II, Ch. 7), as does the heroine's mother in Mary Hays's *Victim of Prejudice* (Vol. I, Ch. 12). (The proverb also reappears in chapter 5 of the final (sixth) volume of *Hugh Trevor* as part of the chapter summary.) Clearly, the attitude that evil communication—which is to say, dealings with the profligate—rather than any innate human propensity toward wickedness would be at the core of corrupt behavior was fundamental to the philosophy of the English Jacobins.

proved the fallacy of the system; and at times tore her hair with frantic sorrow—that she did not continue in the mid-way of guilt, and so preserve some portion of self-approbation, to recompense her, in a small degree, for the total loss of the esteem of all the virtuous world.

But she had gone too far to recede. Could she now have recalled her innocence, even that part she brought with her to London, experience would have taught her to have given up her child, lived apart from him, and once more with the brute creation, rather than to have mingled with her present society. Now, alas! the time for flying was past—all prudent choice was over—even all reflection was gone for ever—or only admitted on compulsion, when it imperiously forced its way amidst the scenes of tumultuous mirth, of licentious passion, of distracted riot, shameless effrontery, and wild intoxication—when it *would* force its way—even through the walls of a brothel.

CHAPTER XXXVII.

IS there a reader so little experienced in the human heart, so forgetful of his own, as not to feel the possibility of the following fact?

A series of uncommon calamities had been for many years the lot of the elder Henry—a succession of prosperous events had fallen to the share of his brother William—The one was the envy, while the other had the compassion, of all who thought about them. For the last twenty years, William had lived in affluence bordering upon splendour, his friends, his fame, his fortune daily encreasing; while Henry, throughout that very period, had, by degrees, lost all he loved on earth, and was now existing apart from civilised society—and yet—during those twenty years, where William knew one happy moment, Henry tasted hundreds.

That the state of the mind, and not outward circumstances, is the nice[1] point on which happiness depends, is but a trite remark: but that intellectual power should have the force to render a man discontented in extraordinary prosperity such as that of the present bishop, or contented in his brother's extreme of adversity, requires illustration.

The first great affliction to Henry was his brother's ingratitude; but reasoning on the frailty of man's nature, and the power of man's temptations, he found excuses for William, which made him support the treatment he had received, with more tranquillity, than William's proud mind

---

1 Precise, exact.

supported his brother's marriage—Henry's indulgent disposition made him less angry with William, than William was with him.

The next affliction Henry suffered, was the loss of his beloved wife—that was a grief which time and change of objects gradually alleviated; while William's wife was to him a permanent grief; her puerile mind, her talking vanity, her affected virtues, soured his domestic comfort; and, in time, he had suffered more painful moments from her society, than his brother had experienced, even from the death of her he loved.

In their children, indeed, William was the happier—his son was a pride and pleasure to him, while Henry never thought upon *his* without lamenting his loss with bitterest anguish. But if the elder brother had in one instance the advantage, still Henry had a resource to overbalance this article. Henry, as he lay imprisoned in his dungeon, and when, after his punishment was remitted, he was again allowed to wander and seek his subsistence where he would,—in all his tedious walks and solitary resting-places, during all his lonely days and mournful nights, had *this resource* to console him:

"I never did an injury to any one: never was harsh, severe, unkind, deceitful: I did not merely confine myself to do my neighbour no harm; I strove to do him service."

This was the resource that cheered his sinking heart amidst gloomy deserts and a barbarous people; lulled him to peaceful slumber in the hut of a savage hunter, and in the hearing of the lion's roar; at times impressed him with a sense of happiness; and made him contemplate with a longing hope, the retribution of a future world.

The bishop, with all his comforts, had no comfort like this—he had *his* solitary reflections too, but they were of a tendency the reverse of these.— "I used my brother ill," was a secret thought of most powerful influence—it kept him waking upon his safe and commodious bed; was sure to recur with every misfortune by which he was threatened, to make his fears still stronger; and came with invidious stabs, upon every successful event, to take from him a part of his joy.—In a word, it was *conscience* which made Henry's years pass happier than William's.

But though, comparatively with his brother, William was the less happy man, yet his self-reproach was not of such magnitude, for an offence of that atrocious nature, as to banish from his breast a certain degree of happiness, a sensibility to the smiles of fortune—nor was Henry's self-acquittal of such exquisite kind, as to chase away the feeling of his desolate situation.

As he fished or hunted for his daily dinner, many a time in full view of his prey, a sudden burst of sorrow at his fate, a sudden longing for some dear society, for some friend to share his thoughts, for some kind shoulder on which to lean his head, for some companion to partake of his repast, would make him instantaneously desist from his pursuit, cast him on the ground in a fit of anguish, till a shower of tears, and his *conscience*, came to his relief.

It was after an exile of more than twenty three years—when, on one sultry morning, after pleasant dreams during the night, Henry had waked with more than usual perception of his misery—that, sitting upon the beach, his wishes and his looks all bent on the sea towards his native land, he thought he saw a sail swelling before an unexpected breeze.

"Sure I am dreaming still!" he cried. "This is the very vessel I saw last night in my sleep!—Oh! what cruel mockery, that my eyes should so deceive me!"

Yet, though he doubted, he leaped upon his feet in transport!—held up his hands, stretched at their length, in a kind of ecstatic joy!—and as the glorious sight approached, was near rushing into the sea to meet it.

For a while hope and fear kept him in a state bordering on distraction.

Now he saw the ship making for the shore, and tears flowed for the grateful prospect. Now it made for another point, and he vented shrieks and groans from the disappointment.

It was at those moments, while hope and fear thus possessed him, that the horrors of his abode appeared more than ever frightful!—Inevitable afflictions must be borne; but that calamity which admits the expectation of relief, and then denies it, is insupportable.

After a few minutes passed in dreadful uncertainty, which enhanced the wished-for happiness, the ship evidently drew near the land—and while Henry, now upon his knees, wept, and prayed fervently for the event; a youth sprang from the barge on the strand, rushed towards him, and falling on his neck, then at his feet, exclaimed—"My father! oh! my father!"

William! dean! bishop! what are your honours, what your riches, what all your possessions, compared to the happiness, the transport bestowed by this one sentence, on your poor brother Henry?

CHAPTER XXXVIII.

THE crosses at land, and the perilous events at sea, had made it now two years, since young Henry first took the vow of a man no longer dependent on the will of another, to seek his father. His fatigues, his dangers were well recompensed! Instead of weeping over a silent grave, he had the inexpressible joy to receive a parent's blessing for his labours. Yet, the elder Henry, though living, was so changed in person, that his son would scarcely have known him in any other than the favourite spot, which the younger (keeping in memory every incident of his former life) knew his father had always chosen for his morning contemplations; and where, previously to his coming to England, he had many a time kept him company. It was to that particular corner of the island that the captain of the ship had generously ordered they should steer, out of the general route, to gratify the filial tenderness he expressed. But scarcely had the interview between the father and the son taken place, than a band of natives, whom the appearance of the vessel had called from the woods and hills, came to attack the invaders. The elder Henry had no friend with whom he wished to shake hands at his departure; the old negro servant who had assisted in young Henry's escape was dead; and he experienced the excessive joy of bidding adieu to the place, without one regret for all he left behind.

On the night of that day whose morning had been marked by peculiar sadness at the louring[1] prospect of many exiled years to come, he slept on board an English vessel, with Englishmen his companions, and his son, his beloved son—who was still more dear to him for that mind which had planned and executed his rescue—his attentive servant, and most affectionate friend.

Though many a year passed, and many a rough encounter was destined to the lot of the two Henrys before they saw the shores of Europe, yet to them, to live or to die together was happiness enough—even young Henry for a time asked for no greater blessing—but, the first glow of filial ardor over, he called to mind, "Rebecca lived in England;" and every exertion which love, founded on the highest reverence and esteem, could dictate, he employed to expedite a voyage, the end of which would be crowned by the sight of her.

CHAPTER XXXIX.

THE contrast of the state of happiness between the two brothers was nearly resembled by that of the two cousins—the riches of young William did not render him happy, nor did the poverty of young Henry doom him to

---

1   Gloomy, dark, threatening.

misery. His affectionate heart, as he had described in his letter to Rebecca, loved *persons* rather than *things*; and he would not have exchanged the society of his father, nor the prospect of her hand and heart, for all the wealth and finery of which his cousin William was the master.

He was right. Young William, though he viewed with contempt Henry's inferior state, was far less happy than he—His marriage had been the very counterpart of his father's; and having no child to create affection to his home, his Study was the only relief from that domestic incumbrance, his wife: and though by unremitting application there (joined to the influence of the potent relations of the woman he hated) he at length arrived at the summit of his ambitious desires, still they poorly repaid him, for the sacrifice he had made in early life, of every tender disposition.

Striding through a list of rapid advancements in the profession of the law, at the age of thirty-eight he found himself raised to a preferment, such as rarely falls to the share of a man of his short experience—he found himself invested with a judge's robe; and, gratified by the exalted office, curbed more than ever that aversion, which her want of charms or sympathy had produced against the partner of his honours.

While William had thus been daily rising in fortune's favour, poor Hannah had been daily sinking deeper and deeper under fortune's frowns: till at last she became a midnight wanderer through the streets of London, soliciting, or rudely demanding money of the passing stranger.—Sometimes, hunted by the watch,[1] she affrighted fled from street to street, from portico to portico—and once, unknowing in her fear which way she hurried, she found her trembling knees had sunk, and her wearied head was reclined, against the pillars that guarded William's door.

At the sudden recollection where she was, a swell of passion, composed of horror, of anger, of despair, and love, gave re-animated strength to her failing limbs; and, regardless of her pursuers' steps, she ran to the centre of the street, and looking up to the windows of the house, cried, "Ah! there he sleeps in quiet, in peace, in ease—he does not even dream of me—he does not care how the cold pierces, or how the people persecute me!—He does not thank me for all the lavish love I have borne him and his child!—His heart is so hard, he does not even recollect that it was he who brought me to ruin."

Had these miseries, common to the unhappy prostitute, been alone the punishment of Hannah—had her crimes and sufferings ended in dis-

---

1 I.e., the watchman: "a constable of the watch who, before the Police Act of 1839, patrolled the streets by night to safeguard life and property" (*OED*).

tress like this, her story had not perhaps been selected for a public recital; for it had been no other than the customary history of thousands of her sex. But Hannah had a destiny yet more severe.—Unhappily, she was endowed with a mind so sensibly alive to every joy, and every sorrow, to every mark of kindness, every token of severity; so liable to excess in passion, that, once perverted, there was no degree of error from which it would with firmness revolt.

Taught by the conversation of the dissolute poor, with whom she now associated, or by her own observation on the worldly reward of elevated villainy, she began to suspect "that dishonesty was only held a sin, to secure the property of the rich; and that, to take from those who did not want, by the art of stealing, was less guilt, than to take from those who did want, by the power of the law."

By false, yet seducing opinions such as these, her reason estranged from every moral and religious tie, her necessities urgent, she reluctantly accepted the proposal, to mix with a band of practised sharpers and robbers; and became an accomplice in negotiating bills forged on a country banker.

But though ingenious in arguments to excuse the deed before its commission; in the act, she had the dread of some incontrovertible statement on the other side of the question. Intimidated by this conviction, she was the veriest bungler in her vile profession—and on the alarm of being detected, while every one of her confederates escaped and absconded, she alone was seized—was arrested for issuing notes they had fabricated, and committed to the provincial jail, about fifty miles from London, where the crime had been perpetrated, to take her trial for—life or death.

CHAPTER XL.

THE day at length is come, on which Hannah shall have a sight of her beloved William!—She who has watched for hours near his door, to procure a glimpse of him going out, or returning home; who has walked miles to see his chariot pass; she now will behold him, and he will see her, by command of the laws of their country.—Those laws, which will deal with rigour towards her, in this one instance are still indulgent.

The time of the assizes,[1] at the county-town in which she is imprisoned, is arrived—the prisoners are demanded at the shire-hall—the jail

---

1 Sessions held periodically in each county of England for the purpose of administering civil and criminal justice.

doors are opened—they go in sad procession.—The trumpet sounds—it speaks the arrival of the judge—and that judge is William.

The day previous to her trial, Hannah had read, in the printed calendar of the prisoners, his name as the learned justice before whom she was to appear. For a moment she forgot her perilous state in the excess of joy, which the still unconquerable love she bore to him, permitted her to taste even on the brink of the grave!—After-reflection made her check those worldly transports, as unfit for the present solemn occasion. But alas! to her, earth and William were so closely united, that, till she forsook the one, she could never cease to think, without the contending passions of hope, of fear, of joy, of love, of shame, and of despair, on the other.

Now fear took place of her first immoderate joy—she feared, that although much changed in person since he had seen her, and her real name now added to many an *alias*—yet she feared that some well-known glance of the eye, turn of the action, or accent of speech, might recall her to his remembrance; and at that idea shame overcame all her other sensations—for still she retained pride, in respect to *his* opinion, to wish him not to know, Hannah was that wretch she felt she was!—Once a ray of hope beamed on her, "that if he knew her, if he recognised her, he might possibly befriend her cause;"—and life bestowed through William's friendship seemed a precious object!—But again, that rigorous honour she had often heard him boast, that firmness to his word, of which she had fatal experience, taught her to know, he would not for any improper compassion, any unmanly weakness, forfeit his oath of impartial justice.

In meditations such as these she passed the sleepless night.

When, in the morning, she was brought to the bar, and her guilty hand held up before the righteous judgment-seat of William—imagination could not form two figures, or two situations more incompatible with the existence of former familiarity, than the judge and the culprit—and yet, these very persons had passed together the most blissful moments that either ever tasted!—Those hours of tender dalliance were now present to *her* mind—*His* thoughts were more nobly employed in his high office—nor could the haggard face, hollow eye, desponding countenance, and meagre person of the poor prisoner, once call to his memory, though her name was uttered among a list of others which she had assumed, his former youthful, lovely Hannah!

She heard herself arraigned, with trembling limbs and downcast looks—and many witnesses had appeared against her, before she ventured to lift her eyes up to her awful judge.—She then gave one fearful glance, and discovered William, unpitying but beloved William, in every feature!

It was a face she had been used to look on with delight, and a kind of absent smile of gladness now beamed on her poor wan visage.

When every witness on the part of the prosecutor had been examined, the judge addressed himself to her—

"What defence have you to make?"

It was William spoke to Hannah!—The sound was sweet—the voice was mild, was soft, compassionate, encouraging!—It almost charmed her to a love of life!—not such a voice as when William last addressed her; when he left her undone and pregnant, vowing "never to see or speak to her more."

She could have hung upon the present words for ever! She did not call to mind that this gentleness was the effect of practice, the art of his occupation; which, at times, is but a copy, by the unfeeling, from his benevolent brothers of the bench.—In the present judge, tenderness was not designed for the consolation of the culprit, but for the approbation of the auditors.

There were no spectators, Hannah, by your side when last he parted from you—if there had, the awful William had been awed to marks of pity.

Stunned with the enchantment of that well-known tongue directed to her, she stood like one just petrified—all vital power seemed suspended.

Again he put the question, and with these additional sentences, tenderly and emphatically delivered——"Recollect yourself—Have you no witnesses? No proof in your behalf?"

A dead silence followed these questions.

He then mildly, but forcibly, added—"What have you to say?"

Here, a flood of tears burst from her eyes, which she fixed earnestly upon him, as if pleading for mercy, while she faintly articulated,

"Nothing, my Lord."

After a short pause, he asked her, in the same forcible but benevolent tone

"Have you no one to speak to your character?"

The prisoner answered,

"No."

A second gush of tears followed this reply, for she called to mind by *whom* her character had first been blasted.

He summed up the evidence—and every time he was compelled to press hard upon the proofs against her, she shrunk, and seemed to stagger with the deadly blow—writhed under the weight of *his* minute justice, more than from the prospect of a shameful death.

The jury consulted but a few minutes—the verdict was—

"Guilty."

She heard it with composure.

But when William placed the fatal velvet[1] on his head, and rose to pronounce her sentence—she started with a kind of convulsive motion—retreated a step or two back, and lifting up her hands, with a scream exclaimed—

"Oh! not from *you!*"

The piercing shriek which accompanied these words, prevented their being heard by part of the audience; and those who heard them, thought little of their meaning, more, than that they expressed her fear of dying.

Serene, and dignified, as if no such exclamation had been uttered, William delivered the fatal speech, ending with—"Dead, dead, dead."

She fainted as he closed the period, and was carried back to prison in a swoon; while he adjourned the court to go to dinner.[2]

CHAPTER XLI.

IF, unaffected by the scene he had witnessed, William sat down to dinner with an appetite, let not the reader conceive that the most distant idea had struck his mind—of his ever having seen, much less familiarly known, the poor offender whom he had just condemned. Still this forgetfulness did not proceed from the want of memory for Hannah—In every peevish or heavy hour passed with his wife, he was sure to think of her—yet, it was self-love, rather than love of *her*, that gave rise to these thoughts—he felt the want of female sympathy and tenderness, to soften the fatigue of studious labour; to soothe a sullen, a morose disposition—he felt he wanted comfort for himself, but never once considered, what were the wants of Hannah.

In the chagrin of a barren bed, he sometimes thought, too, even on the child that Hannah bore him; but whether it were male or female, whether a beggar in the streets, or dead—various and important public occupations forbade him to waste time to enquire. Yet the poor, the widow, and the orphan, frequently shared William's ostentatious bounty. He was the president of many excellent charities; gave largely; and sometimes instituted

---

1   The black cap, literally a square of black cloth, was placed over the white wig of the judge for delivering sentences of death, hence fatal velvet.

2   William's professional indifference recalls lines from the third canto of Alexander Pope's *Rape of the Lock* (1714): "Mean while declining from the Noon of Day,/ The Sun obliquely shoots his burning Ray;/ The hungry Judges soon the Sentence sign,/ And Wretches hang that Jury-men may Dine" (ll. 19–22).

benevolent societies for the unhappy: for he delighted to load the poor with obligations, and the rich with praise.

There are persons like him, who love to do every good, but that which their immediate duty requires—There are servants who will serve every one more cheerfully than their masters—There are men who will distribute money liberally to all, except their creditors—And there are wives who will love all mankind better than their husbands.—*Duty* is a familiar word which has little effect upon an ordinary mind: and as ordinary minds make a vast majority, we have acts of generosity, valour, self-denial, and bounty, where smaller pains would constitute greater virtues.—Had William followed the *common* dictates of charity; had he adopted private pity, instead of public munificence; had he cast an eye at home, before he sought abroad for objects of compassion, Hannah had been preserved from an ignominious death, and he had been preserved from—*Remorse*—the tortures of which he for the first time proved, on reading a printed sheet of paper accidentally thrown in his way, a few days after he had left the town in which he had condemned her to die.

"March the 12th 179-

"The last dying words, speech, and confession; birth, parentage, and education; life, character, and behaviour, of Hannah Primrose, who was executed this morning between the hours of ten and twelve, pursuant to the sentence passed upon her by the Honourable Justice Norwynne.

"HANNAH PRIMROSE was born of honest parents, in the village of Anfield, in the county of ——" [William started at the name of the village and county] "but being led astray by the arts and flattery of seducing man, she fell from the paths of virtue, and took to bad company, which instilled into her young heart all their evil practices, and at length brought her to this untimely end.—So she hopes her death will be a warning to all young persons of her own sex, how they listen to the praises and courtship of young men, especially of those who are their betters; for they only court to deceive.—But the said Hannah freely forgives all persons who have done her injury, or given her sorrow, from the young man who first won her heart, to the jury who found her guilty, and the judge who condemned her to death.

"And she acknowledges the justice of her sentence, not only in respect of the crime for which she suffers, but in regard to many other heinous sins of which she has been guilty, more especially that of once attempting to commit a murder upon her own helpless child, for which guilt she now considers the vengeance of God has overtaken her, to which she is patiently resigned, and departs in peace and charity with all the world, praying the Lord to have mercy on her parting soul.

"POSTSCRIPT TO THE CONFESSION.

"So great was this unhappy woman's terror of death, and the awful judgment that was to follow, that when sentence was pronounced upon her, she fell into a swoon, from that into convulsions, from which she never entirely recovered, but was delirious to the time of her execution, except the short interval in which she made her confession to the clergyman who attended her—She has left one child, a youth about sixteen, who has never forsaken his mother during all the time of her imprisonment, but waited upon her with true filial duty—and no sooner was her fatal sentence passed, than he began to droop, and now lies dangerously ill near the prison from which she is released by death—During the loss of her senses, the said Hannah raved continually on this child—and, asking for pen, ink, and paper, wrote an incoherent petition to the judge, recommending the youth to his protection and mercy. But notwithstanding this insanity, she behaved with composure and resignation, when the fatal morning arrived in which she was to be launched into eternity. She prayed devoutly during the last hour, and seemed to have her whole mind fixed on the world to which she was going—A crowd of spectators followed her to the fatal spot, most of whom returned weeping at the recollection of the fervency with which she prayed, and the impression which her dreadful state seemed to make upon her."

No sooner had the name of "Anfield" struck William, than a thousand reflections and remembrances flashed on his mind to give him conviction, whom it was he had judged and sentenced. He recollected the sad remains of Hannah, such as he once had known her—and now he wondered how his thoughts could have been absent from an object so pitiable, so worthy of his attention, as not to give him even a suspicion who she was, either from her name, or from her person, during the whole trial!

But wonder, astonishment, horror, and every other sensation, was absorbed by——*Remorse:*—it wounded, it stabbed, it rent his hard heart, as it would do a tender one—It havocked on his firm inflexible mind, as it would on a weak and pliant brain!—Spirit of Hannah! look down, and behold all your wrongs revenged! William feels——*Remorse.*

CHAPTER XLII.

A FEW momentary cessations from the pangs of a guilty conscience were given to William, as soon as he had dispatched a messenger to the jail in which Hannah had been confined, to enquire after the son she had left behind, and to give orders that immediate care should be taken of him.— He likewise charged the messenger to bring back the petition she had addressed to him during her supposed insanity; for he now experienced no trivial consolation in the thought that he might possibly have it in his power to grant her a request.

The messenger returned with the written paper, which had been considered by the persons to whom she had entrusted it, as the distracted dictates of an insane mind; but proved to William, beyond a doubt, that she was perfectly in her senses.

"*To Lord Chief Justice NORWYNNE.*

"MY LORD,

"I AM Hannah Primrose, the daughter of John and Hannah Primrose, of Anfield—my father and mother lived by the hill at the side of the little brook where you used to fish, and so first saw me.

"Pray, my lord, have mercy on my sorrows, pity me for the first time, and spare my life. I know I have done wrong—I know it is presumption in me to dare to apply to you, such a wicked and mean wretch as I am; but, my lord, you once condescended to take notice of me—and though I have been very wicked since that time, yet if you would be so merciful as to spare my life, I promise to amend it for the future. But if you think it proper I should die, I will be resigned; but then I hope, I beg, I supplicate, that you will grant my other petition.—Pray, pray, my lord, if you cannot pardon me, be merciful to the child I leave behind—What he will do when I am gone, I don't know—for I have been the only friend he has had ever since he was born.—He was born, my lord, about sixteen years ago, at Anfield, one summer's morning, and carried by your cousin, Mr. Henry Norwynne, to Mr. Rymer's, the curate there—and I swore whose child he was, before the dean, and I did not take a false oath. Indeed, indeed, my lord, I did not.

"I will say no more for fear this should not come safe to your hand, for the people treat me as if I were mad—so I will say no more, only this, that, whether I live or die, I forgive every body, and I hope every body will forgive me—and I pray that God will take pity on my son, if you refuse: but I hope you will not refuse.

"HANNAH PRIMROSE."

William rejoiced, as he laid down the petition, that she had asked a favour he could bestow; and hoped, by his protection of the son, to redress, in a degree, the wrongs he had done the mother. He instantly sent for the messenger into his apartment, and impatiently asked, "If he had seen the boy, and given proper directions for his care?"

"I have given directions, Sir, for his funeral."

"How!" Cried William.

"He pined away ever since his mother was confined, and died two days after her execution."

Robbed, by this news, of his only gleam of consolation—in the consciousness of having done a mortal injury for which he never now by any means could atone, he saw all his honours, all his riches, all his proud selfish triumphs dance before him! They seemed like airy nothings, which in rapture he would exchange for the peace of a tranquil conscience!

He envied Hannah the death to which he first exposed, then condemned her—He envied her even the life she struggled through from his neglect—and felt that his future days would be far less happy than her former existence. He calculated with precision.

CHAPTER XLIII.

THE progressive rise of William, and fall of Hannah, had now occupied nearly the term of eighteen years—added to these, another year elapsed before the younger Henry completed the errand on which his heart was fixed. Shipwreck, imprisonment, and other ills to which the poor and unfriended traveller is peculiarly exposed, detained the father and son in various remote regions until the present period; and, for the last fifteen years, denied them the means of all correspondence with their own country.

The elder Henry was now past sixty years of age, and the younger almost beyond the prime of life. Still length of time had not diminished, but rather had encreased, their anxious longings for their native home.

The sorrows, disappointments, and fatigues which throughout these tedious years were endured by the two Henrys, are of that dull monotonous kind of suffering, better omitted than described: mere repetitions of the exile's woe, that shall give place to the transporting joy of return from banishment!—Yet, much as the younger had reckoned with impatient wishes the hours which were passed distant from her he loved, no sooner was his disastrous voyage at an end, no sooner had his feet trod upon the shore of England, than a thousand wounding fears made him almost doubt, whether it were happiness or misery he had obtained by his arrival. If Rebecca were living, he knew it must be happiness—for his heart dwelt with confidence on her faith—her unchanging sentiments. "But death might possibly have ravished from his hopes what no mortal power could have done." And thus the lover creates a rival in every ill, rather than suffer his fears to remain inanimate.

The elder Henry had less to fear or to hope than his son—yet he both feared and hoped with a sensibility that gave him inexpressible anxiety. He hoped his brother would receive him with kindness, after his long absence, and once more take his son cordially to his favour. He longed impatiently to behold his brother; to see his nephew; nay, in the ardour of the renewed affection he just now felt, he thought even a distant view of Lady Clementina would be grateful to his sight! But still, well remembering the pomp, the state, the pride of William, he could not rely on *his* affection, so much he knew that it depended on external circumstances to excite or to extinguish his love. Not that he feared an absolute repulsion from his brother; but he feared, what, to a delicate mind, is still worse— reserved manners, cold looks, absent sentences, and all the cruel retinue of indifference, with which those who are beloved, so often wound the bosom that adores them.

By enquiring of their countrymen (whom they met as they approached to the end of their voyage) concerning their relation the dean, the two Henrys learned that he was well, and had for some years past been exalted to the bishoprick of ****. This news gave them joy, while it increased their fear of not receiving an affectionate welcome.

The younger Henry, on his landing, wrote immediately to his uncle, acquainting him with his father's arrival in the most abject state of poverty: he addressed his letter to the bishop's country residence, where he knew, as it was the summer season, he would certainly be. He and his father then set off on foot, towards that residence—a palace!

The bishop's palace was not situated above fifty miles from the port where they had landed: and at a small inn about three miles from the bishop's, they proposed (as the letter to him intimated) to wait for his answer, before they intruded into his presence.

As they walked on their solitary journey, it was some small consolation that no creature knew them.

"To be poor and ragged, father," the younger smilingly said, "is no disgrace, no shame, thank heaven, where the object is not known."

"True, my son," replied Henry: "and perhaps I feel myself much happier now, unknowing and unknown to all but you, than I shall in the presence of my fortunate brother and his family: for there, confusion at my ill success through life, may give me greater pain, than even my misfortunes have inflicted."

After uttering this reflection which had preyed upon his mind, he sat down on the road side to rest his agitated limbs, before he could proceed farther. His son reasoned with him; gave him courage; and now his hopes preponderated; till after two days' journey, on arriving at the inn where an answer from the bishop was expected, no letter, no message had been left.

"He means to renounce us." Said Henry trembling, and whispering to his son.

Without disclosing to the people of the house who they were, or from whom the letter or the message they enquired for was to have come, they retired, and consulted what steps they were now to pursue.

Previously to his writing to the bishop, the younger Henry's heart, all his inclinations, had swayed him towards a visit to the village in which was his uncle's former country seat—the beloved village of Anfield—but, respect and duty to him had made him check those wishes—now, they revived again—and with the image of Rebecca before his eyes, he warmly entreated his father to go with him to Anfield, at present only thirty miles distant, and thence, write once more—then wait the will of his uncle.

The father consented to this proposal, even glad to postpone the visit to his dignified brother.

After a scanty repast, such as they had been long inured to, they quitted the inn, and took the road towards Anfield.

CHAPTER XLIV.

IT was about five in the afternoon of a summer's day, that Henry and his son left the sign of the Mermaid, to pursue their third day's journey: the young man's spirits elated with the prospect of the reception he should meet from Rebecca; the elder dejected, at not receiving a welcome from his brother.

The road which led to Anfield necessarily took our travellers within sight of the bishop's palace—the turrets appeared at a distance—and on the sudden turn round the corner of a large plantation, the whole magnificent structure was at once exhibited before his brother's astonished eyes! He was struck with the grandeur of the habitation—and, totally forgetting all the unkind, the contemptuous treatment he had ever received from its owner, (like the same Henry in his earlier years) smiled with a kind of transport "that William was so great a man."

After this first joyous sensation was over, "Let us go a little nearer, my son," said he: "no one will see us, I hope: or if they should, you can run and conceal yourself; and not a creature will know *me*—even my brother would not know me thus altered—and I wish to take a little farther view of his fine house, and all his pleasure grounds."

Young Henry, though impatient to be gone, would not object to his father's desire.—They walked forward between a shady grove and a purling rivulet, snuffed in odours from the jessamine banks, and listened to the melody of an adjoining aviary.

The allurements of the spot seemed to enchain[1] the elder Henry, and he at length sauntered to the very avenue of the dwelling: but just as he had set his daring yet trembling feet upon the turf which led to the palace gates, he suddenly stopped, on hearing, as he thought, the village clock strike seven; which reminded him, that evening drew on, and it was time to go.—He listened again—when he and his son, both together, said "It is the toll of the bell before some funeral."

The signals of death, while they humble the rich, inspire the poor with pride.—The passing-bell gave Henry a momentary sense of equality; and he courageously stept forward to the first winding of the avenue.

He started back at the sight which presented itself!

A hearse—mourning coaches—mutes[2]—plumed horses—with every other token of the person's importance, who was going to be committed to the earth.

Scarce had his terrified eyes been thus unexpectedly struck—when a coffin borne by six men issued from the gates, and was deposited in the waiting receptacle; while gentlemen in mourning went into the different coaches.

A standard-bearer now appeared with an escutcheon,[3] on which the keys and mitre were displayed. Young Henry, upon this, pathetically exclaimed

"My uncle!—It is my uncle's funeral!"

---

1   "Rivet (the attention); to bind, attach (the emotions) closely to an object" (*OED*).

2   Professional attendants hired to grieve at funerals. The presence of mutes here highlights the absence, with the exception of the two Henrys, of any "real mourners" in William's funeral procession.

3   The shield on which a coat of arms is presented. William's insignia, "the key and mitre," reveals his ecclesiastical identity to Henry: a mitre is a headdress worn by a bishop.

Henry, his father, burst into tears.

The procession moved along. The two Henrys, the only real mourners in the train, followed at a little distance—in rags, but in tears.

The elder Henry's heart was nearly bursting—he longed to clasp the dead corpse of his brother, without the dread of being spurned for his presumption.—He now could no longer remember him either as the dean, or bishop; but leaping over that whole interval of pride and arrogance, called only to his memory William, such as he knew him when they lived at home together, together walked to London, and there together, almost perished for want.

They arrived at the church—and while the coffin was placing in the dreary vault, the weeping brother crept slowly after to the hideous spot— His reflections now fixed on a different point. "Is this possible?" said he to himself. "Is this the dean whom I ever feared? Is this the bishop of whom, within the present hour, I stood in awe? Is this William, whose every glance struck me with his superiority? Alas! my brother, and is this horrid abode the reward for all your aspiring efforts? Are these the only remains of your greatness, which you exhibit to me on my return? Did you foresee an end like this, while you treated me, and many more of your youthful companions, with haughtiness and contempt? while you thought it becoming of your dignity to shun and despise us? Where is the difference now, between my departed wife and you? or, if there be a difference, she, perchance has the advantage.—Ah! my poor brother, for distinction in the other world, I trust, some of your anxious labours have been employed; for you are now of less importance in this, than when you and I first left our native town, and hoped for nothing greater, than to be suffered to exist."

On their quitting the church, they enquired of the by-standers, particulars of the bishop's death, and heard he had been suddenly carried off by a raging fever.

Young Henry enquired "If Lady Clementina was at the palace, or Mr. Norwynne?"

"The latter is there"—he was answered by a poor woman: "but Lady Clementina has been dead these four years."

"Dead! Dead!" cried young Henry. "That worldly woman, quitted this world for ever!"

"Yes," answered the stranger: "she caught cold by wearing a new-fashioned dress that did not half cover her, wasted all away, and died the miserablest object you ever heard of."

The person who gave this melancholy intelligence concluded it with a hearty laugh; which would have surprised the two hearers, if they had not before observed—that amongst all the village crowd that attended to see this solemn show, not one afflicted countenance appeared, not one dejected look, not one watery eye. The pastor was scarcely known to his flock—it was in London his meridian[1] lay—at the levee of ministers—at the table of peers—at the drawing-rooms of the great—and now his neglected parishioners paid his indifference in kind.

The ceremony over, and the mourning suite departed, the spectators dispersed with smiling faces from the sad spot; while the Henrys, with heavy hearts, retraced their steps back towards the palace.—In their way, at the crossing of a stile, they met a poor labourer returning from his day's work; who, looking earnestly at the throng of persons who were leaving the churchyard, said to the elder Henry,

"Pray, master, what are all them folk gathered together about? What's the matter there?"

"There has been a funeral." Replied Henry.

"Oh, zooks, what! a burying!—ay, now I see it is—and I warrant, of our old bishop—I heard he was main ill—It is he, they have been putting into the ground, is not it?"

"Yes." Said Henry.

"Why then so much the better."

"The better!" cried Henry.

"Yes, master—though, I should be loath to be where he is now."

Henry started—"He was your pastor, man."

"Ha ha ha—I should be sorry that my master's sheep that are feeding yonder, should have no better pastor—the fox would soon get them all."

"You surely did not know him!"

"Not much, I can't say I did—for he was above speaking to poor folks—unless they did any mischief; and then he was sure to take notice of them."

"I believe he meant well." Said Henry.

"As to what he meant, God only knows—but I know what he *did*."

"And what did he?"

"Nothing at all for the poor."

"If any of them applied to him, no doubt———"

---

1 "Suited to the tastes, habits, capacities, etc." (*OED*); thus William's particular sphere, the arena he has himself singled out as his own.

"Oh! they knew better than all that comes to—for if they asked for any thing, he was sure to have them sent to bridewell,[1] or the workhouse.— He used to say—"*The workhouse was a fine place for a poor man—the food good enough, and enough of it*"—yet he kept a dainty table himself. His dogs, too, fared better than we poor. He was vastly tender and good to all his horses and dogs, I *will* say that for him: and to all brute beasts: he would not suffer them to be either starved or struck—but he had no compassion for his fellow creatures."

"I am sensible you do him wrong."

"That *he* is the best judge of by this time. He has sent many a poor man to the house of correction—and now 'tis well if he has not got a place there himself. Ha ha ha!"[2] The man was walking away, when Henry called to him—"Pray can you tell me if the bishop's son be at the palace?"

"Oh yes, you'll find master there treading in the old man's shoes, as proud as Lucifer!"

"Has he any children?"

"No, thank God! There's been enough of the name—and after the son is gone, I hope we shall have no more of the breed."

"Is Mrs. Norwynne, the son's wife, at the palace?"

"What, master, did not you know what's become of her?"

"Any accident?——"

"Ha ha ha—yes. I can't help laughing—why master she made a mistake, and went to another man's bed—and so her husband and she were parted—and she has married the other man."

"Indeed!" cried Henry amazed.

"Ay, indeed—but if it had been my wife or yours, the bishop would have made her do penance in a white sheet[3]—but as it was a lady, why, it was all very well—and any one of us, that had been known to talk about it, would have been sent to bridewell straight.—But we *did* talk, notwithstanding."

The malicious joy with which the peasant told this story, made Henry believe (more than all the complaints the man uttered) that there had been want of charity and christian deportment in the conduct of the bishop's family. He almost wished himself back on his savage island, where brotherly love could not be less, than it appeared to be in this civilised country.

---

1   A specific London prison, named for (St.) Bride's Well, a holy well that provided the site for a hospital later converted into a house of correction. More generally, the term refers to any prison. In his novel *Fleetwood* (1805), Godwin writes, "I know that the earth is the great Bridewell of the Universe."

2   See Appendix A.1.b for a passage deleted from the second edition.

3   Public punishment for fornication.

CHAPTER XLV.

AS Henry and his son, after parting from the poor labourer, approached the late bishop's palace, all the charms of its magnificence, its situation, which, but a few hours before, had captivated the elder Henry's mind, were vanished—and, from the mournful ceremony he had since been witness of, he now viewed this noble edifice, but as a heap of rubbish piled together to fascinate weak understandings; and to make even the wise and religious man, at times, forget why he was sent into this world.

Instead of presenting themselves to their nephew and cousin, they both felt an unconquerable reluctance to enter under the superb, the melancholy roof—a bank, a hedge, a tree, a hill, seemed, at this juncture, a pleasanter shelter: and each felt himself happy in being a harmless wanderer on the face of the earth, rather than living in splendour, while the wants, the revilings of the hungry and the naked, were crying to heaven for vengeance.

They gave a heart-felt sigh to the vanity of the rich and the powerful; and pursued a path where they hoped to meet with virtue and happiness.

They arrived at Anfield.

Possessed by apprehensions, which his uncle's funeral had served to encrease, young Henry, as he entered the well-known village, feared every sound he heard would convey information of Rebecca's death. He saw the parsonage house at a distance, but dreaded to approach it, lest Rebecca should no longer be an inhabitant.—His father indulged him in the wish to take a short survey of the village, and rather learn by indirect means, by observation, his fate, than hear it all at once from the lips of some blunt relater.

Anfield had undergone great changes since Henry left it.—He found some cottages built where formerly there were none; and some were no more, where he had frequently called, and held short conversations with the poor who dwelt in them. Amongst the latter number was the house of Hannah's parents—fallen to the ground!—He wondered to himself where that poor family had taken up their abode?—Henry, in a kinder world!

He once again cast a look at the old parsonage house—his inquisitive eye informed him, there, no alteration had taken place externally—but he feared what change might be within.

At length he obtained the courage to enter the church-yard in his way to it.—As he slowly and tremblingly moved along, he stopped to read here and there a grave-stone; as mild, instructive, conveyers of intelligence, to which he could attend with more resignation, than to any other reporter.

The second stone he came to, he found was erected *To the memory of the Reverend Thomas Rymer.* Rebecca's father. He instantly called to mind all that poor curate's quick sensibility of wrong, towards *himself;* his unbridled rage in consequence; and smiled to think—how trivial now appeared all, for which he gave way to such excess of passion.

But, shocked at the death of one so near to her he loved, he now feared to read on; and cast his eyes from the tombs accidentally to the church. Through the window of the chancel, his sight was struck with a tall monument of large dimensions, raised since his departure, and adorned with the finest sculpture. His curiosity was excited—he drew near, and he could distinguish (followed by elegant poetic praise) "*To the memory of John Lord Viscount Bendham.*"

Notwithstanding the solemn, melancholy, anxious bent of Henry's mind, he could not read these words, and behold this costly fabric,[1] without indulging a momentary fit of indignant laughter.

"Are sculpture and poetry thus debased," he cried, "to perpetuate the memory of a man, whose best advantage is to be forgotten? Whose no one action merits record, but as an example to be shunned."

An elderly woman, leaning on her stick, now passed along the lane by the side of the church.—The younger Henry accosted her, and ventured to enquire "Where the daughters of Mr. Rymer, since his death, were gone to live?"

"We live," she returned, "in that small cottage across the clover field."

Henry looked again, and thought he had mistaken the word *we*—for he felt assured that he had no knowledge of the person to whom he spoke.

But she knew him, and, after a pause, cried—"Ah! Mr. Henry, you are welcome back. I am heartily glad to see you—and my poor sister Rebecca will go out of her wits with joy."

"Is Rebecca living, and will be glad to see me?" he eagerly asked, while tears of rapture trickled down his face. "Father," he continued in his ecstacy, "we are now come home to be completely happy—and I feel as if all the years I have been away, were but a short week; and as if all the dangers I have passed, had been light as air.—But is it possible," he cried, to his kind informer, "that you are one of Rebecca's sisters?"

Well might he ask; for, instead of the blooming woman of seven-and-twenty he had left her, her colour was gone, her teeth impaired, her voice broken. She was near fifty.

"Yes, I am one of Mr. Rymer's daughters." She replied.

"But which?" Said Henry.

---

1   Ediface; i.e., Lord Bendham's monument.

"The eldest, and the once called the prettiest." She returned. "Though now people tell me I am altered—yet I cannot say I see it myself."

"And are you all living?" Henry enquired.

"All but one: she married and died. The other three, on my father's death, agreed to live together, and knit or spin for our support. So we took that small cottage, and furnished it with some of the parsonage furniture, as you shall see—and kindly welcome I am sure you will be to all it affords, though that is but little."

As she was saying this, she led him through the clover field towards the cottage.—His heart rebounded with joy that Rebecca was there—yet, as he walked, he shuddered at the impression which he feared the first sight of her would make. He feared, what he imagined (till he had seen this change in her sister) he should never heed. He feared Rebecca would look no longer young. He was not yet so far master over all his sensual propensities, as, when the trial came, to think he could behold her look like her sister, and not give some evidence of his disappointment.

His fears were vain.—On entering the gate of their little garden, Rebecca rushed from the house to meet them, just the same Rebecca as ever.

It was her mind, which beaming on her face, and actuating her every motion, had ever constituted all her charms; it was her mind, which had gained her Henry's affection; that mind had undergone no change, and she was the self-same woman he had left her.

He was entranced with joy.

CHAPTER XLVI.

THE fare which the Henrys partook at the cottage of the female Rymers, was such as the sister had described, mean, and even scanty; but this did not in the least diminish the happiness they received in meeting, for the first time since their arrival in England, human beings who were glad to see them.

At a stinted repast of milk and vegetables, by the glimmering light of a little brush-wood on the hearth, they yet could feel themselves comparatively blest, while they listened to the recital of afflictions, which had befallen persons around that very neighbourhood, for whom every delicious viand had been procured to gratify the taste, every art devised to delight the other senses.

It was by the side of this glimmering fire, that Rebecca and her sisters told the story of poor Hannah's fate; and of the thorn it had for ever planted in William's bosom—of his reported sleepless, perturbed nights; and his gloomy, or starting, and half-distracted days: when, in the fulness of *remorse*, he has complained—"of a guilty conscience! of the weariness attached to continued prosperity! the misery of wanting an object of affection!"

They told of Lord Bendham's death from the effects of intemperance; from a mass of blood infected by high seasoned dishes, mixed with copious draughts of wine—repletion of food and liquor, not less fatal to the existence of the rich, than the want of common sustenance to the lives of the poor.

They told of Lady Bendham's ruin since her Lord's death, by gaming— They told, "that now she suffered beyond the pain of common indigence, by the cutting triumph of those, whom she had formerly despised."

They related (what has been told before) the divorce of William; and the marriage of his wife with a libertine[1]—The decease of Lady Clementina; occasioned by that incorrigible vanity, which even old age could not subdue.

After numerous other examples had been recited of the dangers, the evils that riches draw upon their owner; the elder Henry rose from his chair, and embracing Rebecca and his son, said,

"How much indebted are *we* to providence, my children, who, while it inflicts poverty, bestows peace of mind; and in return for the trivial grief we meet in this world, holds out to our longing hopes the reward of the next!"

Not only resigned, but happy in their station; with hearts made cheerful rather than dejected by attentive meditation; Henry and his son planned the means of their future support, independent of their kinsman William— not only of him, but of every person and thing, but their own industry.

"While I have health and strength" (cried the old man, and his son's looks acquiesced in all the father said) "I will not take from any one in affluence what only belongs to the widow, the fatherless, and the infirm; for to such alone, by christian laws—however custom may subvert them—the overplus of the rich is due."

CHAPTER XLVII.

BY forming an humble scheme for their remaining life, a scheme depending upon their *own* exertions alone, on no light promises of pretended friends, and on no sanguine hopes of certain success; but with prudent apprehension, with fortitude against disappointment, Henry, his son, and

---

1   Man notorious for sexual immorality.

Rebecca, (now his daughter) found themselves, at the end of one year, in the enjoyment of every comfort which such distinguished minds knew how to taste.

Exempt both from patronage and from controul—healthy—alive to every fruition with which nature blesses the world; dead to all out of their power to attain, the works of art—susceptible of those passions which endear human creatures one to another, insensible to those which separate man from man—they found themselves the thankful inhabitants of a small house or hut, placed on the borders of the sea.

Each morning wakes the father and the son to cheerful labour in fishing, or the tending of a garden, the produce of which they carry to the next market town. The evening sends them back to their home in joy; where Rebecca meets them at the door, affectionately boasts of the warm meal that is ready, and heightens the charm of conversation with her taste and judgement.

It was after a supper of roots from their garden, poultry that Rebecca's hand had reared, and a jug brewed by young Henry, that the following discourse took place:

"My son," said the elder Henry, "where under heaven, shall three persons be met together, happy as we three are? It is the want of industry, or the want of reflection, which makes the poor dissatisfied. Labour gives a value to rest, which the idle can never taste; and reflection gives to the mind a degree of content, which the unthinking never can know."

"I once," replied the younger Henry, "considered poverty a curse—but after my thoughts became enlarged, and I had associated for years with the rich, and now mix with the poor, my opinion has undergone a total change—for I have seen, and have enjoyed, more real pleasure at work with my fellow labourers, and in this cottage, than ever I beheld, or experienced, during my abode at my uncle's; during all my intercourse with the fashionable and the powerful of this world."

"The worst is," said Rebecca, "the poor have not always enough."

"Who has enough?" asked her husband. "Had my uncle? No—he hoped for more—and in all his writings sacrificed his duty to his avarice. Had his son enough, when he yielded up his honour, his domestic peace, to gratify his ambition? Had Lady Bendham enough, when she staked all she had, in the hope of becoming richer? Were we, my Rebecca, of discontented minds, we have now too little. But conscious, from observation and experience, that the rich are not so happy as ourselves, we rejoice in our lot."

The tear of joy which stole from her eye, expressed more than his words—a state of happiness.

He continued, "I remember, when I first came a boy to England, the poor excited my compassion; but now that my judgment is matured, I pity the rich. I know that in this opulent kingdom, there are near as many persons perishing through intemperance, as starving with hunger—there are as many miserable in the lassitude of having nothing to do, as there are bowed down to the earth with hard labour—there are more persons who draw upon themselves calamity by following their own will, than there are, who experience it by obeying the will of another. Add to this, that the rich are so much afraid of dying, they have no comfort in living."

"There the poor have another advantage," said Rebecca: "for they may defy not only death, but every loss by sea or land, as they have nothing to lose."

"Besides," added the elder Henry, "there is a certain joy, of the most gratifying kind that the human mind is capable of tasting, peculiar to the poor; and of which the rich can but seldom experience the delight."

"What can that be?" cried Rebecca.

"A kind word, a benevolent smile, one token of esteem from the person whom we consider as our superior."

To which Rebecca replied, "And the rarity of obtaining such a token, is what encreases the honour."

"Certainly," returned young Henry: "and yet those in poverty, ungrateful as they are, murmur against that government from which they receive the blessing."[1]

"But this is the fault of education, of early prejudice," said the elder Henry:—"our children observe us pay respect, even reverence, to the wealthy, while we slight or despise the poor. The impression thus made on their minds in youth, they indelibly retain during the more advanced periods of life, and continue to pine after riches, and lament under poverty—nor is the seeming folly wholly destitute of reason; for human beings are not yet so deeply sunk in voluptuous gratification or childish vanity, as to place delight in any attainment which has not for its end, the love or admiration of their fellow beings."

"Let the poor then (cried the younger Henry) no more be their own persecutors—no longer pay homage to wealth—instantaneously the whole idolatrous worship will cease—the idol will be broken."

THE END

---

1   See Appendix A.1.c for the original ending of the novel.

Appendix A: The Composition of the Novel and the Art of Novel Writing

1. Textual Changes from First (1796) to Second (1797) Edition, with Passages Deleted from Second Edition

[Revisions to the first edition of *Nature and Art* fall into three main categories: grammatical, stylistic, and contextual. Largely self-educated, Inchbald expressed, on a number of occasions, uncertainty in grammatical matters; the second edition corrects numerous errors. The major form of stylistic revision entails the placement of commas, which may be shifted or eliminated altogether in order to enhance sentence flow. Contextual changes fall into two main groups. First, the second edition contains modifications of specific words as a means of providing greater clarity, drama, or emphasis. While these are, for the most part, one-word revisions, there is a significant second category of instances in which Inchbald radically alters her text, seemingly in response to criticisms offered by reviewers of the first edition. (For these reviews, see Appendix E.) Six of these changes comprise important additions to the novel by elaborating upon and thereby adding plausibility to the description of Rebecca Rymer, her sequestering of Hannah's infant, the family's detection of the child, and the repercussions of that discovery. Each of these changes is noted in a footnote to the text itself. This appendix prints two passages from the first edition of the novel deleted from subsequent editions, as well as the very different conclusion published in the first edition.

Readers interested in a more detailed comparison between the first and second editions of *Nature and Art* may wish to turn to the Pickering & Chatto edition of the novel (London, 1997), which also contains an appendix listing all major changes from the second to the third (1810) edition.]

a. Passage deleted from Chapter 30

[In deleting this passage, Inchbald may have been addressing the mention of "some improprieties" that appeared in the *Monthly Review* (see Appendix E.4), for she also changed "suckled" to "nursed" in chapter 31.]

She now rose from the earth in haste, and stealing quick on one side, postponed farther gratitude to Henry, for the performance of the most endearing office of a mother. The child greedily received from her bosom the food till then untasted—and on this, feeling more exquisitely the tender, the proud prerogative of a maternal parent, she uttered, with sighs of transport

"Now I am as rich, as happy as your father—as blest as his bride!—for I experience the joy of a conscience relieved from a deadly weight—and I have something to love—something on which to pour that fund of affection which he rejects."

b. Passage deleted from Chapter 44

[The first edition inserts the following exchange.]

"Did he give nothing in charity?"

"Next to nothing. A little weak broth, that runs through one's stomach like mad—a working man, master, can't live on such mess—and my wife wore out more shoe-leather going after it, and lost more time waiting at the door before his fat servants would bring it her, than the thing was worth.—However, as we should not speak ill of the dead, I say nothing against him. So good night, master."

c. Conclusion to First Edition

[The first edition ends on this strangely ironic note. In her subsequent reformulation of the novel's final paragraphs, Inchbald may have had in mind the criticism leveled by the *Moral and Political Magazine* (see Appendix E.5): "The work concludes with a piece of irony so ill placed, that it is painful, and even with some readers is liable to be misunderstood for the serious expression of the writer's sentiment" (September 1796, p. 180).]

"... blessing; and, unlearned as they are, would attempt to alter it.—We leave to the physician the care of restoring our health, we employ the soldier in fighting our battles, and the lawyer in the defence of our fortunes, without presuming to interrupt them in their vocations—then, why not leave, and without molestation, those to govern a kingdom who have studied the science of politics? For though a physician may not always be skilful, a soldier may not always have courage, a lawyer not always honesty, or a minister always good fortune—yet, we should consider, that it is not upon earth we are to look for a state of perfection—it is only in heaven—and there, we may rest assured, that no practitioner in the professions I have named, will ever be admitted to disturb our eternal felicity.["]

2. Letters between Inchbald and William Godwin

a. Letter to Godwin Describing the Travails of Novel Writing (November 1792), cited in C. Kegan Paul, *William Godwin: His Friends and Contemporaries* (London, 1876) Vol. 1: 74–75

[Although the initial referent of this letter is Inchbald's suppressed play, *The Massacre* (withdrawn from publication in 1792), she subsequently refers to the composition of her first novel, *A Simple Story* (1791), which Godwin had read in manuscript, as he was later to read *Nature and Art*.]

Nov. 1792.

SIR, —There is so much tenderness mixed with the justice of your criticism, that, while I submit to the greatest part of it as unanswerable, I feel anxious to exculpate myself in these points where I believe it is in my power.

You accuse me of trusting to newspapers for my authority. I have no other authority (no more, I believe, has half England) for any occurrence which I do not *see*: it is by newspapers that I am told that the French are at present victorious; and I have no doubt but that you will allow that (in this particular, at least) they speak truth.

2ndly. There appears an inconsistency in my having said to you, 'I have no view to any public good in this piece,' and afterwards alluding to its preventing future massacres: to this I reply that it was your hinting to me that it might do harm which gave me the first idea that it might do good.

3rdly. I do not shrink from Labour, but I shrink from ill-health, low spirits, disappointment, and a long train of evils which attend on Laborious Literary work. I was ten months, unceasingly, finishing my novel, notwithstanding the plan (such as you saw it) was formed, and many pages written. My health suffered much during this confinement, my spirits suffered more on publication; for though many gentlemen of the first abilities have said to me things high in its favour, it never was liked by those people who are the readers and consumers of novels; and I have frequently obtained more pecuniary advantage by ten days' labour in the dramatic way than by the labour of this ten months. —Your very much obliged humble servant,

E. INCHBALD.

Leicester Square, 24th.

b. Two undated letters to Godwin on Reading Proofs of his *Caleb Williams* [1794], cited in Kegan Paul, I: 138–40

[According to Kegan Paul, "the letters which follow were written while the story was still in reading, and she wrote in far too hot haste to dream of dating her letters, and usually to sign them" (I: 138).]

Mrs. Inchbald to William Godwin.

(No date.)

God bless you!

That was the sentence I exclaimed when I had read about half a page.

Nobody is so pleased when they find anything new as I am. I found your style different from what I have ever yet met. You come to the point (the story) at once, another excellence. I have now read as far as page 32 (I was then interrupted by a visitor) and do not retract my first sentence. I have to add to your praise that of a most *minute*, and yet most concise method of delineating human sensations.

I could not resist writing this, because my heart was burthened with the desire of saying what I think, and what I hope for.

My curiosity is greatly increased by what I have read, but if you disappoint me you shall never hear the last of it, and instead of 'God Bless,' I will vociferate, God ——m you.'

The Same to the Same

Monday evening.

SIR, —Your first volume is far inferior to the two last. Your second is sublimely horrible—captivatingly frightful.

Your third is all a great genius can do to delight a great genius, and I never felt myself so conscious of, or so proud of giving proofs of a good understanding, as in pronouncing this to be a capital work.

It is my opinion that fine ladies, milliners, mantua-makers,[1] and boarding-school girls will love to tremble over it, and that men of taste and judgment will admire the superior talents, the *incessant* energy of mind you have evinced.

In these last two volumes, there does not appear to me (apt as I am to be tired with reading novels) one tedious line, still there are lines I wish erased. I shudder lest for the sake of a few sentences, (and these particularly marked for the reader's attention by the purport of your preface) a

---

1   A corrupted version of "manteau-maker": one who makes women's robes; a dressmaker.

certain set of people should hastily condemn the whole work as of immoral tendency, and rob it of a popularity which no other failing it has could I think endanger.

This would be a great pity, especially as these sentences are trivial compared to those which have not so glaring a tendency, and yet to the eye of discernment are even more forcible on your side of the question.... But if I find fault it is because I have no patience that anything so near perfection should not be perfection.

c. Undated letter to Godwin Describing his Reading of Her Manuscript, probably "A Satire on the Times" (1794/5), cited in Kegan Paul, I: 140–41

I am infinitely obliged to you for all you have said, which amounts to very nearly all I thought.

But indeed I am too idle, and too weary of the old rule of poetical justice to treat my people, to whom I have given birth, as they deserve, or rather I feel a longing to treat them according to their deserts, and to get rid of them all by a premature death, by which I hope to surprise my ignorant reader, and to tell my informed one that I am so wise as to have as great a contempt for my own efforts as he can have.

And now I will discover to you a total want of *aim*, of *execution*, and every particle of genius belonging to a writer, in a character in this work, which from the extreme want of resemblance to the original, you have not even reproached me with the fault of not drawing accurately.

I really and soberly meant (and was in hopes every reader would be struck with the portrait) Lord Rinforth to represent his Most Gracious Majesty, George the 3rd.

I said at the commencement all Lords of Bedchambers were mirrors of the Grand Personage on whom they attended, but having Newgate[1] before my eyes, I dressed him in some virtues, and (notwithstanding his avarice) you did not know him.

The book is now gone to Mr Hardinge. Mr Holcroft is to have it as soon as his play is over, and though I now despair of any one finding out my meaning, yet say nothing about the matter to Mr Holcroft, but let my want of talent be undoubted, by his opinion conforming to yours.

And there, (said I to myself as I folded up the volumes) how pleased Mr Godwin will be at my making the King so avaricious, and there, (said I to

---

1 London's main prison during this period.

myself) how pleased the King will be at my making him so very good at the conclusion, and when he finds that by throwing away his money he can save his drowning people he will instantly *throw it all away* for flannel shirts for his soldiers, and generously pardon me all I have said on *equality* in the book, merely for giving him a good character.

But alas, Mr Godwin did not know him in that character, and very likely he would not know himself.

d. Letter from Godwin to Inchbald (1 December 1817), cited in Ford K. Brown, *The Life of William Godwin* (London: J.M. Dent, 1926) Vol. I: 320–21

[The following letter, sent to Inchbald with a presentation copy of *Mandeville*, captures the spirit with which Inchbald had earlier critiqued *Caleb Williams*.]

I cannot appear before the world in the character of a novelist,... without recollecting with some emotion the sort of intercourse that passed between us when *Caleb Williams* was in his non-age, and in the vigour of his age. Particularly, I have looked a hundred times with great delight at the little marginal notes and annotations with which you adorned the pages of my writings of that period. Do me the favour to read *Mandeville* with some recollections of the time I allude to; and if, when you have gone through with it, you will oblige me so far as to return the copy with your remarks, I will request your acceptance of a fresh one in exchange for it.

3. Inchbald's Essay on Novel Writing from *The Artist* (1807)

[According to her biographer James Boaden, Inchbald first encountered Prince Hoare—artist, dramatist, secretary to the Royal Academy, and art critic—in February, 1796, the year in which *Nature and Art* was published. When in 1807 Hoare launched the *Artist*, a select journal in which eminent practitioners would write about their various arts, he turned to his friends and contemporaries for contributions. With her background in the theatre and her success as a novelist, Inchbald was an obvious choice. Apparently she agreed to participate in Hoare's enterprise, for Boaden prints a letter from Hoare's sister Mary courteously proposing a number of topics for Inchbald's consideration: "I am sure that nobody could please me so entirely as yourself on the *art* of novel writing—the *art* of dramatic composition—the *art* of conversation: or (if it may be called an *art*) that of propriety of female conduct" (Boaden, II: 362). Although Inchbald's witty essay ostensibly responds to the first of Mary Hoare's suggestions, Inchbald in fact touches upon all four topics. Despite its light tone, Inchbald's article addresses serious issues: her critique of the abuses of fictional composition depends, in large part, upon her belief in the power of fiction to effect important change on both personal and social levels. As in *Nature and Art*, Inchbald demonstrates how individual pride, vanity, or egotism can have far broader social repercussions. Whereas she begins her essay by avowing that she has "not the slightest information to impart, that may tend to produce a good novel" and can therefore only show "how to avoid writing a very bad one," she ends by reminding her readers— including the authors among them—of the responsibilities as well as the pleasures inherent in novel writing.]

The ARTIST. No. XIV. Saturday, June 13, 1807.
TO THE ARTIST

SIR,

IF the critical knowledge of an art was invariably combined with the successful practice of it, I would here proudly take my rank among artists, and give instructions on the art of writing Novels.—But though I humbly confess that I have not the slightest information to impart, that may tend to produce a good novel; yet it may not be wholly incompatible with the useful design of your publication, if I show—how to avoid writing a very bad one.

Observe, that your hero and heroine be neither of them too bountiful. The prodigious sums of money which are given away every year in novels, ought, in justification, to be subject to the property tax; by which regulation, the national treasury, for every such book, would be highly benefitted.

Beware how you imitate Mrs. Radcliffe, or Maria Edgeworth;[1] you cannot equal them; and those readers who most admire their works, will most despise yours.

---

1 Two celebrated novelists of the late eighteenth century. The daughter of a London tradesman, Ann Radcliffe (1764–1823) became the leading practitioner of the Gothic novel. Her suspenseful tales of tyranny and terror met with tremendous popular and financial success; the £500 advance that she received for *The Mysteries of Udolpho* (1794), one of her most successful works, was at the time unprecedented for a novel. A writer of educational treatises and tales for children, Maria Edgeworth (1767–1849) was also a prolific novelist. Edgeworth originated the regional novel with *Castle Rackrent* (1800); in addition, her psychologically complex depictions of London life, of which *Belinda* (1801) is perhaps the most acclaimed, earned her critical renown. Both Maria and her father, Richard Lovell Edgeworth, were great admirers of Inchbald's novels. Inchbald's correspondence with the Edgeworth family is reprinted in Boaden's *Memoirs*.

Take care to reckon up the many times you make use of the words "Amiable," "Interesting," "Elegant," "Sensibility," "Delicacy," "Feeling." Count each of these words over before you send your manuscript to be printed, and be sure to erase half the number you have written;—you may revise again when your first proof comes from the press—again, on having a revise—and then mark three or four, as mistakes of the printer, in your Errata.[1]

Examine likewise, and for the same purpose, the various times you have made your heroine blush, and your hero turn pale—the number of times he has pressed her hand to his "trembling lips," and she his letters to her "beating heart"—the several times he has been "speechless" and she "all emotion," the one "struck to the soul;" the other "struck dumb."

The lavish use of "tears," both in "showers" and "floods," should next be scrupulously avoided; though many a gentle reader will weep on being told that others are weeping, and require no greater cause to excite their compassion.

Consider well before you introduce a child into your work. To maim the characters of men and women is no venial offence; but to destroy innocent babes is most ferocious cruelty: and yet this savage practice has, of late, arrived at such excess, that numberless persons of taste and sentiment have declared—they will never read another novel, unless the advertisement which announces the book adds (as in advertisements for letting Lodgings) *There are no children.*

When you are contriving that incident where your heroine is in danger of being drowned, burnt, or her neck broken by the breaking of an axletree[2]—for without perils by fire, water, or coaches, your book would be incomplete—it might be advisable to suffer her to be rescued from impending death by the sagacity of a dog, a fox, a monkey, or a hawk; any one to whom she cannot give her hand in marriage; for whenever the deliverer is a fine young man, the catastrophe of your plot is foreseen, and suspense extinguished.[3]

Let not your ambition to display variety cause you to produce such a number of personages in your story, as shall create perplexity, dissipate curiosity, and confound recollection. But if, to show your powers of

---

1 Errors noted in a list of corrections attached to a printed book.
2 "The fixed bar or beam of wood, etc., on the rounded ends of which the opposite wheels of a carriage revolve" (*OED*).
3 Perhaps Inchbald had in mind the rescue of Caroline Campinet by the honorable Hermsprong, the eponymous hero of the novel by Robert Bage published in the same year as *Nature and Art*.

invention, you are resolved to introduce your reader to a new acquaintance in every chapter, and in every chapter snatch away his old one; he will soon have the consolation to perceive—they are none of them worth his regret.

Respect virtue—nor let her be so warm or so violent as to cause derision:—nor vice so enormous as to resemble insanity. No one can be interested for an enthusiast[1]—nor gain instruction from a madman.

And when you have written as good a novel as you can—compress it into three or four short volumes at most; or the man of genius, whose moments are precious, and on whose praise all your fame depends, will not find time to read the production, till you have committed suicide in consequence of its ill reception with the public.

There are two classes of readers among this public, of whom it may not be wholly from the purpose to give a slight account. The first are all hostile to originality. They are so devoted to novel reading, that they admire one novel because it puts them in mind of another, which they admired a few days before. By them it is required, that a novel should be like a novel; that is, the majority of those compositions; for the minor part describe fictitious characters and events merely as they are in real life:—ordinary representations, beneath the concern of a true voracious novel-reader.

Such an one (more especially of the female sex) is indifferent to the fate of nations, or the fate of her own family, whilst some critical situation in a romance agitates her whole frame![2] Her neighbour might meet with an accidental death in the next street, the next house, or the next room, and the shock would be trivial, compared to her having just read—"that amiable Sir Altamont, beheld the interesting Eudocia, faint in the arms of his thrice happy rival."

Affliction, whether real or imaginary, must be refined,—and calamity elegant, before this novel-reader can be roused to "sympathetic sensation." Equally unsusceptible is her delicate soul to vulgar happiness. Ease and content are mean possessions! She requires transport, rapture, bliss, extatic joy, in the common occurrences of every day.

She saunters pensively in shady bowers, or strides majestically through brilliant circles. She dresses by turns like a Grecian statue and a pastoral

---

1   One possessed of great intensity of feeling or passionate eagerness in a pursuit; although often, as here, with the unfavorable connotation of over-zealous, even self-delusional.

2   In her early novel, *Mary, A Fiction* (1788), Mary Wollstonecraft displays in the character of Eliza, the protagonist's mother, the disastrous effects of novel reading when employed as substitute satisfaction. Poorly educated and unhappily married, Eliza devours sentimental romances, but can muster little energy for her own family, in particular her daughter.

nymph: then fancies herself as beautiful as the undone heroine in "*Barbarous Seduction*;"[1] and has no objection to become equally unfortunate.

To the healthy, the food is nourishment, which to the sickly proves their poison. Such is the quality of books to the strong, and to the weak of understanding.—Lady Susan is of another class of readers, and has good sense.—Let her therefore read certain well-written novels, and she will receive intimation of two or three foibles, the self-same as those, which, adhering to her conduct, cast upon all her virtues a degree of ridicule.— These failings are beneath the animadversions[2] of the pulpit. They are so trivial yet so awkward, that neither sermons, history, travels, nor biography, could point them out with propriety. They are ludicrous, and can only be described and reformed by a humourist.[3]

And what book so well as a novel, could show to the enlightened Lord Henry—the arrogance of his extreme condescension? Or insinuate to the judgment of Lady Eliza—the wantonness of her excessive reserve?

What friend could whisper so well to Lady Autumnal—that affected simplicity at forty, is more despicable than affected knowledge at fifteen?—And by what better means could the advice be conveyed to Sir John Egoist—to pine no more at what the world may say of him; for that men like himself are too insignificant for the world to know.

A novel could most excellently represent to the valiant General B——, that although he can forgive the miser's love of gold, the youth's extravagance and even profligacy; that although he has a heart to tolerate all female faults, and to compassionate human depravity of every kind; he still exempts from this his universal clemency—the poor delinquent soldier.

The General's wife, too, forgives all injuries done to her neighbours: those to herself are of such peculiar kind, that it would be encouragement to offenders, not to seek vengeance.—The lovely Clarissa will pardon every one—except the mantua-maker who spoils her shape. And good Sir Gourmand never bears malice to a soul upon earth—but to the cook who spoils his dinner.

---

1   Like "Lord Henry," "Lady Susan," et al., Inchbald's invention. Compare Wollstonecraft's account of Eliza, described above: "she read all the sentimental novels, dwelt on the love-scenes, and, had she thought while she read, her mind would have been contaminated; as she accompanied the lovers to the lonely arbors, and would walk with them by the clear light of the moon" (ch. 1).

2   Turning the attention to a subject, often in a critical sense. Wollstonecraft titles chapter five of her *Vindication of the Rights of Woman* "Animadversions on Some of the Writers Who Have Rendered Women Objects of Pity, Bordering on Contempt."

3   Although often used to describe an odd, whimsical, or facetious person, here more likely one who possesses "the faculty of perceiving what is ludicrous or amusing, or of expressing it in speech, writing, or other composition" (*OED*).

That Prebendary[1] is merciful to a proverb—excluding negligence towards holy things—which he thinks himself the holiest. Certain novels might make these people think a second time.

Behold the Countess of L——! Who would presume to tell that once celebrated beauty—that she is now too wrinkled for curling hair; and that her complexion is too faded for the mixture of blooming pink?[2] Should her husband convey such unwelcome news, he would be more detested than he is at present! Were her children or her waiting-maid to impart such intelligence, they would experience more of her peevishness than ever!—A novel assumes a freedom of speech to which all its readers must patiently listen; and by which, if they are wise, they will know how to profit.

The Novelist is a free agent. He lives in a land of liberty, whilst the Dramatic Writer exists but under a despotic government.—Passing over the subjection in which an author of plays is held by the Lord Chamberlain's office,[3] and the degree of dependence which he has on his actors—he is the very slave of the audience. He must have their tastes and prejudices in view, not to correct, but to humour them. Some auditors of a theatre, like some afore-said novel readers, love to see that which they have seen before; and originality, under the opprobrious name of innovation, might be fatal to a drama, where the will of such critics is the law, and execution instantly follows judgment.

In the opinion of those theatrical juries, Virtue and Vice attach to situations, more than to characters: at least, so they will have the stage represent. The great moral inculcated in all modern plays constantly is—for the rich to love the poor. As if it was not much more rare, and a task by far more difficult—for the poor to love the rich.—And yet, what author shall presume to expose upon the stage, certain faults, almost inseparable from the indigent? What dramatic writer dares to expose in a theatre, the consummate vanity of a certain rank of paupers, who boast of that wretched state as a sacred honour, although it be the result of indolence or criminality? Who dares to show to an audience, the privilege, of poverty debased into the instrument of ingratitude?—"I am poor and therefore slighted"—cries the unthankful beggar: whilst his poverty is his sole recommendation to his friends and for which alone, they pay him much attention, and some respect.

---

1 One who receives as his stipend a portion of the revenues of a cathedral or collegiate church.
2 I.e., rouge.
3 As part of his official duties, the Lord Chamberlain licensed plays, thus subjecting the playwright to governmental censorship.

What dramatist would venture to bring upon the stage—that which so frequently occurs in real life—a benefactor living in awe of the object of his bounty; trembling in the presence of the man he supports, lest by one inconsiderate word, he should seem to remind him of the predicament in which they stand with each other; or by an involuntary look, seem to glance at such and such obligations?

Who, moreover, dares to exhibit upon the stage, a benevolent man, provoked by his crafty dependant—for who is proof against ungratefulness?—to become that very tyrant, which he unjustly had reported him?

Again.—The giver of alms, as well as the alms-receiver, must be revered on the stage.—That rich proprietor of land, Lord Forecast, who shall dare to bring him upon the boards of a theatre, and show—that on the subject of the poor, the wily Forecast accomplishes two most important designs? By keeping the inhabitants of his domain steeped in poverty, he retains his vast superiority on earth; then secures, by acts of charity, a chance for heaven.[1]

A dramatist must not speak of national concerns, except in one dull round of panegyrick.[2] He must not allude to the feeble minister of state, nor to the ecclesiastical coxcomb.

Whilst the poor dramatist is, therefore, confined to a few particular provinces; the novel-writer has the whole world to range, in search of men and topics. Kings, warriors, statesmen, churchmen, are all subjects of his power. The mighty and the mean, the common-place and the extraordinary, the profane and the sacred, all are prostrate before his muse. Nothing is forbidden, nothing is withheld from the imitation of a novelist, except—other novels.

E.I.

---

1   *Nature and Art*'s Henry offers a similar critique. When Lord Bendham, an apparent relation to Lord Forecast, asks Henry what he means by "'*the greatest hardship of all,*'" Henry replies: "'It was, my lord, that what the poor receive to keep them from perishing, should pass under the name of *gifts* and *bounty*. Health, strength, and the will to earn a moderate subsistence, ought to be every man's security from obligation'" (ch. 19).

2   "A public speech or writing in praise of some person, thing, or achievement; a laudatory discourse" (*OED*).

Appendix B: "The Prejudice of Education": Philosophical Influences

1. From Jean-Jacques Rousseau, *Émile, ou de l'Éducation* (1762), trans. Barbara Foxley (London: J.M. Dent, 1911)

[From its controversial publication to the present day, Rousseau's treatise-cum-novel has exerted tremendous influence upon the way we think about children and their upbringing. Rousseau's depiction of a proper education for his fictional Émile relates not only to Inchbald's portrayal of her own "natural" man, the younger Henry, but also to the representation of his artificial and corrupted cousin, William. While there are many parts of Rousseau's text that pertain directly to *Nature and Art*, the following excerpts constitute explicit links to Inchbald's novel.]

From Book I

Man is born to suffer; pain is the means of his preservation. His childhood is happy, knowing only pain of body. These bodily sufferings are much less cruel, much less painful, than other forms of suffering, and they rarely lead to self-destruction. It is not the twinges of gout which make a man kill himself, it is a mental suffering that leads to despair. We pity the sufferings of childhood; we should pity ourselves; our worst sorrows are of our own making. (15)

From Book II

Therefore the education of the earliest years should be merely negative. It consists, not in teaching virtue or truth, but in preserving the heart from vice and from the spirit of error. If only you could let well enough alone, and get others to follow your example; if you could bring your scholar to the age of twelve strong and healthy, but unable to tell his right hand from his left, the eyes of his understanding would be open to reason as soon as you began to teach him. Free from prejudice and free from habits, there would be nothing in him to counteract the effects of your labours. In your hands he would soon become the wisest of men; by doing nothing to begin with, you would end with a prodigy of education.

Reverse the usual practice and you will almost always do right. Fathers and teachers who want to make the child, not a child but a man of learning, think it never too soon to scold, correct, reprove, threaten, bribe, teach, and reason. Do better than they; be reasonable, and do not reason with your pupil,... Exercise his body, his limbs, his senses, his strength, but keep his mind idle as long as you can....

But where shall we find a place for our child so as to bring him up as a senseless being, an automaton? Shall we keep him in the moon, or on a desert island? Shall we remove him from human society? (57–58) ...

I know that all these imitative virtues are only the virtues of a monkey, and that a good action is only morally good when it is done as such and not because of others. But at an age when the heart does not yet feel anything, you must make children copy the deeds you wish to grow into habits, until they can do them with understanding and for the love of what is good. Man imitates, as do the beasts. The love of imitating is well regulated by nature; in society it becomes a vice. The monkey imitates man, whom he fears, and not the other beasts, which he scorns; he thinks what is done by his betters must be good.... Imitation has its roots in our desire to escape from ourselves. If I succeed in my undertaking, Émile will certainly have no such wish. So we must dispense with any seeming good that might arise from it.

Examine your rules of education; you will find them all topsy-turvy, especially in all that concerns virtue and morals. The only moral lesson which is suited for a child—the most important lesson for every time of life—is this: "Never hurt anybody." The very rule of well-doing, if not subordinated to this rule, is dangerous, false, and contradictory. Who is there who does no good? Every one does some good, the wicked as well as the righteous; he makes one happy at the cost of the misery of a hundred, and hence spring all our misfortunes. The noblest virtues are negative, they are also the most difficult, for they make little show, and do not even make room for that pleasure so dear to the heart of man, the thought that someone is pleased with us. If there be a man who does no harm to his neighbours, what good must have been accomplished! What a bold heart, what a strong character it needs! (68–69) ...

The apparent ease with which children learn is their ruin. You fail to see that this very facility proves that they are not learning. Their shining, polished brain reflects, as in a mirror, the things you show them, but nothing sinks in. The child remembers the words and the ideas are reflected back; his hearers understand them, but to him they are meaningless. (71)

From Book IV

I have always observed that young men, corrupted in early youth and addicted to women and debauchery, are inhuman and cruel; their passionate temperament makes them impatient, vindictive, and angry; their imagination fixed on one object only, refuses all others; mercy and pity are alike unknown to them; they would have sacrificed mother, father, the whole world, to the least of their pleasures. A young man, on the other hand, brought up in happy innocence, is drawn by the first stirrings of nature to the tender and affectionate passions; his warm heart is touched by the sufferings of his fellow-creatures; he trembles with delight when he meets his comrade, his arms can embrace tenderly, his eyes can shed tears of pity; he learns to be sorry for offending others through his shame at causing annoyance.... Adolescence is not the age of hatred or vengeance; it is the age of pity, mercy, and generosity. Yes, I maintain, and I am not afraid of the testimony of experience, a youth of good birth, one who has preserved his innocence up to the age of twenty, is at that age the best, the most generous, the most loving, and the most lovable of men. (181–82) ...

I do not know whether my young man will be any the less amiable for not having learnt to copy conventional manners and to feign sentiments which are not his own; that does not concern me at present, I only know that he will be more affectionate; and I find it difficult to believe that he, who cares for nobody but himself, can so far disguise his true feelings as to please as readily as he who finds fresh happiness for himself in his affection for others.... (192)

I am aware that many of my readers will be surprised to find me tracing the course of my scholar through his early years without speaking to him of religion. At fifteen he will not even know that he has a soul, at eighteen even he may not be ready to learn about it. For if he learns about it too soon, there is the risk of his never really knowing anything about it.

If I had to depict the most heart-breaking stupidity, I would paint a pedant teaching children the catechism; if I wanted to drive a child crazy I would set him to explain what he learned in his catechism. You will reply that as most of the Christian doctrines are mysteries, you must wait, not merely till the child is a man, but till the man is dead, before the human mind will understand those doctrines. To that I reply, that there are mysteries which the heart of man can neither conceive nor believe, and I see no use in teaching them to children, unless you want to make liars of them. Moreover, I assert that to admit that there are mysteries, you must at least realise that they are incomprehensible, and children are not even capable of this conception! At an age when everything is mysterious, there are no mysteries properly so-called.

"We must believe in God if we would be saved." This doctrine wrongly understood is the root of bloodthirsty intolerance and the cause of all the futile teaching which strikes a deadly blow at human reason by training it to cheat itself with mere words. No doubt there is not a moment to be lost if we would deserve eternal salvation; but if the repetition of certain words suffices to obtain it, I do not see why we should not people heaven with starlings and magpies as well as with children....

Let us beware of proclaiming the truth to those who cannot as yet comprehend it, for to do so is to try to inculcate error. It would be better to have no idea at all of the Divinity than to have mean, grotesque, harmful, and unworthy ideas; to fail to perceive the Divine is a lesser evil than to insult it. (220–21) ...

What precautions we must take with a young man of good birth before exposing him to the scandalous manners of our age! These precautions are painful but necessary; negligence in this matter is the ruin of all our young men; degeneracy is the result of youthful excesses, and it is these excesses which make men what they are.... Such are the despicable men produced by early debauchery; if there were but one among them who knew how to be sober and temperate, to guard his heart, his body, his morals from the contagion of bad example, at the age of thirty he would crush all these insects, and would become their master with far less trouble than it cost him to become master of himself.

However little Émile owes to birth and fortune, he might be this man if he chose; but he despises such people too much to condescend to make them his slaves. Let us now watch him in their midst, as he enters into society, not to claim the first place, but to acquaint himself with it and to seek a helpmeet worthy of himself.

Whatever his rank or birth, whatever the society into which he is introduced, his entrance into that society will be simple and unaffected; God grant he may not be unlucky enough to shine in society; the qualities which make a good impression at the first glance are not his, he neither possesses them, nor desires to possess them. He cares too little for the opinions of other people to value their prejudices, and he is indifferent whether people esteem him or not until they know him. His address is neither shy nor conceited, but natural and sincere, he knows nothing of constraint or concealment, and he is just the same among a group of people as he is when he is alone. Will this make him rude, scornful, and careless of others? On the contrary; if he were not heedless of others when he lived alone, why should he be heedless of them now that he is living among them? He does not prefer them to himself in his manners, because he does not prefer them to himself in his heart, but neither does he show them an indifference which he is far from feeling; if he is unacquainted with the forms of politeness, he is not unacquainted with the attentions dictated by humanity. He cannot bear to see any one suffer; he will not give up his place to another from mere external politeness, but he will willingly yield it to him out of kindness if he sees that he is being neglected and that this neglect hurts him; for it will be less disagreeable to Émile to remain standing of his own accord than to see another compelled to stand....

Although when he makes his entrance into society he knows nothing of its customs, this does not make him shy or timid; if he keeps in the background, it is not because he is embarrassed, but because, if you want to see, you must not be seen; for he scarcely troubles himself at all about what people think of him, and he is not the least afraid of ridicule. Hence he is always quiet and self-possessed and is not troubled with shyness. All he has to do is done as well as he knows how to do it, whether people are looking at him or not; and as he is always on the alert to observe other people, he acquires their ways with an ease impossible to the slave of other people's opinions. We might say that he acquires the ways of society just because he cares so little about them....

He who loves desires to be loved. Émile loves his fellows and desires to please them. Even more does he wish to please the women; his age, his character, the object he has in view, all increase this desire. I say his character, for this has a great effect; men of good character are those who really adore women. They have not the mocking jargon of gallantry like the rest, but their eagerness is more genuinely tender, because it comes from the heart. In the presence of a young woman, I could pick out a young man of character and self-control from among a hundred thousand libertines.... (300–03)

2. From Thomas Day, *The History of Sandford and Merton* (1783–89)

[This popular children's book describes the education of two boys from different social classes. The wealthy land-owner Mr. Merton, displeased with the spoiled and arrogant behavior of his son Tommy, sends him to be educated by the local vicar, Mr. Barlow, who has already taken upon himself the tutelage of Harry Sandford, son of a local farmer. Explicitly didactic in nature—the main narrative of the two boys is continually interspersed with exemplary tales—the book's overtly dualistic arrangement bears obvious relevance to the structure of Inchbald's novel.]

From Chapter I

But at the mansion-house, much of the conversation, in the meantime, was employed in examining the merits of little Harry. Mrs Merton acknowleged his bravery and openness of temper; she was also struck with the very good-nature and benevolence of his character, but she contended that he had a certain grossness and indelicacy in his ideas, which distinguish the children of the lower and middling classes of people from those of persons of fashion. Mr Merton, on the contrary, maintained, that he had never before seen a child whose sentiments and disposition would do so much honour even to the most elevated situations. Nothing, he affirmed, was more easily acquired than those external manners, and that superficial address, upon which too many of the higher classes pride themselves as their greatest, or even as their only accomplishment;... "Indeed, the real seat of all superiority, even of manners, must be placed in the mind: dignified sentiments, superior courage, accompanied with genuine and universal courtesy, are always necessary to constitute the real gentleman; and where these are wanting, it is the greatest absurdity to think they can be supplied by affected tones of voice, particular grimaces, or extravagant and unnatural modes of dress; which, far from becoming the real test of gentility, have in general no other origin than the caprice of barbers, tailors, actors, opera-dancers, milliners, fiddlers and French servants of both sexes. I cannot help, therefore, asserting," said he, very seriously, "that this little peasant has within his mind the seeds of true gentility and dignity of character; and though I shall also wish that our son may possess all the common accomplishments of his rank, nothing would give me more pleasure than a certainty that he would never in any respect fall below the son of farmer Sandford." ...

[Mr. Barlow discusses his ideas with Mr. Merton.]

"Poverty, that is to say, a state of labour and frequent self-denial, is the natural state of man; it is the state of all in the happiest and most equal governments, the state of nearly all in every country; it is a state in which all the faculties, both of body and mind, are always found to develope themselves with the most advantage, and in which the moral feelings have generally the greatest influence. The accumulation of riches, on the contrary, can never increase, but by the increasing poverty and degradation of those whom Heaven has created equal; a thousand cottages are thrown down to afford space for a single palace....

"[H]e that undertakes the education of a child, undertakes the most important duty in society, and is severally answerable for every voluntary omission. The same mode of reasoning, which I have just been using, is not applicable here. It is out of the power of any individual, however strenuous may be his endeavours, to prevent the mass of mankind from acquiring prejudices and corruptions; and, when he finds them in that state, he certainly may use all the wisdom he possesses for their reformation. But this rule will never justify him for an instant in giving false impressions where he is at liberty to instil truth, and in losing the only opportunity which he perhaps may ever possess, of teaching pure morality and religion. How will such a man, if he has the least feeling, bear to see his pupil become a slave, perhaps to the grossest vice; and to reflect with a great degree of probability that this catastrophe has been owing to his own inactivity and improper indulgence? May not all human characters frequently be traced back to impressions made at so early a period, that none but discerning eyes would ever suspect their existence? Yet nothing is more certain; what we are at twenty depends upon what we were at fifteen; what we are at fifteen upon what we were at ten; where shall we then place the beginning of the series?"

From Chapter VII

Harry was destitute of the artificial graces of society, but he possessed that natural politeness and good nature, without which all artificial graces are the most distracting things in the world. Harry had an understanding naturally strong; and Mr Barlow, while he had with the greatest care preserved him from all false impressions, had taken great pains in cultivating the faculties of his mind. Harry, indeed, never said any of those brilliant things which render a boy the darling of the ladies; he had not that vivacity, or rather impertinence, which frequently passes for wit with superficial people; but he paid the greatest attention to what was said to him, and made the most judicious observations upon subjects he understood.

From Chapter VIII

[Tommy, influenced by a group of peers who have been visiting him, badly mistreats Harry, to the great chagrin of Mr. Merton.]

"Alas, sir," answered Mr Barlow, "what is the general malady of human nature but this very instability which now appears in your son? Do you imagine that half the vices of men arise from real depravity of heart? On the contrary, I am convinced that human nature is infinitely more weak than wicked, and than the greater part of all bad conduct springs rather from want of firmness than from any settled propensity to evil."

"Indeed," replied Mr Merton, "what you say is highly reasonable; nor did I ever expect that a boy so long indulged and spoiled should be exempt from failings. But what particularly hurts me is to see him proceed to such disagreeable extremities without any adequate temptation—extremities that, I fear, imply a defect of goodness and generosity—virtues which I always thought he had possessed in a very great degree."

"Neither," answered Mr Barlow, "am I at all convinced that your son is deficient in either. But you are to consider the prevalence of example, and the circle to which you have lately introduced him. If it is so difficult even for persons of a more mature age and experience to resist the impressions of those with whom they constantly associate, how can you expect it from your son? To be armed against the prejudices of the world, and to distinguish real merit from the splendid vices which pass current in what is called society, is one of the most difficult of human sciences." ...

[The following dialogue is sub-headed "Tommy's Altered Opinions."]

Tommy.—You know, sir, that when I first came to you, I had a high opinion of myself for being born a gentleman, and a very great contempt for everybody in an inferior station.

Mr Barlow.—I must confess you have always had some tendency to both these follies.

Tommy.—Yes, sir; but you have so often laughed at me upon the subject, and shown me the folly of people's imagining themselves better than others, without any merit of their own, that I was grown a little wiser. Besides, I have so often observed, that those I despised could do a variety of things which I was ignorant of, while those who are vain of being gentlemen can do nothing useful or ingenious; so that I had begun to be ashamed of my folly. But since I came home I have kept company with a great many fine gentlemen and ladies, who thought themselves superior to all the rest of the world, and used to despise every one else; and they have made me forget everything I learned before.

Conclusion

And now Mr Merton, having made the most affectionate acknowledg-
ment to all this worthy and happy family,[1] ... summoned his son to
accompany him home. Tommy arose, and with the sincerest gratitude
bade adieu to Harry and all the rest. "I shall not be long without you,"
said he to Harry; "to your example I owe most of the little good that I can
boast: you have taught me how much better it is to be useful than rich or
fine; how much more amiable to be good than to be great. Should I ever
be tempted to relapse, even for an instant, into any of my former habits,
I will return hither for instruction, and I hope you will again receive me."
Saying this, he shook his friend Harry affectionately by the hand, and,
with watery eyes, accompanied his father home.

3. From William Godwin, *The Enquirer: Reflections on Education, Manners and Literature in a Series of Essays* (London: G.G. and J. Robinson, 1797)

[This collection of essays, while less well-known than Godwin's earlier
Enquiry Concerning Political Justice (first published 1793), deals more specifically with education, devoting more than half of its essays to that topic.
The correlations between Godwin's "principles" and those presented,
albeit in fictional form, in Inchbald's novel are striking; it seems likely
that, given her social and intellectual connections to Godwin,[2] Inchbald
was one of those to whom Godwin refers in his Preface to *The Enquirer* as
follows: "The Essays are principally the result of conversations, some of
them held many years ago, though the Essays have all been composed for
the present occasion. The author has always had a passion for colloquial
discussion; and, in the various opportunities that have been afforded him
in different scenes of life, the result seemed frequently to be fruitful both
of amusement and instruction" (vii).]

From Part I, Essay IX: Of the Communication of Knowledge

The most desirable mode of education therefore, in all instances where it
shall be found sufficiently practicable, is that which is careful that the

---

1   I.e., the family of the Sandfords, whom Mr. Merton has just rewarded for their care of his son
    with a team of excellent horses.
2   See Introduction, pp. 17–18.

acquisitions of the pupil shall be preceded and accompanied by desire. The best motive to learn, is a perception of the value of the thing learned. The worst motive, without deciding whether or not it be necessary to have recourse to it, may well be affirmed to be constraint and fear. There is a motive between these, less pure than the first, but not so displeasing as the last, which is desire, not springing from the instrinsic excellence of the object, but from the accidental attractions which the teacher may have annexed to it.

According to the received modes of education, the master goes first, and the pupil follows. According to the method here recommended, it is probable that the pupil should go first, and the master follow. If I learn nothing but what I desire to learn, what should hinder me from being my own preceptor?...

There are three considerable advantages which would attend upon this species of education.

First, liberty. Three fourths of the slavery and restraint that are now imposed upon young persons would be annihilated at a stroke.

Secondly, the judgment would be strengthened by continual exercise. Boys would no longer learn their lessons after the manner of parrots. No one would learn without a reason, satisfactory to himself, why he learned; and it would perhaps be well, if he were frequently prompted to assign his reasons. Boys would then consider for themselves, whether they understood what they read. To know when and how to ask a question is no contemptible part of learning....

Thirdly, to study for ourselves is the true method of acquiring habits of activity. The horse that goes round in a mill, and the boy that is anticipated and led by the hand in all his acquirements, are not active. I do not call a wheel that turns round fifty times in a minute, active. Activity is a mental quality.... (78–82)

From Part I, Essay XII: Of Deception and Frankness

The child that any reasonable person would wish to call his own or choose for the object of his attachment, is a child whose countenance is open and erect. Upon his front sit fearless confidence and unbroken hilarity. There are no wrinkles in his visage and no untimely cares. His limbs, free and unfettered, move as his heart prompts him, and with a grace and agility infinitely more winning than those of the most skilful dancer. Upon the slightest encouragement he leaps into the arms of every thing that bears a human form. He welcomes his parent returning from a short absence, with a bounding heart. He is eager to tell the story of his joys and adventures. There is something in the very sound of his voice, full, firm, mellow, fraught with life and sensibility; at the hearing of which my bosom rises, and my eyes are lighted up. He sympathizes with sickness and sorrow, not in a jargon purposely contrived to cajole the sufferer, but in a vein of unaffected tenderness. When he addresses me, it is not with infantine airs and in an undecided style, but in a manner that shows him fearless and collected, full of good sense, of prompt judgment, and appropriate phraseology. All his actions have a meaning; he combines the guilelessness of undesigning innocence with the manliness of maturer years. (108–09)

From Part I, Essay XIII: Of Manly Treatment and Behaviour

It has sometimes been a question among those who are accustomed to speculate upon the subject of education, whether we should endeavour to diminish or increase the distinction between youth and manhood, whether children should be trained to behave like men, or should be encouraged to the exercise of manners peculiar to themselves.

Pertness and primness are always in some degree ridiculous or disgusting in persons of infant years. There is a kind of premature manhood which we have sometimes occasion to observe in young persons, that is destructive of all honest and spontaneous emotion in its subjects. They seem as if they were robbed of the chief blessing of youth, the foremost consolation of its crosses and mortifications——a thoughtless, bounding gaiety. Their behaviour is forced and artificial. Their temper is unanimating and frigid. They discuss and assert, but it is with a borrowed judgment. They pride themselves in what is eminently their shame; that they are mere parrots or echoes to repeat the sounds formed by another. They are impertinent, positive and self-sufficient. Without any pretensions to an extraordinary maturity of intellect, they are destitute of the modesty and desire of information that would become their age. They have neither the graces of youth nor age; and are like forced plants, languid, feeble, and, to any just taste, unworthy of the slightest approbation....

It is desirable that a child should partake of both characters, the child and the man. The hilarity of youth is too valuable a benefit, for any reasonable man to wish to see it driven out of the world. Nor is it merely valuable for the immediate pleasure that attends it; it is also highly conducive to health, to the best and most desirable state both of body and mind. Much of it would be cultivated by adults, which is now neglected; and would be even preserved to old age; were it not for false ideas of decorum, a species of hypocrisy, a supersubtle attention to the supposed minutiae of character, that lead us to check our spontaneous efforts, and to draw a veil of gravity over the innocent, as well as the immoderate, luxuriance and wantonness of our thoughts....

The whole branch of this education undoubtedly requires the delicate preserving of a certain medium. We should reason with children, but not to such a degree as to render them parrots or sophists. We should treat them as possessing a certain importance, but not so as to render them fops and coxcombs. We should repose in them a certain confidence, and to a certain extent demand their assistance and advice, but not so as to convey a falsehood to their minds, or make them conceive they have accomplishments which they have not.

In early youth there must perhaps be some subjection of the pupil to the mere will of his superior. But even then the friend need not be altogether lost in the parent. At a certain age the parental character should perhaps be wholly lost. There is no spectacle that more forcibly extorts the approbation of the human mind, than that of father and child, already arrived at years of discretion, who live together like brethren. There is no more unequivocal exhibition of imbecility, than the behaviour of a parent who, in his son now become a citizen at large, cannot forget the child; and who exercises, or attempts to exercise, an unseemly authority over him. The state of equality, which is the consummation of a just education, should for ever be borne in mind. We should always treat our children with some deference, and make them in some degree the confidents of our affairs and our purposes. We should extract from them some of the benefits of friendship, that they may one day be capable of becoming friends in the utmost extent of the term. We should respect them, that they may respect themselves. We should behold their proceedings with the eyes of men towards men, that they may learn to feel their portion of importance and regard their actions as the actions of moral and intelligent beings. (111–18)

Appendix C: Literary Cross-Currents: Political Critique in Inchbald's Jacobin Contemporaries

1. The "Noble Savage" and the British Aristocracy, from Robert Bage, *Hermsprong* (1796), ed. Pamela Perkins (Peterborough, ON: Broadview Press, 2002)[1]

[Any "free and wild being who draws directly from nature virtues which raise doubts as to the value of civilization," the noble savage emerged from the combination of colonial travel narratives, classical and medieval conventions, and the speculations of philosophers and men of letters. (See Hoxie N. Fairchild, *The Noble Savage: A Study in Romantic Naturalism* [New York: Columbia University Press, 1928] 2.) Inchbald's younger Henry manifests a significant example of the noble savage as a true outsider, a native visitor whose novel point of view provides an opportunity for satire or reform: although raised on a "savage island" off the coast of Africa, he proves himself far more civilized than his genteel British cousin. A European raised in America, the eponymous hero of Robert Bage's novel *Hermsprong*, published in the same year as *Nature and Art*, furnishes a different version of the noble savage archetype. The following excerpts describe the unorthodox manner and background of Hermsprong who, although he enters the village of Grondale as a stranger, eventually proves himself the rightful heir to Lord Grondale's estate.]

From Chapter 8

[Maria Fluart describes Hermsprong in a letter to her friend Caroline Campinet, the daughter of Lord Grondale.]

About the sixth day, Mr. Sumelin introduced us to a gentleman from France, an American born, I believe, but having property in France, had been there some years; and not liking, I suppose, the politics of that country, had been selling his property; remitting part of the produce to Mr. Sumelin, to whom he had been recommended by a house in Philadelphia, in order to have it invested in the English funds.

How shall I describe this young stranger to you, my dear? He looks like a man, I think, and yet I have seen but few men look like him. He is not an Adonis,[1] like Mr. Fillygrove; nor does he resemble that accomplished personage in dress or manners.

The latter are indeed, rather open and engaging, than graceful. There is an ease about him, but it is an unstudied, unimitated ease. It seems his own; and becomes him so well, that he acquires our own good will, almost before he has spoke. That his conversation will support his credit with ladies in general, is more than I dare affirm.… By the bye, he has a very ugly name; Hermsprong; it sounds monstrous Germanish. (89)

[In Vol. III, ch. 3, Hermsprong describes himself to the two young women.]

"Of myself, Miss Campinet, I have nothing to say, but that the active part of my life was spent like that of other young Indians, whose very sports are athletic, and calculated to render man robust, and inure him to labour and fatigue. Here I always found my superiors. I could not acquire the speed of many of my companions, my sense of smelling was less acute,—my sagacity inferior. I owe this probably to the sedentary portion of my life, spent with my father in learning languages, in mathematics, in I know not what. My father, always thinking of Europe, was desirous I should have a taste, at least, of the less useful, but more ornamental parts of knowledge. In consequence, I am superficial. I have a mouthful of many sciences, a meal of none. In this I believe I resemble the generality of young Englishmen. It is fashion here—and surely a people more obedient to fashion have never existed—never can exist."

"Such was the life I led amongst the aborigines of America; I am fond on the remembrance of it. I never there knew sickness, I never there felt ennui, I even loved some of my copper-coloured companions—"

"And none of your companionesses?" asked Miss Fluart.

"Oh no,—I was too young. Love is there a simple lesson of nature. They never experience its pains; they never refine upon its pleasures. Yet the modesty of their young women is uncommon. They have delicacy also, and respecting men, a timidity of which here I have not seen many examples." …

"What more have I to tell my lovely hearers, but that I grew up in the grace of God, and in the keeping of many of the ten commandments. That I could almost run up a tree like a squirrel; almost catch an antelope;

---

1   From Greek mythology, a beautiful youth loved by Aphrodite.

almost, like another Leander,[1] have swam over a sea to a mistress, had I had one. That at the end of ten years, my father found himself affluent to his own satisfaction; and meditated a return to Philadelphia. This was prevented by the war that gained England the loss of her colonies. Two years after, I lost my father by an inflammatory fever; an incalculable loss; for his instructions were my daily benefit; his fond affection, my daily happiness. Almost the affliction sunk my mother to the grave. She wrote to France. She asked again of her father forgiveness; but she asked nothing else. On the contrary, she informed him that she had wealth sufficient to enable her to spend the remainder of her life where and how she pleased. No other possible plea could so soon have disposed my grandfather to compassion. He forgave her now with all his heart." ...

"Before the expiration of a year, by the kind aid of Mr. Germersheim, we were safe in France. I was then sixteen; my grandfather thought I was too wild and rude. The ladies of our affinities were shocked to see me enter a room so ungracefully; so they sent me to learn to dance. My grandfather thought proper that I should be well skilled in book-keeping. Of the latter school, however, I did not like the confinement; of the former, the frivolity and grimace. I told my mother this, and desired her leave to run over France, in the way I had been over great part of America since my father's death; that is, on foot, attended only by a man to carry a few changes of linen et cetera—. Perhaps I should not have obtained her consent, had not a great decrease of plumpness and animal spirits, made her apprehensive I was beginning to suffer by so great a change of habits. In seven years, then, I had made excursions half over Europe; in which time I lost first my grandfather, and little more than two years since, my mother. I have succeeded to the fortunes of both; and not liking the situation of things in France, I sold all I was able, and have dispersed the money into different banks, principally in England, Italy, and America. Lastly, I have come over into England, to look at it; resolved, if I did not find it more suited to my taste than the rest of Europe, to return to America; buy 30,000 acres of land, and amuse myself with peopling a desart." (252–55)

2. Corruption in Church and State

[In keeping with the Jacobin critique of institutions rather than human nature per se, two novels written contemporaneously with *Nature and Art*

---

1   A Greek youth who swam the Hellespont every night to be with his beloved, Hero, a priestess of Aphrodite. When he drowned while swimming to her, she committed suicide.

provide parallel accounts of the dishonest and hypocritical workings of England's political and religious systems. Whereas Holcroft's *Hugh Trevor* offers dual examples of plagiarism comparable to that between the elder William and the "learned" bishop, Bage's *Hermsprong* presents the contrast between the wealthy and corrupt Dr. Blick and his poor but honest vicar, Mr. Woodcock.]

a. From Thomas Holcroft, *The Adventures of Hugh Trevor* (1794–97)

[Holcroft's second novel, whose publication was interrupted by the Treason Trials of 1794,[1] tells the story of the eponymous narrator's search for a profession, so that he might support and thus marry the woman he loves. In the process of that search, Holcroft exposes first family and religious pride, then the corruption of the universities, the nobility, political and religious hierarchies, and the legal system. Unable to find an untainted form of professional work, Hugh is ultimately saved by the discovery of a long-lost uncle, from whom he inherits an estate.

The following excerpts from Volume 2 describe Hugh's encounters, after having attended Oxford, with a nobleman and a bishop desirous of appropriating Hugh's well-meaning abilities for their own purposes. Although Hugh's naïve willingness to comply with their proposals recalls that of William senior, Holcroft's choice of a first-person point of view allows his character a degree of self-consciousness denied to William. In this first section, Hugh makes the acquaintance of a nobleman with political aspirations and soon determines that they concur in their criticism of the current government.]

From Chapter 5

I answered his lordship that I should be equally glad, if I could contribute to the good government and improvement of mankind by correcting their present errors; and that the vices I had mentioned, and every other vice I could discover, I should always think it my duty to oppose.

'That,' answered his lordship, 'is right, Mr. Trevor! You speak my own sentiments! Opposition, strong, severe and bitter, is what I am determined on! Your principles and mine are the same, and I am resolved he[2] shall repent of having made me his enemy! We will communicate our thoughts to each other, and as you are a young man whose talents were

---

1 See Introduction, p. 16.
2 I.e., the Prime Minister.

greatly esteemed at **** college, and who know how to place arguments in a striking form, I have no doubt of our success. I will make him shake in his seat!'

His lordship then drew a whole length picture first of his own griefs, and next of the present state of representation, and the known dependence and profligacy of the minister's adherents, which highly excited my indignation. My heart exulted in the correction which I was determined to bestow on them all; and I made not the least doubt but that I should soon be able to write down the minister, load his partizans with contempt, and banish such flagitious[1] proceedings from the face of the earth.

With these all sufficient ideas of myself, and many professions of esteem and friendship from the earl, I retired to begin a series of letters, that were to rout the minister, reform the world, and convey my fame to the latest posterity....

I could not disguise from myself that the motives of his lordship were not of the purest kind: but I had formed no expectations in favour of his morals; and, if the end at which he aimed was a good one, his previous mistakes must be pardoned. He had engaged me in a delightful task, had given me an opportunity of exerting my genius and of publishing my thoughts to the world, and I sat down to my labours with transport and zeal.

From Chapter 6

My letter had appeared, signed Themistocles,[2] his lordship's known political cognomen.[3] It was the first in which he had declared openly against the minister. His sentiments in consequence of this letter were become public, and many of the minority, desirous of fixing in their interest one whom they had before considered rather as their opponent than their friend, came to visit and pay him their compliments.

The resolute manner in which I had purposely and uniformly shewn him that I must be treated as his equal had produced its intended effect: I was dismissed with no haughty nod, but came and went as I pleased, and frequently bore a part in their conversation. I had still an open ear for vanity, which was not a little tickled by the frequent terms of applause and admiration with which Themistocles was quoted. His lordship did me

---

1 "Extremely wicked or criminal: heinous, villainous" (*OED*).
2 Athenian general and statesman (527?–460? BCE), who commanded the Athenian fleet at the Battle of Salamís, during which the Persians were defeated.
3 "A distinguishing name or epithet given to a person or assumed by himself; a nickname" (*OED*).

the justice to inform his visitors that the letter was written by me. We had indeed conversed together; they were his thoughts, his principles, and it was true he had made such additions and corrections as were necessary. Then, proceeding to invectives against the minister, he there dropped me, and my share of merit.

The mortification of this was the greater because truth and falsehood were so mingled that, however, inclined I might be, I knew not which was to do myself justice. But the praise, which they bestowed wholly on his lordship and which his lordship was willing to receive, I very unequivocally took to myself. It gave me animation; the pen was seldom out of my hand, and the exercise was sanative.[1]

From Chapter 7

New honours awaited me. My lord the bishop was come to town, of which Enoch[2] had providently taken care to have instant notice. Among the other good things I had related to myself, I had not forgotten to tell Enoch of the several sermons I had written;…

Though the door was the door of a bishop and we had the text in our favour, "Knock and it shall be opened,"[3] yet Enoch, no doubt remembering his own good breeding, was too cautious to ask if his lordship were at home. He bade the servant say that a clergyman of the church of England and a young gentleman from Oxford, bringing letters from the president of ****** college and other dignitaries of the university, requested an audience.

The message was delivered, and we were ushered into a parlour, the walls of which were decorated with the heads of the English archbishops, surrounding Hogarth's modern midnight conversation.[4] There was not a book in the room; but there were six or eight newspapers. With these we amused ourselves for some time, till the approach of the bishop was announced by the creaking of his shoes, the rustling of his silk apron, and the repeated hems with which he collected his dignity.

The moment I saw him, his presence reminded me of my old acquaintance, the high-fed brawny doctors of Oxford. His legs were the pillars of

---

1 Curative, healing.
2 Enoch Ellis, a minor clergyman who has befriended Hugh.
3 Matthew 7:7: "Ask, and it shall be given you; seek, and ye shall find; knock, and it shall be opened unto you."
4 William Hogarth (1697–1764) was a satirical painter and engraver famous for his exposure of contemporary mores and behavior (often sexual behavior). The room's bizarre juxtaposition of the sacred with the profane thus parallels the bishop's own corrupt persona.

Hercules, his body a brewer's butt,[1] his face the sun rising in a red mist. We have been told that magnitude is a powerful cause of the sublime; and if this be true, the dimensions of his lordship certainly had a copious and indisputable claim to sublimity. He seemed born to bear the whole hierarchy. His mighty belly heaved and his cheeks swelled with the spiritual inflations of church power. He fixed his open eyes upon me and surveyed me from top to toe. I too made my remarks. 'He is a true son of the church,' said I.—The libertine sarcasm was instantly repelled, and my train of ideas was purified from such irreverent heresy—'He is an orthodox divine! A pillar of truth! A Christian Bishop!' Thought is swift, and man assents and recants before his eyes can twinkle.

I delivered my credentials and he seated himself in a capacious chair, substantially fitted to receive and sustain its burden of divinity, and began to read. My letters were from men high in authority, purple-robed and rotund supporters of our good *Alma Mater*,[2] and met with all due respect. Clearing his sonorous throat of the obstructing phlegm, with which there seemed to be danger that he should sometime or other be suffocated, he welcomed me to London, rejoiced to hear that his good friends of the university were well, and professed a desire to oblige them by serving me.

I briefly explained to him my intention of devoting myself to the church, which he highly commended; and Enoch, who far from being idle all this time had been acting over his agreeable arts, soon found an opportunity of informing the right reverend father in God what powerful connexions I had, how well skilled I was in classical learning, and how deeply read in theology, how orthodox my opinions were, and to give a climax which most delighted me added that, young as I was, had already obtained the character of a prodigious fine writer!

He did not indeed say all this in a breath; he took his own time, for his oratory was always hide bound; but he took good care to have it all said. His secret for being eloquent consisted rather in action than in language, and now with the spiritual lord as before with the temporal, he accompanied his speech, with those insinuating gesticulations which he had rarely found unsuccessful. He had such a profound reverence for the episcopacy, [bowing to the ground] was so bitter an enemy to caveling[3] innovators, [grinning malignity] had so full a sense of his own inferiority [contorting his countenance, like a monkey begging for gingerbread] and humbled himself so utterly in the presence of the powers that be that,

---

1 A large cask for wine or ale.
2 I.e., Oxford University.
3 I.e., caviling: critical or complaining.

while he spoke, the broad cheeks of the bishop swelled true high church satisfaction; dilating and playing like a pair of forge bellows.

My modesty was his next theme, and with it was coupled the sermons I had written, not omitting the one I had brought in my pocket. But his young friend was so bashful! was so fearful of intruding on his lordship! as indeed every one must be, who had any sense of what is always due to our superiors! Yet as the doctrines of his young friend were so sound, and he was so true a churchman, it might perhaps happen that his lordship would have the condescension to let one of his chaplains read him the sermon of his young friend? He was sure it would do him service with his lordship. Not but he was almost afraid he had taken an unpardonable liberty, in intruding so far on his lordship's invaluable time and patience.

Evil communication corrupts good manners. I could not equal the adulation of Enoch; but, when I afterward came to canvas my own conduct, I found I had followed my leader in his tracks of servility quite far enough.

His lordship, to indicate his approbation of our duplex harangue, graciously accepted the sermon to peruse, informed me of his day and hour of seeing company, and invited me and my friend to become his visitors: … with which mark of holy greeting Enoch and I, well pleased, were about to depart.

[The bishop discovers that Hugh has an interest in writing against nonconformity.]

'These are weighty matters. The church was never more virulently and scandalously attacked than she has been lately! The most heretical and damnable doctrines are daily teeming from the press! Not only infidels and atheists, but the vipers which the church has nurtured in her own bosom are rising up to sting her! Her canons are brought into contempt, her tests trampled on, and her dignitaries daily insulted! The hierarchy is in danger! The bishops totter on their bench! We are none of us safe.'

To the reality of his picture I readily assented. 'But,' said I, 'my lord, we have the instruments of defence in our own power: we have the scriptures, the fathers, the doctors of our church and all the authorities for us. The only thing we want is a hero, qualified to bear this cumbrous armour, and to wield these massy weapons.' […]

His lordship agreed that the truth was all on our side: and for his part he wished it to be thundered forth, so as at once to crush and annihilate all heretics, and their damnable doctrines!

'Since I am encouraged by your lordship,' said I, 'this shall be the first labour of my life; and, though I grant it is Herculean, I have little doubt of executing it effectually.' His lordship, though not quite so certain of my success as I was, in the name of the church, again gave his hearty assent; and we, with smiles, thanks, and bows in abundance, took our leave: …

From Chapter 8

… During this intercourse, and particularly in these conversations, I had sufficient opportunities of studying his lordship's[1] character. He was self-ish, ignorant, positive, and proud: yet he affected generosity, talked on every subject as if it were familiar to him, asserted his claim to the most undeviating candour, and would even affect contempt for dignitaries and distinctions, when they were not the reward of merit. "A nobleman might by accident possess talents; but he was free to confess that the dignity of his birth could not confer them. He would rather be Mr. *** (Mr. *** was present) than a prince of the blood. He panted to distinguish himself by qualities that were properly his own, and had little veneration for the false varnish of ancestry. Were that of any worth, he had as much reason to be vain as any man perhaps in the kingdom: his family came in with the Conqueror, at which time it was respectable: it had produced men, through all its branches, in whose names were no disgrace to history.' Then summoning an additional quantity of candor he added—'There have been many fools among them, no doubt; and I am afraid some knaves; but what have I to do with their knavery, folly, or wisdom? Society, it is true, has thought fit to recompense me for their virtues: such is the order of things. But I cannot persuade myself that I have received the least tarnish from any of their vices. I am a friend to the philosophy of the times, and would have every man measured by the standard of individual merit.'

From Chapter 9

The bishop … one day gave me a hint that he should be glad to see me the next time alone. Without suspecting the motive, I was careful to comply with the request; and the ensuing morning, the right reverend dignitary, no other person being present, gave me to understand that he had read my sermon with satisfaction.

---

1   This is the nobleman referred to in Chapters 5 and 6, above.

After this and various other circumlocutory efforts and hints, he at last spoke more plainly. The subject was a good one, and he had an inclination to deliver it himself, at one of the cathedrals where he intended to preach. But then it must be in consequence of a positive assurance, from me, that I should react with discretion. He did not want sermons; he had enough: but this pleased him: though, if it were known it were a borrowed discourse, especially borrowed from so young a man not yet in orders, it might derogate from episcopal dignity.

Enraptured at the fund of self approbation which I collected from all this, I ardently replied, 'I knew not how to express my sense of the honour his lordship did me; that I could neither be so absurd as to offend his lordship nor so unjust as to be insensible of his favours; that I held the sacerdotal[1] character to be too sacred to suffer any man to trifle with it, much less to be guilty of the crime myself; and that, if his lordship would oblige me by fulfilling his kind intention, my lips should be irrevocably and for ever closed. The honour would be an ample reward, and, whatever my wishes might be, it was more than I could have hoped and greater perhaps than I deserved.'

It might well be expected that at this age I should fall into a mistake common to mankind, and consider secrecy as a virtue; yet I think it strange that I did not soon detect the duplicity of my conduct, nor imagine that there was any guilt in being the agent of deceit. But this proves that my morality had not yet taught me rigidly to chastise myself into truth; nor had it been in the least aided by the example of the agreeable Enoch. Perhaps I did not even, at the moment, suspect myself to be guilty of exaggeration.

[The Bishop delivers Hugh's sermon, much to the latter's enormous disappointment.]

His voice was thick, his delivery spiritless, and his cadences ridiculous. His soul was so overlaid with brawn and dignity that, though it heaved, panted, and struggled, it could never once get vent. Speaking through his apoplectic organs, I could not understand myself: it was a mumbling hubbub, the drone of a bagpipe, and the tantalizing strum strum of a hurdy-gurdy![2] Never was hearer more impatient to have it begin; never

---

1 "Befitting or characteristic of a priest, priestly" (*OED*).

2 "A musical instrument rustic in origin resembling the lute or guitar, and having strings (two or more of which are tuned so as to produce a drone), which are sounded by the revolution of a rosined wheel turned by the left hand, the notes of the melody being obtained by the action of keys which 'stop' the strings and are played by the right hand" (*OED*).

was hearer better pleased to have it over! Every sentence did but increase the fever of my mind....

His lordship however had no sooner descended than he was encircled by as many flatterers as thought they had any right to approach: among whom, to my shame be it spoken, I was one. I did not indeed applaud either his discourse or his delivery; I was not quite so depraved, nor so wholly forgetful of the feelings he had excited! but I laboured out an aukward panegyric[1] on the important duties he had to fulfil, and on the blessing it was to a nation, when worthy persons were chosen to fill such high offices. Thus endeavouring to quiet my conscience by a quibble, and with a half faced lie make him believe what it was impossible I could mean.

The discourse too was praised abundantly. It was divine! His lordship had never delivered more serious and alarming truths! But though no man could be better convinced that in reality this was all fact, yet coming from them I knew it to be all falsehood. They could not characterize what they could not hear; and the maukish[2] adulation curdled even upon my digestive stomach.

The lesson however certainly did me good, though it had yet but little influence upon my conduct.

[Hugh subsequently learns that the lord for whom he had written letters opposing the reigning party has now switched sides.]

'We must now vere about, and this was the business for which I wanted you. A good casuist[3] you know, Mr. Trevor, can defend both sides of a question; and I have no doubt but that you will appear with as much brilliancy, as a panegyrist, as you have done, as a satirist.'

How long I remained in that state of painful stupefaction into which I had been thrown, at the very commencement of this harangue, is more than I can say: but, as soon as I could recover some little presence of mind, I replied—'You, my lord, no doubt have your own reasons; which, to you, are a justification of your own conduct. For my part, when I wrote against the minister, it was not against the man. A desire to abash vice, advance the virtuous, and promote the good of mankind, were my

---

1   Elaborate praise.
2   Both the meanings "imbued with sickly or false sentiment; lacking in robustness" and "having a nauseating taste" (*OED*) seem applicable here.
3   "A theologian (or other person) who studies and resolves cases of conscience or doubtful questions regarding duty and conduct" (*OED*), although often with a negative connotation of quibbling or evasiveness.

motives!'—'Mr. Trevor, I find you are a young man: you do not know the world'——The scene with the bishop was acting over again, and I felt myself bursting once more with indignation. With ineffable contempt in every feature of my face, I answered—'If a knowledge of the world consists in servility, selfishness, and the practice of deceit, I hope I never shall know it.'—'You strangely forget yourself, Mr. Trevor!'—'I am not of that opinion, my lord. I rather think, it was the man who could suppose me capable of holding the pen of prostitution that strangely forgot himself!'

His lordship hemmed, rang his bell, hummed a tune, and wished me a good morning; and I rushed out of his apartment and hurried up to my own, where I found myself suddenly released from all my labours, and at full leisure to ruminate on all the theological and political honours that were to fall so immediately and profusely upon me.

And here it is worthy of remark that I did not accuse myself; for I did not recollect that I had been in the least guilty. Yet when the earl had asked me to write letters, that were to be supposed by the public the production of his own pen, I had then no qualms of conscience; and when the bishop invited me to favour falsehood, by attributing my best written sermon to him, I concurred in the request with no less facility. When deceit was not to favour but to counteract my plans, its odious immorality then rushed upon me. Men are so much in a hurry, to obtain the end, that they frequently forget to scrutinize the means. As for my part, far from supposing that I had been a participator in guilt, I felt a consciousness of having acted with self-denying and heroic virtue. This was my only armour, against the severe pangs with which I was so unexpectedly assaulted.

b. From Robert Bage, *Hermsprong* (1796), ed. Pamela Perkins (Peterborough, ON: Broadview Press, 2002)

[These selections contrast Dr. Blick, the avaricious clergyman whose patron is the proud and vindictive Lord Grondale, with his humane and devoted curate, Mr. Woodcock. Although he speaks of himself below in the third person, Gregory Glen is the novel's narrator, a resident in the village of Grondale and a friend to Hermsprong. As the illegitimate son of "a blooming girl, brought up in a cottage" (ch. 1) and the neighborhood squire, Glen provides, through his own history, a narrative critique of the corrupt élite similar to that proffered in *Nature and Art*.]

From Chapter 3

The next person upon the canvas is Dr. Blick, rector of Grondale and Sithin; a man perfectly orthodox in matters of church and state, such as these bad times require; and, thank heaven, we have plenty of them. Dr. Blick's merit was great indeed; I cannot say it had been fully rewarded. Hitherto he had arisen in the church no higher than a poor canon, which, with the product of three livings; for he had one in commendam, scarce produced him 1000 *l.* a year.[1] But if he joins to that merit, which now leads to honours, the agreeable art of assentation,[2] no man knows to what dignities he may arise. Dr. Blick could not accuse himself of any neglect of this art, where the application might be useful; more especially to his patron, Lord Grondale; whose peculiar merit he conceived to be such, that even a bishopric,[3] could he be induced to ask it for a friend, would scarce be refused him by administration. He was therefore much devoted to his lordship; ...

From Chapter 11

A sight of the encampment put Mr. Hermsprong in mind of his rencontre with Dr. Blick.[4] Mr. Glen did not seem in the humour for panegyric; for his portrait of the Doctor was rather unfavourable. That he united pride with meanness; that he was as haughty to his inferiors, as cringing to superiors. An eternal flatterer of Lord Grondale, he did not even presume to preach against a vice, if it happened to be a vice of his patron. "And yet," said Glen, "this man is rich; has great church preferment, two good livings, and a stall;[5] keeps his chariot, and does not chuse to marry."

"I hope," said Mr. Hermsprong, "you are not now giving a general picture of the English clergy?"

---

1   A relatively low position in the church hierarchy, a canon officiates within a cathedral. Clergy in the Church of England could hold more than one living, deputizing their responsibilities in the parish to a curate (such as Mr. Woodcock). The phrase "in commendam" is used of an ecclesiastic living "which a bishop or other dignitary was permitted to hold along with his own preferment" (*OED*). Glen is of course being ironic here: recall that the living given to William senior at the beginning of *Nature and Art* brought £500 a year.

2   "The action of assenting to the opinions of another; *esp.* obsequious or servile expression or act of assent" (*OED*).

3   Office or position of a bishop.

4   In chapter 6 Hermsprong, while out walking, had met and been unpleasantly interrogated by Dr. Blick.

5   I.e., a position within a cathedral.

"By no means," replied Mr. Glen; "as individuals, I think them generally worthy; and if you desire to see a contrast to Dr. Blick, you may find it in his curate; a man of learning; of high probity; simple in his manners; attentive to his duties; and so attached to his studies, that he may be said to be almost unacquainted with mankind. This man is married; has four daughters; and from the bountiful rector of Grondale has forty-five pounds per annum, for doing half the duties of Grondale, and the whole of Sithin, a village a mile hence, where he resides. It is true, he derives about an equal revenue from his patrimonial fortune, otherwise it would be impossible his family could be supported."(98)

From Chapter 13

[Hermsprong has a second distasteful encounter with Dr. Blick.]

"Is this," Mr. Hermsprong asked, "a general specimen of the English clergy?"

"By no means," replied Mr. Glen; "except a certain portion of rancour against those who differ from them in religion or politics (an effect probably springing from their *l'espirit du corps*,) they are in general rather amiable than otherwise. But they are men. Sometimes, in their too earnest desire of the good things here below, they are apt to forget those above. They are wise, however; and if unfortunately they are assaulted by any violent cupidities,[1] they commonly take the proper means of obtaining them. Doctor Blick, for example, having been seized with that capital disorder, the love of accumulation, has fulfilled himself with a prudent quantity of adulation, which has answered his purpose well; he has church preferment to near 1000 *l*. per annum; and has not, I am told, laid aside his expectations of a bishopric."

"And is the want of this agreeable quality," asked Hermsprong, "to be assigned as the cause of Mr. Woodcock's not rising in the church?"

"Alas!" replied Glen, "not having been in the way of subjects on whom to practise, he has not taken the trouble to acquire it. Nor is this the only point of contrast betwixt himself and his reverend master. Besides, taking care not to lose any thing of his dues, by a foolish lenity, or by a love of peace, the Doctor knows it is his duty rather to govern than to teach his flock; and he governs *à la royale*, with imperious airs, and

---

1   Inordinate desire or appetite, especially for wealth or possessions.

imperious commands. Woodcock, on the contrary, is one of the mildest of the sons of men. It is true, he preaches humility, but he practices it also; and takes pains, by example, as well as precept, to make his parishioners good, in all their offices, their duties, and relations. To the poor, he is indeed a blessing; for he gives comfort, when he has nothing else to give. To him they apply when sick; he gives them simple medicines; when they are in doubt, he gives them wholesome counsels. He is learned too, and liberal in his opinions; but of manners so simple, and so ignorant of fashion and folly, that to appear in the world would subject him to infinite ridicule." (107–08)

3. Seduction and Prostitution

[The story of Hannah Primrose, the seduced maiden who is impregnated and abandoned by the younger William, and whose desultory attempts to sustain herself and her child result in imprisonment and death, furnishes a crucial part of the novel's plot as well as providing a major source of its social critique. Novels by several of Inchbald's radical contemporaries, most notably Mary Wollstonecraft and Mary Hays, employed similarly powerful narratives of betrayal and despair as key elements of their feminist polemic. As their titles imply, both Wollstonecraft's *Wrongs of Woman* and Hays's *Victim of Prejudice* follow Inchbald's novel in attacking the sexual double standard that condemned—and often destroyed—women while absolving the men who mistreated them. As the following narratives, embedded within their respective novels, demonstrate, women's oppression can cut across socioeconomic lines: for both Wollstonecraft's working-class character and Hays's more privileged one, the destitution and despair that result from sexual betrayal take a similarly harrowing, indeed relentless, form.]

a. From Mary Wollstonecraft, *The Wrongs of Woman: or, Maria*, in *Posthumous Works* (London, 1798)

Chapter V

[Touched by the love that has blossomed between Maria, imprisoned against her will in a madhouse by a brutal husband, and her fellow prisoner, Darnford, their keeper Jemima tells them her story.]

"My father," said Jemima, "seduced my mother, a pretty girl, with whom he lived fellow-servant; and she no sooner perceived the natural, the dreaded consequences, than the terrible conviction flashed on her—that she was ruined. Honesty, and a regard for her reputation, had been the only principles inculcated by her mother; and they had been so forcibly impressed, that she feared shame, more than the poverty to which it would lead. Her incessant importunities to prevail upon my father to screen her from reproach by marrying her, as he had promised in the fervour of seduction, estranged him from her so completely, that her very person became distasteful to him; and he began to hate, as well as despise me, before I was born.

"My mother, grieved to the soul by his neglect, and unkind treatment, actually resolved to famish herself; and injured her health by the attempt; though she had not sufficient resolution to adhere to her project, or renounce it entirely. Death came not at her call; yet sorrow, and the methods she adopted to conceal her condition, still doing the work of a house-maid, had such an effect on her constitution, that she died in the wretched garret, where her virtuous mistress had forced her to take refuge in the very pangs of labour, though my father, after a slight reproof, was allowed to remain in his place—allowed by the mother of six children, who, scarcely permitting a footstep to be heard, during her month's indulgence, felt no sympathy for the poor wretch, denied every comfort required by her situation.

"The day my mother died, the ninth after my birth, I was consigned to the care of the cheapest nurse my father could find; who suckled her own child at the same time, and lodged as many more as she could, in two cellar-like apartments.

"Poverty, and the habit of seeing children die off her hands, had so hardened her heart, that the office of a mother did not awaken the tenderness of a woman; nor were the feminine caresses which seemed a part of the rearing of a child, ever bestowed on me....

[Jemima's subsequent mistreatment by a cruel step-mother is followed by even greater abuse at the hands of the woman to whom she becomes apprenticed, the keeper of a cheap clothing shop.]

"I shudder with horror, when I recollect the treatment I had now to endure. Not only under the lash of my task mistress, but the drudge of the maid, apprentices and children, I never had a taste of human kindness to soften the rigour of perpetual labour. I had been introduced as an object of abhorrence into the family; as a creature of whom my step-mother, though she had been kind enough to let me live in the house with her own child, could make nothing. I was described as a wretch, whose nose must be kept to the grinding stone—and it was held there with an iron grasp....

"Thus was I the mark of cruelty till my sixteenth year; and then I have only to point out a change of misery; for a period[1] I never knew. Allow me first to make one observation. Now I look back, I cannot help attributing the greater part of my misery, to the misfortune of having been thrown into the world without the grand support of life—a mother's affection. I had no one to love me; or to make me respected to enable me to acquire respect. I was an egg dropped on the sand; a pauper by nature, hunted from family to family, who belonged to nobody—and nobody cared for me. I was despised from my birth, and denied the chance of obtaining a footing for myself in society. Yes; I had not even the chance of being considered as a fellow-creature—yet all the people with whom I lived, brutalized as they were by the low cunning of trade, and the despicable shifts of poverty, were not without bowels,[2] though they never yearned for me. I was, in fact, born a slave, and chained by infamy to slavery during the whole of existence, without having any companions to alleviate it by sympathy, or teach me how to rise above it by their example. But, to resume the thread of my tale—

"At sixteen, I suddenly grew tall, and something like comeliness appeared on a Sunday, when I had time to wash my face, and put on clean clothes. My master had once or twice caught hold of me in the passage; but I instinctively avoided his disgusting caresses. One day however, when the family were at a methodist meeting, he contrived to be alone in the house with me, and by blows—yes, blows and menaces, compelled me to submit to his ferocious desire; and, to avoid my mistress's fury, I was obliged in future to comply, and to skulk to my loft at his command, in spite of increasing loathing.

"The anguish which was now pent up in my bosom, seemed to open a new world to me: I began to extend my thoughts beyond myself, and grieve for human misery, till I discovered with horror—ah! what horror!—that I was with child. I knew not why I felt a mixed sensation of despair and tenderness, excepting that, ever called a bastard, a bastard appeared to me an object of the greatest compassion in creation.

---

1   End, cessation.
2   Pity or compassion, from the internal organs as the "seat of the tender or sympathetic emotions" (*OED*).

"I communicated this dreadful circumstance to my master, who was almost equally alarmed at the intelligence; for he feared his wife, and public censure at the meeting. After some weeks of deliberation had elapsed, I in continual fear that my altered shape would be noticed, my master gave me a medicine in a phial, which he desired me to take, telling me, without any circumlocution, for what purpose it was designed. I burst into tears, I thought it was killing my self—yet was such a self as I worth preserving? He cursed me for a fool, and left me to my own reflections. I could not resolve to take this infernal potion; but I wrapped it up in an old gown, and hid it in a corner of my box.

"Nobody yet suspected me, because they had been accustomed to view me as a creature of another species. But the threatening storm at last broke over my devoted head—never shall I forget it! One Sunday evening, when I was left, as usual, to take care of the house, my master came home intoxicated, and I became the prey of his brutal appetite. His extreme intoxication made him forget his customary caution, and my mistress entered and found us in a situation that could not have been more hateful to her than me. Her husband was 'pot-valiant,' he feared her not at the moment, nor had he then much reason, for she instantly turned the whole force of her anger another way. She tore off my cap, scratched, kicked, and buffeted me, till she had exhausted her strength, declaring, as she rested her arm, 'that I had wheedled her husband from her. But could anything better be expected from a wretch, whom she had taken into her house out of pure charity?' What a torrent of abuse rushed out? till, almost breathless, she concluded with saying—'that I was born a strumpet; it ran in my blood, and nothing good could come to those who harboured me.'

["]My situation was, of course, discovered, and she declared that I should not stay another night under the same roof with an honest family. I was therefore pushed out of doors, and my trumpery thrown after me, when it had been contemptuously examined in the passage, lest I should have stolen any thing.

"Behold me in the street, utterly destitute! Whither would I creep for shelter? To my father's roof I had no claim, when not pursued by shame;—now I shrunk back as from death, from my mother's cruel reproaches, my father's execrations. I could not endure to hear him curse the day I was born, though life had been a curse to me. Of death I thought, but with a confused emotion of terror, as I stood leaning my head on a post, and starting at every footstep, lest it should be my mistress coming to tear my heart out. One of the boys of the shop passing by, heard my tale, and immediately repaired to his master, to give him a description of my situation; and he touched the right key—the scandal it would give rise to, if I were left to repeat my tale to every enquirer. This plea came home to his reason, who had been sobered by his wife's rage, the fury of which fell upon him when I was out of her reach, and he sent the boy to me with half-a-guinea, desiring him to conduct me to a house, where beggars, and other wretches, the refuse of society, nightly lodged.

"This night was spent in a state of stupefaction, or desperation. I detested mankind, and abhorred myself.

"In the morning I ventured out, to throw myself in my master's way, at his usual hour of going abroad. I approached him, he 'damned me for a b——, declared I had disturbed the peace of his family, and that he had sworn to his wife never to take any more notice of me.' He left me; but, instantly returning, he told me that he should speak to his friend, a parish officer, to get a nurse for the brat I laid to him; and advised me, if I wished to keep out of the house of correction, not to make free with his name.

"I hurried back to my hole, and, rage giving place to despair, sought for the potion that was to procure abortion, and swallowed it with a wish that it might destroy me, at the same time that it stopped the sensations of new-born life, which I felt with indescribable emotion. My head turned round, my heart grew sick, and in the horrors of approaching dissolution, mental anguish was swallowed up. The effect of the medicine was violent, and I was confined to my bed several days; but, youth and a strong constitution prevailing, I once more crawled out, to ask myself the cruel question, 'Whither I should go?' I had but two shillings left in my pocket, the rest had been expended, by a poor woman who slept in the same room, to pay for my lodging, and purchase the necessaries of which she partook.

"With this wretch I went into the neighbouring streets to beg, and my disconsolate appearance drew a few pence from the idle, enabling me still to command a bed; till, recovering from my illness, and taught to put on my rags to the best advantage, I was accosted from different motives, and yielded to the desire of the brutes I met, with the same detestation that I had felt for my still more brutal master. I have since read in novels of the blandishments of seduction, but I had not even the pleasure of being enticed into vice.

"I shall not," interrupted Jemima, "lead your imagination into all the scenes of wretchedness and depravity, which I was condemned to view; or mark the different stages of my debasing misery. Fate dragged me through the very kennels of society; I was still a slave, a bastard, a common property. Become familiar with vice, for I wish to conceal nothing from you,

I picked the pockets of the drunkards who abused me; and proved by my conduct that I deserved the epithets, with which they loaded me at moments when distrust ought to cease.

"Detesting my nightly occupation, though valuing, if I may use the word, my independence, which only consisted in choosing the street in which I should wander, or the roof, when I had money, in which I should hide my head, I was sometime before I could prevail on myself to accept of a place in a house of ill fame, to which a girl, with whom I had accidentally conversed in the street, had recommended me. I had been hunted almost into a fever, by the watchmen of the quarter of the town I frequented; one, whom I had unwittingly offended, giving the word to the whole pack. You can scarcely conceive the tyranny exercised by these wretches: considering themselves as the instruments of the very laws they violate, the pretext which steels their conscience, hardens their heart. Not content with receiving from us, outlaws of society (let other women talk of favours) a brutal gratification gratuitously, as a privilege of office, they extort a tithe of prostitution, and harass with threats the poor creatures whose occupations afford not the means to silence the growl of avarice. To escape from this persecution, I once more entered into servitude...

[Jemima subsequently leaves that position as servant to become the kept mistress of a cultured yet dissolute man, in whose company she begins to educate herself through reading and conversation. When he suddenly dies intestate, she must once again search for work, but with little success.]

"How often have I heard," said Jemima, interrupting her narrative, "in conversation, and read in books, that every person willing to work may find employment? It is the vague assertion, I believe, of insensible indolence, when it related to men; but, when with respect to women, I am sure of its fallacy, unless they will submit to the most menial bodily labour; and even to be employed at hard labour is out of the reach of many, whose reputation misfortune or folly has tainted.

"How writers, professing to be friends to freedom, and the improvement of morals, can assert that poverty is no evil, I cannot imagine....

"Not to trouble you," continued she, "with a detailed description of all the painful feelings of unavailing exertion, I have only to tell you, that at last I got recommended to wash in a few families, who did me the favour to admit me into their houses, without the most strict enquiry, to wash from one in the morning till eight at night, for eighteen or twenty-pence a day. On the happiness to be enjoyed over a washing-tub I need not comment; yet you will allow me to observe, that this was a wretchedness of situation peculiar to my sex. A man with half my industry, and, I may say, abilities, could have procured a decent livelihood, and discharged some of the duties which knit mankind together; whilst I, who had acquired a taste for the rational, nay, in honest pride let me assert it, the virtuous enjoyments of life, was cast aside as the filth of society. Condemned to labour, like a machine, only to earn bread, and scarcely that, I became melancholy and desperate.

"I have now to mention a circumstance which fills me with remorse, and fear it will entirely deprive me of your esteem. A tradesman became attached to me, and visited me frequently,—and I at last obtained such a power over him, that he offered to take me home to his house. Consider, dear madam, I was famishing: wonder not that I became a wolf!—The only reason for not taking me home immediately, was the having a girl in the house, with a child by him—and this girl—I advised him—yes, I did! would I could forget it!—to turn out of doors: and one night he determined to follow my advice.—Poor wretch! she fell upon her knees, reminded him that he had promised to marry her, that her parents were honest!—What did it avail?—She was turned out.

"She approached her father's door, in the skirts of London,—listened at the shutters,—but could not knock. A watchman had observed her go and return several times—Poor wretch!"——The remorse Jemima spoke of seemed to be stinging her to the soul, as she proceeded.

"She left it, and, approaching a tub where horses were watered, she sat down in it, and, with desperate resolution, remained in that attitude—till resolution was no longer necessary.

"I happened that morning to be going out to wash, anticipating the moment when I should escape from such hard labour. I passed by, just as some men, who were going to work, drew out the stiff, cold corpse.—Let me not recal the horrid moment!—I recognized her pale visage; I listened to the tale told by the spectators, and my heart did not burst. I thought of my own state, and wondered how I could be such a monster!—I worked hard; and, returning home, I was attacked by a fever. I suffered both in body and mind. I determined not to live with the wretch. But he did not try me; he left the neighbourhood. I once more returned to the wash-tub.

[After sustaining an injury she is admitted into a hospital, but is discharged for lack of money before her wound has fully healed.]

"After my dismission, I was more at a loss than ever for subsistence, and not to weary you with a repetition of the same unavailing attempts, unable to stand at the washing-tub, I began to consider the rich and poor as natural enemies, and became a thief from principle.—I could not now cease to reason, but I hated mankind. I despised myself, yet I justified my conduct. I was taken, tried, and condemned to six month's imprisonment in a house of correction. My soul recoils with horror from the remembrance of the insults I had to endure, till branded with shame, I was turned loose in the street, pennyless. I wandered from street to street, till, exhausted by hunger and fatigue, I sunk down senseless at a door, where I had vainly demanded a morsel of bread. I was sent by the inhabitant to the workhouse, to which he had surlily bid me go, saying, 'he paid enough conscience to the poor,' when, with parched tongue, I implored his charity. If those well-meaning people, who exclaim against beggars, were acquainted with the treatment the poor receive in many of these wretched asylums, they would not stifle so easily involuntary sympathy, by saying that they have all parishes to go to, or wonder that the poor dread to enter the gloomy walls. What are the common run of work-houses, but prisons, in which many respectable old people, worn out by immoderate labour, sink into the grave in sorrow, to which they are carried like dogs!" …

"True," rejoined Darnford, "and, till the rich will give more than a part of their wealth, till they will give time and attention to the wants of the distresssed, never let them boast of charity. Let them open their hearts and not their purses, and employ their minds in service, if they are really actuated by humanity; or charitable institutions will always be the prey of the lowest order of knaves."

Jemima returning, seemed in haste to finish her tale. "The overseer farmed the poor of different parishes, and out of the bowels of poverty was wrung the money with which he purchased this dwelling, as a private receptacle for madness. He had been a keeper at a house of the same description, and conceived that he could make money much more readily in his old occupation. He is a shrewd—shall I say it?—villain. He observed something resolute in my manner, and offered to take me with him, and instruct me how to treat the disturbed minds he meant to intrust to my care. The offer of forty pounds a year, and to quit a work-house, was not to be despised, though the condition of shutting my eyes and hardening my heart was annexed to it.

"I agreed to accompany him; and, four years have I been attendant on many wretches, and"—she lowered her voice,—"the witness of many enormities. In solitude my mind seemed to recover its force, and many of the sentiments which I imbibed in the only tolerable period of my life, returned with their full force. Still what should induce me to be the champion for suffering humanity?—Who ever risked any thing for me?—Who ever acknowledged me to be a fellow-creature?"—

Maria took her hand, and Jemima, more overcome by kindness than she had ever been by cruelty, hastened out of the room to conceal her emotions.

b. From Mary Hays, *The Victim of Prejudice* (1799), ed. Eleanor Ty (Peterborough, ON: Broadview Press, 2nd edition, 1998)[1]

[Unaware of her parentage, the heroine Mary is raised in rural retreat by a guardian, Mr. Raymond. Under his progressive and benevolent care she grows up the physical and intellectual equal of William Pelham, a gentleman's son who is being educated by her guardian. When Mary and William fall innocently in love, Mr. Raymond removes Mary to a coastal village, although he fails to give her the reason why she "*can never be the wife of William Pelham*" (33). There Mary receives a packet from her guardian in which he describes his relation to her dead mother, also named Mary, who, after having been seduced and abandoned by another, had entrusted her daughter to his care. The letter printed below furnishes the story of Mary's mother, the novel's first "victim of prejudice"; the heroine Mary will subsequently become another such victim when she is raped and sequestered by the profligate aristocrat Sir Peter Osborne.]

From Volume I, Chapter XII

"'*To* MR. RAYMOND.

"'How far shall I go back? From what period shall I date the source of those calamities which have, at length, overwhelmed me?—Educated in the lap of indolence, enervated by pernicious indulgence, fostered in artificial refinements, misled by specious, but false, expectations, softened into imbecility, pampered in luxury, and dazzled by a frivolous ambition, at the age of eighteen, I rejected the manly address and honest ardour of the man[2] whose reason would have enlightened, whose affection would have supported me; through whom I might have enjoyed

---

1 © 1998 Eleanor Ty. Reprinted with permission.
2 I.e., Mr. Raymond.

the endearing relations, and fulfilled the respectable duties, of mistress, wife, and mother; and listened to the insidious flatteries of a being, raised by fashion and fortune to a rank seducing my vain imagination, in the splendour of which my weak judgement was dazzled and my virtue overpowered.

"'He spoke of tenderness and honour, (prostituted names!) while his actions gave the lie to his pretentions. He affected concealment, and imposed on my understanding by sophistical pretences. Unaccustomed to reason, too weak for principle, credulous from experience, a stranger to the corrupt habits of society, I yielded to the mingled intoxication of my vanity and my senses, quitted the paternal roof, and resigned myself to my triumphant seducer.

"'Months revolved in a round of varied pleasures; reflection was stunned in the giddy whirl. I awoke not from my delirium, till, on an unfounded, affected, pretence of jealousy, under which satiety veiled itself, I found myself suddenly deserted, driven with opprobrium from the house of my *destroyer*, thrown friendless and destitute upon the world, branded with infamy, and a wretched outcast from social life. To fill up the measure of my distress, a little time convinced me that I was about to become a mother. The money which remained from my profuse habits was nearly exhausted. In the prospect of immediate distress, I addressed myself to the author of my woes. Relating my situation, I implored his justice and mercy. I sought in vain to awaken his tenderness, to touch his callous heart. To my humble supplications no answer was vouchsafed. Despair, for awhile, with its benumbing power, seized upon my heart!

"'Awakening to new anguish, and recalling my scattered faculties, I remembered the softness and the ease of my childhood, the doating fondness of my weak, but indulgent, parents. I resolved to address them, resolved to pour out before them the confession of my errors, of my griefs, and of my contrition. My lowly solicitations drew upon me bitter reproaches: I was treated as an abandoned wretch, whom it would be criminal to relieve and hopeless to attempt to reclaim.

"'At this crisis, I was sought out and discovered by a friend (if friendship can endure the bond of vice) of my destroyer; the man who, to gratify his sensuality, had entailed, on an unoffending being, *a being who loved him*, misery and certain perdition. My declining virtue, which yet struggled to retrieve itself, was now assailed by affected sympathy, by imprecations on the wretch who had deserted me, and an offer of asylum and protection.

"'My heart, though too weak for principle, was not yet wholly corrupted: the modest habits of female youth were still far from being obliterated; I suspected the views of the guileful deceiver, and contemned them with horror and just indignation. Changing his manners, this Proteus[1] assumed a new form; prophaned the names of humanity, friendship, virtue; gradually inspiring me with confidence. Unable to labour, ashamed to solicit charity, helpless, pennyless, feeble, delicate, thrown out with reproach from society, borne down with a consciousness of irretrievable error, exposed to insult, to want, to contumely, to every species of aggravated distress, in a situation requiring sympathy, tenderness, assistance,—From whence was I to draw fortitude to combat these accumulated evils? By what magical power or supernatural aid was a being, rendered, by all the previous habits of life and education, systematically weak and helpless, at once to assume a courage thus daring and heroic?

"'I received, as the tribute of humanity and friendship, that assistance, without which I had not the means of existence, and was delivered, in due time, of a lovely female infant. While bedewing it with my tears, (delicious tears! tears that shed a balm into my lacerated spirit!) I forgot for awhile its barbarous father, the world's scorn, and my blasted prospects: the sensations of the injured woman, of the insulted wife, were absorbed for a time in the stronger sympathies of the delighted mother.

"'My new friend, to whose tender cares I seemed indebted for the sweet emotions which now engrossed my heart, appeared entitled to my grateful esteem: my confidence in him became every hour more unbounded. It was long ere he stripped off the mask so successfully assumed; when, too late, I found myself betrayed, and became, a second time, the victim of my simplicity and the inhuman arts of a practised deceiver, who had concerted with the companion of his licentious revels, wearied with his conquest, the snare into which I fell a too-credulous prey.

"'Evil communication, habits of voluptuous extravagance, despair of retrieving a blasted fame, gradually stifled the declining struggles of virtue; while the liberal manners of those, of whom I was now compelled to be the associate, rapidly advanced the corruption;

"'Took off the rose
"'From the fair forehead of an innocent love,
"'And plac'd a blister there.[2]

"'In a mind unfortified by principle, modesty is a blossom fragile as lovely. Every hour, whirled in a giddy round of dissipation, sunk me deeper in shameless vice. The mother became stifled in my heart: my visits to my

---

1   In Greek mythology the son of Poseidon, who was able to change his shape at will.
2   Changed slightly from William Shakespeare, *Hamlet* (III.iv.42–44).

infant, which I had been reluctantly prevailed upon to place with a hireling, were less and less frequent. Its innocence contrasted my guilt, it revived too powerfully in my heart the remembrance of what I was, the reflection on what I might have been, and the terrible conviction, which I dared not dwell upon, of the fate which yet menaced me. I abstained from this soul-harrowing indulgence, and the ruin of my mind became complete.

"'Why should I dwell upon, why enter into, a disgusting detail of the gradations of thoughtless folly, guilt, and infamy? Why should I stain the youthful purity of my unfortunate offspring, into whose hands these sheets may hereafter fall, with the delineation of scenes remembered with soul-sickening abhorrence? Let it suffice to say, that, by enlarging the circle of my observation, though in the bosom of depravity, my understanding became enlightened: I perceived myself the victim of the injustice, of the prejudice, of society, which, by opposing to my return to virtue almost insuperable barriers, had plunged me into irremediable ruin. I grew sullen, desperate, hardened. I felt a malignant joy in retailing upon mankind a part of the evils which I sustained. My mind became fiend-like, revelling in destruction, glorying in its shame. Abandoned to excessive and brutal licentiousness, I drowned returning reflection in inebriating potions. The injuries and insults to which my odious profession exposed me eradicated from my heart every remaining human feeling. I became a monster, cruel, relentless, ferocious; and contaminated alike, with a deadly poison, the health and the principles of those unfortunate victims whom, with prac-tised allurements, I entangled in my snares.[1] Man, however vicious, how-ever cruel, reaches not the depravity of a shameless woman. *Despair* shuts not against him every avenue to repentance; *despair* drives him not from human sympathies; *despair* hurls him not from hope, from pity, from life's common charities, to plunge him into desperate, damned, guilt.

"'Let the guileful seducer pause here, and tremble! Let the sordid voluptuary, the thoughtless libertine, stop amidst his selfish gratifications, and reflect! Oh! Let him balance this tremendous price, this deplorable ruin, against the revel of an hour, the revel over which satiety hovers, and to which disgust and lassitude quickly succeed! Boast not, vain man, of civil refinements, while, in the bosom of the most polished and populous cities, an evil is fostered, poisoning virtue at its source, diffusing through every rank its deadly venom, bursting the bonds of nature, blasting its

---

1   Mary's "odious profession" is of course prostitution; thus she endangers her clients' health by infecting them with venereal disease.

endearments, destroying the promise of youth, the charm of domestic affections, and hurling its helpless victims to irremediable perdition.

"'The evening, which completed my career of crime, roused my slumbering conscience. To *murder* I was yet unfamiliarized. In the instant when remorse, with its serpent-sting, transfixed my heart, I beheld, with unspeakable confusion and anguish, the man who had, with honourable tenderness, sought the chaste affection of my youth. A thousand poignant emotions rushed upon my soul: regret, shame, terror, contrition, combined to convulse my enfeebled frame. Through the dead silence of the night, amidst the prison's gloom, contending passions rent my tortured spirit: in the bitterness of despair, I dashed my wretched body against the dungeon's floor; tore, with my nails, my hair, my flesh, my garments; groaned, howled, shrieked, in frantic agony. Towards morning, a stream of blood gushed from my nose and lips, and, mingling with a flood of tears, a kindly and copious shower, recalled me from the verge of insanity. The first collected thought which returning sense presented was, a determination to avoid the man whose value I had learned too late, and by whom I had been beloved in my days of peace and innocence. I procured, as the day advanced, the implements of writing, and traced the characters delivered to your hand; presaging, but too truly, your humane solicitude.

"'At this period, I felt suddenly awakened, as it were, to a new existence. The prospect of death, by bounding the future, threw my reflections upon the past. I indulged in the mournful prospect; I committed it to paper; while, as my thoughts were methodized, my spirit became serene.

"'Lowly and tranquil, I await my destiny; but feel, in the moment that life is cut short, dispositions springing and powers expanding, that, permitted me to unfold themselves, might yet make reparation to the society I have injured, and on which I have but too well retaliated my wrongs. But it is too late! *Law* completes the triumph of injustice. The despotism of man rendered me weak, his vices betrayed me into shame, a barbarous policy stifled returning dignity, prejudice robbed me of the means of independence, gratitude ensnared me in the devices of treachery, the contagion of example corrupted my heart, despair hardened and brutality rendered it cruel. A sanguinary policy precludes reformation, defeating the dear-bought lessons of experience, and, by a legal process, assuming the arm of omnipotence, annihilates the being whom its negligence left destitute, and its institutions compelled to offend.

"'Thou, also, it may be, art incapable of distinction; thou, too, probably, hast bartered the ingenuous virtues, the sensibility of youth, for the despotism, the arrogance, the voluptuousness of man, and the unfortunate daughter of an abandoned and wretched mother will spread to thee her innocent arms in vain. If, amidst the corruption of vaunted civilization, thy heart can yet throb responsive to the voice of nature, and yield to the claims of humanity, snatch from destruction the child of an illicit commerce, shelter her infant purity from contagion, guard her helpless youth from a pitiless world, cultivate her reason, make her feel her nature's worth, strengthen her faculties, inure her to suffer hardship, rouse her to independence, inspire her with fortitude, with energy, with self-respect, and teach her to contemn the tyranny that would impose fetters of sex upon her mind.

"MARY."

Appendix D: Africa and the Sierra Leone Colony

[As the novel provides very little description of the education of the younger Henry, it also offers scant depiction of the West African setting in which the son lived from infancy until the age of 12, and the father for a total of 24 years. This appendix provides a context for the novel's oblique yet significant African component by focusing on documents related to the late eighteenth-century settlement of Sierra Leone. Although we are given little information about the father's voyage other than the fictitious name of "Zocotora Island" (ch. 10), the novel later makes an explicit link to that settlement by stating that the son hoped, nine years later, to "procure a passage" on a ship that was part of "the intended expedition to Sierra Leone" (ch. 32).

As the historian Christopher Fyfe (*A History of Sierra Leone* [Oxford University Press, 1962]) has noted, "The hope of making a fortune in the slave trade attracted many European adventurers to Sierra Leone and its vicinity. Some settled on the Banana Islands ... Others settled along the many river banks" (8). Such slave trading existed simultaneously with British plans, spearheaded most powerfully by the abolitionist Granville Sharp, to create in Sierra Leone a "Free Colony" for the "Black Poor" living in London. Begun in 1786 as a government-sponsored scheme for the repatriation of freed African slaves, many of whom had fought for the British during the Revolutionary War, the colony founded in Sierra Leone in 1787 was soon destroyed by a combination of climate, illness, and the hostility of slave traders and the indigenous African tribes. Revitalized by Abolitionists in 1791 as the private humanitarian and commercial endeavor "The Sierra Leone Company," the venture reestablished what was left of the initial community and in 1792 gained a new settlement of Africans from Nova Scotia. Granville Sharp's original self-governing charter was replaced, once the Sierra Leone Company took over, by a system of white governance; Sierra Leone became a crown colony in 1808 and gained national independence in 1961.

Africa and the "African Question" were very much part of the British cultural imaginary during the years in which Inchbald was writing *Nature and Art*, largely through written descriptions by freed black slaves or travelers to the region. The *Interesting Narrative* of Olaudah Equiano, a West African kidnapped and sold into slavery in the West Indies, details some of the problems involved in the planning of the first, government-funded settlement to Sierra Leone. Alexander Falconbridge, who had earlier traveled as a doctor on slave ships and subsequently become a vehement abolitionist, was sent to direct the repurchasing of land and to resettle the remaining settlers in 1791; he was accompanied by his new wife Anna Maria, whose "Letters" provide compelling representations of that endeavor, as well as of the natural setting and African natives and customs absent from Inchbald's novel. For more information on Sierra Leone, see Helen Thomas, *Romanticism and Slave Narratives: Transatlantic Testimonies* (Cambridge University Press, 2001).]

1. From Olaudah Equiano, *The Interesting Narrative of the Life of Olaudah Equiano, or Gustavus Vassa, the African. Written by himself* (1789), ed. Angelo Costanzo (Peterborough, ON: Broadview Press, 2001)[1]

[After having been captured at the age of 10 or 11 from his native west Africa (modern day Nigeria), Olaudah Equiano was taken to the Caribbean and then to Virginia. There he was bought by a British naval officer, Michael Henry Pascal, who renamed him Gustavus Vassa after a Swedish freedom fighter. Working for several masters on both British and American merchant and military vessels, he was eventually able, through trading and saving, to buy his freedom from the Quaker merchant, Robert King, in 1766, at the age of 21. Although he continued to work on commercial sailing vessels, Equiano eventually settled in London, where he allied himself with important abolitionist leaders and became an active member of the Sons of Africa, a group of black abolitionists. Believing initially in the cause of black resettlement as an ameliorative measure for the many freed slaves living in England—a means of bettering slaves' position while still tolerating the institution of slavery itself—Equiano worked as Commissary of Stores for the Sierra Leone project before accusing his superiors of corruption, an experience he describes in the excerpt below. His *Interesting Narrative*, a first-hand account of the slave-trade controversy by a native African and former slave turned loyal British subject, added a significant voice to the raging debates over slavery and the slave trade. Published as an explicitly abolitionist text, Equiano's best-selling *Narrative* went through eight editions in the five years after its 1789 publication and was also translated into several languages.]

---

1   © 2001 Angelo Costanzo. Reprinted with permission.

On my return to London in August [1786], I was very agreeably surprised to find, that the benevolence of government had adopted the plan of some philanthropic individuals, to send the Africans from hence to their native quarter, and that some vessels were then engaged to carry them to Sierra Leone; an act which redounded to the honour of all concerned in its promotion, and filled me with prayers and much rejoicing.

There was then in the city a select committee of gentlemen for the black poor, to some of whom I had the honour of being known; and as soon as they heard of my arrival, they sent for me to the committee. When I came there, they informed me of the intention of government; and as they seemed to think me qualified to superintend part of the undertaking, they asked me to go with the black poor to Africa. I pointed out to them many objections to my going; and particularly I expressed some difficulties on the account of the slave dealers, as I would certainly oppose their traffic in the human species by every means in my power. However, these objections were over-ruled by the gentlemen of the committee, who prevailed on me to go; and recommended me to the honourable Commissioners of his Majesty's Navy, as a proper person to act as a commissary for government in the intended expedition; and they accordingly appointed me in November 1786, to that office, and gave me sufficient power to act for the government in the capacity of commissary, ... I proceeded immediately to the executing of my duty on board the vessels destined for the voyage, where I continued till the March following.

During my continuance in the employment of government I was struck with the flagrant abuses committed by the agent, and endeavoured to remedy them, but without any effect. One instance, among many which I could produce, may serve as specimen. Government had ordered to be provided all necessaries (slops, as they are called, included) for 750 persons; however, not being able to muster more than 426, I was ordered to send the superfluous slops, &c. to the king's stores at Portsmouth; but, when I demanded them for that purpose from the agent, it appeared they had never been bought, though paid for by government. But that was not all, government were not the only objects of peculation; these poor people suffered infinitely more; their accommodations were most wretched; many of them wanted beds, and many more cloathing and other necessaries....

I could not silently suffer government to be thus cheated, and my countrymen plundered and oppressed, and even left destitute of the necessaries for almost their existence. I therefore informed the Commissioners of the Navy of the agent's proceeding; but my dismission was soon after procured by the means of a gentleman in the city, whom the agent, conscious of his peculation, had deceived by letters, and whom, moreover, empowered the same agent to receive on board, at the government's expense, a number of passengers, contrary to the orders I received. By this I suffered a considerable loss in my property: however, the commissioners were satisfied with my conduct, and wrote to Capt. Thompson, expressing their approbation of it.

Thus provided, they proceeded on their voyage; and at last, worn out by treatment, perhaps not the most mild, and wasted by sickness, brought on by want of medicine, clothes, bedding, &c. they reached Sierra Leone just at the commencement of the rains. At that season of the year it is impossible to cultivate the lands, their provisions therefore were exhausted before they could derive any benefit from agriculture; and it is not surprising that many, especially the Lascars,[1] whose constitutions are very tender, and who had been cooped up in ships from October to June, and accommodated in the manner I have mentioned, should be so wasted by their confinement as not long to survive it.

Thus ended my part of the long-talked-of expedition to Sierra Leone; an expedition, which, however unfortunate in the event, was humane and politic in its design; nor was its failure owing to government; every thing was done on their part; but there was evidently sufficient mismanagement, attending the conduct and execution of it, to defeat its success. (242–45)

2. Letter from First Governors of Sierra Leone Settlement (1788) [Prince Hoare, *Memoirs of Granville Sharp* (London, 1820) 321–23]

Mr. James Reid, Chief in Command in the New Colony of Sierra Leone, to Granville Sharp, Esq. (extract):

Sierra Leone, September, 1788

Dear Friend,
We did not find our arrival at our new settlement according to our wishes; for we arrived in the rainy season, and very sickly, so that our people died very fast, on account of our lying exposed to the weather, and no houses, only what tents we could make, and that was little or no help to us, for the rain was so heavy it beat the tents down. But now, thank God, we have got houses, such as the country will afford, and does middling well; and we that are in being try every experiment in regard of proving the land,

---

1   Sailors from the East Indies.

to be sensible what it will produce, and find the more we cultivate the better the land seems to turn out, in regard of the country roots and herbs. But our English seeds do not thrive; none that we have brought out with us, as we have tried them; but that is owing to the seeds being too old.

There is one thing that would be very helpful to us; if we had an agent or two out here with us, to carry on some sort of business in regard of trade, so that we could rely a little sometimes on them for a small assistance, until our crops were fit to dispose of, and then pay them. It would be of infinite service to all the poor settlers, as provisions are scarce to be got—no, not one mouthful sometimes—which oblige us to dispose of all our clothes, and other few necessaries that we have: though, God knows, they are not much, for we are almost naked of every thing....

3. The Sierra Leone Company's Declaration (1791)

Substance of the Report of the Court of Directors of the Sierra Leone Company to the General Court, held in London on Wednesday the 19th of October, 1791, pp. 51–54. (Reprinted from Christopher Fyfe, *Sierra Leone Inheritance* [London: Oxford University Press, 1964] 116–17.)

[The sponsors of this trading company, which took over the Sierra Leone settlement after its initial destruction, were among the most zealous opponents of the slave trade. The following declaration shows how they blended business and philanthropy.]

... For the sake of acquainting the Princes and Chiefs, as well as the natives in general, with the real views of the Company, and for the sake also of counteracting misrepresentations that might be made concerning them, they propose to send over the following printed Declaration:—

'The Sierra Leone Company established by the British Parliament do hereby declare, that they will send out goods from England and take all kinds of African produce in exchange; that they will not deal in slaves themselves, nor allow any slave trade on their ground.

'They will always have a large store of European goods for sale, and a force sufficient to defend it.

'They wish always to keep peace, and will make no war unless they are first attacked; but they will suffer no one to be ill treated on their ground, nor to be seized and carried off into slavery; but will themselves punish their own people for any crimes fairly proved to have been committed by them.

'Black and white settlers will all be equally governed, and will have their persons and property secured, according to the laws of Great Britain.

'Schools for reading, writing and accounts, will be set up by the Company, who will be ready to receive and instruct the children of such natives as shall be willing to put them under their care.'

4. From Anna Maria Falconbridge, *Narrative of Two Voyages to the River Sierra Leone, During the Years 1791–92–93* (London, 1794)

From Letter I (London, 5 January 1791)

Mr. Falconbridge is employed by the St. George's Bay Company[1] to carry out some relief for a number of unfortunate people, both blacks and whites, whom Government sent to the river Sierra Leone, a few years since,[2] and who in consequence of having had some dispute with the natives, are scattered through the country, and are just now as I have been told, in the most deplorable condition.

He (Mr. Falconbridge) is likewise to make some arrangements for collecting those poor creatures again, and forming a settlement which the company have in contemplation to establish, not only to serve them, but to be generally useful to the natives.

From Letter III (Bance Island, 10 February 1791)

You will readily believe my heart was gladdened at the sight of the mountains of Sierra Leone, which was the land we first made.

Those mountains appear to rise gradually from the sea to a stupendous height, richly wooded and beautifully ornamented by the hand of nature, with a variety of delightful prospects.

I was vastly pleased while sailing up the river, for the rapidity of the ship through the water afforded a course of new scenery almost every moment, till we cast anchor here: Now and then I saw the glimpse of a native town, but from the distance and new objects hastily catching my eye, was not able to form a judgment or idea of any of them; but this will be no loss, as I may have frequent opportunities of visiting some of them hereafter....

---

1 The writer uses an earlier name for the Sierra Leone Company (before its incorporation in June 1791).

2 I.e., the earlier settlement of 1787, decribed by Olaudah Equiano, above, pp. 209–10.

The master of her,[1] and several of the people to whose assistance Mr. Falconbridge is come, and who had taken refuge here, came to visit us.

They represented their sufferings to have been very great; that they had been treacherously dealt with by one *King* Jemmy, who had drove them away from the ground they occupied, burnt their houses, and otherwise devested them of every comfort and necessary of life; they also threw out some reflections against the Agent of this island; said he had sold several of their fellow sufferers to a Frenchman, who had taken them to the West Indies.

[The Falconbridges have an audience with his Majesty Naimbana, King of Sierra Leone, his Queen, and Mr. Elliotte Griffiths, their interpreter.]

After setting nigh half an hour, Naimbana made his appearance, and received us with seeming good will: he was dressed in a purple embroidered coat, white sattin waistcoat and breeches, *thread stockings*, and his left side emblazoned with a flaming star; his legs to be sure were *harliquined*, by a number of holes in the stockings, through which his black skin appeared.

Compliments ended, Mr. Falconbridge acquainted him with his errand, by a repetition of what he wrote the day before: and complained much of King Jemmy's injustice, in driving the settlers away, and burning their town.

The King answered through Elliotte, (for he speaks but little English) that Jemmy was partly right—the people had brought it on themselves; they had taken part with some Americans, with whom Jemmy had a dispute, and through that means drew the ill will of this man upon them, who had behaved, considering their conduct, as well as they merited; for he gave them three days notice before he burned their town, that they might remove themselves and all their effects away; that he (Naimbana) could not prudently re-establish them, except by consent of all the Chiefs—for which purpose he must call a court or palaver; but it would be seven or eight days before they could be collected; however, he would send a summons to the different parties directly, and gave Falconbridge timely advice when they were to meet.

Falconbridge perceived clearly nothing was to be effected without a palaver, and unless the King's interest was secured his views would be frustrated, and his endeavours ineffectual; but how this was to be done, or what expedient to adopt, he was at a loss for....

---

1   The Lapwing, a cutter that had earlier sailed from England to Sierra Leone.

At length, trusting that the praise-worthy purposes he was aiming at insured him the assistance of the King of Kings he resolved to try what good words would do....

He then entreated the King would use all his might to prevent any unfavourable prejudices which a refusal to reinstate the Settlers, or to confirm the bargain made with Captain Thompson, might operate against him in the minds of his good friends the King of England and the St. George's Bay Company.

The King said he liked the English in preference to all white men, tho' he considered every white man as a *rogue*, and consequently saw them with a jealous eye; yet, he believed the English were by far the honestest, and for that reason, notwithstanding he had received more favors from the French than the English, he liked the latter much best.

From Letter III [sic] (Granville Town, Sierra Leone, 13 May 1791)

[There is a successful meeting, in which Falconbridge is allowed to repurchase land for settlement.]

Falconbridge now had effected the grand object; he was next to collect and settle the miserable refugees: no time was to be lost in accomplishing this; the month of February was nearly spent, only three months of dry weather remained for them to clear their land, build their houses, and prepare their ground for a crop to support them the ensuing year;...

The spot they were driven from, was to be preferred to any other part; but by treaty it was agreed they should not settle there: There were other situations nearly as good, and better considerably than the one fixed on; but immediate convenience was a powerful inducement.

Here was a small village, with seventeen pretty good huts, which the natives had evacuated from a persuasion that they were infested by some evil spirits; but as they made no objection to our occupying them, we gladly took possession, considering it a fortunate circumstance to have such temporary shelter for the whole of our people.

When those from Pa Boson's had joined us, Falconbridge called them all together, making forty-six, including men and women; and after representing the charitable intentions of his coming to Africa, and issuing to them such clothing as were sent out in the Lapwing; he exhorted in the most pathetic language, that they might merit by their industry and good behaviour the notice now taken of them, endeavour to remove the unfavourable prejudices that had gone abroad, and thereby deserve further favours from their friends in England; who, besides the cloaths they had already received, had sent them tools of all kinds, for cultivating their land, also arms and ammunition to defend themselves, if necessary; that these articles would be brought on shore when they got a storehouse built; where they would be lodged for their common good and occasional use; he then concluded this harangue by saying,—he named the place GRANVILLE TOWN, after their friend and benefactor, GRANVILLE SHARP, Esq. at whose instance they were provided with the relief now afforded them.

I never did, and God grant I never may again, witness so much misery as I was forced to be a spectator of here: Among the outcasts were seven of our country women,[1] decrepid with disease, and so disguised with filth and dirt, that I should never have supposed they were born white; add to this, almost naked from head to foot; in short, their appearance was such as I think would exhort compassion from the most callous heart; but I declare they seemed insensible to shame, or the wretchedness of their situation themselves; I begged they would get washed, and gave them the cloaths I could conveniently spare: Falconbridge had a hut appropriated as a hospital, where they were kept separate from the other settlers, and by his attention and care,[2] they recovered in a few weeks....

Nature seems to have been astonishingly sportive in taste and prodigality here, both of vegetable and animal productions, for I cannot stir out without admiring the beauties or deformities of her creation.

Everything I see is entirely new to me, and notwithstanding the eye quickly becomes familiarized, and even satiated with views which we are daily accustomed to; yet there is such a variety here as to afford a continual zest to the sight.

To be frank, if I had a little agreeable society, a few comforts, and could endure the same good health I have hitherto enjoyed, I should not be against spending some years of my life in Africa; but wanting those sweeteners of life, I certainly wish to return to where they may be had.

---

1   These women had been part of the earlier settlement. Fyfe notes that there had been 70 white women on that voyage, along with 290 black men, 41 black women, 11 black children, and 38 officials or craftsmen with their families (*History of Sierra Leone*, 19).

2   Falconbridge was a physician.

From Letter IV (Granville Town, 8 June 1791)

The tract of country now called Sierra Leone, is a Peninsula one half the year, and an island the other—that is, during the rains the Isthmus is overflowed.

The river, which was formerly called *Tagrin*, now takes its name from the country; at its entrance it is about ten miles from one Promontory to the other, but here, it is scarcely half that distance across, and a few miles higher up it becomes very narrow indeed.

It is not navigable for large vessels any higher than Bance Island, but small craft may go a great distance up.

Besides the islands I have mentioned, there are several others, uninhabited, between this and Bance Island.

Granville town is situated in a pretty deep bay, on the south-side of the river, about nine miles above Cape Sierra Leone, fifteen below Bance Island, and six from Robana.

Half a mile below us is the town of one *Pa Duffee*; two miles lower down is *King Jemmy*'s; and beyond him is *Queen Yamacubba*'s, and two or three small places; a mile above us *Signior Domingo* lives, and a little higher one *Pa Will*.

I have been at all these places, and find a great similitude in the appearance of the people, their behaviour, mode of living, building, amusements, &c....

Their chief amusement is dancing: in the evening men and women assemble in the most open part of the town, where they form a circle, which one at a time enters, and shews his skill and agility, by a number of wild comical motions.

Their music is made by clapping of hands, and a harsh sounding drum or two, made out of hollowed wood covered with the skin of a goat.

Sometimes I have seen an instrument resembling our guitar, the country name of which is *bangeon*.

The company frequently applaud or upbraid the performer, with bursts of laughter, or some odd disagreeable noise; if it is moonshine, and they have spirits to drink, these dances probably continue until the moon goes down, or until day light.

From Letter V (London, 30 September 1791)

[According to Fyfe, "The passage from England to Sierra Leone normally took three or four weeks. The return passage, when ships had to sail out to mid-Atlantic for a wind to carry them north might take much longer" (*History of Sierra Leone*, 19). The Falconbridges' difficult voyage back to London may shed some light on the travails experienced by Henry and his father on their prolonged return from Africa; moreover, the harrowing description of the Falconbridges' encounter with five men who had been abandoned on a seemingly deserted island certainly supports Inchbald's depiction of the elder Henry's destitution.]

The Lapwing was badly equip'd for sea; the crew and passengers amounted to nine: four of the former were confined with fevers, and consequently there were only four, (and but one a sailor) to do the ship's duty....

We had not been at sea a week, when all our live stock were washed or blown overboard, by repeated and impetuous tornadoes—so that we had not a thing left but the flower [sic] and salt provisions; however, we were in hopes of getting in a few days to Saint Jago, one of the Cape De Verd Islands, where the loss of our stock might be replaced.

In this we were disappointed, for instead of a few days, a continued interruption of calms and boisterous weather, made it six weeks before we reached that Island; during the whole of which time I was confined to my cabin, and mostly to my bed, for it rained incessantly....

I recovered my strength and spirits during the short time we were at that place [St. Jago], as did all our sick; indeed it was necessary and lucky, for it enabled us to contend against misfortune, and conquer the hardships, and inconveniencies, which afterwards attended us.

We had fine moderate weather the first twenty-four hours, and got the length of St. Vincent, one of the same islands, where, falling calm, we came to anchor....

The boat's crew had scarcely landed, when we were greatly astonished and alarmed to behold from the cutter (for we lay no distance from the shore) five *naked human beings*, who had just started up from behind a hilloc, running towards them—however, our fears were quickly abated, by seeing the boat returning.

The master was one that went on shore, and he understood a little Portuguese, in which language these victims to barbarity addressed, and told him, they had, several months past, been banished from an adjacent island, called Mayo, and landed where they then were in the deplorable condition he beheld them.

The Lapwing was the first vessel that had anchored there since their exilement, and they begged and prayed we would take them off—they did not care where!

This we could not do with any kind of discreetness, from the danger of starving them and ourselves....

Our Skipper ... then enquired, ... for what they were banished? ... no further answer could be obtained, than their having offended the Governor of Mayo, who was a *Black* man.

They were miserably emaciated, and a hapless melancholy overhang'd their countenances.—When we first came up, joyful smiles beamed through the cloud, which soon darkened when they learnt there was no prospect of being relieved....

We offered to take any one of them, but not one would consent to separate or share any good fortune the whole could not partake of....

Appendix E: Contemporary Reviews and Critical Preface

1. [Mary Wollstonecraft], *Analytical Review* 23 (January–June 1796): 511–14

The present novel, though written with a more philosophical spirit than the simple story, has not, on that very account, perhaps, an equally lively interest to keep the attention awake. The reason may be easily traced, without derogating from the abilities of the author. Virtuous prejudices produce the most violent passions; and, consequently, are the powerful engines to be employed in depicting the adventures, that become interesting in proportion as they exhibit the conflicts of feeling and duty, truly or falsely eliminated.

This work abounds with judicious satirical sallies, and with those artless strokes which go directly to the heart. In fact, were we to characterize Mrs. Inchbald's talent, we should unhesitatingly say *naivete*. The story of Hannah Primrose we found particularly affecting: the catastrophe giving point to a benevolent system of morality. The transitions, however, from one period of the history to another, are too abrupt; for the incidents, not being shaded into each other, sometimes appear improbable. This we think the principal defect of the work on the whole. The chapters conclude with a degree of laboured conciseness, which seems to disconnect them, or rather snaps the thread of the fiction. The reader jumps with reluctance over eighteen years; and is forced to reason about the fate of the favourite hero, which was before a matter of feeling.

The making a young modest woman, with some powers of mind, acknowledge herself the mother of a child that she humanely fostered, in the presence of the man she loved, is also highly improbable, not to say unnatural.

Some of the conversations are written with dramatic spirit; we shall select two or three, as specimens of a production we wish to recommend to the youths of both sexes.

[The reviewer here cites the following three passages: the dialogue between Henry and William in chapter 21; the conversation between Henry and Hannah in chapter 30; and the two Henrys' encounter with the poor man in chapter 44.]

"M[ary Wollstonecraft]."

2. *Monthly Mirror: Reflecting Men and Manners*, Vol. I (March 1796): 289

These volumes we strongly recommend to the perusal of novel readers in general. They embrace a pathetic and well digested narrative, wherein the dark side of human nature is but too justly depleted, and we fear many a fair reader in contemplating the character of William, "will find a moral of her own."

The opening is simple, and the eye has only to wander over a few pages before the heart must confess an interest. From its commencement to its close, propriety is kept in view, and every page displays an imagination guided by nature, and a mind watchful over the best interests of the rising generation.

Mrs. Inchbald was left a widow at a very early period, and should she be induced to change her situation, we have only to wish she may meet with her *own* Henry.

3. *Critical Review* 16 (March 1796): 325–30

The talents of Mrs. Inchbald, as a novelist and dramatic writer, are too well known to the world, to require any encomium in addition to those they have already received. Success is undoubtedly, in the common concerns of life, but a bad criterion of merit; yet in literature it may be laid down as an axiom, that where a large portion of applause and success attends a writer, there must be something either of the useful or the pleasing to attract public attention.

The present work is entirely of a moral nature; and its tendency appears to be, to render the great less infatuated with their fancied advantages, less anxious in the pursuit of wealth and honours, which produce little solid happiness,—and the poor less disposed to murmur at that humble lot which Providence has assigned them,—since 'In this opulent kingdom there are near as many persons perishing through intemperance, as starving with hunger—there are as many miserable in the lassitude of having nothing to do, as there are, bowed down to the earth with hard labour—there are more persons who draw upon themselves calamity by following their own will, than there are, who experience it by obeying the will of another. Add to this, that the rich fear dying, so much, they have no comfort in living.'[1]

---

1 From chapter 47.

As we wish not to anticipate the interest which will be excited by this performance, we shall only remark of the story, that the moral already mentioned is exemplified in the history of two brothers, who, commencing their career of life under precisely the same circumstances, are thrown into situations diametrically opposite. The pathos is touched by Mrs. Inchbald with a masterly hand; nor is her skill inferior in delicate and pointed sarcasm.... The misapplication and misconception of words by this amiable semi-barbarian contain much humour and satire ...

The story of Hannah Primrose is in the highest degree interesting and affecting. We shall close our extracts from a work which has afforded us uncommon pleasure, by the account of the condemnation to death of this unfortunate female by the very man by whom her honour had been betrayed, and by whom she had been left to infamy and want—to consequent prostitution and theft, the crime for which she was arraigned. [The reviewer here provides a lengthy quotation from chapter 40.]

4. *Monthly Review* 19 (April 1796): 453

This work will do much credit to the talents of the fair writer: the incidents are highly interesting; the language, if not splendid and highly polished, is at least pure and easy; the sentiments are just; and the satire is keen and pointed without descending to personality. We might deviate from this general praise, in criticizing some improbabilities, some impossibilities, and some improprieties: but we must not dilate. The candid observations of a discerning friend, after having perused this work, might enable Mrs. Inchbald to render it, and any subsequent production, more secure from the attacks of rigid criticism.

5. *The Moral and Political Magazine*, Vol. 1 (June–September 1796)

a. June 1796: 19–26

A new object was given to moral writers of every description, by that profound observation—that the miscarriages and unhappiness of private life, for the most part, flow from the mistakes of civil institutions.

It was easy to see that the novelist, in reciting a tale of domestic distress, might pause to unfold the connexion between the misery he was describing and its ultimate cause in the errors of government. But the work of the politician in this shape was destructive of the immediate design of the novelist, which was to engage the mind in scenes of action from which he could never suffer it for a moment to be withdrawn. Voltaire, in his Candide, and other political romances, and Dean Swift in his Gulliver's Travels, were successful enough in concealing their art. But those productions were mere satires; and failed in the main object of a tale which is to excite sympathy, and in its best effect, which is to induce new and better propensities into the reader. The work of the politician, and that of the novelist, in its fullest extent, were not, however, incompatible. Notwithstanding the influence of Rousseau's Eloisa[1] in engrossing the faculties of the soul, an accurate observer will be more interested by the writer as he is a politician in that work, than a poet and novellist [sic]. In a work of recent date, and in this country, this combination of characters in the writer is not less complete than in the foregoing instance. Although, in the novel of Caleb Williams,[2] the action is never at rest, and although the passion and circumstances of the tale keep the mind in almost an excess of emotion, yet we no sooner begin to take a critical retrospect of the work than we are at a loss to decide whether the skill of the fabulist or the politician be the greater.

To aspire to enter a class among writers in which is to be found the names of Rousseau and Godwin, demanded at least sufficient courage for any task. But Mrs. Inchbald, in making the attempt in the work we are reviewing, has vindicated her claim by other qualities. In a former novel, entitled *A Simple Story*, she had displayed an accurate understanding of the workings of the human heart; and, in the present, she has combined that knowledge with a penetrating insight into the character of political society.

The following is an outline of the fable of this work.

William and Henry, the sons of a country shopkeeper who had died insolvent, come to London with a hope no higher than to get a plain livelihood. The elder (William) is a good scholar, having received an education at a grammar school, and is of a haughty and impracticable temper. The younger is illiterate, but of exquisite sensibility of mind; and, as he is persuaded his brother William knows all things better than himself, and has beside the most ardent affection for him, his will is, in most instances, the creature of his brother's.

Their common qualities of sobriety, industry, and honesty, can scarcely keep them from starving in the metropolis; and when they are on the

---

1 Based on the medieval story of Abelard and Eloise, Rousseau's epistolary novel *Julie, ou la Nouvelle Héloïse* (1761) was enormously popular through the eighteenth century, going through ten English editions before 1800.

2 Godwin's widely popular and influential novel was published in 1794. Inchbald read the novel in manuscript; for her response, see Appendix A.2.b.

precipice of reprobating these qualities, they are preserved from this profanation by Henry recollecting that he can play on the fiddle.

No sooner is it known that Henry can play most excellently on the violin than he is caressed by the great, and partakes of their fare. Thus living in plenty, Henry would gladly, in the simplicity of his heart, teach his learned and morose brother to play on the violin. But driven from this expedient by William's anger, he proposes to send him to one of the universities, where he concludes the qualifications of the scholar, in which William excels, will procure him as many dinners, suppers, and friends, as Henry's violin furnished in London.

William goes: but, notwithstanding his Latin and Greek, he would have starved if the affectionate Henry had not supplied him with money. Henry, frequently pressed by his great friends to receive some mark of their favour, answers in every case, that he has a brother who is a very learned man, and for whom he should be happy to procure some little preferment, but is always repulsed with these unfortunate questions:— Can the learned man play on any instrument?—Can he sing?—Till one fortunate evening, at the conclusion of a concert, a great man shakes him by the hand, and promises a living of five hundred a year to his brother, in return for the entertainment Henry had just given him.

The incumbent dies. William is ordained, and presented to the living. Ungrateful man! he now hates more than ever the friendly violin, the instrument of his elevation. Henry's affection never abates, from William's pride; and, in a year or two, by his interest, he procures him a deanery.

The dean now seriously remonstrates with Henry, on his useless occupation; and intimates the degradation he suffers, in hearing his frivolous accomplishment praised in all companies. Henry, perceiving he has lost his brother as an intimate friend, searches for one to fill up his affectionate heart, and marries.

The wife of Henry is a public singer. The dean upbraids him with the disgrace attending his choice; and, marrying the daughter of a poor Scotch earl, while he invites Henry to the wedding, he does not condescend to invite his sister-in-law. Henry resents this insult; and, among the many he had received from his brother, it is the only one he does resent.

In the words of the charming writer of this work, "If Henry's wife was not fit company for Lady Clementina, it is to be hoped she was company for angels; she died within the first year of her marriage, a faithful and affectionate wife, and a mother."

Henry, soon after losing the use of his right hand by a fall from his horse, and losing at the same time most of his friends, sets sail with his infant son, in company with other adventurers, to people an unfrequented part of a large island in Africa.

The dean is extremely moved when he receives this intelligence; for he loved his brother, and, beside, could not but remember the many things he had done for him, and the many insults he had endured in requittal. "But (to speak in the accurate language of the writer) the avocations of an elevated life erase the deepest impressions." The dean, running in the circle of ambition and pride, forgets his brother. He allies himself to a friend of a different description, a bishop of patrician descent, in whose company a great portion of his time rolls away, at the levees of the powerful, and he passes the remainder in his closet in writing books of which the bishop takes all the reputation, although he has all the labour.

While the dean is thus engaged, Lady Clementina, the lady of the dean, passes her time in attending routs, and in talking of herself; and her son William (whom she bore to the dean within a twelvemonth after their marriage) passes his time with persons hired to teach him "to walk, to ride, to talk, to think like a man—*a foolish man instead of a wise child as nature designed him to be!*

"This unfortunate youth is never permitted to have one conception of his own; all is taught him; he is never once asked, *what he thinks?* but men are paid to tell him *how to think.* He is taught to revere such and such persons, however unworthy of his reverence; to believe such and such things, however unworthy his credit; and to act so and so, on such and such occasions, however unworthy of his feelings."

Mr. Norwynne, (*Norwynne* is the dean's family name, and though the boy is yet at school he is called *mister*,) is now arrived at the age of thirteen, when a letter is delivered to the dean, and with it the messenger brings a boy of nearly the same age as Mr. Norwynne. The letter is from Henry, the brother of the dean, and the boy is his son. The letter states, that the whole party of adventurers, of which, he was one, were cut off by the savages, except himself. He was heart-broken for his comrades; and yet on the whole, he could not say the savages were much to blame—the adventurers had no business in invading their territories; and if the savages had invaded England, they would have fared the same. Henry, having gained some strength in his hand during the voyage, and pleasing the king of the savages with playing on his violin, was spared; and his child was granted to his lamentations, when on the point of being put to death. But the weakness in his hand returning, the king of the savages supposed Henry *would not* entertain him with music, and threw him into prison, and threatened to kill his child if he did not play. In this sad case, he found an opportunity, by means of a faithful savage, of sending his child on board of an English vessel lying at a small distance from the island, with a charge to the captain to deliver him to the dean—thus, with the genuine sensibility of his character, giving up his sole comfort, and delivering himself over to despair, to benefit his child.

He described the young Henry (for he was named after his father) to be tractable, affectionate, and sincere—but very ignorant: the father had no books, and had taught him little of the manners of his native country, thinking he would learn them time enough if he ever saw it; and if not, it was as well he should never know them: he had given him a disrelish for the faults of the savages; had taught him to love and to do good to his neighbour, whoever that neighbour might be, or whatever his failings—falsehood of every kind he included in the precept as forbidden, for he did not think any one could love his neighbour and deceive him: and he trained him up in a contempt for all frivolous vanity, and all indulgencies he was never likely to obtain.

This letter and this circumstance revive the dean's recollection of the many kind things his brother Henry had done for him, and he resolves to repay them all in the person of his child. He adopts the boy, and young William and young Henry are brought up together to man's estate.

The young Henry is the counterpart of his father, except (as may be supposed) that his simplicity is even greater. Very perplexing indeed, is it to his uncle, his cousin, and the bishop (who is a constant visiter at the dean's) to explain to him the propriety of our European sentiments and manners, in some cases.

We will exhibit Henry, for the purpose of his being better known, in one or two of those discussions.

'Observing his uncle one day offended with his coachman, and hearing him say to him in a very angry tone "You shall never drive me again;'

'The moment the man quitted the room, Henry (with his eyes fixed in the deepest contemplation) repeated five or six times in a half whisper to himself,

"You shall never drive me again—you shall never drive me again.'

'The dean at last asked 'what he meant by thus repeating his words?'

"I am trying to find out what *you* meant,' said Henry.

"What! do not you know,' cried his enlightened cousin, 'Richard is turned away? he is never to get upon our coach-box again, never to drive any of us any more.'

"And was it pleasure to drive us, cousin? I am sure I have often pitied him; it rained sometimes very hard when he was on the box, and sometimes Lady Clementina has kept him a whole hour at the door all in the cold and snow; was that pleasure?'

"No,' replied young William.

"Was it honour, cousin?'

"No,' exclaimed his cousin with a contemptuous smile.

"Then why did my uncle say to him, as punishment 'he should never'—

"Come hither, child,' said the dean, 'and let me instruct you; your father's negligence has been inexcusable. There are in society' (continued the dean) 'rich and poor; the poor are born to serve the rich.'

"And what are the rich born for?'

"To be served by the poor.'

"But suppose the poor would not serve them?'

"Then they must starve.'

"And so poor people are permitted to live, only upon condition that they wait upon the rich?'

"Is that a hard condition? or if it were, they will be rewarded in a better world than this.'

"Is there a better world than this?'

"Is it possible you do not know there is?'

"I heard my father once say something about a world to come; but he stopt short, and said I was too young to understand what he meant.'

"The world to come' (returned the dean) 'is where we shall go after death; and there no distinction will be made between rich and poor; all persons there will be equal.'

"Aye, now I see what makes it a better world than this. But cannot this world try to be as good as that?'

"In respect to placing all persons on a level, it is utterly impossible; God has ordained it otherwise.'

"How! has God ordained a distinction to be made, and will not make any himself?'

The dean is compelled to give up his contest with Henry, in this case. He cannot make him apprehend the use of the poor in the creation, nor the reasons why God has made all persons equal in a better state, and rejected that impartial scheme in this world.

In the following discussion, the dean and his son William are more successful; but then they are aided by the learning and sagacity of the bishop.

"Sir,' said William, to his father one morning as he entered the room, 'do you hear how the cannons are firing, and the bells ringing?'

"Then I dare say,' cried Henry, 'there has been another massacre.'

'The dean called to him in anger, 'Will you never learn the right use of words? You mean to say a battle.'

"Then what is a massacre?' cried the frightened, but still curious Henry.

"A massacre,' replied his uncle, 'is when a number of people are slain—'

"I thought,' returned Henry, 'soldiers had been people!'

"You interrupted me,' said the dean, 'before I finished my sentence—certainly, both soldiers and sailors are people, but they engage to die by their own free will and consent.'

"What! all of them?'

"Most of them.'

"But the rest are massacred?'

'The dean answered, 'The number that go to battle unwillingly, and by force, are few; and for the others, they have previously sold their lives to the state.'

"For what?'

"For soldiers' and sailors' pay.'

"My father used to tell me, we must not take away our own lives; but he forgot to tell me, we might sell them for others to take away.'

"William,' (said the dean to his son, his patience tired with his nephew's persevering nonsense) 'explain to your cousin the difference between a battle and a massacre.'

"A massacre,' said William, rising from his seat, and fixing is eyes alternately upon his father, his mother, and the bishop (all of whom were present) for their approbation, rather than the person's to whom his instructions were to be addressed; 'a massacre,' said William, 'is when human beings are slain, who have it not in their power to defend themselves.'

"Dear cousin William,' (said Henry) 'that must ever be the case, with every one who is killed.'

'After a short hesitation, William replied, 'In massacres, people are put to death for no crime, but merely because they are objects of suspicion.'

"But in battle,' said Henry, 'the persons put to death are not even suspected.'

'The bishop now condescended to end this disputation by saying emphatically

"Consider, young savage, that in battle neither the infant, the aged, the sick nor infirm are involved, but only those in the full prime of health and vigour.'

'As this argument came from so great and reverend a man as the bishop, Henry was obliged, by a frown from his uncle, to submit, as one refuted; although he had an answer at the veriest tip of his tongue, which it was torture to him not to utter. What he wished to say must ever remain a secret. The church has its terrors as well as the law, and Henry was awed by the dean's tremendous wig, as much as Paternoster Row is awed by the attorney-general.'

[*To be concluded in the following Magazine.*]

b. July 1796: 79–83 [Continued]

Henry never loses the delicate parts of his character. His sympathy is excited by every one's pleasure and every one's misery: he trespasses on no man's peace for his own gratification: and he never miscals virtue and vice, in compliance with rules contrived for the convenience of a depraved state of society.

"I know I am called proud.' One day said William to Henry.

"Dear cousin,' replied Henry, 'it must be only then by those who do not know you: for to me you appear the humblest creature in the world.'

"Do you think so?'

"I am certain of it; or would you always give up your opinion to that of persons in a superior state, however, inferior in their understanding? Would, else, their weak judgment immediately change yours, though, before, you had been decided on the opposite side? Now indeed, cousin, I have more pride than you, for I never will stoop to act or to speak contrary to my feelings.'

"Then you will never be a great man.'

"Nor ever desire it, if I must first be a mean one.'

Such is Henry. His cousin is, as nearly as possible, the reverse. He is unmindful of the peace of others: and, in the pursuit of plans of aggrandizement, is observant of the rules of society, when his own free will, sincerity, and duty to his neighbour, are to be the sacrifice.

The dean has a country seat at a village called Anfield; and there William and Henry fall in love.

'If (says the writer) passions that were pursued on the most opposite principles can receive the same appellation. William, well versed in all the licentious theory, thought himself in love, because he perceived a tumultuous impulse cause his heart to beat, while his fancy fixed on a certain object, whose presence agitated yet more his breast.

'Henry thought himself not in love, because, while he listened to William on the subject, he found their sensations did not in the least agree.

'William owned to Henry, that he loved Hannah, the daughter of a cottager in the village, and hoped to make her his mistress.

'Henry felt that his tender regard for Rebecca, the daughter of the curate of the parish, did not inspire him even with the boldness to acquaint her with his sentiments, much less to meditate one design that might tend to her dishonour.

'While William was cautiously planning, how to meet in private, and accomplish the seduction of the object of his passion, Henry was endeavouring to fortify the object of *his* choice with every virtue. He never read a book from which he received improvement, that he did not carry it to Rebecca—never knew a circumstance which might assist towards her moral instruction, that he did not hasten to tell it her!'

William succeeds in his designs upon Hannah. He then forsakes her (to marry the niece of a nobleman of great interest) and treats her with great obduracy. Hannah bears a child to him; and being neglected by him, and cast upon the world to seek for her bread, with the complicated disadvantages arising from the habits of a youth nursed with extreme indulgence by fond parents, and from the want of character, endures many miseries, in company with her poor child, and falls, by successive degrees, into a state of great depravity; till, being concerned in uttering forged notes, she is tried for the offence, and condemned to die.

Eighteen years pass during the progressive degradation of Hannah: and, in that period, the dean is made a bishop, and his son (who had been bred to the bar) is raised, by the interest of his wife's relations, joined to his own knowledge of society, to the high station of lord chief justice of one of the courts.

William is the judge of Hannah. She becomes acquainted with this awful aggravation of her fate previous to the trial. Hannah had a soul thrilling with the tenderest feelings of human nature; and in the midst of all her miseries, through all the time of her unhappy life after she was abandoned by William, her love for him had never suffered diminution. When this William (now lord chief justice Norwynne) asks her, with an assumed gentleness, "the art of his occupation," *what defence she has to make?* she is lost in unutterable reflections on the present! on the past! Again the judge puts the question, and Hannah remains in silence. The question is repeated again,—*What have you to say?* and she answers,— *Nothing, my lord*. The judge demands *if she has no one to appear to her character?* and she bursts into tears, remembering by *whom* that character was first destroyed. But when *William* places the fatal velvet on his head, and rises to pronounce the sentence of the law upon Hannah, she starts back with a convulsive motion, and, lifting up her hands, exclaims with a scream—"Oh! Not from you!"

The judge, "serene and dignified, as if no such exclamation had been uttered, delivers the fatal speech."

Hannah is carried from the bar in a senseless state, and a few days afterwards is executed.

Her wrongs are soon avenged on William, who, ignorant that this poor woman is the Hannah he had seduced, accidentally reads an account of her death, including her confession, in which she mentions her name and the place of her birth, and recites her unhappy story, but, with the returning sensibility of her innocent years, forbears to name the despoiler of her peace.

In this account it was stated, that she had left a child, a youth about sixteen, who never forsook his mother, during her confinement, but with true filial duty waited on her, and who had drooped from the passing of the fatal sentence, and then lay dangerously ill: and that she had left a petition, addressed to the judge, relative to his child.

William, awakened to the barbarity of his deeds, sends for the child, and the petition. He is informed that the boy died two days after his mother's execution. The petition is delivered to William, and is in the following eloquent pathetic terms:

"*To Lord Chief Justice NORWYNNE.*

"My Lord, I am Hannah Primrose, the daughter of John and Hannah Primrose, of Anfield; my father and mother lived by the hill at the side of the little brook where you used to fish, and where you first saw me.

"Pray, my lord, have mercy on my sorrows, pity me for the first time, and spare my life. I know I have done wrong; I know it is presumption in me to dare to apply to you, such a wicked and mean wretch as I am; but, my lord, you once condescended to take notice of me, and though I have been very wicked since that time, yet if you would be so merciful as to spare my life, I promise to amend it for the future. But if you think it proper I should die, I will be resigned; but then I hope, I beg, I supplicate, that you will grant my other petition. Pray, pray my lord, if you cannot pardon me, be merciful to the child I leave behind. What he will do when I am gone, I don't know; for I have been the only friend he has had ever since he was born. He was born, my lord, about sixteen years ago, at Anfield, one summer's morning, and carried by your cousin, Mr. Henry

Norwynne, to Mr. Rymer's, the curate there; and I swore whose child he was, before the dean, and I did not take a false oath. Indeed, indeed, my lord, I did not.

"I will say no more for fear this should not come safe to your hand, for the people treat me as if I were mad; so I will say no more, only this, that, whether I live or die, I forgive every body, and I hope every body will forgive me; and I pray that God will take pity on my son, if you refuse: but I hope you will not refuse.

                         "HANNAH PRIMROSE."

The wrongs of Hannah are now fully and terribly avenged. The judge is delivered up a prey to *remorse*. 'It wounded, it stabbed, it rent his hard heart, as it would do a tender one. It havocked on his firm inflexible mind, as it would on a weak and pliant brain. He saw all his honours, all his riches, all his proud selfish triumphs dance before him! They seemed like airy nothings, which in rapture he would exchange for the peace of a tranquil conscience!

'He envied Hannah the death to which he exposed, then condemned her. He envied her even the life she struggled through from his neglect— and felt, that his future days, would be far less happy than her former existence. He calculated with precision.'

                    [*To be continued.*]

c. September 1796: 177–180 [Concluded]

While the younger William is engaged in the scenes of a depraved life, reaping its ineffectual pleasures and its substantial sorrows, his cousin Henry is performing an act of filial duty and devotion. He no sooner reaches the age of manhood, and is released from a dependence upon the will of another, than he makes a vow to go in search of his father: and a little before the time that William entered into public life, he bade farewel to his lover, and proceeded to the coast of Africa.

The elder Henry still lived. The savages had released him from his prison, and permitted him to roam and seek his subsistence at his pleasure.

The elegant writer of this work has drawn a fine picture of the state of the brothers, during the last twenty years: and has shown the younger tasting of happiness in the hunter's hovel, within the hearing of the lion's roar; and the elder drinking of the bitterness of reflection and sorrow on his safe commodious bed. It was *conscience* that caused all the difference in this point between them. Exterior circumstances seemed to pronounce the BISHOP *fortunate*, and HENRY *miserable*. The internal state of the brothers exposed the fallacy of these appearances.

Yet Henry's susceptible mind could not fail to feel his forlorn condition.

'As he fished or hunted for his daily dinner, many a time in full view of his prey, a sudden burst of sorrow at his fate, a sudden longing for some dear society, for some friend to share his thoughts, for some kind shoulder on which to lean his head, for some companion to partake of his repast, would arrest his pursuit, cast him on the ground in a fit of anguish, till a shower of tears, and his *conscience*, came to his relief.

'It was on a sultry morning, when, after pleasant dreams during the night, he had waked with more than usual perception of his misery, that, sitting upon the beach, his wishes and his looks all bent on the sea towards his native land, he thought he saw a sail swelling before an unexpected breeze.

"Sure I am dreaming still!' he cried. 'This is the very vessel I saw last night in my sleep!—Oh! what cruel mockery, that my eyes should so deceive me!'

'Yet, though he doubted, he leaped upon his feet in transport!—held up his hands, stretched at their length, in a kind of ecstatic joy!—and as the glorious sight approached, was near rushing into the sea to meet it.

'For a while hope and fear kept him in a state bordering on distraction.

'Now he saw the ship making for the shore, and tears flowed for the grateful prospect. Now it made for another point, and he vented shrieks and groans from the disappointment.

'It was at those moments, while hope and fear thus possessed him, that the horrors of his abode appeared more than ever frightful! Inevitable afflictions must be borne; but that calamity which admits the expectation of relief, that is afterwards denied, is insupportable.

'After a few minutes passed in dreadful uncertainty, which enhanced the wished-for happiness, the ship evidently drew near the land; a boat was launched from her; and while Henry, now upon his knees, wept, and prayed fervently for the event; a youth sprang from the barge on the strand, rushed towards him, and falling on his neck, then at his feet, exclaimed—'My father! oh! my father!"

The father and son return to England, and learn the prosperous condition of the bishop and the judge. They proceed to the country palace of the former, the elder Henry with many alarms lest he should be received in an unkind manner by his brother.

They approach the bishop's noble domain, and come in sight of the turrets of his magnificent palace. The elder Henry is struck with the grandeur of the scene, and cannot wholly forbear to look back with complacency on the part he had taken in raising his brother's fortunes. While these thoughts are revolving in his mind, the road, by a sudden angle, brings him into an avenue in the front of the palace. The circumstances of an approaching funeral present themselves: a sumptuous coffin is borne out of the house: they learn it bears the remains of the bishop: and they silently follow the funeral procession—*the only mourners in the scene.*

The bishop died, hated by the poor for his selfishness, his pride, and his tyranny. Lady Clementina had gone before, having destroyed herself by wearing a new-fashioned dress that occasioned a cold, and brought her to the grave. The judge was living—but with a mind wounded by the infidelity of his wife, from whom he had been divorced, and languishing a prey to contrition for all the evils he had brought upon the tender, and, till he poisoned her peace, the happy Hannah.

After the funeral of the bishop is ended, the father and son, without chusing to see their lofty relation, proceed to the village of Anfield. The younger Henry and Rebecca meet again. They are married; and, together with the father of Henry and two of Rebecca's sisters (her father being dead)[1] they maintain themselves, in a state of ease, and with contentment of mind, by the produce of a garden and by fishing.

We have given several pages to the consideration of this novel, because of its uncommon power of at once diffusing political and moral sentiments, and of engaging and gratifying the imagination.

A critic who should seek for the observance of the rules of this species of composition, without being very highly capable of revelling in the delight the great masters of these rules proposed as their end, would complain, no doubt, of the structure of the story. It is true, the action, after commencing with two persons, and proceeding so far as extremely to interest us in their fortunes, becomes subordinate to the history of other persons who nearly swallow up all sympathy for the former. But the passion that is excited, though the object be changed, is still the same, and is so imperceptibly and perfectly transferred, that we come to the end of the story, at least without being very eager to question the writer about the propriety of the change.

Separate parts of this fiction are wrought up with a hand guided by the finest genius. The whole of the story of Hannah is a masterpiece of exquisite and glowing painting. It is impossible to say of this part, whether feel-

---

1   Although Rebecca's sisters are indeed living, the household that Inchbald describes at the novel's conclusion includes only the two Henrys and Rebecca.

ing or judgement had the ascendancy in the production. The descent of Hannah from virtue and happiness to the abyss of vice and misery is natural, inevitable! And no one, we think, can read that story, and be the author or victim of such ruin.

The younger William, in a conversation with his cousin Henry, endeavours to excuse his design of seducing Hannah, by saying he had told her he could not marry her, and if she yielded to his desires, she had only herself to reproach.

Henry[1] answers this exclamation, "Oh, heaven!"

"What makes you exclaim so vehemently?" says William.

"An idea," replies Henry, "of the bitterness of that calamity which inflicts self-reproach! Oh, rather deceive her!—leave her the consolation to reproach you rather than herself!"

Is it possible to touch the canvas with a finer pencil?

The plan of the work, as it is formed to produce a political effect, is conducted with equal vigour. The design is to exhibit the effect of selfishness, vain-glory, and a desire of rank and exterior grandeur on the one hand, and of sensibility and benevolence on the other.

In the former part of this plan, the writer has displayed great art in placing personages on the stage who are the representatives of a species. Their vices are inseparable from their order.—What is the fruit? Is it happiness, is it tranquillity to themselves? Let the reader of this work say, when he had summed up their enjoyments!—Is it a benefit and a blessing to others? It would be an insult to ask that question of one whose heart was bleeding with the sorrows of this tale. In fine, the inherent vices of a bad system are detected in their silent action on private life.

The writer has not so completely succeeded in the exhibiting a contrast to the depravity and miseries of society. The two Henries are indeed innocent; but they are ignorant: and innocence is not virtue, nor ignorance happiness.

There is another considerable fault in the work; but it is not like the former, of a political kind. It is a fault of composition. The work concludes with a piece of irony so ill placed, that it is painful, and even with some readers is liable to be misunderstood for the serious expression of the writer's sentiments.[2]

---

1   William in original review.
2   See Appendix A.1.c for the original (1796) ending, to which the reviewer here refers.

6. Anna Laetitia Barbauld, Preface to *The British Novelists* Series, Vol. 27 (1810)

To readers of taste it would be superfluous to point out the beauty of Mrs. Inchbald's novels. The *Simple Story* has obtained the decided approbation of the best judges. There is an originality both in the characters and the situations which is not often found in similar productions. To call it a *simple story* is perhaps a misnomer, since the first and second parts are in fact two distinct stories, connected indeed by the character of Dorriforth, which they successively serve to illustrate....

It is a particular beauty in Mrs. Inchbald's compositions, that they are thrown so much into the dramatic form. There is little of mere narrative, and in what there is of it, the style is careless; but all the interesting parts are carried on in dialogue:—we see and hear the persons themselves; we are but little led to think of the author, and it is only when we have done feeling that we begin to admire.

The only other novel which Mrs. Inchbald has given to the public is *Nature and Art*. It is of a slighter texture than the former, and put together without much attention to probability; the author's object being less to give a regular story, than to suggest reflections on the political and moral state of society. For this purpose two youths are introduced, one of whom is educated in all the ideas and usages of civilized life; the other (the child of Nature) without any knowledge of or regard to them. This is the frame which has been used by Mr. Day[1] and others for the same purpose, and naturally tends to introduce remarks more lively than solid, and strictures more epigrammatic than logical, on the differences between rich and poor, the regard paid to rank, and such topics, on which it is easy to dilate with an appearance of reason and humanity; while it requires a much profounder philosophy to suggest any alteration in the social system, which would not be rather Utopian than beneficial.

There is a beautiful stroke in this part of the work, where Henry, who, according to Rousseau's plan,[2] had not been taught to pray till he was of an age to know what he was doing, kneels down for the first time with great emotion; and on being asked if he was not afraid to speak to God, says, "To be sure I trembled very much when I first knelt, but when I came to the words 'Our Father who art in heaven,' they gave me courage, for I know how kind a father is."

---

1   Thomas Day, author of *The History of Sandford and Merton* (1783–89). For selections from this work, see Appendix B.2.

2   *Émile, ou de l'Éducation* (1762). For extracts from Rousseau, see Appendix B.1.

But by far the finest passage in this novel is the meeting between Hannah and her seducer, when he is seated as judge upon the bench, and, without recollecting the former object of his affection, pronounces sentence of death upon her. The shriek she gives, and her exclamation, "Oh, not from you!" electrifies the reader, and cannot but stir the coldest feelings.

Judgement and observation may sketch characters, and often put together a good story; but strokes of pathos, such as the one just mentioned, ... can only be attained by those whom nature has endowed with her choicest gifts.

One cannot help wishing the author had been a little more liberal of happiness to poor Henry, who sits down contented with poverty and his half-withered Rebecca.

There is another wish the public has often formed, namely, that these two productions were not the *only* novels of such a writer as Mrs. Inchbald.

Select Bibliography

Editions of *Nature and Art*

Inchbald, Elizabeth. *Nature and Art.* 2 vols. London: G.G. & J. Robinson, 1796.

———. *Nature and Art.* "Second Edition, Corrected and Improved." 2 vols. London: G.G. & J. Robinson, 1797.

———. *Nature and Art.* "A New Edition, with the Last Corrections by the Author." *The British Novelists*, Vol. 27, with a Preface by Mrs. Barbauld. London: Rivington, 1810.

———. *Nature and Art.* Facsimile of 1st edition. Intro. Jonathan Wordsworth. Oxford and New York: Woodstock Books, 1994.

———. *Nature and Art.* Facsimile of 2nd edition. Intro. Caroline Frankline. London: Routledge/Thoemmes, 1995.

———. *Nature and Art.* Ed. and Intro. Shawn L. Maurer. London: Pickering Women's Classics, 1997.

Inchbald Biography and Bibliography

Boaden, James. *Memoirs of Mrs Inchbald, including her Familiar Correspondence with the Most Distinguished Persons of her Time, to which are added "The Massacre" and "A Case of Conscience."* 2 vols. London: Bentley, 1833.

Brown, Ford K. *The Life of William Godwin.* London: J.M. Dent, 1926.

Cauwel, Janice Marie. "Authorial 'Caprice' vs. Editorial 'Calculation': The Text of Elizabeth Inchbald's *Nature and Art.*" *Bibliographical Society of America* 72 [1978]: 169–85.

———. "A Critical Edition of *Nature and Art* (1796) by Elizabeth Inchbald." PhD Dissertation, University of Virginia, 1976.

Jenkins, Annibel. *I'll Tell You What: The Life of Elizabeth Inchbald.* Lexington: University of Kentucky Press, 2003.

Joughin, G. Louis. "An Inchbald Bibliography." *Studies in English* (University of Texas) 14 (July 1934): 59–74.

Littlewood, S.R. *Elizabeth Inchbald and Her Circle: The Life Story of a Charming Woman.* London: O'Connor, 1921.

Manvell, Roger. *Elizabeth Inchbald: England's Principal Woman Dramatist and Independent Woman of Letters in Eighteenth-Century London.* Lanham, MD and London: University Press of America, 1987.

Paul, C. Kegan. *William Godwin: His Friends and Contemporaries.* Boston: Roberts Brothers, 1876.

Sigl, Patricia. "The Elizabeth Inchbald Papers." *Notes and Queries* 227 [June 1982]: 220–24.

Nature and Art: Early Critical Studies

Gregory, Allene. *The French Revolution and the English Novel.* New York and London: G.P. Putnam's Sons, 1915.

Kavanagh, Julia. *English Women of Letters: Biographical Sketches.* 2 vols. London: Hurst and Blackett, 1863.

MacCarthy, B.G. *The Female Pen: Women Writers and Novelists 1621–1818.* 1946. New York: NYU Press, 1994.

McKee, William. *Elizabeth Inchbald, Novelist.* Washington: Catholic University of America, 1935.

Recent Studies of *Nature and Art*: Articles, Essays, and Book Chapters

Kelly, Gary. *The English Jacobin Novel 1780–1805.* Oxford: Clarendon, 1976.

Maurer, Shawn Lisa. "Masculinity and Morality in Elizabeth Inchbald's *Nature and Art*." *Women, Revolution, and the Novels of the 1790s.* Ed. Linda Lang-Peralta. East Lansing: Michigan State University Press, 1999. 155–76.

Rogers, Katharine M. "Elizabeth Inchbald: Not Such a Simple Story." *Living By The Pen: Early British Women Writers.* Ed. Dale Spender. New York and London: Teachers College Press, 1992. 82–90.

Scheuermann, Mona. *Her Bread to Earn: Women, Money and Society from Defoe to Austen.* Lexington: University of Kentucky Press, 1994.

———. *Social Protest in the Eighteenth-Century English Novel.* Athens: Ohio State University Press, 1986.

Schofield, Mary Anne. *Masking and Unmasking the Female Mind: Disguising Romances in Feminine Fiction, 1713–1799.* Newark: University of Delaware Press, 1990.

Ty, Eleanor. *Unsex'd Revolutionaries: Five Women Novelists of the 1790s.* Toronto: University of Toronto Press, 1993.

Recent Studies of *Nature and Art*: Significant Mention

Butler, Marilyn. *Jane Austen and the War of Ideas.* 1975. Oxford: Clarendon, 1987.

Jones, Vivien. "Placing Jemima: Women Writers of the 1790s and the Eighteenth-Century Prostitution Narrative." *Women's Writing* 4, 2 (1997): 201–220.

Spencer, Jane. *The Rise of the Woman Novelist.* Oxford: Basil Blackwell, 1986.

Spender, Dale. *Mothers of the Novel.* London: Pandora, 1986.

Staves, Susan. "British Seduced Maidens." *Eighteenth-Century Studies* 14 (1980–81): 109–34.